NIGHTS OF THE
LONG KNIVES

A resident of long standing is murdered in a luxury apartment overlooking Lake Lugano. Painstaking inquiries by the Swiss police disclose that the victim, Norden, a quiet and scholarly German expatriate, once belonged to the most formidable and exclusive of all SS units: the Wesel Group.

The discovery of Norden's diaries takes us back to a spring day in 1933, when SS Sturmbannführer Wesel visits a cadet camp in search of 'human material' for Hitler's earliest and deadliest secret weapon: a small band of ruthless and dedicated young men who will stop at nothing to fulfil their leader's objectives.

Once recruited, Norden and his five companions are subjected to the ultimate in physical and psychological training – a conditioning process so rigorous that it equips them to carry out any mission, however brutal or nonsensical. They perform their assignments like laboratory animals, killing and maiming to order, terrorizing or assassinating Hitler's opponents in the dawn of the Nazi era.

We follow the activities of the Wesel Group throughout the pre-war years and beyond, witnessing their involvement in the liquidation of Hitler's homosexual henchman Röhm, in the Spanish Civil War, in the Gleiwitz incident that triggered World War II, and in the pilot scheme that provided a model for every extermination camp from Auschwitz to Belsen.

But no amount of conditioning and indoctrination can entirely neutralize the pull of human emotion. Greed, fear and revenge finally prove stronger than esprit de corps, and the trail that began in 1933 ends, more than forty years later, in a bloodstained Lugano apartment. Or does it? The denouement is not complete until the last page has been turned.

by the same author

OFFICER FACTORY

THE NIGHT OF THE GENERALS

WHAT BECAME OF GUNNER ASCH

THE REVOLT OF GUNNER ASCH

GUNNER ASCH GOES TO WAR

BROTHERS IN ARMS

THE 20TH OF JULY

THE FOX OF MAULEN

CAMP 7 LAST STOP

UNDERCOVER MAN

WHO'S IN CHARGE HERE?

HERO IN THE TOWER

A TIME FOR SCANDAL

A TIME FOR TRUTH

A TIME FOR PAYMENT

NIGHTS OF THE LONG KNIVES

Hans Hellmut Kirst

TRANSLATED BY J. MAXWELL BROWNJOHN

COLLINS
St James's Place London 1976

William Collins Sons & Co Ltd
London · Glasgow · Sydney · Auckland
Toronto · Johannesburg

First published in Germany under the title
Die Naechte der Langen Messer
First published in Great Britain 1976
© Hoffmann und Campe Verlag, Hamburg 1975
© In the English translation by
Wm Collins Sons & Co Ltd 1976

ISBN 0 00 222409 7

Set in Monotype Imprint
Made and Printed in Great Britain by
William Collins Sons & Co Ltd Glasgow

Contents

'Everyone must know that, if he raises his hand to smite the State, his fate is certain death.'

Adolf Hitler addressing the Reichstag on 18 July 1934

'Thine honour is loyalty.'

SS motto

'The executioner, too, belongs to the sovereign's train.'

Medieval saying

'Whatsoever has to be done we must do with unexampled severity, sworn determination and German thoroughness.

We owe it to our nation, our Fatherland and beloved Führer. Our hour has struck.'

From *Maxims* by Waldemar Wesel

'Even death has its funny side.'

Free translation from the Old Testament

PROLOGUE
IN LUGANO

Springtime in Lugano was extravagantly beautiful this year – it nearly always was. Although a pale mantle of snow still clung to the surrounding peaks, the tulip-trees fringing the lakeside promenade erupted with almost sensual delight as their delicate pink blossom strove to prevail over the glacial whiteness of the mountains above. The streets glistened with rain, but nobody minded the wet. The inhabitants of Canton Ticino seemed to revel in the moist spring weather.

In Viale Cattaneo, one of the smartest streets in this imposing Swiss town, in a house near the spacious park, lay the body of a man. It had been there for several days. By the time it was found, decay had set in.

Excerpts from statements made by Rossana Bossi, 56, widowed mother of eight. A resident of Varese, Italy, Signora Bossi travelled thrice weekly to Lugano, crossing the Swiss–Italian border at the Ponte Tresa to do one day's cleaning for each of three employers: the owner of a fashion boutique, a German-Swiss bank executive, and – every Monday at a fifth-floor apartment in Viale Cattaneo – a certain Signor Norden.

'A middle-aged German gentleman – about fifty-five, I'd say. He seemed *molto simpatico*. I had to clean his apartment once a week. It was no trouble – no dirt to speak of, never mussed up his sheets, hardly used the kitchen at all. I put him down as a *letterato* – a literary gentleman of some kind. He had piles of books and sheets of paper covered with handwriting, but no typewriter.

'He always spoke Italian to me. Just like one of those radio announcers – no trace of a foreign accent. He usually went for a walk while I was doing the housework.

'Where to? The cemetery, probably – he spent a great deal of time there. He used to visit a grave near the back wall – an unmarked grave. He often put flowers on it. Very generous of him, even if flowers don't cost much round here. He was generous to me too. My money was always waiting for me on the kitchen table, even before I started cleaning. A 50-franc note plus a 5-franc piece on the side, regular as clockwork. He meant it as a tip, I suppose.

'Well, this Monday I found the door of his apartment unlocked. The smell hit me as soon as I walked in. Really awful it was. Signor Norden was lying beside his bed, not on it. His face was all twisted and horrible-looking, and his white shirt – he always wore white shirts – was caked with blood. I called the police right away.'

The CID duty officer at Lugano, a subdistrict administered by the Ticinese cantonal police headquarters at Bellinzona, was Detective Inspector Luigi Fellini. As usual, he was not over-burdened with work. Lugano seldom witnessed cases of sudden and violent death. Not even the traffic division encountered many of those. Fraud, embezzlement and forgery were generally dealt with by banks and businessmen acting among themselves. As for undesirables, the Aliens Department expelled them promptly and without ceremony.

Anyone who aspired to live in the canton of Ticino soon discovered it was inadvisable to make a nuisance of himself, least of all within the jurisdiction of such an outwardly placid police force. Although Inspector Fellini betrayed few signs of professional ambition, he was gifted with infinite perseverance.

Fellini presented himself at Viale Cattaneo with an air of idle curiosity. Corpses were – to repeat – a rare spectacle, but he soon realized that the corpse confronting him was even more exceptional than most.

This did not prevent him from giving an impression of pure routine. His first step was to interview Signora Bossi, allowing her to talk freely, asking few questions and making no notes. Then he waited patiently for a preliminary medical report.

The police surgeon looked puzzled. 'Take a look at that body. The chest has been mangled – blown apart – probably by a single slug from a gun of outsize calibre.'

Fellini shrugged, privately speculating that it might have been an antique hand-gun, perhaps a heavy 18th-century duelling pistol. Alternatively, a sawn-off shotgun fired at point-blank range.

He notified his immediate superior in Bellinzona and recommended that a firearms expert be sent for at once. 'Preferably one of the Zürich bunch,' he added, meaning Switzerland's premier forensic science team.

The expert from Zürich, a man named Brucker, boarded a Traffic Division helicopter and touched down at Lugano's Agno Airport just two hours later.

Results of preliminary inquiries into the Lugano killing.

1. Report from the Aliens Department:
Heinz-Hermann Norden, born Stettin 1 May 1913, West German national. Herr Norden applied for a resident's permit in 1963 on grounds of ill health, supporting his application with a medical certificate. His stated intention was to study Italian and engage in specialized research for German-Italian dictionaries on architecture, the fine arts and music. He also produced the banker's guarantee required by law.

Investigation of Herr Norden's background yielded nothing of an adverse nature.

2. Statement by Dr Dino Bolla, attorney-at-law:
It was in 1963, on the recommendation of a respected Munich colleague, that Herr Norden invited me to become his legal representative with special responsibility for financial and tax matters. He possessed assets valued at SF750,000, officially described as the proceeds of a family inheritance. These I invested and administered on his behalf. He was an agreeable but extremely retiring man who seemed wholly engrossed in his work as a scholar of independent means. At all events, I felt no qualms about acting for him.

3. Statement by Sergio Bernasconi, Lugano cemetery director:
The grave to which you refer is No. 217, situated beside the outer wall and a little to the right of centre. It contains the remains

13

of an unidentified person, female, presumed to be the victim of a climbing accident. Her body was found near the San Bernardino Pass early in July 1960. Although it was somewhat mutilated and slightly decomposed, the deceased had obviously been a woman of outstanding beauty – blonde and slender despite her age, which was then estimated at 40-plus. Your colleagues in Bellinzona will have a more detailed file on the subject. I only remember that it never proved possible to identify her with absolute certainty.

Towards the end of 1960 or early in 1961 – anyway, that winter – I was contacted by a Count von der Tannen of the German Federal Republic, an elderly gentleman of extremely distinguished appearance. After inspecting the dead woman's personal effects, studying photographs of her body and interviewing various witnesses, he concluded that she might have been his missing daughter Elisabeth – a supposition which the authorities could neither dismiss nor confirm with any degree of certainty.

Then, in the autumn of 1963, Plot No. 217 acquired a highly conscientious benefactor in the person of Signor Norden. He commissioned a white marble walkway, arranged for the grave to be planted with carefully selected perennials, and purchased a 50-year lease from the cemetery administrators.

He often brought fresh flowers, too. His floral tributes were particularly impressive on three days in the year: May 1st, July 1st – the unidentified woman's putative date of death – and October 10th.

4. *Preliminary report by Karl Brucker, ballistics expert of Zürich:*
The projectile recovered during the post mortem examination of Norden's body permits the following conclusion to be drawn: it was not a handmade or hand-moulded lead ball of the kind generally used in antique firearms, but – almost certainly – a steel-jacketed slug of modern manufacture, though its calibre can only be described as exceptional.

In other words, the bullet recovered from Norden's body corresponds to none of the internationally accepted small arms calibres. Those commonly found in pistols and revolvers are 6.35, 7.65 and 9 mm., as in the German 08 army pistol. This, however, is a considerably heavier bullet – possibly of 10 mm. diameter or more. My department has no record of any standard

14

hand-gun which would fire such a projectile.

5. Interim report from Detective Inspector Fellini to cantonal police headquarters at Bellinzona:

A thorough search of Norden's apartment has yielded the following items:

(*a*) Notes for a projected work on Italian fascist terms and phrases systematically compared with their German National Socialist equivalents.

(*b*) Three keys concealed behind books, the latter being definitive works on Nazi Germany in general and the structure of the SS in particular. All three are obviously keys to safe-deposit boxes, possibly in Lugano – where we have upwards of 40 financial institutions – or somewhere just across the Italian border, e.g. Varese, Luino or Milan.

(*c*) A plain calling-card, ivory in colour and of good quality. The killer may have tossed it at his victim's body. If so, he threw it so hard that it slid between the wall and the bed and landed in an accumulation of dust beneath. Boldly scrawled on it in slanting capitals were the words:

'LAST RESPECTS FROM DIETMAR.'

6. Further report from ballistics expert Karl Brucker of Zürich:

Checks on modern hand-guns of this exceptionally large calibre produced no immediate results, neither here nor at the Federal Crime Bureau in Wiesbaden, West Germany. Our German colleagues at first suspected the weapon employed was a rifle or shotgun, there being only two comparatively rare types that seemed to fill the bill: a Belgian 48 mm. elephant gun specially designed for big game hunting, and a Soviet Maxim K11, reportedly used by prison-camp guards because of its great spread and high velocity.

I decided to seek a second opinion from Professor Erwin Müller of Basle, a collector and expert of international repute. He has a wide knowledge of firearms and ammunition, especially 20th-century hand-guns of European provenance. His comments:

'Hand-guns of the suspected calibre are seldom used, and no such weapon has ever, so far as I can determine, been mass produced.

'It is none the less fair to assume that in 1933 or 1934 a weapon of similar calibre was specially designed and manufactured in limited numbers by the Solingen firm of Wolf & Kustermann, whose chief gunsmith was a man named Grabert, since deceased. This hand-gun appears to have been produced for a small but important SS special service unit.

'Between 1940 and 1942, I myself compiled a report on all that was known about the weapon in collaboration with a German police officer named Dickopf. Herr Dickopf had fled Nazi Germany under the threat of political persecution and came to work with us in Switzerland.

'A copy of our wartime report is being dispatched to you by express post. Even though much of it is conjecture, I would ask you to treat the relevant information as confidential.'

Ticino's cantonal CID chief was an amiable-looking man on the threshold of fifty. Reputed to be one of the canton's foremost connoisseurs of Merlot wine, he drove an ancient Fiat and wore a perpetual smile which seemed mild and meditative until one looked into his eyes, which were keen and clear – almost chilly.

The superintendent's apparent motive in driving over from Bellinzona was to drink a glass of wine with Fellini. In practice, this meant splitting a bottle. A choice Merlot, naturally, but not to be found on any wine list. This particular bottle reposed in the cellar of a quiet little back-street restaurant near the station and was drunk with thinly sliced salami and peasant bread from the Maggio Valley. Conversation at first centred on regional dishes, in this instance *polenta veneziana* and its astonishing range of culinary uses.

Afterwards they strolled to the big park on Lugano's lakeside promenade. Passing the caged deer and the children's playground, they headed for one of the numerous benches like two tourists intent on enjoying the scenery.

Fellini realized his boss had not selected the spot at random. They were close to the house where Norden's body had been found – so close that the setting sun would have cast its shadow across their bench.

The superintendent cleared his throat. 'Any idea what you're up against?'

'One murder's much like another,' Fellini said, almost defensively.

'They're all different, take it from an old hand. I did a stint with the Italian CID in Milan before I came here. That brought me into contact with a whole assortment of killings. The corpses that made a real impression on me belonged to poor innocents who'd been eliminated through no fault of their own – those were the ones that aroused my hunting instincts. Then again, there were a few occasions when I felt the victim had it coming to him. That's the kind of hunch I've got now, Fellini.'

Fellini was clearly puzzled. 'What are you trying to do, Commissario, nudge me?' He shrugged. 'If you really want to know what I think about this case, I'm inclined to think it's a hangover from the Hitler-Mussolini era – maybe an attempt to eliminate a dangerous rival or a traitor in the ranks. It wouldn't be the first time these bastards have conducted a private purge. I wish they wouldn't shit on my doorstep, that's all.'

The superintendent's expression was almost morose. 'I'm afraid I see no reason to reject your theory, *caro* Fellini – in fact I think it verges on understatement. This looks like more than a belated execution in the name of fascist solidarity. It could be something even hotter to handle – like an act of political fratricide.'

'What gives you that idea? Not my official reports, surely?'

'They're a model of cautious objectivity, I'm glad to say. We never indulge in speculation of any kind, not officially, but having read the report by that firearms expert . . . Well, let's say I don't feel too sanguine about the case.'

'But that doesn't absolve us from our duty to investigate it, Commissario.'

'I'm afraid not.' The superintendent gave a sudden grimace. 'Know what I kept thinking as I ran through the file? Let the swine exterminate each other and good riddance! As far as I'm concerned, there can't be enough dead bodies of the Norden variety.'

Fellini stared at his boss. 'You're not suggesting we let matters rest?'

'No, of course not,' growled the superintendent, 'even if it does go against the grain.'

'Would you prefer us to hand the case over – say to the West German police? Either that or call the Federal Crime Bureau at Wiesbaden and request their assistance?'

'Neither, Fellini. This is your case, and if I know you, you'll want to keep it. *Bene*, see what you can do.'

'I will, Commissario. Any suggestions or instructions?'

'No, I'm giving you a free hand for the moment, more or less. Those keys – have you managed to locate the safe-deposit boxes?'

'Not yet.'

'What about Norden's books and papers? Have you had them vetted by an expert?'

'There are plenty of German or German-speaking writers living here. I thought of asking one of them.'

'Fine, as long as you don't pick a retired Nazi. Concentrate on Norden's background. The more you discover about the man himself the closer you'll get to his killer. Lots of luck – you'll need it. By the way, I advise you to keep the body on ice for as long as possible. Somebody may ask to see it.'

Extracts from a study compiled jointly by Professor Erwin Müller of Basle and Chief Superintendent Alois Dickopf, subsequently head of West Germany's Federal Crime Bureau, Wiesbaden. Begun during World War II, their report embodied conjectures about the use of a non-standard hand-gun on a number of exceptional occasions.

(*a*) 24 hours before Louis Barthou, the French Foreign Minister, was assassinated alongside King Alexander of Yugoslavia in Marseilles on 9 October 1934, the local security chief was shot dead by two unidentified men who escaped. Ballistics experts from the forensic laboratory at Lyons, acknowledged to be the finest in France, were unable to identify the firearms used.

(*b*) A hand-gun of exceptional calibre was also used in the murder of Ernst vom Rath, a third secretary at the German Embassy in Paris, on 7 November 1938, allegedly by a Jew named Herschel Grynszpan.

(*c*) More murders were committed with weapons of comparable or identical calibre on the occasion of the *Kristallnacht* of 9–10 November 1938. The victims were prominent Jewish citizens of Munich, Berlin and Frankfurt.

(*d*) Later incidents of a similar nature, some officially documented, occurred in Vienna during the so-called liberation of Austria by Nazi Germany, when numerous political opponents were systematically murdered.

Attention is also drawn to the fake attack on the Gleiwitz radio station in Silesia, which provided Hitler with an official pretext for attacking Poland in 1939 and was carried out by a hand-picked unit of SS men who ruthlessly gunned down a number of their compatriots in the process. The successful attempt on Heydrich's life in Prague in 1942 seems likewise to have involved the use of these unusual weapons, in addition to hand-grenades.

(*e*) Further inquiries – regrettably unsupported by firm evidence – indicate that the same special hand-guns were first employed in the murder of Röhm and his lieutenants at the end of June 1934.

(*f*) Even in the case of Hitler's demise at his Berlin command post in 1945, Soviet findings suggest that his skull was shattered prior to cremation by a slug of exceptionally large calibre.

Norden's literary remains were examined by HH, an author of international reputation. Resident in Ascona, near Lugano, HH had spent much of his pre-war life in Austria before fleeing from the Nazis to France. Always a German at heart, he fought the Germans until France fell and then escaped to the United States. He later acquired US citizenship and served for several years as an officer with the American forces of occupation in Germany.

HH eventually settled in the Italian south of Switzerland. He was a brilliant polyglot, and it was said that he could – had he wished – have written his books in any one of four languages. As he smilingly admitted to his few friends, however, he dreamt in German, and that was the language he wrote in.

'You wanted my opinion,' he told Fellini, 'so here it is. I've spent hours wading through Norden's books and papers. My prevailing impression is that he must have been a fanatical and unrepentant Nazi. His political beliefs had the intensity of a religious faith.

'Your man didn't bother to defend Nazi Germany – in his view, there was no need. It's obvious he took the Third Reich's historical immortality for granted, so he confined himself to evolving an updated philosophical basis for Nazism.

'He didn't base it solely on the theories of Rosenberg, who wrote *The Myth of the 20th Century*. His direct inspiration was a man named Waldemar Wesel, whose *Maxims* were approved reading in Nazi Germany. They were only written for the inner circle, but then, who else mattered?

'Norden was busy re-casting Wesel's ideas in a definitive work. Projected title, with apologies to the late Adolf Hitler: *Unser Kampf – our* struggle!'

Progress report by Inspector Luigi Fellini of Lugano:
Two of the three safe-deposit boxes for which keys were found in Norden's apartment have now been located.

Key No. 1 fitted a Lock Box at the Società Banca Svizzera, Lugano, an affiliate of the Schweizerischer Bankverein of Basle and Zürich. It was found to contain US 100-dollar bills totalling nearly $2 million, also just under £1 million in pound notes, though these were quickly discovered to be forgeries.

Key No. 2 opened a deposit box at the First National Bank. This contained about 80 sheets of manuscript headed *Heinz-Hermann Norden*, *Autobiographical Notes* and a thick wad of papers including passports, travel documents, press clippings and special permits of various kinds.

Fellini reviewed his haul with mingled delight and dismay. 'Almost too good to be true,' he muttered, and sent the new batch of papers for appraisal by HH in Ascona.

They held the author spellbound. His first reaction was to dismiss the autobiographical notes as the figments of a fevered imagination. Then he recalled that this world of unbridled human behaviour had actually existed: more than that, it had endured for twelve years, almost to the day, under the sole and undisputed aegis of Nazi Germany.

Statements made by Dr Maximilian Isaac Londoner, together with some details of his personal background:

Dr Londoner was a surgeon of international standing, German-born but a naturalized US citizen. A cancer specialist, he had originally practised in Munich, where he performed a number of breast cancer operations made doubly sensational by his extreme youth and innovative surgical techniques. For reasons that were never fully explained, he emigrated to the States in 1935 and was welcomed with open arms by Boston University.

He had previously – in 1933 – persuaded his widowed mother, Ruth Golda Londoner, to settle in Lugano. Frau Londoner quickly fell in love with the scenic charms of Ticino and its inhabitants' leisurely way of life. She took only a few months to master Italian, and was soon addressed by everyone as 'Signora' Londoner. Her devoted son visited her every spring.

This year, as usual, the surgeon's visit included a reunion with HH. The two were childhood friends, having attended the same school. They celebrated their reunion at a first-class restaurant serving Tuscan wines and Roman specialities, but it was not until the coffee that Dr Londoner tentatively embarked on a confession which HH, as he admitted later, found 'simply staggering'.

'It was a few days ago,' Dr Londoner began. 'I'd been lunching with my mother at the Hotel Meister, where she lives. I was delighted by her appetite, her energy and vitality – her lively approach to things in general. She's over eighty, don't forget. A while back she was invited to contribute to a Jewish cemetery, but she refused. Maternity hospitals and nursery schools interested her far more than a collection of mouldering bones.

'Anyway, I left her feeling well fed and thoroughly pleased with life. Then I went for a stroll along the promenade. I was feeling vaguely euphoric, but it didn't last. All at once I caught sight of a man. His face was horrifyingly familiar.

'I'd only seen him once before, and that was nearly forty years ago. I've become an old man since then, but he seemed virtually unchanged. The same silky fair hair, the same icy blue eyes – the look of a man who rides roughshod over everything and everyone in his way. I recognized him right away.'

'Are you positive?' HH asked. 'Sure you aren't suffering from a trauma – the Jewish one? Nobody could blame you after all that happened, Max, but it didn't happen to you alone. You're still alive, remember. You weren't among the millions they butchered – you got away.'

Dr Londoner nodded. 'I know, but there's one episode in my life I've never discussed with a living soul until now. One summer evening in 1935, just as I emerged from my Munich operating theatre, I was arrested and bundled off, bloodstained gown and all. After a harrowing trip in a cattle-truck with about 30 fellow-prisoners, all Jewish, I ended up somewhere in the Bavarian Forest not too far from Munich.

'That was where I met Siegfried, standing there at the gate like an Arno Breker statue. We might have been bugs, the way he looked us over. Then he sorted us into two groups with a jerk of the thumb, meaning this one to the right, that one to the left. In other words, summary execution or a lingering death.'

'But you survived,' HH said.

'Sure, but I can't pretend I owe my survival to heroism. It was because of money invested by some friends of mine. One of the guards – I think his name was Hagen, though they also called him Dietmar – was ready to make a deal. Anyway, I was released. I got out via Switzerland and made it to the States.'

'And now you think you've had another brush with this Siegfried – the man who condemned you to death with a jerk of his thumb. Are you absolutely sure it was him? Did he recognize you?'

'He stared straight through me, but that doesn't mean much. How many mass murderers make an individual note of their victims? After feeling sick and dizzy for a moment or two, I followed him back to his hotel, the Paris. He was registered there under the name S. Fried.'

'Can you tell me the exact date of this encounter, Max?'

'Yes, it was the day after my mother's birthday.'

Which happened to be the day on which a German expatriate named Norden was gunned down in his Viale Cattaneo apartment.

THE WESEL GROUP

1 Recruiting an Elite

Extract from the autobiographical notes of Heinz-Hermann Norden:
'1 May 1933. My 20th birthday – probably the most momentous
day in my life. I spent it at a special training camp near Prien
on the Chiemsee, undergoing a two-week endurance and physical
efficiency course for selected members of the SS.

'Here I met the man to whom I owe so infinitely much:
Waldemar Wesel, my master and mentor. Here too I met my
chief rival, if not mortal enemy. Or rather, I began to see him in
his true colours. But what was that in comparison with the
historic challenge ahead?

'This marked the true beginning of my life. It has not been a
life without significance.'

1 May 1933 was a crisp, clear day. In the dawn hours, tatters of
mist had drifted towards the camp from the near-by lake, but these
were soon dispersed by a refreshing breeze which encouraged the
human frame to give of its best.

The camp consisted of tents pitched round a flagpole from
which, fluttering proudly in the breeze, flew the swastika flag:
black emblem on a white disk on a red background. Fifty SS
cadets were drawn up on parade, each one hand-picked from among
several hundred candidates in accordance with the motto, *The
Best shall be First!*

The camp commander was a man named Bertram, known as
'Bull' Bertram, a sinewy heavyweight who had been a front-line
officer in the Great War and was reputed to have won a chestful
of medals. He customarily turned out stripped to the waist,
wearing only the pants of a tan track suit, muscular as a prize-
fighter.

'Right, boys!' he bellowed. 'Show us what you're made of.'

Stop-watches and tape-measures were used to make an accurate
record of cadet progress in cross-country running, long-jumping,

long-distance swimming, weight-lifting and scaling ropes, poles and trees.

It had taken Bull Bertram only four days to split his 50 cadets into five groups. Among those assigned to Group 1, the most promising, was Heinz-Hermann Norden, whose energy and dogged determination had won him a clear lead over all but one of the rest.

The only cadet within spitting-distance of Norden was a youth named Hagen, who contested each event with grim perseverance. He had beaten Norden in the long-jump by just over 10 centimetres but trailed by nearly 2 minutes in the 10-kilometre cross-country race. Today's trial event was No. 13, heaving the stone, an ancient Germanic sport.

Norden was not only determined to beat Hagen but confident of doing so. Though less muscular, he had the better technique. His first throw beat Hagen's by nearly 50 centimetres, but Hagen more than halved this advantage at the next attempt. The contest soon developed into a duel between the two front-runners – a duel destined to endure, on the athletic field and off.

Meanwhile, both contestants became aware that Bertram had been joined by a stranger. Slim and elegant with piercing eyes, he was not the type of man to go unnoticed despite his elaborately countrified Bavarian costume: square-toed brogues, leather shorts and piped jacket.

Bertram greeted the stranger with obvious respect and shook hands warmly. A moment later there came a renewed cry of 'Right, boys! Show us what you're made of.'

With his next throw, Norden achieved a distance that shattered the camp record. Hagen almost matched it. The rest trailed far behind.

'Remarkable,' observed the visitor, who had been watching intently. 'Is this for my benefit, Bertram, or are they really above average?'

'The pick of the bunch, Sturmbannführer,' Bertram told him. 'Probably the finest human material I've processed in the last six months.'

'I'd like to meet them both, but individually. Norden first.'

Wolfgang Bertram, described as an athletics coach, commenting on the episode nearly 40 years later:

I always was the athletic type and still am – just that, nothing more. I may be over 70 but I still go mountain-climbing and play tennis and a good game of golf.

Yes, I ran a training camp in those days. My job was to toughen the cadets up, but that's as far as it went. If the authorities took advantage of my honest endeavours, they did so without my knowledge or consent. All that interested me was healthy minds in healthy bodies.

Certainly I remember the day that SS major turned up at the camp. It wasn't a routine visit, you see. I'd been warned to expect him by Reichsführer Himmler himself – in the strictest confidence, of course. As for knowing what he wanted, I had absolutely no idea.

'So you're Norden,' said the visitor. 'First name Heinz-Hermann.'

His voice was soft, with an underlying sibilance. It became almost snakelike when he hissed the letter S and developed into a snarl when he rolled his Rs. 'My name is Wesel, Sturmbannführer Wesel. I'm here on a special assignment, but don't be alarmed. It's purely for your information, understand?'

'Yessir!' barked Norden, standing at attention with textbook poise. 'Yessir – I think so.'

'At ease! And address me simply as Wesel. In other words, forget for the moment that I'm your senior officer. I don't attach any importance to the outward trappings of rank. What concerns me is mutual trust and co-operation, understand?'

'Yessir. You mean we're both members of a unit pledged to absolute loyalty and ready for anything.' Norden uttered this quotation from the SS training manual as if he were undergoing an oral examination.

Waldemar Wesel nodded approvingly as his clear, cold eyes studied the figure in front of him. Norden stood just over six feet tall, a slim but sturdy youth with the resilience of a steel spring and the lithe grace of a wild animal. He had a smooth, vacant face, flaxen hair, a high forehead and pale blue eyes.

'I gather you matriculated a year ago. You received excellent marks in nearly every subject, so why didn't you go on to university? Why didn't you apply for a post in the civil service or join the army with a view to becoming an officer? What made you join the SS?'

'I felt I had to obey the call of duty, Sturmbannführer – Herr Wesel, I mean. We Germans are living in an age of radical change: the new era heralded by our leader Adolf Hitler. If possible, I want to share in it.'

'Well said, but have you any idea what the new era may entail? How far are you prepared to go?'

'I can't conceive of anything I wouldn't be willing to do in the service of our Führer.'

'That sounds promising, Norden.' Waldemar Wesel's expression conveyed that he was not displeased with Norden's attitude but far from fully satisfied. With the sunlight gleaming on his sleek head, he started to stroll round the athletic field. Norden, a respectful two paces to his left, listened attentively to the monologue that followed.

Its theme was that their beloved Germany had been robbed of a well-deserved victory in the last war and was now surrounded by enemies: the British, French and Americans – 'all of whom we'd have polished off, given a fair chance!'

Worse still, they were threatened from within by their hereditary enemies: back-stabbers, besmirchers of national honour, week-kneed liberals, socialist pigs, communists – and, most dangerous of all, that bane of the German race, the Jews!

'In other words, Norden, we must clean house! The Weimar Republic inflicted fifteen years of systematic destruction on this country. Our task is to obliterate the past and rise above it.'

'Only one man can help us do that – the Führer!'

'Exactly, but do you see what a monumental purge the country's going to need? Are you ready to do your part?'

'I certainly am, Sturmbannführer. There's a new age dawning, here and now. I mean to be part of it.'

Excerpts from a report by the Institute of Modern History, Munich:
At least three people surnamed Wesel (not Wessel) are listed as having belonged to the politico-educational wing of the SS and

its special agencies:

1. Wesel, Kurt, National Socialist pamphleteer, later war correspondent, subsequently editor of a post-war newspaper in Southern Germany. Died in 1972.

2. Wesel, Erich. Radio commentator, author and lecturer. Died just after the war.

3. Wesel, first name variously recorded as Waldemar, Walter or Walt, nickname Waldi. Fate unknown. Reputed to be one of the Third Reich's most influential back-room boys. Although never officially entered in any contemporary personnel list, Waldemar Wesel may be assumed to have belonged to Hitler's inner circle, like Heydrich, who was allegedly a close friend of his.

Wesel may also be regarded as one of the ideological trailblazers of National Socialism. Two of his books attracted special attention, at least in the relevant quarters. These were *Nothing Ventured, Nothing Gained* (1931) and *A Future Written in Blood* (1932), both published by Franz Eber Associates of Munich. Each one was dedicated to Adolf Hitler, in the first referred to as 'the front-line soldier', in the second as 'the redeemer of the German soul'.

'You seem to be a conscientious youngster, Norden,' Wesel said graciously as they continued to circle the lakeside camp site. 'Would you describe your allegiance to the Führer as absolute and unqualified?'

'Yessir.'

'Good,' said Wesel, 'because that's who I've come from. I'm here at his personal command.'

Norden was overcome. It was as if he could see his beloved Führer, standing just behind Wesel and staring directly into his eyes.

Wesel's satisfaction grew. Now strolling along like a couple of old comrades, they left the athletic field behind and walked together down a crunchy gravel path bordered by sunlit meadows of lush green grass.

The SS major asked endless questions. He seemed to want to know all there was to know about his young companion. Did he have any personal commitments – was there a girl he planned to marry? Alternatively, was he aware of any homosexual tendencies? That was no disqualification in itself but could be important, so Norden mustn't take offence at the question. Finally, could he conceive of a situation so unnerving it would affect his capacity to act with the requisite speed and determination?

Norden's response to all these inquiries was an unequivocal negative.

'The Führer,' Wesel went on, 'has commissioned me to recruit an élite unit, a nucleus of our country's finest young men. This might seem an enormity to some – certainly to those incapable of recognizing the signs of the times. To those who realize that nothing in life is free, and that we must fight for the attainment of our objectives, nothing could be more natural.' He paused. 'Are you ready to join that struggle?'

'Yes, Sturmbannführer,' said Norden.

'Even if it entails self-sacrifice, self-denial and hardship? Even if it means being utterly ruthless, no matter towards whom – yourself included. What is your attitude to comradeship?'

'Comradeship,' Norden recited, 'is the basis of our SS brotherhood.'

'What about Hagen? Does he belong in that category?'

'Of course, Sturmbannführer.'

'I get the impression you don't think much of him.'

'Not as a person,' Norden agreed with engaging candour. 'Perhaps it's because he doesn't quite share my outlook – and vice versa. But of course, that doesn't alter the fact that we're comrades pledged to a common cause. Nothing else matters.'

'I've more or less decided to offer you a place in this crack unit I spoke of,' Wesel said. 'I can only accept a handful of recruits. Do you want to join?'

'Yessir,' said Norden. 'I'm ready for anything.'

'That's settled, then.' Wesel sounded tolerably pleased. 'However, that brings you face to face with an immediate decision.'

The SS major gazed into the distance with a contemplative smile. His eyes roved across the dark and lustrous waters of the Chiemsee to the mountains defining the western horizon. Their peaks were still dusted with snow.

'Let's assume, Norden, that I proposed to enrol Hagen in this unit as well as yourself, but only with your prior consent. What would your decision be? Think carefully.'

'I should await your orders, Sturmbannführer, and obey them without question.'

Statements made by Brigadeführer Clausen of SS Operational Headquarters and taken from a Nuremberg trial transcript:
I was unaware of any élite formations specially trained for exceptional assignments and invested with unlimited powers. To be more precise, no such units were officially listed in our files.

I did, however, hear rumours that hand-picked units of this nature – probably two or three in all – had come into being from 1933 onwards. A few reports on the subject, presumably inspired by ill-disposed political exiles, did in fact appear in the so-called international press – not only in *The Times* of London but the *Neue Zürcher Zeitung* and *New York Times*. The details they contained seemed highly suspect, and they were officially classified as deliberate scare-mongering.

I cannot, however, entirely dismiss the possibility that such units did exist and were financed by one of Reichsführer Himmler's special funds. Between 1933 and 1939, Himmler disbursed 50 to 60 million marks free from public accountability – a budget which trebled or quadrupled in later years.

Waldemar Wesel's name is not unknown to me, but I can tell you nothing about his special functions from, say, 1933 onwards. I do recall that he was promoted General of the Waffen-SS in 1938 or 1939, presumably at Himmler's personal behest and in recognition of special services to the Führer and Fatherland.

Precisely what services, I can't say. No, really not. Even to a man in my position, some things were a closed book.

'Bertram, my friend,' Wesel told the camp supervisor, 'you've got a very promising bunch here. But I'm going to rob you of your best man – Norden.'

'For my money, Hagen's a match for him,' Bertram declared. 'He's a crack shot with a pistol. Why not treat yourself to a demonstration of his marksmanship?'

Wesel didn't hesitate, especially as the handling of firearms came high on his list of priorities. He already knew the marksmanship rating of his protégé, Norden, from the personal record submitted by Bertram. It was well above average, but watching Hagen in action might help complete his assessment of the pair. Hagen appealed to him, somehow – he looked cold-blooded in a saturnine way Wesel found highly attractive. The SS major was a good judge, if not of all men, at least of his own kind.

There followed a repeat of Test No. 20, 'Pistol-shooting from a Standing Position without Support.' Marksmanship ratings were based on the time taken to empty an eight-round magazine and the number of hits scored. It was an almost light-hearted proceeding because the plywood target represented an unmistakably Jewish individual seen in profile facing left: ringlets, nose hooked like a synagogue key, chin adorned with an oriental beard. This target, one of a special batch supplied by the Reich Ordnance Depot in Munich, was humorously referred to as 'Moses'.

Bertram roared, 'Open fire!'

The members of Group 1 blazed away at their national anathema. They drilled it at random, scoring numerous hits in the dummy's trunk and head. Sturmbannführer Wesel watched them as if supervising the efforts of a party of enthusiastic schoolchildren.

'Now Norden!' Bertram decreed briskly. 'Run out a new target.'

Heinz-Hermann Norden looked serene but alert. He turned his back as the target was run out, the pistol dangling casually from his right hand. On the command 'Fire!' he whirled and started shooting. He emptied his magazine of all eight rounds – all eight landed in the dummy's head.

Waldemar Wesel gave Bertram a congratulatory nod. 'Norden's good. Can anyone here beat him – Hagen, say?'

'Two guns for Hagen!' shouted Bertram. 'Right, boy, let's see your speciality.'

'Yessir,' said Hagen, sounding supremely self-confident.

He took one loaded pistol in each hand and weighed them for a moment. Then he planted his legs slightly apart. Releasing the safety-catches with his thumbs, he drew a deep breath and said 'Ready!'

Bertram gave permission to fire. Hagen raised each gun in turn, first with the left hand, then with the right, and emptied their respective magazines: a total of sixteen rounds fired with bewildering speed.

The echoes died away. And there on the dummy with the Jewish features, standing out clearly against its cardiac region, was a swastika.

'Well,' Bertram said proudly to his visitor, 'was I exaggerating?'

Wesel nodded. 'I'll have a chat with Hagen as well.'

The interview took place in the butts a minute later. The two men stood facing each other, screened from view by thick banks of earth. Wesel looked Hagen over, appraising him inch by inch like a valuable item of breeding stock.

'Where did you learn to shoot like that?'

'My father was a gamekeeper,' Hagen said. 'I could drop a royal stag first shot, even as a boy. My dad was found murdered a few years ago, by the way. They said he'd been killed by poachers, but I figure he was murdered by socialists or communists. He was a very patriotic type.'

'And who taught you the swastika trick?'

'I thought it up myself. It didn't take too long to perfect – only two years – but now I can do it in my sleep.'

Waldemar Wesel found it hard not to betray excessive admiration. 'I watched you very closely while you were shooting, Hagen. It struck me that you kept both eyes open – wide open. That breaks all the accepted rules of aiming. The backsight and foresight should be aligned with one eye only.'

'One eye's all I've got,' Hagen said. 'I lost the sight of the other two years ago, at a Party meeting. The hall was attacked by some Bavarian nationalists egged on by local Jews. There was a fight and I got clobbered. Everyone's called me Hagen since then, after the one-eyed character in the Nibelung story.'

'So it isn't your real name?'

'My real name's Dietmar.'

'Hagen will do,' Wesel said. Abruptly, he added, 'What do you think of Norden?'

'Nobody better.'

'Any reservations?'

'None at all. We're both in the same outfit. That means I

respect him – all the way.'

Wesel studied Hagen intently. His estimated value was rising by leaps and bounds.

'I'm told you had a brother who was infected with Catholicism, Hagen. He caught the disease at school, I gather. From the Jesuits.'

'My brother's dead,' Hagen replied. 'Has been ever since that assembly-room riot at Weilheim two years back – the one where I lost an eye. He got his head bashed in. By me, in self-defence, of course.'

Wesel stroked his chin. 'In that case, may I take it you're ready to pledge yourself heart and soul to the Führer and his cause, allowing nothing to stand in your way?'

'Nothing and no one.'

'That's all I wanted to know.' Wesel's words signified that Hagen, né Dietmar, was destined for enrolment with Norden in the Wesel Group. The bargain was sealed with a symbolic act to which the Sturmbannführer attached great importance: an intense and conspiratorial handshake.

A little later that day, 1 May 1933, Wesel sauntered up to the camp commander.

'I'm taking the pair of them, Bertram - Norden and Hagen. Have them ready to move out in half an hour, complete with all their gear. They're mine from now on, so forget them. As far as you're concerned, they never existed.'

2 The Oath-taking

During the afternoon of that memorable day – it was still 1 May 1933 – Sturmbannführer Wesel's big black Mercedes purred through the Upper Bavarian countryside. Some two hours after leaving Prien on the Chiemsee it neared the outskirts of Wolfratshausen. Wesel sat up front with the civilian driver while Norden and Hagen occupied the rear seats.

Silence had reigned throughout the trip. Not a word passed between the four until Wesel addressed the man at his side.

'Head for the hill,' he said, 'as usual.' The driver didn't even nod.

They drove through Wolfratshausen, then up a winding road to the Starnberger See. Passing a picturesque village, the car continued its steep ascent until, quite suddenly, it pulled up and the hum of the engine died. Before them rose an almost conical hill surmounted by a lone tree: a massive oak of formidable aspect. A German oak – probably several centuries old.

Wesel got out and strode towards it. At a nod from the driver, Norden and Hagen hurried after him.

Once at the summit, the Sturmbannführer leant against the gnarled trunk of the symbolic tree and, with an almost benedictory gesture, indicated the panorama below him.

They all gazed out across the little township far beneath, out into a vast tract of countryside extending as far as the mountains, which were still visible. They even thought they could detect, just forward of this mountainous backdrop, the shimmer of the Chiemsee beside which their camp had stood.

'This,' Wesel said portentously, 'is an historic spot. Our Führer Adolf Hitler has often called a halt beneath this oak on his trips to the German Alps, which he loves so dearly. This is the very spot, too, where he made the decision to build arterial roads of vast size and extent, motorways running from Hamburg to Berchtesgaden, Berlin to Munich, Königsberg to Berlin – a unique road network capable of facilitating the movement of troops with a speed of which only Napoleon dreamed before him. That is,' he added, 'if our enemies ever force us to mobilize.'

Norden nodded, genuinely stirred by these heroic visions. Hagen found it easier to hold his emotions in check, but even his silence had an ecclesiastical quality.

All at once, as if deliberately bringing them back to earth, Wesel said: 'We didn't come here just to admire the view. You're going to sign two sworn statements, an oath of unqualified allegiance to the Führer and a pledge of absolute secrecy. Then we can get down to business, not before.'

Documents found among the personal effects of Heinz-Hermann Norden exactly 40 years later in Lugano.

1. Oath of allegiance:

I, Heinz-Hermann Norden, born at Stettin on 1 May 1913, hereby declare my willingness to render absolute obedience to my Führer Adolf Hitler. This absolute and unqualified duty of obedience applies only to my Führer or to those persons directly appointed and invested with authority by him.

This I affirm and swear on my honour.

2. Pledge of secrecy:

I, Heinz-Hermann Norden, born at Stettin on 1 May 1913, hereby undertake conscientiously, loyally and promptly to carry out all the orders and assignments given me, and to treat them as State secrets of the utmost confidentiality.

I further undertake never to discuss these matters with an outsider or to divulge details thereof by word of mouth or in writing. The discussion and evaluation of orders and instructions devolves solely on my immediate superior, acting with the Führer's personal authority.

This pledge will, of course, remain fully effective in the event of my retirement or dismissal from the service.

Waldemar Wesel took possession of the documents after they had been read, signed, and sealed with another handshake. Stowing them carefully in his briefcase, he said, 'You are now members of the élite unit which the Führer has personally directed me to recruit.'

36

Norden and Hagen treated their new commanding officer, who was still leaning nonchalantly against Hitler's oak, to a look of heroic pride or oxlike trust, whichever.

'Your probationary period,' Wesel continued, 'will take the form of an intensive training course lasting four to six weeks. I'm sure you'll more than measure up to the demands I make on you. I've seldom been disappointed by men of my own calibre.

'You will spend this crucial introductory period as my guests – or rather, guests of the Führer. Board, accommodation and clothing will be provided free of charge. You will also receive pocket money – to begin with, 250 marks a week.'

Hagen gave an involuntary start. 'But that's a thousand a month!'

'If all goes according to plan, you'll have no money worries from now on. Once you complete your probationary period, you go to work in earnest. You'll find your assignments arduous but rewarding.

'After graduation, you will be appointed to senior SS rank. You'll also be given access to bank accounts regularly augmented by awards for merit. Your initial credit balance will be a five-figure sum of which the first digit will, I believe, be 2 in the first place and 5 shortly afterwards.'

Hagen's eyes shone. He was evidently engaged in some mental arithmetic. 'Not bad!' he said.

But Norden, like a climber scaling more exalted heights, asked, 'Shall we also have the honour of meeting our Führer?'

'That,' Wesel replied as though presenting them with a blank cheque, 'is his earnest expectation.'

'When?'

'As soon as you've successfully completed your primary training and I can inform the Führer that my team is complete and fully operational. You'll be six men in all, by the way. The other four are already installed at the former Villa Salomon in Feldafing on the Starnberger See, which is where we're bound for now. Most of the locals are farmers, but a number of the larger estates have been acquired by the Party. There's an administrative college and two all-year-round training camps for members of the Hitler Youth and German Girls' League. Last but not least, plumb in the middle of them, there's us.'

Still leaning against Hitler's oak, the SS major beckoned to his driver, who headed for the tree at a brisk trot despite his ponderous build. He stationed himself in front of Wesel, not army-fashion but in an unmistakably disciplined way.

'This,' announced Wesel, 'is a member of our group, Driver Sobottke.'

'Pleased to meet you,' Norden said politely, and shook hands. Hagen, who preferred to remain aloof, merely stated his name and nodded.

Sobottke smirked at the new recruits. 'Don't worry, I won't be giving you any orders – not authorized to. I just pass them on and offer a helping hand if necessary.'

'We'll get along all right.' Hagen gave the driver a challenging stare. 'If I need any help, I'll ask.'

'I should add,' Wesel put in, 'that our friend Sobottke is a martyr to the cause. They gave him life imprisonment for direct complicity in two murders.'

'I spent nearly ten years inside,' Sobottke amplified, grinning broadly. He seemed almost to relish the recollection. 'They put me away in 1923. I really made three hits, not two, but they couldn't prove it, plus another couple they never knew about – or didn't want to. Talk about law and order! Those Weimar cops didn't know their ass from their elbow.'

Visibly surprised and impressed, Norden and Hagen stared at the big, genial-looking man as if he were a species of mythical beast.

'Those were the days when patriots had to take the law into their own hands,' Wesel explained. 'In 1923 a number of treacherous subversives were executed by an organization to which I myself belonged – one with which the Führer also maintained links. Even at that time, Sobottke was the strong right arm of one such patriotic group. Naturally, he was among the very first to be released when we came to power.'

Hagen walked over to the driver, grasped his hand and gave it a powerful squeeze. 'It'll be a pleasure working with someone like you.'

They reached Feldafing before sunset. The road leading uphill from the centre of the village terminated abruptly in a stone wall the height of a bull elephant. Centuries-old trees loomed beyond, half glimpsed through wrought-iron gates of Bavarian baroque craftsmanship. Sobottke sounded his horn – two shorts and a long.

While the car was still idling outside in the lane, a woman materialized at the gates of the property across the way. She was tall, full-bosomed and decidedly Nordic, wearing a clinging blue silk dress. Waving a matching scarf, she hailed the car cheerfully.

'Heil Hitler, Herr Wesel!'

'Heil Hitler,' Wesel responded tersely. Although barely able to conceal his repugnance, he strove to remain civil. He removed his hat and raised his right arm in the Nazi salute.

'Give them another toot,' he snarled at Sobottke under his breath.

As soon as the sound of the horn had died away, the voice of the voluptuous blonde rang out once more. 'Do drop in some time, Herr Wesel – *any* time.' Her eyes veered towards the two young men in the back of the car, alight with interest. 'Don't hesitate to say if I can help. That's what neighbours are for.'

'Many thanks for your kind offer, my dear Frau Franke,' Wesel called back, still studiously polite. 'And please give my best regards to your husband.'

Information about Frau Franke volunteered subsequently by Driver Sobottke:

She was always pestering us, particularly the first few months. Then it stopped. Wesel couldn't bear her but he couldn't afford to offend her either.

The husband of this Frau Franke – Hermine, I think her first name was – was a big wheel in the Party with a lot of grateful sidekicks on his payroll. He hardly ever showed his face in Feldafing – they probably kept him too busy in Berlin, pinching his secretary's ass and other people's money, I'd wager – but I'm only guessing.

Anyway, his wife seemed to be feeling left out. It was getting cobwebs on it, if you know what I mean. She had a good body, even if she wasn't sweet sixteen. What's more, she was as hot as a bitch in season – or so they said.

Hardly surprising, the way she played up to Wesel – not him personally, of course, but his recruits. She never stopped trying – 'let me be neighbourly, help to boost the boys' morale, do my bit for Führer and Fatherland . . .'

It was a tricky set-up and Wesel knew it. Her old man was a Party bigwig, don't forget, and that made her hard to handle.

At long last a gardener bustled up. He opened the gate, swept off his hat and deferentially lowered his gaze to the expanse of immaculate white gravel at his feet.

The driver rounded a 90-degree bend, then headed straight for the Villa. At the main entrance, dignified by a white portico, the new arrivals were greeted by a reception committee of two. One was a sturdy but attractive young woman, the other a lissom young man with a winning smile and a melodious voice.

Wesel indicated the latter. 'This is Raffael,' he explained, 'our group secretary and steward. Raffael is directly responsible to me and looks after my personal welfare. Your own needs will be attended to by Clara here.'

Clara discreetly sized up the newcomers. She was a rustic beauty, a flower of the Bavarian backwoods, almost graceful despite her opulent figure.

'You say she's going to attend to our needs?' Hagen observed enthusiastically. 'All of them, Sturmbannführer?'

'It's all or nothing in this outfit,' Wesel said dispassionately. 'Our very existence is the supreme exception – a passport to any behaviour that doesn't disrupt or endanger our band of brothers. Do that and you endanger yourself.'

'I see,' said Hagen, falling back a pace.

Wesel smiled indulgently. 'You've still got plenty to learn. Start by moving into your quarters. You'll join the others for supper at 20.00 precisely.'

From Heinz-Hermann Norden's autobiographical notes:

The accommodation at Feldafing was remarkably luxurious. The top floor of the new wing contained separate quarters for each of us. Not just bedrooms but three-room suites. The furnishings were high-quality and brand new. Even Hagen was temporarily at a loss for words.

Although what happened next may seem innocuous, it immediately put me on my guard. Hagen made another attempt to assert himself at my expense, and that I refused to tolerate.

Norden and Hagen were conducted up a staircase covered in thick, footstep-muffling carpet to the first floor of the Villa. Here Raffael paused outside the two empty suites reserved for them.

'Both apartments are exactly the same size,' he explained politely. 'The furniture's the same too, but the basic colour-scheme varies. One's beige and the other's grey. Oh yes, and one has a view of the lake. The other looks out over the garden.'

Hagen eyed Norden warily. 'Mind if I take first pick?'

'You bet I do.'

'What's that supposed to mean?' Hagen took a cautious but belligerent step towards Norden. 'Trying to call the tune already? Who the hell do you think you are?'

'You'll find out soon enough.'

'Just a minute, gentlemen,' Raffael broke in. 'This won't do at all. One of the Sturmbannführer's cardinal rules is equality. We're all on the same footing here – nobody takes precedence over anybody else.'

'I accept that,' Norden said simply.

'So what are you grousing about?' Hagen snapped.

Raffael went for a quick compromise. 'You may find you're arguing about nothing. Each set of rooms has a lot to recommend it.'

'Fine,' said Hagen. 'In that case I'll take the one with the lake view.'

'That's my choice too,' retorted Norden.

'Look,' Raffael said, 'how would it be if you toss for it – and the winner gets first choice?'

Hagen shrugged. 'It's all right with me.'

'Count me out,' Norden said flatly. 'I'm opposed to gambling in any form. On principle.'

The secretary's late-gothic angel-face turned pink. Coming from a frame as willowy as his, Raffael's subdued voice had a surprisingly incisive ring. 'Right, here's what we'll do. Apartments 5 and 6 will be allocated alphabetically. No. 5 goes to you, Hagen. Norden, you get No. 6. Kindly move in at once.'

'Are you authorized to make such a decision?' Hagen demanded.

'I am,' Raffael replied calmly.

This gave Norden the apartment he had wanted in the first place – the one with the view of the lake. Hagen felt he'd suffered a temporary setback, but there was always a next time.

The first evening meal Norden and Hagen were privileged to share in this exclusive company began at 8 p.m. on the dot.

The dining-hall was dominated by a long refectory table neatly laid with antique silver cutlery, hand-cut Murano glassware, choice Lyons napery and Meissen china. Blood-red hot-house roses were massed in bowls of a pale Nordic blue.

Smartly attired in black full-dress SS uniform, snow-white shirt and patent leather shoes, Waldemar Wesel stood just inside the door. He extended his right hand and gripped the hands that shot out to take it as if acknowledging a sixfold oath of allegiance. Sixfold because the newcomers were flanked by another four young men of similar height and build, their gaze and bearing expressive of the same hardy self-assurance.

'First, gentlemen, let's fortify ourselves,' Wesel told his recruits. 'I'll introduce you as we go, but there's no hurry. We'll have plenty of time to get used to each other, so let's not rush things.'

He took his place at the head of the table, waving Norden and Hagen into the chairs on either side of him.

'As to what this is all about, gentlemen, Goethe put it in a nutshell: *Grim weeks, gay festivities*. From now on we work as hard as we play. Our unit is up to strength. All that remains is to get it operational as quickly as possible.'

Wesel rose, glass in hand, and looked at each one in turn, beginning with Norden and ending with Hagen. Then he rapped out:

'To our homeland, our nation, our Leader!'

Contrary to their expectations, the recruits were not called upon to sing the Horst Wessel Song. The Sturmbannführer simply drained his glass at a gulp and they followed suit.

Wesel looked supremely happy. His hour had struck.

Extracts from the transcript of a post-war interview between Stephan Sobottke and Captain Douglas G. Scott of US Military Intelligence:

I've spent a lifetime driving cars. I started by chauffeuring the boss of some association or other, just after the first war. I was even drafted to drive for the Nazis later on – strong-armed would be a better word. Got myself wounded three times in World War II driving staff cars under fire. Now I own a fleet of cabs.

What went on inside that villa at Feldafing? I only wish I could tell you, Captain, honestly.

I was billeted in an annexe and acted as chauffeur. Abroad? Yes, sometimes. I took them anywhere I was ordered.

Who belonged to the outfit? There were about half a dozen of them. Where did they come from and what did they do? Search me!

No, I can't tell you their names either. I don't think they ever used their real names. Believe me, Captain, the place was a closed book.

Leave well alone, that's what I told myself.

Memorandum appended to the above by Captain Scott:

Sobottke was interrogated several times. From what he let slip, coupled with statements by former members of the villa's staff, the six inmates were as follows:

1. *Siegfried*, probably the son of a Rhineland schoolmaster. Commonly referred to at Feldafing as 'Snow White', he seems to have been dumb but docile – in other words, a lethal instrument in the hands of those who knew how to manipulate him.

2. *Hermann*. He was reputed to be highly intelligent and determined, witness his Feldafing nickname 'Hell-bent Hermann'. We may assume with some certainty that he was a ruthless and violent criminal with several previous convictions.

3 and 4. *Berner and Bergmann*, also known as 'the Siamese Twins'. These two appear to have been inseparables who enjoyed

a relationship based on homosexual attraction.

5 and 6. The last two to join the group and – as far as one can judge at this point in time – probably the most important.

First, *Norden*: a starry-eyed idealist who unflinchingly obeyed 'the dictates of his conscience'. Human life meant nothing to him.

Last of all, *Hagen*, sometimes known as Dietmar: a cool, calculating and completely ruthless character who stopped at nothing, even where his so-called comrades were concerned.

From the pre-1933 writings of Waldemar Wesel.

On responsibility:
Always remember you are a German! As such, you owe a profound debt to your nation, its values and achievements. Never waver in this belief, even when abused, derided or persecuted for its sake. The spirit of nationhood is all-transcending.

On the Germanic heritage:
Bear in mind that you are a link in a chain more than a thousand years old. Resolve to be a strong link – one that will never break. Your distant ancestors once defied the Roman Empire so effectively that Europe, the hub of the civilized world, has since been inconceivable without the German people.

On the Leader of the Germans:
The process that began with Hermann of the Cherusci, who inflicted a crushing defeat on the Roman legions in the Teutoburger Wald, has continued ever since. It has not, however, been fostered with the requisite will to succeed. We have renounced whole empires in the course of history. This must never happen again. Our guarantee that it will not is Adolf Hitler.

This became clear to me in the course of a private interview during which the Führer told me, 'Comrade Wesel, there are great things in store – gigantic things. I am firmly resolved to face them, true to our common realization that anything which fails to destroy us can only augment our strength. As fire is to tempered steel, so shall war be to Greater Germany!'

3 Basic Training

Martial music, the Führer's favourite march, the *Badenweiler*, roused the upper floor of the former Villa Salomon early next morning.

The six recruits showed no surprise. Their reactions were swift and sure. Nobody could have guessed that they had little more than three hours' sleep behind them.

As soon as the march had died away, Raffael hailed Wesel's half-dozen, 'Heil Hitler, gentlemen! It's 06.00 on the 2nd of May 1933. Parade for breakfast at 07.30. Order of dress: No. 5, or civilian clothes. Till then, personal hygiene and physical exercise. Take as much exercise as you like, but not less than thirty minutes.'

The first to hit the open air was Norden, wearing a white T-shirt, navy-blue shorts and black gymshoes. Close on his heels came Hagen, naked except for a pair of skin-tight briefs. He was followed almost at once by Berner and Bergmann, in russet track-suits. This advance party was joined by Raffael himself, resplendent in lilac bathrobe and canary silk scarf. The morning air was very chill.

They doubled to the far corner of the garden, where numerous items of apparatus were set out. In addition to a horizontal bar, parallel bars, wall-bars, Swedish horse, long horse and trampoline, there were exercise mats arrayed with iron dumb-bells in three sizes, shot for putting, fencing equipment, medicine balls, hand-balls and footballs.

Sobottke, temporarily functioning as a gymnasium attendant, leant against the perimeter wall sipping coffee from a thick blue-and-white china mug and munching an oven-fresh roll.

There was no sign of Wesel, but he was there none the less. Wearing a pale blue version of Raffael's silk bathrobe, he had stationed himself just inside one of the french windows with a pair of binoculars.

Norden set off on several laps round the garden punctuated by flying angels over the long horse. Hagen selected the heaviest pair of dumb-bells, whirled them round his head and released them in turn. Each landed some forty metres away. Berner and Bergmann were bombarding one another with medicine balls – playfully, to all appearances, but the smack of leather on flesh indicated they were hurling them with considerable force.

Siegfried turned up a few moments later, also in sports gear. He cleared the pieces of apparatus in quick succession, omitting none. As ever with Siegfried, each exercise was performed with ritual solemnity.

Hermann was the last to appear. He leapt for the horizontal bar, took a couple of swings and launched himself into a triple grand circle. It was a display that would have graced any open championship.

Waldemar Wesel had reverted to Bavarian costume for his team's first communal breakfast, but this time with a Franconian flavour: deerskin breeches and a vivid green forester's shirt with braces and a cross-strap the width of a man's hand.

His recruits stood rigidly at attention, registering that deference to higher authority which never failed to delight him. In this respect, as in so many others, Wesel was a connoisseur.

'Right, gentlemen,' he said. 'You have been selected to join a unit of the most exclusive kind. That being so, I would ask you to bear the following in mind: nothing must be allowed to surprise or unnerve you from now on. As of now, you cease to be governed by the rules to which ordinary mortals are subject. There will be moments in your lives when you feel like lords of creation, personal instruments of the Führer's will. There will also, and inevitably, be times when you feel yourselves tested to the limit of human endurance. These ordeals must be withstood in the spirit of the front-line soldier. They are only one side of the coin that constitutes your reward.'

'What's the other?' Hagen demanded eagerly.

Wesel threw back his head and laughed. 'A full life, my friend. The best quarters, the fastest cars, the finest training. Above all, complete authority over fellow-mortals of inferior status – power of life and death. It's a challenge. Are you ready to meet it?'

Hagen led the chorus of assent.

'In that case we can start breakfast.' Wesel indicated the massive oak sideboard at the end of the room. It was a sea of plates and dishes heaped with a prodigal assortment of delicacies.

'Look at that, gentlemen. The finest food Europe can offer, and all for you.'

Raffael, who had been standing discreetly in the background, minced to the fore. He reeled off the brimming dishes: 'Deep-sea crabs and goat's cheese from Norway; Swedish herrings, fresh and pickled, marinaded or in vinegar; eels, jellied, smoked or bottled in a special sauce, from Denmark; grilled sausages, eggs and bacon *à l'anglaise*; salami from Lake Garda and mortadella from Bologna, both of the finest quality; three dozen assorted French cheeses . . .'

'A magnificent spread,' Wesel cut in, 'and quite appropriate to our privileged status. We can feed like this at any time, gentlemen – or not, as the case may be. Why not? Because we must learn, very early on, to resist temptation in all its forms. Let's start right away.'

He summoned Clara, who had prepared the feast. She appeared without delay. 'You rang, sir?' she said, hovering expectantly.

'Clara,' decreed Wesel, 'get rid of this pig-swill at once – all of it. The staff can gorge themselves on it if they choose. Throw the rest in the trash-can.'

Clara was impassive. 'Very good, sir. Will that be all?'

'No, bring us some bread. Good stale peasant bread, and make sure it's at least a week old. We'd also like some beef dripping, coarse salt and sliced onions. Oh yes, and half a dozen bottles of mineral water.'

'Nothing else, sir?' inquired Clara.

'Nothing else, my dear. What more do we need?'

From statements made in later years by Clara Heidegger:

So what's all the fuss about? It was a good position – housekeeper, officially, though I had to do some cleaning as well. A couple of dailies came in three times a week to do the rough work under my supervision. Breakfast was my job. I usually came on duty at about 6 a.m. and knocked off after lunch.

What are you hinting at? I didn't live in – never spent a night on the premises. What's more, the residents were none of my business. Anyway, I'm the proud mother of four grown-up children and happily married to a fine man – he works for the Munich City Council. I'm not going to have my life ruined by dirty-minded insinuations.

I can tell you this much. The gentleman in charge of the place never looked twice at me – that's right, Herr Wesel. He was too wrapped up in that boy-friend of his.

Herr Wesel did himself proud, and that's putting it mildly. You should have seen his suite on the ground floor! The office was as bare as a monk's cell. Then came his study, all gloss paint, plate glass and leather. Finally there was his bedroom. Out of this world, it was – like Cleopatra's boudoir in a Hollywood movie, not that his tastes were any business of mine.

The work wasn't hard and I got through it quickly. The six upstairs apartments were no trouble because the gentlemen kept those tidy themselves. They made their own beds and swabbed the wash-basins and floors like a bunch of cleaning-women.

Did anything strike me as unusual? Nothing much, except that I wasn't allowed in any of the upstairs rooms on my own. There were other standing instructions too, like always leave the doors wide open, never dust the desks, don't touch books or papers of any kind.

I didn't find life particularly exciting, not till Norden appeared on the scene. He appealed to me somehow. That would have been fine if it hadn't been for Hagen. To put it crudely, he fancied me.

It was really embarrassing, the way they fought over me, but I couldn't help feeling flattered. What girl wouldn't have?

09.00. The curriculum prescribed a lecture on 'Elementary Tactics'. Place: Common-Room No. 3. This, as Raffael explained, was the so-called Unit Library.

Lined with leather-bound volumes in oak shelves, the library had been installed by the late Herr Salomon but reorganized by Wesel – in other words, intellectually deloused and ideologically expanded. In practical terms, this meant out with Heine and in with Kolbenheyer, Zöberlein and Eckart. Karl Bücher was ousted, Fontane dislodged, and Goethe tolerated but banished to the top shelf.

At eye-level, dominating the wall on which most light fell, nestled Hitler's *Mein Kampf*, Rosenberg's *Myth of the 20th Century*, several crisp new editions of Houston Stewart Chamberlain and, of course, the works of Waldemar Wesel bound in dark brown leather. Each of these definitive expressions of the spirit of the new age was represented by half a dozen copies.

In the middle of the room stood a massive oak table flanked by six high-backed chairs, their hard seats sheathed in ox-hide but devoid of any form of padding.

'Please pretend this table is round,' Wesel enjoined his men. 'It's immaterial where you sit. No chair confers greater privileges than any other.'

'Except that I've got the light in my eyes,' Hagen pointed out. 'Norden hasn't.'

'I'll trade places if you like,' Norden said swiftly. 'The light doesn't bother me. I'm not sensitive.'

'Neither am I,' Hagen retorted.

Wesel brusquely raised his hand. 'I won't have these ridiculous fits of temperament, gentlemen, get that straight once and for all. You're here to receive instruction from me or my appointed subordinates. My orders must be obeyed unquestioningly and without the slightest attempt to jockey for position, is that perfectly clear?' He looked round sharply. 'Well, is it?'

It was. Wesel's half-dozen were gratifyingly quick to learn their lessons.

The Sturmbannführer noted this with satisfaction, then swung round to face the library door just as somebody opened it from the outside.

'Ah,' he said curtly, 'Detective Superintendent Müller.'

The newcomer must have tipped the scales at 250 pounds, if not more, but he was surprisingly light on his feet. The twinkle in his piggy eyes belied a permanent air of somnolence.

The six recruits instantly christened him 'Hippo', but their initial amusement soon yielded to burgeoning respect. They were face to face with one of their greatest mentors.

Information filed by Captain Scott of US Military Intelligence and based on personal research:

The true role of the Wesel Group, which I was ultimately assigned to investigate, defied immediate comprehension. The one thing I did spot very fast was that the murderous intensity common to all its members could only have been generated by the interaction of several factors, among them a power-crazed and inflexible determination to destroy at the bidding of higher authority.

Wesel devoted these months to assembling a Satan's brood of dedicated killers and systematically training them to a supreme pitch of efficiency. Later developments at Auschwitz were, I submit, the natural outcome of his pioneering work in this field.

To exploit the full potential of this sinister unit, Wesel welded its members into an élite. They underwent a crash course administered by the finest available experts in every branch of instruction. One of these appears to have been a man whose identification poses considerable problems. He was probably named Müller.

People with this surname, if it really was his name, are as numerous in Germany as grains of sand. The inner circle of the SS had its share, e.g. 'Synagogue' Müller of Stuttgart, who specialized in arson, or 'Peg-leg' Müller of Hanover, an inquisitor whose victims seldom survived interrogation. Another sinister member of the black brotherhood was the man who later became known as 'Gestapo' Müller, a divisional chief at the SS Security Department. This Müller was a brilliant detective and one of the most dedicated killers of his day.

It has not been possible to establish beyond doubt that the Müller at Feldafing was identical with the 'Gestapo' Müller of later years. I personally consider it probable.

The man named Müller lumbered in, panting a little. He paused near the door and surveyed the men entrusted to his not so tender mercies. Intrigued, they stared back.

Müller nodded at Wesel and Raffael in an unmistakable token of dismissal. Not a word was uttered until the door had closed behind them.

'Well,' he said in a mild voice, 'which one of you is the best pistol-shot?'

'Me, I reckon,' Hagen replied without hesitation. 'I never score less than 90 per cent with either hand.'

'Me neither,' Norden said, 'except that I don't turn it into a circus act. I'm a straight right-hander.'

'What about the rest of you?' Müller asked.

Siegfried spoke up next. 'I can hit the hand on a church-tower clock at fifty metres.'

Prompted by a friendly glance from Müller, Berner and Bergmann confessed that they were better at close combat. 'But then, even a gunman has to get close to his target.'

Müller regarded his students with growing interest. He slumped into the chair vacated by Wesel and folded his hands over his paunch. 'What firearms have you had most experience with so far?'

Automatic pistols, came the swift response. Automatics of standard calibre – any kind available.

Müller snorted contemptuously. 'Glorified amusement arcade stuff, gentlemen! No automatics, that's the rule from now on. Can anyone tell me why?'

Norden put his hand up. 'Could it be something to do with spent cartridge-cases, Superintendent? An automatic ejects them when you fire – they leave your signature on a job. Is that it?'

'Right.' Müller blinked sleepily. 'But first there's something else. Kindly don't address me as Superintendent. My name's Müller, and don't take it into your heads to christen me Fatso. I was thin as a rake a few years back, but that was when I drank. These days I can't afford to breathe fumes over our Führer, so now I stick to candies. My personal habits are none of your business, though, is that clear? You've got enough problems of your own.'

They all stared at him in surprise – respectfully too, as the occasion seemed to demand. Some of them even ventured a sympathetic smile.

Müller was also smiling now, but grimly. 'So let's stick to the point. If automatics are out, what's the practical alternative?'

'We use revolvers.' Now it was Hagen who leapt into the breach. He'd been sitting there tensely, his one good eye darting from

Müller to Norden and back. 'Revolvers don't eject cartridge-cases. The trouble is, we don't have any.'

'Yes you do,' Müller said flatly. 'I got you some.'

'American models, Herr Müller?'

'The very best. A dozen – six for immediate use and six to be held in reserve. Plenty of ammunition too.'

'When can we try them out?'

'As soon as you like. The guns are waiting for you downstairs. Let's adjourn to the indoor range.'

The Villa soon received a visitor in the Junoesque person of Frau Hermine Franke, blithely determined to play the good neighbour. Raffael failed to head her off – after all, she was the wife of a senior Nazi official – so Wesel was forced to receive her.

He did so in the drawing-room. Frau Franke, radiant in steel-blue, strode possessively towards her host, arms extended. Wesel contrived a smile.

'Naughty, naughty!' she cried archly. 'You've been positively elusive lately. Don't tell me you're frightened of me!'

'Nothing could be further from the truth,' Wesel assured her, just as loudly but with far less conviction. He strove to dodge her and take refuge behind a large armchair. 'How's my esteemed friend, your husband?'

'Flourishing, I gather.' Frau Franke subsided on to a sofa. She settled herself in the exact centre, leaving two cramped spaces on either side of her. Wesel, who had recoiled still further, was warmly invited to choose between them. 'He sends his regards.'

'How kind. Please remember me to him when you're next in touch. I hope he doesn't mind you visiting me in my lair.'

'Far from it, Sturmbannführer.' Hermine Franke gave Wesel an eloquent smile. 'I spent the best part of an hour on the phone to him only yesterday, busy though he is. "I can't sit here twiddling my thumbs," I told him. "I propose to make myself useful, as every German woman should." And do you know what he said? "Carry on!" Those were his exact words.'

'Useful?' Wesel repeated, looking apprehensive. 'But not here, surely? My dear Frau Franke, people might misunderstand your motives. Your husband and I are privileged to be close associates of the Führer. The least breath of scandal . . .'

'But my dear man, I've no designs on you – none at all.' She looked him in the eye and burst out laughing. 'All I want, and my husband fully approves, is to share in this great and decisive moment in our nation's history. I want to help to create a harmonious atmosphere – help you with my own personal assets. In other words, as a woman of Germany.'

'Help me?' Wesel parried. 'What precisely did you have in mind?'

'It's those cadets of yours – such nice young men. They deserve a little pampering, a few home comforts.'

'From you?' Even a man like Wesel had his tribulations. 'You mean . . .'

Hermine Franke spread her legs a fraction. The skirt drew tight across her thighs in a way which might have titillated anyone but Wesel.

Brightly, she went on, 'I could organize some coffee parties for them, show them the beauties of our local countryside, stimulate their cultural interests. Wouldn't you welcome that?'

'Of course,' Wesel hastened to assure her. 'If the opportunity arises – yes, of course. And now . . .' He showed her almost unceremoniously to the door. 'Many thanks, Frau Franke. Your offer of help is greatly appreciated, believe me. I'll be in touch.'

'Soon?' she asked eagerly.

Wesel nodded and handed her over to Raffael, who escorted her to the main gate. There he kissed her hand in farewell, a civility she acknowledged with a faint purr of approval.

'I *do* like old-fashioned good manners,' she sighed.

Raffael hurried back to Wesel. He found him slumped exhausted on the drawing-room sofa. The Sturmbannführer demanded champagne.

'If there's one thing more frightful than a woman, it's a German woman – or rather, what that creature means by the term. To think she's the wife of a Reichsleiter!'

Raffael shrugged. 'We'll have to do something about her.'

'We will.' Wesel's composure had returned. 'You don't think I'm going to have my plans fouled up by a sex-starved bitch who scents a chance of getting laid? Laid by our boys? Like hell!

It isn't on their training schedule.'

Even the unflappable Clara was driven to near distraction at least once a week. This was on so-called rest days, which did not occur with any regularity – on Saturdays or Sundays, for example – but were determined arbitrarily by Wesel and never announced in advance.

Rest days were heralded by a different kind of musical reveillé. In place of the *Badenweiler March*, Raffael broadcast the dulcet strains of a Viennese waltz recorded by the Marek Weber Orchestra. If any of the Villa's inmates realized that Herr Weber was not only Jewish but of Polish origin, it seemed to cause them no concern.

Thus began the rest day, which lasted for as long as Wesel deemed fit – sometimes well into the afternoon. Dependable little Clara had her work cut out on days like these. Instead of laying the dining-room table, she had to serve breakfast to each of the six men individually. The easiest needs to satisfy were those of Berner and Bergmann in Rooms 3 and 4. A single tray sufficed for both because they were always to be found in one bed or the other.

Hermann, in Room 1, could also be described as relatively undemanding. If he didn't have to get up, he slept. All Clara had to do was put a bottle of mineral water in his room.

Siegfried, the occupant of Room 2, was harder to please because he blithely uttered a variety of special requests, e.g. grilled kidneys or smoked cheese. Needless to say, he got whatever he asked for.

As for Norden, Clara betrayed a certain predilection for waiting on him. There were many things about him that appealed to her: his quiet reserve, his courtesy, his modesty. Today, as usual, he sat up in bed when she appeared but drew the blankets up to his chin.

'Feel like anything special, Herr Norden?' she said coaxingly, leaning towards him a little. 'You only have to say.'

'Please don't go to any trouble on my account, Fräulein Clara. I wouldn't dream of asking for anything special.'

'But you can, Herr Norden.' She winked encouragingly. 'Anything you like.'

'Delighted you feel that way, Fräulein Clara, but don't you think it might lead to complications? We'd better not get too involved.'

'Why so bashful?' Clara sat on the bed, intensely aware of the blanket-shrouded bulge of his thighs. 'People can please themselves in this place – Herr Wesel says so. We can do as we like, out of hours.'

The door of Norden's room was open according to orders. Hagen chose that moment to barge in and stand there with his hands on his hips. 'Hey!' he called brightly. 'Where's my breakfast? I'm famished.'

'Coming right away,' Clara said, jumping to her feet.

Hagen grinned broadly. 'Far be it from me to butt in, Clara. I'm the tactful type. If I'd caught you in Norden's bed, either underneath or on top, I'd have beaten a hasty retreat, but you're just sitting around. Why? Won't he, or *can't* he?'

'Shut your mouth!' Norden said angrily. 'Stop trying to needle me.'

'I only want to prove which of us is smarter, in bed and out. You're welcome to hold hands with Clara if that's how you get your kicks. I can offer her more than that. Like an unforgettable fuck – one that'll make her knees tremble.'

'Get out, you filthy swine!' roared Norden.

'I'm going. Clara can come too if she likes. No reason why she shouldn't, is there?'

Clara stiffened. 'I refuse to be treated like a public convenience, Herr Hagen. My life's my own and I'm the one who decides how I spend it. *And* what company I keep.' With that, she stalked haughtily out of the room.

Hagen stared after her with a connoisseur's eye. 'I'll screw that girl sooner or later.' He turned to Norden. 'I'll screw her with you watching – want to bet?'

'Don't be too sure,' Norden snapped. 'If anybody gets screwed, it could be you.'

The next bout of target practice at Feldafing, where American police specials were now in use, produced a number of outstanding performances.

The range was 25 metres, the light of early evening only fair, the target a life-size human silhouette. Each member of the group was allowed three shots.

Norden scored three hits in the heart. Berner and Bergmann peppered the dummy's feet – 'a dancing lesson', as they called it. Siegfried shattered both knee-caps and one elbow 'to immobilize the swine', and Hermann cut an isosceles triangle at the point where the genitals would have been. Hagen drilled both eyes and placed his third shot neatly in mid-forehead.

Müller nodded, curtly but not unappreciatively. His students were making good progress, at least in one of their ten or a dozen branches of instruction. They still had plenty to learn, but time was short. Wesel, clearly thirsting for action, had stressed this only yesterday.

'Right, gentlemen,' said Müller. 'So you've dropped your man. He goes down. Maybe he twitches a little, then he's dead. So far so good, but what happens next?'

Hagen reacted with his usual speed. 'You get the hell out of it.'

'With a gun in your hand?' asked Norden.

'You can always stuff it in your pocket or a shoulder-holster.'

'What about fingerprints?'

'Prints can be wiped off with a handkerchief.'

'A handkerchief could get lost in the rush – it could help to incriminate you. They can tell your blood group by analysing your saliva these days.'

Müller cut them short. 'Right, that's enough amateur dramatics. Whatever mission you're engaged on, there mustn't be any prints at all. You're going to have to learn to do even the most delicate jobs in gloves, and that includes shooting in them. It isn't as easy as it sounds, but we'll practise and go on practising till it's second nature.'

The six young men nodded obediently.

'The point is,' Müller went on, 'you can get away with murder – and I mean murder – as long as you know the basic rules of criminal investigation. You can even be caught in the act. The one thing you can never afford to do is supply the police with solid and incontrovertible evidence. Our next lesson will be on how to avoid doing just that.'

From Captain Scott's notes on his post-1945 investigations:

Hard as I tried to pinpoint the function and significance of the Wesel Group, many things remained obscure. For instance, the identity of the man in the cellar.

It proved impossible to build up a detailed picture of who he could have been. All I could learn was that a man, said to be elderly, had been confined in a locked room at the far end of the cellar, where the Villa's dry stores and wine-racks were also situated.

Wesel had sole charge of the keys to these premises. He occasionally issued them to Raffael. Müller was also entrusted with them at times, but I formed the impression from statements made by Sobottke that Müller possessed a spare or duplicate key.

The man in the cellar was sighted on several occasions, but only at a distance and generally after nightfall. Witnesses described him as walking in the garden 'with slow, careful steps'. He did not appear to be under restraint or guard.

The cellar inmate's voice is said to have been soft and gentle, especially when he conversed with Müller, who often accompanied him. I was even informed that Müller addressed him by the familiar German '*du*'. Strange as this may sound, anything was conceivable in the Germany of those days.

Hermine Franke, next-door neighbour of the Wesel Group, persevered in her efforts to establish the most human of all human contacts with its members. Combating her endeavours was easier said than done.

Frau Franke refused to give up. She repeatedly tried to telephone Wesel, only to be informed each time by Raffael that the Sturmbannführer was out. She made several attempts to enter the grounds but was politely turned away. It was only when her quarry unwisely decided to take a stroll through the village that she ran him to earth.

Wesel found himself cornered by Frau Franke as soon as the gardener closed the gate behind him. He contorted his face into a mirthless smile and gave her a Hitler salute.

Hermine Franke's voice throbbed with indignation. 'What's the meaning of this, Sturmbannführer? Am I not to be trusted with your men?'

'Of course, but . . .'

'I should hope so!' she barked. 'Especially in view of my husband's express injunction to do something positive. Are you deliberately trying to keep me from my patriotic duty?'

'God forbid!' Wesel replied, looking agonized.

'Then kindly take action. I propose to give a dinner party tomorrow night, to mark my husband's birthday. Will you come – you and your men, I mean?'

Wesel controlled himself with difficulty. He felt confident of his ability to cope with most things, even the demands of his Führer, but this Valkyrie irritated him beyond endurance.

'My dear Frau Franke,' he said, 'my men and I are engaged on a special assignment of the most exacting and confidential nature. Our duties keep us occupied night and day.'

'So my husband tells me,' she replied, 'but that's precisely why you need relaxation. You will come, won't you?'

'Very well, if you insist – why not?' Wesel donned an affable expression. 'Dinner tomorrow, then. I'm afraid we can't all attend but I'll send you two of my best men, Cadets Berner and Bergmann. I feel certain you'll enjoy their company.'

'Good,' Hermine Franke nodded approvingly. 'They'll do to begin with.'

Berner and Bergmann reported to Wesel as soon as they returned from dinner. The Sturmbannführer heard them out with a feline glint in his eye.

BERNER: 'An unspeakable woman, Herr Wesel. She fed and watered us like prize cattle. Then she went to work on us – emotional freedom, modern morality, sexual emancipation – that sort of crap. I felt sick, the way she swung her tits and wiggled her ass at us.'

BERGMANN: 'She was always brushing up against us and putting her hand on our knees. We let her get on with it the way you told us. She didn't actually rape us, but there's no mistaking what's she's after. She wants to get laid.'

'She does, does she?' mused Wesel.

Berner looked aghast. 'You surely don't expect *us* to oblige,

Sturmbannführer?'

'Well,' Wesel said, 'I naturally had a reason for picking you two to handle this assignment. We aren't here to service the wives of senior Party members after all, and you seem to be in less danger than the rest of us.'

'By now,' Wesel declared a few days later, 'we've all come to know each other a little better. I'm happy to say we've made a promising start – but only a start. It's time to move on to other things. In plain language, the halcyon days of target practice are temporarily a thing of the past. I'm now going to familiarize you with some of the purgatories of human existence. It's midsummer, a season of the year when garbage and rotting entrails and spilt blood smell even riper than usual. You'll need to get used to those, so now's your chance. This is the curriculum for your next phase of instruction.'

He passed out some mimeographed sheets. Their wording was admirably succinct.

'*Week 1*,' Wesel read out, '*garbage collection, maintenance and clearance of rubbish-dumps and sewage works.*' He looked up. 'In other words, confrontation with accumulated filth must not be allowed to stifle our appreciation of life's supreme values.'

'*Week 2*,' he went on, '*lessons in practical anatomy involving the dissection of human cadavers.*' He paused again. 'Death, gentlemen, is an inseparable part of life. We must learn to take it in our stride.'

Finally: '*Week 3, abattoir work, with special emphasis on the slaughter of animals.*' He smiled. 'We must inure ourselves to the sight of blood – just as long as it's inferior. The sort common to cattle and certain debased members of the human race. Think about it!'

The Sturmbannführer squared his shoulders. 'Once this is over we shall know more about many things. Ourselves, our role, and the limits of our capacity to act in the service of the Führer – if any . . .'

They withstood this ordeal too, discounting a few minor complications.

Siegfried could watch blood flow by the gallon but found it hard to endure the smell. Hermann developed an allergy to sewage. Human excrement turned his stomach, though he was never actually sick. Berner and Bergmann came within an inch of flunking in anatomy.

Norden did his best to exhibit total imperturbability. He performed each of his allotted tasks with the same almost reverent dedication. The only time he looked pale and preoccupied was on his third day at the abbattoir, when a consignment of gently bleating lambs arrived for slaughter, but the moment soon passed.

Hagen strove to demonstrate throughout these reeking, stinking, sanguinary ordeals that nothing on earth could unnerve him. He busily shovelled excreta, ripped out intestines and transported carcasses as if they were Christmas packages. On his fifth day at the charnel-house he actually beat the foreman slaughterer's previous record by nearly 15 per cent.

Once and only once did Hagen come near to vomiting, and that was when one of his fellow-trainees, probably Berner or Bergmann, was humorous enough to secrete a severed penis in his midday soup.

All in all, Wesel felt entitled to pat himself on the back. His men had displayed exceptional powers of concentration, admirable self-control and unwavering devotion to duty under extreme stress. His system was working well.

'The past three weeks,' he told them approvingly, 'have taken us another important step along the arduous road to our final objective. I congratulate you on living up to my expectations. However, your sternest ordeals are still to come. I shall be introducing you to one of them in the next few days, but first I have to deal with a problem that threatens to disrupt our work.'

Waldemar Wesel flew to Berlin in a special aircraft placed at his disposal by the Chancellery, having previously phoned Reichsleiter Franke to request an interview. The Reichsleiter's official car, a black and hearselike Mercedes, was waiting for him at Tempelhof Airport.

Less than an hour later he was closeted with Franke in his office: leather, oak, oriental rugs, sparsely filled bookshelves, heaps of files. Above and beyond the desk, an oil portrait of the Führer.

A fat man with the genial manner but sharp eyes of a con man, Martin Franke was one of the Party's leading personnel chiefs and wielded considerable influence over its financial allocations. He was also reputed to be one of Hitler's most trusted subordinates and, therefore, worthy of respect.

'My dear fellow,' he began, 'the Führer has kept me privately informed of your special assignment, so I'm quite prepared for some substantial calls on our funds. You'll always find me a receptive audience. Well?'

'Perhaps we could discuss finance some other time, Martin. My current problems are rather different, I'm afraid. To make matters worse, they involve your private life.'

'My wife, you mean?' Franke laughed contemptuously. 'If I know you, Waldi, you're well aware of what's wrong with my marriage.'

Wesel's eyes narrowed. 'I've a rough idea.'

'The fact is, I married Hermine in a weak moment – years ago, when I was still a junior civil servant.' The Reichsleiter spoke freely – he knew he could, in Wesel's presence. 'Since then we've drifted apart, as they say.'

'So I've heard, off the record. One of your secretaries is reputed to have had a couple of children by you.'

Franke laughed again. 'Your information isn't a hundred per cent correct, Waldi – it was two secretaries and one child apiece. In recent months, though, I've fallen for somebody else. Good looks, lots of class. She's already pregnant.'

'Congratulations,' Wesel said drily. 'That should make it easier for you to be firm with your wife. Her unfortunate activities are giving me and my men a lot of trouble.'

'You don't say!' Franke grinned. 'Giving you trouble, is she? *You*, Waldi? Trouble you can't handle? I don't believe it. Why, the Führer was only talking about you the other day. If anyone's a born trouble-shooter, he said, it's Wesel.'

'If I smell trouble,' Wesel replied with a smile, 'it's only because the source isn't just any female but the wife of a Reichsleiter.'

'Maybe, but don't forget that our official commitments always take priority. Just because women happen to be married to us, it doesn't stop them being a secondary consideration. Perhaps I ought to mention something else. The child this lady of my choice is expecting – I want it to bear my name. Do I make myself clear?'

'In that case,' Wesel said, already pondering on the shape of things to come, 'may I take the precaution of asking you a very special favour? Your wife occupies the house next door to my training centre at Feldafing. If it fell vacant for any reason, I'd like to take it over. We could use it to house instructors, visitors, domestic staff and guards. That would mean we had the Villa completely to ourselves, and I value my privacy.'

'Done,' said Franke. 'If the house falls vacant it's yours. Its purchase will be financed by one of our special contingency funds.'

Wesel took his leave in a mood of comradeship and gratitude. The two men's handshake could not have been more cordial.

Wesel had already reached the door when Franke, who was standing behind his desk, added a confidential rider.

'Something's just occurred to me, Waldi,' he said anxiously. 'It's about my wife. The poor creature has a number of failings, but there's one that worries me more than most. She insists on bathing in the lake at night, preferably in the nude. I've warned her about it time and time again, as many of our friends can testify. Anything might happen . . .'

The man from the cellar first surfaced on the day after Wesel's students had completed their garbage-dump, dissecting-room and slaughter-house ordeals, but not without intensive preparation. Every event at the Villa was carefully pre-planned.

Wesel did not let his cat out of the bag at once. Before doing so, he summoned Müller.

'Is he ready?'

Müller nodded. 'He is.'

'Are we likely to have any trouble?'

'Depends who with, Sturmbannführer.' Propping his bulk against the door behind which the man from the cellar was presumably waiting, Müller stared at Wesel with overwhelming scepticism. 'Wouldn't it be better if we left him where he belongs – in the dungeons of the new era?'

'Better or worse, what's the difference? We must never shirk an opportunity to enlighten the young. Let's get down to business, Herr Müller. For the benefit of our students, kindly outline the man's special function.'

Müller did so with deliberate brevity, carefully watching the attentive faces of the Group. 'Very well,' he said, 'I'm now at liberty to introduce a certain Herr Breslauer – Professor Aaron Breslauer, psychologist, doctor of medicine, doctor of philosophy. As for his special function, he's been instructed to make intellectual mincemeat of you by arguing against virtually every aspect of our work here.'

'In other words,' Wesel said briskly, 'he's a devil's advocate. That's why I selected him – as an intellectual challenge to the lot of you. All right, now's your chance to beat him at his own game.'

Leisurely, Müller opened the door behind him. He looked at nobody while doing so – in fact his eyes seemed to be shut.

Slightly bent but walking with a neat, light step, a short, dapper-looking little man entered the library. He blinked at the sudden flood of light from the window, a faint smile on his wrinkled face. His hair was a luminous silver-grey, but his eyes, or what could be seen of them between half-closed lids, were crystal clear.

'That's a Jew!' Hagen blurted out. 'Or I'm a Dutchman,' he added.

'Right first time,' Wesel said.

'What's he doing here?'

'He is to us as night is to day, winter to summer, moon to sun.'

'A Jew here, with us?'

'Yes, and you're going to argue with him,' decreed Wesel, ' – hard and convincingly.'

Hagen looked dazed. 'Argue with a Jew?'

'Treat it as a confrontation with the absolute antithesis of all we are,' Wesel recommended. 'Listen to his arguments and counter them, refute them with logic, reduce them to ideological absurdity. Do that and you'll be utterly liberated – free and fit for anything.'

4 Great Days before Dark Deeds

Anything Wesel demanded of his team was done, and everything he ordained had its purpose. Not that this precluded the occasional emergence of problems, some of them deliberately contrived by Wesel himself and one of them undoubtedly being 'the man from the cellar'.

It was not easy for the members of the Wesel Group to debate with him so calmly, least of all for Norden, who often declared that everything within him rebelled against 'that creature'.

The Sturmbannführer casually brushed Norden's objection aside. 'That's just the effect I'm aiming at.'

Wesel's students were often confronted with 'that creature' in the weeks and months that followed – often, but with the usual systematic irregularity. Sometimes they saw him four or five times in a single week, sometimes not at all for weeks on end. Their encounters took place at a wide variety of times: sometimes in the morning, generally in the late afternoon, occasionally in the middle of the night. These debates, which the training schedule designated with an 'S' for Semitism, were usually convened round the fireplace in the drawing-room. Breslauer would lean against the chimney-breast while the members of the group occupied a semi-circle of armchairs ranged at a meaningful distance from him. Müller, who seemed to take a special interest in the Jew's welfare, was almost invariably present. Wesel attended far less often. Neither Müller nor Wesel made any comment. They merely listened, noting every word and observing every face.

It became clear that Breslauer enjoyed a wide measure of freedom to conduct these sessions as he pleased. The attainment of Wesel's objective was independent of this. The Sturmbann-führer wanted to stir his men up, stimulate their mental reactions, nurture their swiftly maturing sense of superiority.

BRESLAUER: 'You just mentioned the word "race". How would you define it?'

SIEGFRIED: 'Every human being belongs to a specific race because he was born into it. His destiny is ruled by that circumstance alone.'

BRESLAUER: 'But there are racial mixtures too. What about people who are racially indeterminate? How would you classify them?'

HERMANN: 'Why should we even try? There's only one certainty from our angle: racial mixtures are always impure and we refuse to have any truck with them on principle. Absolute racial purity is the sole criterion.'

HAGEN: 'Even in the case of recognizably pure races, you have to draw a distinction between the superior and the inferior, e.g. Aryan and Semitic.'

BRESLAUER: 'Are you quite sure? Isn't it just possible that a fair cross-section of any race would be found to include superior and inferior individuals?'

NORDEN: 'But the Aryan-Germanic race, to which our Führer belongs . . .'

BRESLAUER: 'Ah! Perhaps you'd be kind enough to tell me which of that gentleman's physical characteristics are unmistakably Aryan or Germanic?'

Moments like these, which were far from infrequent, called for extreme self-control on the part of those who attended such debates. The extent of their restraint was noted with care, either by Müller or by Wesel. The young men surpassed themselves – in fact they eventually came to believe that they had plumbed the mystery of the proceedings. Most were inclined to regard 'that Yid' as a paid provocateur who had been systematically forced upon them, a talkative old man whose days – of this they soon became convinced – were already numbered. They began to wonder which of them would be entrusted with his liquidation.

Hagen volunteered first, if only to get an edge on Norden, but Wesel's response was surprisingly negative – perhaps because Müller happened to be present at the time.

'Decisions of that kind are my sole responsibility,' the Sturmbannführer told Hagen. 'If I ever consider such a step expedient I'll let you know. You don't strike me as well schooled enough to be let loose on subhuman elements. You still have a lot to learn –

isn't that so, Herr Müller?'

'They still have a craze for playing Red Indians,' said Müller. 'Anyone they take a dislike to, they want to scalp. They haven't grasped the essential point, which is something else.'

Wesel and Müller were sitting in the drawing-room drinking imported Scotch with plenty of ice and a dash of soda. Silence enveloped them. The staff had left the Villa hours before. The men, or four of them at least, were already asleep.

The only two absentees were Berner and Bergmann, who had received yet another invitation to dine with Frau Franke. Wesel and Müller were patiently awaiting their return.

They did not have to wait much longer. Berner and Bergmann soon appeared, wearing evening dress. The Siamese Twins looked slightly drunk but delighted with themselves as they clicked their heels to Wesel and his companion. Müller peered at his watch. It was eleven minutes after midnight.

'Well?' said Wesel.

'Sturmbannführer,' Bergmann reported without the flicker of an eyelid, 'there's been the most frightful accident. We couldn't help it – it was just one of those things.'

'You don't mean . . . Not Frau Franke?'

'Yes,' Berner broke in. 'She got a cramp while taking a dip in the lake. We tried to save her but she sank like a stone. There was nothing we could do.'

'How dreadful,' Wesel said mournfully. 'I assume,' he added in the same breath, 'that neither of you had anything to do with this tragedy?'

'Of course not, Sturmbannführer,' Bergmann assured him. He glanced at Berner, who nodded. 'We just happened to be there. Nobody else was, only us, but it wasn't our fault.'

'I'm sure it wasn't.' Wesel gave them a look of implicit trust. 'However, we mustn't allow this incident to cast the faintest shadow of suspicion on our unit. I shall ensure that it doesn't. Herr Müller, how would you suggest we regularize matters?'

'Let's see,' said Müller. He splashed another generous snort of Scotch into his glass, breathing heavily. Then he proceeded to fire off a series of questions to which he demanded swift and cogent answers. The next fifteen minutes were his alone.

MÜLLER: 'Can you fix the time of Frau Franke's death?'

BERNER: 'Almost to the minute. It happened at 11.30.'

MÜLLER: 'Are there likely to be any marks on the body – lacerations or contusions that might have been caused by violent pressure or blows with an instrument, blunt or sharp?'

BERGMANN: 'Certainly not. All we did was grab her by the ankles when she dived, and . . .'

MÜLLER: 'Right. Where is the body now?'

BERNER: 'Exactly where it went under. Why, should we have hauled it ashore?'

Müller dismissed this abruptly. 'At least I've taught you that much. The removal of a body from the scene of a crime – accident, I mean – automatically creates grounds for suspicion. All right, go on. When did you finish dinner, including dessert and coffee, and why do you think I'm asking?'

BERGMANN: 'Because an autopsy can establish when somebody ate their last meal, almost to the minute. It can't fix the time when alcohol was swallowed, before a meal or afterwards.'

'Right again,' said Müller. 'So when did you finish eating?'

'Just after ten.'

'Good.' Müller glanced at Wesel. 'Well, Sturmbannführer?'

'I spent the evening sitting here re-reading *Mein Kampf*,' Wesel said. 'When Berner and Bergmann came in, I looked at the clock. It said ten-thirty. Right, you two?'

'Right, Sturmbannführer. Ten-thirty on the dot.'

'I can swear to that,' Wesel went on, 'and so can Raffael, who let them in at the front gate. That should be good enough for anyone, shouldn't it?'

'It ought to be,' said Müller. 'To recap, none of us had any connection with the unfortunate woman's death, which occurred an hour later. If any busybody from the local CID claims otherwise, he'll get nowhere fast.'

Wesel expressed his full concurrence. It was inconceivable that anyone would dare allege that the wife of a senior Party official and close associate of the Führer had been immoral enough to bathe in the nude with two young men. 'Nobody could afford to suggest such a thing,' he concluded.

Nobody did. The official verdict was accidental death by drowning.

Frau Franke was buried in state. Prominent among the mourners: Martin Franke and Waldemar Wesel. The whole occasion was fraught with solemnity. The brown-shirted SA provided a ruffle of drums at the cemetery gate, the SS a raven-black guard of honour. There were wreaths by the score, including one from the Führer himself.

Berner and Bergmann had requested the honour of helping to carry the coffin. Cotton-wool clouds drifted across an azure sky.

Reichsleiter Franke, who bore himself with a manly composure verging on dignity, registered grief mingled with pride. He nodded to his friend and colleague.

'So that's that, Waldi. Any complications?'

'None,' Wesel murmured reverently. Misty-eyed, he watched the coffin being lowered into the grave. Tears seemed to glisten on the cheeks of Frau Franke's two last dinner-guests, but they were only rain-drops deposited by an intermittent summer shower that greatly added to the melancholy nature of the proceedings.

'My boys are definitely coming along,' Wesel continued, still speaking out of the corner of his mouth. 'Prompt service, eh? All the same, there's still room for improvement.'

From Maxims *by Waldemar Wesel. On orders and their purposeful implementation:*

Many people can obey orders. They are docile, submissive, even devout. That is worth a great deal in itself.

Not many can obey orders with conviction. Conviction blossoms only where people feel a direct response, a sacred flame burning within. Such are the predestined lieutenants of the great.

The ability to grasp the full implications of an order, yet act on it without flinching, is granted to only a handful of men – those who combine faith with conviction and knowledge. They are the knights and custodians of their own particular Grail: a sacred resolve which is simultaneously cold as ice and hot as molten lava. This quality must be systematically encouraged.

Operations undertaken for the above purpose:

1. Tree-planting

Followed by his team, Wesel set off for the back garden of the Villa. Here, as instructed, Sobottke had laid out six standard roses, each with a stem four feet long, a leafy crown dotted with crimson blooms, and vigorous roots. Six spades stood ready, driven into the ground.

'Right, gentlemen,' called Wesel, 'get cracking!'

Each man started, with diligent and practised spadework, to dig a pit three feet square, three feet deep. They might have been participating in an unusual form of athletic contest. Hagen won it in a bare ten minutes, only seconds before Norden's pit was likewise pronounced adequate.

Wesel issued his next command after a two-minute breather. 'Now comes the planting, gentlemen. These are special rose-trees. They have to be planted roots uppermost.'

Minutely observing their reactions as he spoke, he was gratified to note that their surprise lasted for only a moment or two. Then they set to work as ordered. None of them had shown any undue hesitation. Five minutes later the roots of half a dozen rose-trees protruded four feet into the air.

2. Book-burning

A bonfire was blazing fiercely in the Villa's stable yard. Sobottke had fed it with branches, logs and pieces of broken furniture.

It was a cold, crisp day wreathed in wisps of late autumnal mist. Last night's frost still lay where the sun had failed to penetrate.

The six men welcomed the crackling warmth of the fire. Wesel had summoned them outside in the middle of an English lesson which, in accord with one of his own mottoes – 'Creature comforts are an aid to life and learning' – they had been permitted to attend in light indoor clothes. Now they were standing in the sunless stable yard, fanned by a northerly breeze that kept the temperature close to zero. They edged forwards and held out their hands to the blaze.

Close by stood a table laden with books, and beside it hovered Wesel, wearing a heavy Bavarian cape and an encouraging smile.

'Right,' he said. 'The code-word for this exercise is "book-burning". The first of its kind took place in Berlin on the 10th of May this year, under the aegis of Dr Goebbels. It was an unparalleled success, except that the books were burnt at random – that's to say, unselectively. We're going to repeat the process, but with more method.'

The proceedings opened in a comparatively uneventful way.

Wesel tossed books to each of his men, who hurled them into the flames without hesitation. The fire blazed up in a wonderfully warming manner which more than compensated for the stench of burning glue and leather.

Consigned to the flames were volumes by Erich Maria Remarque, 'that traitor to the concept of front-line comradeship', and Arnold Zweig, 'an unscrupulous bolshevik peace-monger', Kurt Tucholsky and Erich Kästner, 'immoral degenerates', Thomas and Heinrich Mann, 'middle-class navel-contemplators', Lion Feuchtwanger and Stefan Zweig, 'cultural assholes', Jakob Wassermann and Alfred Döblin, 'money-grubbing exhibitionists', and a gaggle of American novelists – Dreiser, Lewis, Sinclair, Steinbeck and Dos Passos – all of whom, irrespective of whether Wesel adjudged them plutocratic or socialist, were categorized as 'a decadent shower of shit'.

Next, however, Hermann was thrown a book by Alfred Rosenberg, a Reichsleiter and Nazi dignitary. Entitled *The Myth of the 20th Century*, it passed for one of the authoritative literary manifestations of National Socialism because it sought and proclaimed 'the new man'.

'This one too?' asked Hermann, taking out insurance. 'Is that an order?'

Wesel just nodded, fractionally but unmistakably. In Wesel's opinion, Rosenberg owed his prominence to a variety of misconceptions and back-stage manœuvres. Rosenberg's book was a mere farrago of platitudes and journalistic hot air compared with which his, Wesel's, *Maxims* were a crystalline fount of enlightenment.

Rosenberg's *Myth* soared into the flames.

Wesel did not stop to relish the spectacle for long. He quickly reached for the next book and tossed it to Hagen. It was his own *Maxims*, a special leather-bound edition blocked in gold. Hagen took once glance at it and threw it in the fire.

'You burnt my book?' Wesel said, almost taken aback. 'Without hesitation? Why?'

'Because you ordered me to.' Hagen felt absolutely confident he had done the right thing. He was adapting himself to Wesel and Wesel's ideas with growing precision. 'It's your book. You can do or order us to do anything you like with it.'

Ever wary, Hagen omitted to utter the rest of what he was thinking, namely: if Rosenberg deserved a singe, why not Wesel?

'Good man,' said the Sturmbannführer. He spoke hurriedly and with an obvious effort. 'Prompt and unquestioning implementation of orders, that's what I like to see.'

He handed the next book to Norden with an elaborate air of unconcern. Norden took it, glanced down and froze in disbelief. He had drawn Hitler's *Mein Kampf*. It took him three seconds to reach a decision.

Then he said, 'No, Sturmbannführer!'

'Why not?' Wesel demanded.

'In the first place, you never gave me a direct order – you merely handed me the book. Secondly, nobody can issue a direct order for the destruction of this book. I know we're totally subject to your authority, but there's one person with an even greater claim on our obedience: the Führer.'

'Meaning what, Norden?'

'Meaning that if the Führer ever personally instructed me to burn his book, I should do so, but only then. Otherwise not.'

'Excellent,' Wesel said at once, ' – perfectly put. You can keep the book, Norden. It belongs to you because you saved it from the flames. Who knows? It may one day bear a personal dedication from the Führer himself.'

Almost forty years later, the inscribed volume was found among Heinz-Hermann Norden's effects in Lugano. The dedication read:

'To my faithful comrade-in-arms and trusted subordinate, with warmest regards and in joint expectation of our Greater German future.' Below it was a boldly scrawled initial which soared upwards like a rocket, then fell away obliquely as though plummeting into the void. It stood for Adolf Hitler.

Another ideological debate took place soon afterwards in the presence of Detective Superintendent Müller.

Isolated as ever, the man from the cellar was standing beside the drawing-room fire with his hands clasped together and his gaze fixed on nobody in particular. He opened the debate in a low but resonant voice.

'You recently employed a term which strikes me as a trifle vague: "racially valuable." I'd very much like to know what you understand by it.'

'That's easy,' said Siegfried. 'It means precisely what you, being a Jew, are not and can never be.'

Müller, who rarely intervened in these ideological exchanges, did so now. 'Come, come, gentlemen! Kindly stick to the rules. No personal remarks, please. Objective arguments only.'

Breslauer showed no sign of irritation or resentment. He continued to debate the point as if confronted by the attentive, interested, sceptical students to whom he had been accustomed for decades as a university professor. He numbered Einstein among his friends, had been a regular visitor to Thomas Mann's home in Munich and conducted an extensive correspondence with Ebert, first president of the Weimar Republic. And now he was here.

'People of every age have believed in their ability to draw crucial and socially relevant distinctions. For instance, between master and slave, Christian and heathen, Rome and the rest of the world; between different systems of armament, different trades, different ideologies. Their criterion was based solely on the views of those who happened to be in power at the time.'

Objection by Hermann: 'What about the right of the stronger, the superior, the more resolute? Hasn't that always been the decisive law of nature?'

BRESLAUER: 'Of all the men who have claimed the centre of the world stage, none was more than a transient figure. Nothing in the historical process is absolutely final.'

HAGEN: 'Except the Führer's Germany – or don't you accept that?'

BRESLAUER: 'Very few empires in recorded history have survived for longer than two or three hundred years. Hitler has proclaimed a Thousand-Year Reich. It's not only utopian, it's a downright historical absurdity.'

HAGEN: 'You obviously haven't grasped what Hitler means to the world. How many years do you give us – the Führer, I mean?'

BRESLAUER: 'Maybe ten. A dozen at most.'

HAGEN: 'Why?'

BRESLAUER: 'Because everything points to the inevitability of a global war. Hitler could have his way with Germany for decades to come, but he and his nation aren't alone on this planet. His very existence is a challenge. Once it's taken up, that'll be the end of him.'

The Villa that had housed the late Frau Franke was officially handed over on a fine, mild Sunday. The widower turned up in person.

'Sturmbannführer Wesel,' he declared, 'I couldn't refrain from seizing this opportunity to convey, both to you and to your splendid young team, my warm appreciation of all you have achieved here. I wanted to be present when the property was transferred to your safekeeping.'

Wesel, flanked by his six cadets, responded in kind. 'Reichsleiter Franke, my honoured friend and colleague, we thank you! We thank you for your understanding, your goodwill, your convincing demonstration of the ties that unite all loyal followers of the Führer.'

They shook hands, secure in the knowledge of what really united them. Then, shoulder to shoulder, they marched across the narrow lane separating the grounds of the Villa from those of the late Frau Franke's country retreat. It was, so to speak, a formal act that consecrated the house and set the seal on its formal acquisition.

The Reichsleiter's joyous sentiments were justified for more reasons than one. Hermine's death left him a free agent and the sale of his country house had swelled his coffers. Last but not least, he had cemented the invaluable friendship of a man who, like himself, belonged to the Führer's inner circle.

The Franke villa, cheaply purchased less than a year earlier from the heirs of a murdered enemy of the State, made an ideal extension to Wesel's training centre. It would not only act as a luxurious guest-house for visiting instructors and senior Party officials but provide the domestic and ancillary staff – Sobottke, the cook, Clara and others – with comfortable quarters close to their place of work.

'I should appreciate it,' the Reichsleiter continued humbly, 'if my wife could be commemorated in some modest fashion.'

'But of course, Martin,' Wesel said at once. 'We'll call your former house the Hermine Franke Building and put up a plaque to her. Will that do?'

Franke looked almost overwhelmed. 'Thank you, Waldemar. Your sympathy and kindness mean more than I can say. That's why I've ventured to present your unit with a small token of my esteem. You'll find it down at the landing-stage.'

It was a large and glossy power-boat, all varnished wood and gleaming chrome – a custom-built craft with an inboard engine by Rolls-Royce. Probably the handsomest and fastest boat on the Starnberger See.

'Splendid!' exclaimed Wesel. His men clustered round, wide-eyed. 'Just what we needed. Does it have a name yet?'

'I took the liberty of having one inscribed,' Franke replied solemnly. 'On the bows, where it should be – in gold lettering. I hope you don't mind, Waldemar?'

The name was *Hermine*. They all stared at it in reverent silence. Even Wesel was temporarily speechless.

Statement taken in San Francisco, California, from Bernd G. Breslauer, realtor:

Sure, that's right. Professor Breslauer was an uncle of mine. He lived in Munich, Germany, till 1933. Nothing fancy, just a three-room apartment stuffed with books.

He lived alone. His wife had died of cancer late in 1930. He was an international authority on Freudian analysis. Very creditable, but it didn't buy him much in the way of luxuries.

Early in February 1933 he was arrested. He smuggled a message out before they came for him – 'I suppose I'm on some list or other.' We didn't hear anything further for over a year. Then, in 1934, he was granted an exit visa and turned up here. All he had with him was one little bag with a few clothes in it. No books at all.

We made him welcome, naturally. Apart from anything else, he was a big man in his field. Only a few days after he arrived here a telegram came from Albert Einstein; 'Delighted you made it,' it said. 'When do we get together?'

Uncle Aaron moved into the two attic rooms we fixed up for him, but he didn't do much studying or writing, just sank into apathy. His silence got us down, to be honest. Still, it turned out later that he was working on some kind of think-tank project for his friend Einstein.

He did go out walking occasionally. People he steered clear of on principle, autos he was less good at dodging. Even when he did come downstairs, which wasn't often, he sat there brooding. The only person who ever got a smile out of him was our daughter Ruth, who was ten at the time. He taught her chess – she's still up to pro standard.

One night I came out with it. 'Look, Uncle,' I said, 'what did they do to you?'

I remember every word of his reply. 'Your question needs rephrasing, my boy,' he said. 'What did you *let* them do to you, Uncle? – that's nearer the mark.'

He didn't say anything else for a couple of minutes. Then he went on, 'I don't know the answer to your question but I'm working on one. Whether it's a cause for hope or fear, I can't say. I only know this much: I'd probably be dead right now if it wasn't for a man named Müller. I still wonder if the world wouldn't be a better place if he'd never existed – but that's another question that defeats me.'

But the real mystery came later. In 1935, after he'd been with us for upwards of a year, Uncle Aaron decided to go back to Europe. We begged him not to but he packed up and left. Just a few clothes – no books. We never heard what became of him.

Müller looked reprovingly at the man from the cellar. 'My dear fellow,' he said, the concern in his voice tinged with an unmistakable note of warning, 'much as I admire your intellectual honesty, you have a suicidal turn of phrase. You'll talk yourself into the morgue if you carry on this way.'

'I thought I was ordered to be systematically provocative – to force your young men to think. Aren't I doing it?'

'With a vengeance. You bring your arguments down on their heads like a hammer – I can almost hear the crunch of bone. It amuses me personally, but it's a wasted labour of love on your part. You'll never get through to them, so lay off. Try and restrain yourself a little.'

Breslauer's expression was faintly indulgent. 'It's your doing that I'm here at all. You got me into this. Why?'

'For three reasons. In the first place, if you weren't here you'd have ended up in a concentration camp, dead by now – you're no athlete, old man. Secondly, you provide these political apprentices with a perfect stooge because you still believe in the superiority of mind over matter, even in these glorious days. Last of all, anyone involved in this thing, like me, can use some insurance. I may need a character witness – a prestige Jew – and you're mine.'

'So you really value my survival?'

Müller nodded firmly. 'We've made a deal, Wesel and I. You play ball with us for a year. Then you can go where you like, spend the rest of your life as you please. Till then you've got to toe the line, otherwise I won't answer for the consequences.'

They had first met in summer 1931, over the body of a girl student who'd committed suicide. Müller suspected murder and wanted to nail someone for it, but he'd never heard arguments as lucid and cogent as those deployed by Breslauer, the dead girl's tutor. They not only convinced him but filled him with respect for the professor's powers of logic and persuasion.

They met often from then on, sometimes spending whole days deep in discussion. They'd struck up a kind of friendship.

'You never know,' Breslauer said quietly, 'I may succeed in getting them to think after all. If not all six, at least a couple. Wouldn't that be worth any sacrifice you care to name?'

'Breslauer, my friend, haven't you got it into your honest Jewish head what's going on here? It's open season in Greater Germany. Jews and subversives are fair game.'

'And you're out hunting with the rest of the pack?'

'Don't think I had no option, old friend – the choice was mine.

It's all the same to me. I don't have anybody or anything left to lose. Both my brothers were killed in the last war. My sister was raped and murdered by French African troops during the occupation of the Ruhr. My father was so appalled by our national decline, as he saw it, that he put a bullet in his head. My mother threw herself in front of a train. In 1930 I got married. My wife died giving birth to our first child, probably as a result of criminal negligence. I did my best to prove it but failed. The world's a cess-pit, I tell you, and Germany's three parts under.'

Breslauer seemed troubled by the realization of what motivated his protector. 'You're no patriot, Müller. You obviously loathe Germany – you want to help destroy it. Is that your only reason for being here? Do I have that fear to contend with as well?'

Müller's laugh was loud but mirthless. Doing his best to sound casual, he said, 'You always make the same dangerous mistake, Professor – you say what you think. With me you can afford to, but only with me. Our supermen don't like home truths, especially when they're out of tune with the times, so watch your tongue. You're my prestige Jew, remember? I'm going to save your neck even if I risk my own in the process.'

'We now come,' Waldemar Wesel informed his attentive students after a communal breakfast, 'to another important phase in your specialized training. For five days in each of the next three weeks, you will be attached to the staff of a concentration camp, namely Dachau. The intervening weekends will be devoted to seminars at which the experience you gain will be analysed and assessed.'

Wesel's 'graduated schedule' took the following form:

Week 1. Initiation into the special features of the concentration camp system. Practical experience of general guard duties. Reception of incoming consignments and disposal of casualties. Length of shift: twelve hours daily.

Week 2. Personal care and supervision of individual detainees. Selection and transference procedures, utilization of manpower, search and segregation methods.

Week 3. Attendance at interrogations and special man-management sessions, their evaluation and practical use. Direct participation in advanced forms of interrogation and corrective treatment.

'The whole course has already been exhaustively discussed with Sturmbannführer Eicke, the camp commandant,' Wesel explained. 'He's awaiting you with open arms, so to speak. I sincerely trust – correction, I'm absolutely positive – that you won't let me down.'

There was little fear of that, but Wesel was a believer in thorough briefings.

'Even during this operation you will remain directly subordinate to me alone – administratively, financially and disciplinarily. Volunteer no information about me or your unit. Refer anyone who questions you to the camp commandant or the Central Security Department, who will get in touch with me. The same applies if anything unforeseen occurs, though I hardly think it likely.'

One of the preparatory lectures was delivered by Detective Superintendent Müller. His theme: interrogation.

'The interrogator possesses an invariable advantage over his subject. He can decide which factors to concentrate on and which to avoid. The interrogator is a kind of hunter – he can stalk his quarry or lurk in a well camouflaged hide, but he must be able to bide his time. The development of patience is his only guarantee of a clean kill.

'Experience teaches us that nobody hands out information on a plate. Keep asking questions – ask the same ones over and over again, but always make a note of the answers you get. You'll soon become aware they don't all tie up. After several hours of questioning, discrepancies are bound to creep in. Identify and analyse them, systematically evaluate and exploit them. Then you'll get somewhere.

'The ultimate stage, which one seldom fails to attain, is mental exhaustion – a kind of induced bewilderment that destroys the subject's capacity for logical thought. If he's genuinely guilty he'll abandon his evasive tactics and fall back on prepared lies, and behind them – very close behind, in many cases – you'll find the truth.'

Interrogation techniques were also the subject of a discourse by

SS-Obersturmführer Alfons Lederhuber, who headed the 'Inquiry Section' at Dachau concentration camp.

'First of all,' he said, surveying his six new assistants, 'welcome aboard. I can use help. The traffic's heavy, so we have to work fast to get through our daily quota.

'Another thing. We aren't dealing with suspects here. These people are convicted criminals: public enemies, traitors, political offenders, defeatists, subversives and Jews. Our methods are geared to the fact that they're all liars and inferior beings. We don't appeal to their better nature. They don't have any, so we simply knock their teeth out or kick them in the ass – or the balls, which works even better. Then they turn talkative, most of them. In a small proportion of cases we have to resort to subtler methods. They may spit blood but they spit out the truth as well, and we're devoted to the truth round here.

'Don't worry about your lack of experience. If you're half as smart as I hope you are, you'll pick up the technique in no time.'

The three weeks at Dachau could be accounted another unqualified success for Wesel's brilliant organizing skill and his men's outstanding efficiency. They were crowned by a gala dinner in 'medieval German' style, i.e. stodgy, greasy and abundant.

Between the various courses, including carp stewed in ale and roast sucking-pig, Waldemar Wesel reviewed his students' achievements with the aid of some bulky progress reports lying beside his plate. He leafed through them carefully even though he knew their contents almost by heart.

'First I must tell you that the camp commandant has congratulated me on your high standard of training, a compliment I'm happy to pass on.' Wesel proceeded to list several gratifying items from Eicke's record of their activities.

Siegfried's prize performance consisted in persuading a socialistically inclined trade union leader to talk within ten minutes. After a series of full-blooded blows on both ears, he whimperingly confessed to having embezzled funds and wangled himself some extra bread rations. Hermann's vigilance had been responsible for the discovery of a 10-metre escape tunnel which he filled in, having previously waited until the would-be escapers were on site. Berner and Bergmann were commended for their swift recognition of homosexual elements, three of whom had offered resistance and been beaten into a pulp. Hagen had specialized in Jews. Thanks to his intensive treatment, five had confessed to malicious slanders on the Führer and another seven to involvement in a treasonable conspiracy. The inevitable outcome was a twelve-name addition to the commandant's 'wastage' list.

Last of all, Norden. In accord with Wesel's instructions, he had been given an assignment of major importance: a Roman Catholic bishop. After first reducing him to tears, he induced him to confess that he despised the Führer – an admission he did not long survive.

Wesel's lip curled. 'What did you do, choke him?'

'No, just talked to him,' said Norden, 'using his own arguments – I even quoted the Bible. He started cursing the Führer but his heart must have given out. He suddenly dropped dead. All Lederhuber said was, "A dead man is a closed file – one more problem solved."'

They drank to that. All night long.

The next day – or rather, because Wesel had proclaimed a rest day, late afternoon – the peace was abruptly shattered by a series of dull but penetrating thuds interspersed with bellows of rage.

Raffael, Wesel's secretary and watch-dog, raced to the scene. Hagen and Norden had attacked each other in the upstairs passage. They were rolling around, swapping punches and snarling while their four fellow-students looked on with the detached amusement of passers-by watching a dog-fight.

'Stop it!' Raffael shrilled. 'Stop it at once!'

Nobody took any notice. The situation showed signs of deteriorating. A large mirror got smashed and two wall-lights were swept from the corridor wall. Raffael rushed off, to reappear a minute later with his lord and master.

Waldemar Wesel was attired in an ankle-length nightshirt of monastic brown. His cheeks were slightly flushed, presumably with indignation. He clapped his hands and, without unduly raising his voice, said, 'Stop this nonsense at once!'

Norden and Hagen were too closely entwined to hear the order.

Not so the other four, who hurled themselves at their battling comrades and tore them apart. Norden and Hagen came to attention, chests heaving.

'You will both report to me in ten minutes,' Wesel said, punching out the words like a machine-press. 'In my office, in uniform. The rest of you, stand by.'

'Yessir!' came the sixfold response.

Ten minutes later Wesel was sitting at his desk in an SS uniform adorned with sundry war medals and the Party's gold badge. Norden and Hagen stood rigidly at attention in front of him, likewise in black tailored uniforms but without any insignia.

Wesel waited for them to speak.

'Sorry, Sturmbannführer,' Hagen blurted out, 'but it wasn't my fault. Norden flipped his lid.'

'I was provoked,' snapped Norden, 'in the most outrageous manner. By Hagen.'

'Silence, the pair of you,' Wesel said coldly. 'There can be no excuse for what went on in my presence, no excuse and no satisfactory explanation. Incidents of this kind must never occur in our unit – never, do you hear? Now tell me how it happened.'

'It was that little whore Clara,' Hagen said. 'She started it all.'

'No she didn't,' Norden corrected him stubbornly. 'You did.'

From Clara Heidegger's reminiscences:

All hell broke loose that morning. As usual on a day when there was no set time for getting up, I had to serve breakfast in the young gentlemen's rooms after knocking to see who was awake. Hagen was the first.

Knowing the kind he was, I brought him something he could really get his teeth into. Smoked blood- and liver-sausage, farmhouse butter with wood-baked wholemeal bread, and a double-strength pot of coffee.

Well, I'd hardly put the tray down when he grabbed my arm and tried to drag me into bed with him. I thought it was funny at first, especially as I felt sure I was strong enough to fight him off if I tried. Then he rammed his hand up between my legs and I let out a yell.

Next thing I knew, Norden came rushing in as if he'd only been waiting for the word. A really nice boy, Norden was. To tell you the truth, I wouldn't have minded if it had been him that . . . But then, he always was a gentleman, especially when it came to the opposite sex.

Anyway, he sprang to the defence of my honour, as they say in books. He rushed at Hagen, dragged him out of bed and started hitting him, like I said.

Wesel listened to Clara's report dispassionately and thanked her politely. Then he recalled Norden and Hagen and summoned the other four. A minute later his men were standing in front of him like six expectant black statues.

'First,' he began, 'I won't tolerate physical violence between group members. Intellectual rivalry is fine – it promotes determination and efficiency – but there's no room for amateur pugilists in this outfit. I shall assume that this fracas was an exception to the general rule and will never recur. Secondly,' he went on, 'I find myself compelled to give those directly involved a severe reprimand – their first and last. In future I shall summarily dismiss anyone who becomes embroiled in incidents of this kind.' His sapphire eyes shone with menace.

'Thirdly, I condemn the behaviour of the rest of you. You should have taken prompt action to ensure that I was spared such a degrading spectacle. These matters are best settled in private.

'Fourthly, as regards the special status of Clara. Clara is an employee who does her work and does it well. No restrictions are imposed on her extramural activities. She can associate with anyone she pleases in return for a guaranteed fee of 50 marks, but rape is out – understand? Which brings me to a fifth point to which I've probably devoted insufficient attention until now. You're young men, and young men need an outlet for their surplus energy. If your condition is as critical as all that, perhaps you require treatment.'

Wesel's keen ears detected a murmur of relief and approval. Deftly, he picked up the phone, asked the switchboard for a Munich number from his address-book and demanded to speak to Sturmbannführer Webermayer. After a brief but cordial exchange of salutations, Wesel stated his requirements.

'Book me some rooms in one of your better-class establishments – preferably Leopoldstrasse. This evening, for six, and no excuses, you old rogue – you know me! I insist on your very best personnel, and that includes the delectable Fräulein Schulze. Right?'

Wesel must have been assured that all was in order. He replaced the receiver with a satisfied air and turned to his men.

'Fine, it's all arranged. You can vent your frustrations in a five-star bordello – at SS expense, of course. The main thing is to get your blood pressure back to normal.'

Sobottke chauffeured the six men to Leopoldstrasse in the Mercedes. They were warmly received by the officer in charge, Sturmbannführer Webermayer, who greeted them with an impeccable Hitler salute.

Pertinent information was imparted while they drank a glass of mediocre German bubbly in the downstairs lounge. They soon learned that there were rules to be observed, even here, but it did not dull their sense of anticipation as they lolled in the inevitable red velvet armchairs. Doubtless at Wesel's behest, Webermayer treated them to a preliminary moral pep talk.

'I want you to regard this house as a continuance of the Græco-Roman classical tradition, as an establishment devoted to relaxation in refined surroundings – the kind of relaxation that provides a renewed stimulus after mental or physical exertion. Once again, gentlemen, welcome to you all!'

Webermayer pressed a bell-push and the room was invaded by six females who tripped in wearing smiles and little else. He then withdrew, but not before singling one of them out for special attention.

'Allow me to present Fräulein Schulze. She will familiarize you with our house rules.'

A woman of wholly indeterminate age, possibly in her mid-20s, possibly ten years older, Erika Schulze was an attractively proportioned Nordic beauty. She scrutinized the six prospects carefully, taking her time. Then she sat down between Norden and Hagen, gestured to her five companions, who introduced themselves, and said, 'For a start, let's get acquainted.'

This did not take long. Hagen was the first to make his choice, which fell on an Arabian pocket Venus. Siegfried disappeared soon afterwards with a big-eyed North German blonde who claimed to be Scandinavian. Hermann picked a dainty French girl of exceptional mammary proportions and suffered her to lead him off.

Berner and Bergmann, inseparable as ever, took what was left. This comprised a Viennese named Mitzi and a signorina from Bologna with Madonna-like features and a generously upholstered figure. In return for their basic fee plus the promise of a special bonus, the two girls were encouraged to stage a Lesbian marathon while the Siamese Twins looked on, locked in a fond embrace.

Only two people remained in the pink-lit salon: Norden and Erika Schulze, who continued to sip fizz and exchange meaningful glances. Minutes passed in silence.

'Somebody special, are you?' Erika asked at length.

'*You* are,' Norden replied impulsively. 'I can tell!'

'Maybe, but I can't always afford to be choosy. Business comes first. Isn't it the same with you?'

'Much the same,' Norden said. Gently but fervently, he brushed her hand with his lips.

She drew him towards her – down on her.

'You!' she moaned expertly. 'You're wonderful – one in a million!' It sounded like high commendation but was only high-class routine. Erika Schulze had a natural talent for her trade. She was an undisputed pro.

'You're unique!' he echoed, suddenly finding himself beneath her.

A minute or two later Erika rolled off him and lay there with the spurious air of exhaustion and fulfilment she generally assumed on such occasions. An almost stupefying wave of perfume enveloped her and Norden like the scent of invisible jasmine.

Norden, tenderly stroking her breasts, said, 'You're a very special person, Erika.'

She snuggled against him. 'You certainly make me feel like one, Heinz-Hermann.'

'We were made for each other.'

Erika propped herself on one elbow and studied his face. The first thing she detected was tenderness, but tenderness alloyed with a kind of resolute concern. And concern, so experience had taught her, was often underlaid by sentiments of a more possessive

84

nature. She hurriedly qualified what he had just said.

'We're good together, that's all.'

'Yes,' he said promptly, 'because we fell in love at first sight.'

'Don't be complicated, darling,' Erika retorted, perturbed. 'Keep your mind on your work.' She ignored his further protestations – she had often heard similar ones before.

But never from someone like Norden.

The Group's successful introduction to the Leopoldstrasse brothel was promptly extended to a full 48-hour visit on direct orders from Wesel.

However, the Sturmbannführer's talent for indoctrination and organization was such that he did not leave his men to stew uninterruptedly in their own juice. Instead, he offered them a series of carefully selected cultural diversions.

One such was a visit to the Alte Pinakothek, Munich's most celebrated art gallery, where they were encouraged to study Altdorfer's huge *Battle of Arbela*, dedicated to the memory of Alexander the Great, and some fleshily erotic canvases by Rubens – to name only a few of Wesel's favourite paintings. Then came expeditions to the Deutsches Museum enlivened by informative lectures on the Germanic spirit of invention and its wealth of creative contributions to the development of railroads, the internal combustion engine, electricity, telephony and aeronautics.

But perhaps the most seminal experience of all was a tour of the *Degenerate Art* exhibition that had been staged at the Hofgarten by culturally vigilant Nazi officials. Here, among other gruesome monstrosities, could be seen dishcloth daubs by Nolde, scrawls by Klee, Kandinsky's bomb-bursts of colour with their suggestion of chronic diarrhœa, the moronic infantilisms of Franz Marc, who favoured blue horses, red earth and green skies, and some more daubs by Lovis Corinth which, having been perpetrated after his second stroke, prompted any healthy-minded person to inquire why his brushes and paints hadn't been confiscated after the first.

'Nauseating,' was Hagen's verdict, 'but my stomach's stronger than most. They only make me laugh.'

'They're very instructive all the same,' Norden said earnestly. 'You have to know what total degeneracy looks like before you can appreciate true values. It strengthens your determination to defend them.'

Hagen winked at the others, confident of their approval. 'I may not be a culture-vulture like you, Norden, but I know enough about art to say this much: my girl in Leopoldstrasse has got more technique in her left tit than this lot put together.'

Whereupon they were driven back to Leopoldstrasse for a further spell of recreation.

As soon as these relaxing two days were up, Wesel swung back into action.

Summoned to the library, the six found him alone in front of the blackboard. Inscribed on it in white chalk were the words 'Ester – Synagogue – Leonhard'.

'We now come,' Wesel announced in a brisk but encouraging tone, 'to the last and most important of your preliminary tests. If you pass them, as I'm sure you will, I shall be able to report our unit fully operational. The Führer wishes to be personally informed of the outcome of these three missions. I hope you realize what that means, gentlemen.'

Their silence demonstrated that they were entirely alive to the gravity of the situation.

'Three special missions,' Wesel repeated, 'each to be carried out by a two-man team. I have already selected the teams and their objectives. How you carry out your allotted tasks is your own affair. No modes of procedure will be suggested – you must devise your own. I shall limit myself to defining your respective targets.'

He did so in a businesslike manner.

Project 1, christened 'Ester', involved a former trade union leader of that name who still nursed left-wing sympathies. He was to be cornered in his third-floor 'lair' in Schwanthalerstrasse and taught a lesson. Entrusted with this educational task: Berner and Bergmann.

Project 2, code-named 'Synagogue', referred to the Jewish place of worship at the rear of Lenbachplatz in Munich. 'An outlandish and provocative piece of architecture which dares to ape the Romanesque style – in brick, what's more! Leave your mark on it, and think of something original.' Responsible for this second mission: Siegfried and Hermann.

Finally, Project 3: a writer named Leonhard, resident in Teng-strasse. 'A bleeding heart who enjoys parading his conscience in public. A definite outsider – lots of foreign connections. I want him eliminated.' This mission went to Norden and Hagen.

'How much time do we have?'

'One week,' Wesel told them. 'That should give you ample time to study your objectives in depth before taking swift and effective action. No mistakes, please. I expect absolute perfection.'

Wesel was not disappointed.

Each of the three teams had an entirely free hand. Raffael dealt with equipment requisitions, Müller was available for advice on investigative methods, and Sobottke took care of transportation.

Preparations were soon complete. Every mission went according to plan, though not without a few shortcomings which were little more than minor blemishes. Their cause lay less with the principal actors than with a still deficient sense of purpose in certain members of the general public and – regrettably – certain sections of official-dom as well. Many citizens were just not fully permeated by the spirit of the new age. Their conversion was obviously going to take time.

Project 'Ester', at least, was a total and unqualified success. Berner and Bergmann pulled it off without a hitch. Disguised as handymen, the two men carefully researched every aspect of their target. They struck with due speed, at supper-time.

The two dungaree-clad intruders had only to flash their re-volvers to send the 'working-class traitor,' plus wife and two child-ren, scuttling into the lavatory. Having bolted the door, they demolished the apartment, smashing all that lent itself to destruc-tion with the axes they'd brought along in a sack. Then they bellowed 'Heil Hitler!' and left.

'Without a single interruption,' reported the Siamese Twins. 'There wasn't a soul to be seen on the stairs – nobody lifted a finger to stop us.'

Project 'Synagogue' was just as carefully planned. Siegfried and Hermann completed their task without difficulty because the building and the streets surrounding it were deserted in the small hours. Using a bucket of phosphorescent crimson paint – a brainwave of Hermann's – they daubed the outer walls with man-sized swastikas punctuated by the Nazi slogan 'Perish Judah!' This produced a decorative effect impossible to overlook and to remove.

The two heroes had scarcely departed when some misguided nocturnal strollers called the fire brigade. After briefly inspecting the graffiti, the firemen returned to their Blumenstrasse depot and left the morning shift to tackle them.

Meanwhile, the incident had become the talk of the town. It attracted large numbers of sightseers including a local correspondent of the London *Times*, but Wesel did not mind if the Jew-infested British Isles received some intimation of which way the German wind was blowing. One day, when world Jewry was expiring in a welter of blood, not red paint, people would remember this portent from the 'Capital of the Movement'.

Project 'Leonhard' created the strongest impact, although the possibility of an official investigation lent it an element of risk. Working in harness, Norden and Hagen set a supreme example. Hagen broke the door down with a single mighty kick. Norden dashed into the apartment, revolver at the ready. The author, that 'insidious subverter of the masses', was seated at his desk. He stared at the intruders in dismay, but only for a split second. Then Norden shattered his skull with a well-aimed bullet.

'You jumped the gun!' Hagen shouted angrily. 'Why didn't you leave him to me? I'd set my heart on killing the swine!'

At that moment the author's wife rushed in and threw herself on his lifeless body in a belated attempt to shield him. Hagen finished her at once with another single shot, this time in the heart. Then, for good measure, a child appeared – a little girl of about ten, wearing a long nightie and clutching a doll in her arms. She gazed at them helplessly, uncomprehendingly, before Hagen gunned her down.

Norden's expression was grave when they reported the completion of their task to Wesel. 'In my view,' he said, 'Hagen went too far.'

'It was essential,' Hagen retorted. 'Our personal safety demanded it. Some children have a photographic memory for faces – Müller taught us that. What were we supposed to do, risk being identified?'

'She was still a minor,' Norden said coldly. 'Her testimony wouldn't have carried any weight.'

Wesel looked stern. 'Am I to understand, Norden, that you're lodging a formal complaint against your team-mate?'

'Of course not, Sturmbannführer.'

'Good, just as I thought. To those in the service of Fatherland and Führer, sacrifices are not only necessary but unavoidable.'

Nobody disputed the point.

Satisfied, Wesel went on: 'Gentlemen, you've passed your last major test. A great day looms ahead – the day when our sworn brotherhood is ceremonially inaugurated by the Führer himself, Adolf Hitler!'

The great day was not slow in coming. Early on the morning of 20 April 1934, the 45th birthday of Germany's beloved leader, Wesel gathered his men around him. He gazed deep into each pair of eyes in turn, lingeringly. Wesel appreciated the value of the pregnant pause.

'From today,' he declared, 'our group embarks on its existence as a self-contained and independent special service unit. You will be under my command but directly responsible to the Führer.'

Their eyes widened, but they were even more impressed when Wesel, reading from a typewritten sheet, made the following announcement:

First, and with immediate effect, the members of the Wesel Group were appointed Untersturmführer, or second-lieutenants in the SS. Their appointment was official and carried the corresponding rate of pay. Wesel himself jumped three rungs of the ladder and became a Brigadeführer.

Secondly, personal bank accounts had been opened in their names and credited with a five-figure sum representing their preliminary bonus. Half of it was deposited with the Deutsche Bank in Munich, the balance with the Schweizerischer Bankverein in Zürich. Raffael was holding the relevant cheque-books.

Thirdly, they would be issued with passports – initially two each: a German passport and one purporting to be issued by another European country, the latter dependent on their linguistic aptitudes.

Fourthly, the Group's motor pool was to be enlarged by the

purchase of some more first-class German cars, e.g. Mercedes and Horch, and one or two American models from the Studebaker and Packard ranges. These vehicles would be available for recreational as well as operational use.

Fifthly, living quarters could now be refurnished and redecorated to match the tastes and inclinations of their occupants, whose wardrobes were to be supplemented with suits, shirts, underclothes and footwear, all custom-made in accordance with personal requirements.

'But that's not all, gentlemen,' Wesel told his six disciples, who continued to stare at him in rapturous amazement. 'I'm now at liberty to inform you that you're to visit the Führer. Adolf Hitler has expressed a wish to meet you personally!'

5 The Rewards of Power

The German air was pure and clear that April morn. The skies were cloudless and the sun shone bright – 'Führer-weather!' as Wesel described it over breakfast.

He urged them to tuck in, but not only to fortify themselves for their historic midday encounter with the Führer at Munich's Brown House, national headquarters of the Nazi Party. Even before leaving the Villa they were to meet the man who had, with Wesel himself, been a spiritual co-founder of their enterprise. 'I'm sure you'll take to him and vice versa. He knows all about every last one of you.'

But even that failed to exhaust the day's store of surprises. After coffee the newly promoted Brigadeführer invited his junior officers to join him in a bottle of brandy dating from 1889, when Hitler first saw the light at Braunau am Inn. Wesel warmed his balloon glass in both hands, sniffing the contents appreciatively. Then he rose and looked gravely round the table.

'With your promotion to the rank of Untersturmführer, gentlemen, you are now enrolled in the officer corps of the SS. That imposes special obligations but it also confers exceptional privileges. One of them is the right to use the second person singular when addressing your brother officers, irrespective of rank. Any problems, Hagen?'

'Certainly not, Brigadeführer. Thank you.' Hagen employed the familiar German '*du*' without a flicker of hesitation.

They all rose and toasted each other, the six newly fledged officers prefacing their first sip with an expectant glance at their powerful friend and mentor.

After breakfast, to their great surprise and profound delight, came a special presentation. They were summoned to the Brigadeführer's office for what they assumed would be a final inspection. Smartly drawn up before him, they saw Wesel make a sweeping gesture towards the six capacious cardboard boxes on his desk. Each of them bore a name.

Wesel handed them over one by one. No words, just a brief but hearty handshake. The boxes contained dress uniforms of the deepest black, also caps, ceremonial dirks and patent leather shoes. Three gleaming silver stars on the collar badges proclaimed their new rank: Untersturmführer!

'Don't thank me, gentlemen. The gratitude is on my side. Raffael has gone to great lengths to see that every item fits you – no alterations will be needed. Always ensure that your bearing does justice to the uniform you wear, particularly today.'

They reassembled in the drawing-room just before 10.00, this time resplendent in their new dress uniforms. It was a noble sight. Wesel's men seemed to emit an aura which filled him with pride.

'Fine,' he said, 'but stay on your toes. Our visitor is a stickler for military perfection. If we can't provide it, who can?'

Their visitor arrived at the Villa on time, almost to the second. Punctuality was one of his fads – one of several they would come to know in due course. Raffael greeted him outside and ushered him into the drawing-room, then vanished as quickly as he could. Although Raffael was tougher than he looked, there was something about this man that made his blood run cold.

Once in the room, the newcomer seemed to ignore everyone but Wesel. He strode up to him and the two senior officers gripped each other by the shoulders in a virile embrace. Then Wesel stepped aside to reveal his men. The visitor scrutinized their rigid forms with keen, almost avid, attention.

Finally he said, 'So these are your blue-eyed boys.'

Wesel nodded. The visitor came nearer, a slim man with the long narrow face of a horse, jutting nose, small asymmetrical eyes and strongly protuberant lips. He raised his arm in the Nazi salute.

'Heil Hitler, gentlemen. My name is Heydrich.'

The voice was remarkable. Clear, high-pitched and harsh, with the crisp and imperious tone of someone used to giving orders.

'Gentlemen,' said Heydrich, 'you have equipped yourselves to meet the Führer in person. If you have any questions, ask them now.'

Silence.

'Very good.' Heydrich had apparently taken this for granted. 'No questions – very good. In that case, Waldi, I can inform the Führer that your men are present and correct.'

Wesel cocked an eyebrow. 'Won't Himmler be doing that himself?'

'The Reichsführer,' Heydrich replied with a sardonic grin, 'is otherwise engaged. He and his aides are practising Indian meditation techniques. He seems to think it's an Aryan pastime.'

Wesel grinned back.

Adolf Hitler received the Wesel Group in his study on the first floor of the Brown House, a palatial room designed by his court architect and meaningfully dominated by a portrait of Frederick the Great, King of Prussia.

Hitler entered the room at twelve-thirty. On Heydrich's recommendation and in consultation with Reichsleiter Franke, he had reserved half an hour for this audience. At 1 p.m. he was due in the sumptuous Senatorial Hall, with its brick-red leather chairs, there to preside over a grand birthday banquet attended by leading representatives of the Party, government and armed forces.

He walked over to his desk, turned, and studied each of his visitors in succession.

'Welcome, gentlemen. You will understand why I refrain from offering you any form of alcoholic beverage. You are members of our younger generation and guarantors of our national future. I want that future to be happy and carefree but not irresponsible and self-indulgent. Liquor and tobacco are the enemies of moral fibre. As I'm sure you're aware, I abhor strong drink and have not smoked since I was a young man. My early days were Spartan in the extreme.'

Waldemar Wesel stiffened to attention and saluted. 'My Führer, I beg leave to report that no member of my unit smokes. No cigarettes, no cigars – not even an occasional pipe.'

'Excellent, Wesel, excellent.' Hitler graciously inclined his head. 'I could provide your men with many arguments in favour of total abstinence, but not now. Later perhaps, when we're less pressed for time. Can that be arranged, Heydrich?'

'Certainly, my Führer,' said Heydrich.

Hitler nodded and turned back to Wesel. 'I have made a thorough study of your new book on the nature of obedience. It lies on my desk, permanently within reach. You have put my innermost thoughts into words.'

'Thank you, my Führer!'

Hitler proceeded to harangue his visitors as if addressing a Party rally. He spoke in a loud, harsh voice with guttural over- and undertones. Sometimes his eyes had a far-away expression, sometimes they merely looked vacant, sometimes they followed the movements of his hands, which seemed to carve words out of the air by main force.

'I look upon Comrade Wesel as one of our Movement's ideological pioneers,' he concluded. 'He is one of the very few thinkers to have proclaimed what is, from our point of view, the only true path to political greatness. If I am to tread that path, I need men pledged to absolute allegiance. Men like yours, Wesel. Can I depend on you – all of you?'

'Yes, my Führer!' Wesel replied. He prompted his companions with a glance.

'Yes, my Führer!' they barked simultaneously.

Adolf Hitler accepted these expressions of loyalty as a matter of course. Once more he gazed into each pair of eyes. Then he said:

'I have seldom felt as secure as I have in your company, gentlemen. I trust that we shall have many more opportunities to pursue what has, I feel sure, been a productive exchange of views. I shall send for you again before long.'

Late in the afternoon of that memorable 20 April, the Villa in Feldafing witnessed the start of a celebration which lasted into the small hours. Vast quantities of champagne were consumed.

Waldemar Wesel was absent. Together with Heydrich, he had lingered in the vicinity of Germany's birthday boy, Adolf Hitler. Müller had retired to the cellar with Breslauer, giving orders that he was not to be disturbed, and the domestic staff had been granted a night off.

This left Wesel's minions unattended except by Raffael, who had received telephoned instructions from Wesel to draw on the Villa's stocks for anything that might be required in the way of

94

liquid refreshment.

On this occasion, Raffael showed himself faintly uncooperative. The only person to have been left out, unwarmed by the glow of the Führer's approval, he displayed a sullen reluctance to act as wine waiter.

His actual words were, 'If you must get drunk, help yourselves.'

This drew a massive retort from Hagen, the party's self-appointed spokesman. 'Just a minute,' he called. 'Who the hell do you think you are?'

'Not your errand-boy,' Raffael replied defiantly.

A ripple of amusement ran round the table. It stopped short at Hagen. 'Raffael,' he said, 'if you want to keep your ass in commission, do as you're told.'

Raffael gaped at him. 'Are you threatening me?'

'You're damn right I am.'

'Raffael's under my protection,' Norden broke in.

'You don't say!' Hagen's voice was blurred but incisive. 'Fancy your chances with him, do you?'

'How dare you suggest such a thing!'

'You couldn't afford to try it anyway. You'd be poaching on Wesel's preserves.'

'Nobody,' Norden said with menace, 'is authorized to give Raffael orders except the Brigadeführer.'

'Look, I'm just as fond of Raffael as you are.' Hagen's tone became bantering. 'I hope he feels the same about me – for his sake. Is that right, Raffael?'

Raffael shrugged.

'Fine, so why not be a good boy and do as you're told?'

Raffael complied, outwardly at least, by shuttling back and forth with the crates of drink required to render the party dead drunk and ripe for bed. This took time.

At some stage in the interminable proceedings, Berner leant confidentially towards Bergmann. 'Did you get a good look at Heydrich? Anything strike you about him?'

'Only his rear end.'

'Sorry to disappoint you both,' sneered Raffael. 'Heydrich isn't like Röhm. He's a married man with an eye for the opposite sex. They say he got fired from the Navy for screwing the ass off a shipping magnate's daughter. The shipping magnate happened to be a buddy of Admiral Raeder.'

Norden looked stern. 'Herr Heydrich's private life is his own concern, not ours. Is that clear, Raffael?'

'Of course, Norden,' Raffael replied hastily. 'Please don't get me wrong.' He glanced at Hagen, who was still glowering in his direction. 'Besides, he's an artistic kind of person.'

'How artistic?' asked Hermann. 'Like Wesel, you mean?'

'Heydrich plays the violin,' Raffael confided. 'But only among friends.'

Hermann wagged his head in drunken disapproval. 'They say Einstein plays the fiddle too. A prize pig of a Jew, Einstein!'

'What's all this, Raffael?' Hagen demanded sharply. 'Are you comparing Gruppenführer Heydrich with a Jewish fiddler?'

'You're crazy,' Raffael protested. 'I never even mentioned Einstein, Hermann did.'

But Hagen refused to give up. He reached for a tumbler, filled it to the brim with schnapps and held it out.

'Right, knock that back, and no stopping for breath. The toast is Heydrich.'

Raffael cradled the tumbler in both hands. He looked despairingly round the table, but they were all watching him like Hagen now, Norden included.

He shut his eyes and drank. The empty glass slipped through his fingers, fell to the floor and smashed. Then he collapsed, retching.

'So he can't drink either,' was Hagen's contemptuous verdict. Ponderously, he rose and walked over to Raffael, grabbed him by both lapels, hauled him erect and rammed him against the nearest wall. Raffael seemed to stick there, ashen-faced and wide-eyed with terror.

'Listen, you!' growled Hagen. 'Don't ever try and make trouble for us – any of us, have you got that straight, rose-petal?'

'Let him go,' Norden said, half irritably, half amused. 'He's out on his feet.'

'Shurrup!' Hagen snapped. 'Haven't you caught on yet? This little worm takes us for a bunch of knuckleheads. He thinks he can play one of us off against the other. If you ever try it again, Raffael, I'll kill you!' He pulled Raffael towards him and slammed him back against the wall. Raffael slumped to the floor, then struggled up and tottered out of the room, avoiding everybody's eye.

Hagen ostentatiously wiped his hands on a napkin. 'He had that coming. He'll think twice before he crosses any one of us. What is it Wesel always says? *Principiis obsta* – nip your troubles in the bud. Let's drink to that!'

Early next morning, on 21 April, Wesel proclaimed a general alert. The Six paraded in the drawing-room under his sardonic gaze. Red-eyed and bleary from too little sleep and too much liquor, they were naked under their bathrobes. According to Raffael, they couldn't have had more than three or four hours' sleep. Raffael himself was pale as death and could barely stand. He had spent half the night puking in Wesel's lavatory.

Wesel gave his men an encouraging wink. 'You don't look too good. We must take some remedial measures. I recommend a brisk trot down to the lake. Anyone object?'

Nobody did.

'Fine,' said Wesel. 'Then we'll meet at the landing-stage in fifteen minutes. Sports gear – track-suits and gym-shoes. Let's enjoy the dawn in our own way.'

It was a clear day, mild and almost windless, but the waters of the lake retained the winter chill. An early *Föhn*, or warm alpine breeze, had the effect of bringing the mountains so near they seemed within reach.

Wesel sat pensively at the wheel of the power-boat, ignoring the huddled figure of Raffael beside him. The other six had taken their places on the upholstered bench-seats.

When they were almost in the middle of the lake, equidistant from Feldafing and the mountains, Wesel killed the engine. 'Now, gentlemen,' he said with a smile, 'let's assume the boat's a write-off. It's sinking – it isn't there any more. What's the answer?'

'I get it, Brigadeführer,' said Norden, ' – a mock alert!' Fully clothed, he promptly jumped overboard and struck out for the shore.

'Norden catches on fast,' Wesel said brightly. 'Anyone else for a swim?'

Berner and Bergmann leapt over the side followed by Siegfried and Hermann.

Hagen hesitated for a moment. 'What about Raffael? Want me to give him a helping hand?'

'I don't count,' protested Raffael.

'He's one of us, isn't he?' Hagen said.

Wesel gave a brisk nod of agreement. Raffael needed a lesson too, after his repulsive display of inebriation.

'Right, man, in you go!' shouted Hagen. He grabbed Raffael, hefted him off his feet and threw him into the water. Then he dived in after him.

Hagen swam close beside Raffael, a grin of encouragement on his face. Raffael floundered along, gasping and spluttering. Hagen slapped him vigorously on the back – so vigorously Raffael would have gone under but for his tormentor's last-minute assistance.

'You can make it if I want you to,' Hagen said, 'and I do – for now. Get me?'

'I get you,' Raffael gasped.

'I'm your friend,' Hagen continued, towing him towards the shore in a lifeguard's grip, 'but it takes two to be friends, understand?'

'Yes,' spluttered Raffael. 'Just as long as I . . .'

Hagen hauled his limp form ashore. He'd saved the boy's life, and that, he felt, should create a sense of obligation. It also created unforeseen complications.

It was Norden who carried Raffael to his room after Hagen had left him lying on the lake-shore. He dumped him on his bed, undressed him and towelled him down hard.

Raffael's slender body took on a faint flush. He opened his eyes, recognized Norden and smiled, painfully but with unmistakable gratitude. Then he said, 'You're a pal. Not like Hagen – he's a swine!'

'All right, all right,' Norden said soothingly. 'Call him that if it makes you feel better, but forget you ever said it. I already did.'

'But you shouldn't, Norden – you're the last person.' Raffael sat up. His voice sounded tense and strained. 'He's as much your enemy as mine. He hates us both.'

'I never heard you say that, Raffael. Hagen isn't my enemy or yours. You can depend on me to help you any time, but not against another member of the Group.'

Raffael fell back as if Norden had struck him. A tremor ran through his body. Then he rolled over and buried his face in the pillow. 'Everything's so terrible here,' he groaned. 'It's like having claustrophobia – you can hardly breathe. *I* can't, anyway. I've *had* this place!'

The Wesel Group's visits to the brothel in Leopoldstrasse had developed into a smooth routine. A phone call ensured that all was in readiness by the time they arrived – the same accommodation, the same playmates. It became a matter of course that Norden should be allotted the main attraction, the prepossessing Fräulein Schulze. Erika always earned her money even when, as now, she only provided a sympathetic audience.

Norden squeezed her hand. 'You mean an awful lot to me, Erika.'

'That's nice,' she said, gazing expectantly at him.

The lighting was a subdued pink. A heavy, cloying pall of scent hung over the room.

'When you come down to it,' Norden confided, 'we're two of a kind.'

'How do you mean?'

'I mean we're both exceptions, in our own way. That's why we belong together.'

'Any time, darling, but what are you getting at? Fancy something special tonight?'

'Mutual redemption,' Norden said solemnly, 'that's what I'm getting at – mutual redemption and fulfilment!'

Erika found it hard to disguise her alarm at the direction the conversation was taking.

'You should have been a preacher,' she said, looking at him uncertainly. Then she burst out laughing. 'My God, you don't mean you want to *marry* me?'

Before Norden could make the appropriate declaration, there was a rap on the door and Hagen barged in.

Norden's eyes flashed. 'How dare you! Get out – you've no business in here!'

Hagen regarded the two naked figures with a broad grin. 'Keep your shirt on, I didn't mean to break anything up. Wesel just phoned. We've got to report immediately.'

'Why?'

'Ask him yourself,' Hagen replied tartly. 'All I know is, there's a crisis at the Villa. You'd better shift yourself, old son. This instalment's over.'

Waldemar Wesel had summoned Müller for an urgent consultation which transcended their normal working relationship. They eyed each other in silence across the Brigadeführer's private study. Wesel's expression was perceptibly worried, Müller's undisguisedly curious.

'For a man with your success rate, Brigadeführer, you don't look happy. What's the matter this time?'

'It's Raffael,' Wesel replied after some hesitation. 'I'm anxious about him, very anxious.'

'Raffael?' Müller raised his eyebrows. 'I wouldn't have thought he'd give you much trouble. What's he done?'

'He's disappeared,' Wesel confided.

'Disappeared?' Müller looked sceptical. 'Maybe he went for a walk. He probably needed some fresh air.'

'Walk, hell! He's walked out. He must have left here hours ago.'

Müller's eyes narrowed. 'What makes you think he's gone for good?'

'He took some of his belongings – underclothes, toilet articles, everything he'd need.' Desperately, Wesel added, 'He's left me.'

Müller strove with difficulty to conceal his glee. He simulated the businesslike reactions of a detective.

'Is he well-heeled? Does he have a valid passport? Any contacts abroad?'

'No, no,' Wesel said. 'I've always kept him short of funds and his passport's still in my safe.'

'In that case,' Müller observed briskly, 'he can't have gone far.'

'Will you be able to locate him?'

'Is it that important to you?'

'Yes! Find him, Herr Müller. I want him back at all costs.'

'Dead or alive?' drawled Müller.

'Alive. He'll have to account for his behaviour to me personally. Are you sure you can track him down?'

'Pretty sure,' Müller said, combining encouragement with caution. 'As long as you give me an entirely free hand.'

'Meaning what?'

'Access to Raffael's personal file, for one thing. I want all the confidential information about him you possess, and that includes any relevant extracts from Vice Squad records. In addition, I want to search his quarters and personal effects. I'll have to know all there is to know about him.'

'Agreed,' said Wesel. He was obviously prepared to make greater concessions than usual. 'Anything else?'

'Once I've completed my preliminary investigation, I may have to enlist the co-operation of the police.'

'But don't let him fall into their hands!' Wesel exclaimed anxiously. 'My reasons will be obvious when you've studied his personal file. He must be handed over to nobody but me.'

'I think I understand.' Müller was still relishing the situation. 'So the police can assist in running him to earth but we actually bag him.'

'You propose to use our men, Müller? This is a personal matter.'

'Perhaps, Brigadeführer, but why not convert it into an exercise? It could provide an additional test of our efficiency. And by the way, Brigadeführer, this might be an ideal opportunity for you to fulfil a certain undertaking you gave me.'

'What are you driving at, Müller?' Wesel shrugged. 'Very well. Raffael's recapture is worth something to me, so name your price.'

'Breslauer's release. By that I mean safe conduct to a foreign port, his fare and expenses, and a full set of internationally valid papers. Fair exchange is no robbery. I deliver Raffael, you release Breslauer. Is it a deal?'

Wesel nodded without undue hesitation. 'As long as there's no fuss, Herr Müller. I'm sure you appreciate the importance of discretion.'

Müller assembled the six young officers for what seemed at first to be just another training session.

'This is a trace-and-search exercise,' he began casually. 'In other words, we're going to locate a missing person. Routine procedure, that's all.'

Hermann was the first to respond. 'Before you can find a missing person you have to know his identity. Who are we looking for?'

'Raffael.' Müller's dispassionate tone was belied by his keen-eyed scrutiny of the faces round him.

'You mean our tame fairy got cold feet?' Hagen sneered.

'Looks like it,' Müller replied blandly. 'Maybe *you* can explain how he got them?'

Hagen back-pedalled fast. 'Raffael's an honorary member of the Group,' he said. 'I respect the fact. Besides, I saved his life the other day. That speaks for itself, doesn't it?'

There was a snort of contempt from Norden. Müller glanced quickly at him and said, 'Well, doesn't Hagen's explanation satisfy you?'

'No,' Norden said coldly. 'For some time now, I've had the impression that Raffael feels Hagen is a threat to his personal safety.'

'Impressions aren't evidence,' Müller retorted. 'Let's stick to the known facts, shall we, unless you've got a better idea?'

Norden shook his head.

'Good. Fact No. 1 is this: Raffael has disappeared and it's your job to find him.'

'So it's a man-hunt,' Siegfried said. 'Is he fair game – I mean, are we allowed to bring him in feet first?'

'Not under any circumstances,' Müller replied. 'You're to track him down without harming a hair on his head, and don't forget it. As soon as I've briefed you, gentlemen, get going and good hunting!'

Müller's plan of campaign for the recapture of Raffael.

Raffael's radius of operations will probably be restricted by his limited circle of friends, old haunts and potential places of accommodation. Being experts on this aspect of the social scene, Berner and Bergmann will cover some of the more notorious establishments – a preliminary list of nine is at their disposal. Hagen and Hermann can comb the unofficial lodging-houses. A list of those is also available.

Norden and Siegfried are assigned to investigate Raffael's immediate circle, including his parents, who are resident in Nuremberg. A former fiancée of Raffael's is also said to be living there, as is his closest boyhood friend, Joseph Rosenberg. I can supply the addresses.

All lines of inquiry must be pursued vigorously but with discretion. Should any problems arise, contact me at once. In the event of a genuine emergency, however, make a note of the following name and address: Winter, Chief Clerical Officer, Commissioner's Secretariat, Police Headquarters, Munich. Herr Winter is authorized to deal with any unforeseen complications. You will identify yourselves to him as follows: 'Wesel Group, Müller.'

Information given by Herbert Winter of Munich, retired chief clerical officer, Police Department.

I was a junior civil servant in those days, at the start of the Third Reich. My choice of career had been more or less dictated by family tradition. My grandfather was a respected member of the Royal Bavarian judiciary, my father a lawyer and university lecturer. My own objective prior to 1933 was a post in the Ministry of Justice, but first I had to do a stint at Munich Police Headquarters, where I functioned as a co-ordinator.

Although not in any way exceptional, it was a job requiring considerable tact. In the simplest terms, 'co-ordination' entailed settling disputes within the Commissioner's sphere of authority, promoting interdepartmental harmony and ensuring that no two operations overlapped or were duplicated.

We still regarded law and justice as identical in those far-off days. If another department requested our assistance and pronounced itself competent to deal with a certain matter, there was seldom any reason to withhold our wholehearted co-operation.

Wesel, did you say? Never heard of him. Did I know somebody named Müller? I knew plenty of Müllers, but – yes, just a minute, there's one I recall in particular – a homicide expert of international standing. He'd been seconded for special duties – at the request of the Chancellery, so rumour had it. That meant he was more or less directly responsible to Hitler.

One had to bear his special status in mind, of course. What it

103

amounted to was that Müller could play the entire Police Department like a piano. He was a virtuoso performer, take it from me.

Information supplied by Alfred Warmbruder, also known as 'Alfredo', owner of a series of clubs frequented by homosexuals (1931, the Oasis, Munich; 1940, the Mirage, Zürich; 1953 onwards, the Shadows, Los Angeles):

They were nice boys, most of them. I don't just mean from the business angle – I wasn't so much interested in that. Most of them needed help, you see. They were given a dog's life, especially in Munich, even though some of my best customers were senior officers in the SA – you know, the Brownshirts.

Nothing much happened till the end of April 1934. That was when these two heavies turned up at the club. Hagen and Hermann, they called each other. The first thing they did was line my customers up against the wall and frisk them. As if any of *us* would have packed a gun . . .!

Next, they smashed up my lovely little club – just *ruined* the décor. After that they questioned us about somebody called Raffael. They questioned us so hard I had to call an ambulance.

One of my members produced papers to prove he was an SA officer, but they worked him over just the same. 'A pig's a pig,' they told him, 'officer or no officer.'

The police did turn up eventually – I managed to get word to them, though they took their time arriving.

Hagen and Hermann didn't turn a hair. 'Hands off,' one of them yelled. 'You'd better check with Headquarters first. Herr Winter'll soon tell you if you're authorized to muscle in. Just say "Wesel Group, Müller." He'll get the message.'

Five minutes later the police backed off fast. Whoever these two were, Headquarters must have given them the green light. Then they really started working us over.

'We're looking for somebody named Raffael,' they said. 'Early 20s, peaches-and-cream complexion, blond wavy hair, big blue eyes, trusting expression, ladylike manners. What do you know about him? Who does he spend his time with? When did you last see him? Where does he usually hang out?'

They put five people in hospital, trying to extract addresses from them. They extracted some, too. Unfortunately, one belonged to an American newspaperman who'd made a name for himself helping refugees to emigrate.

Up till then he'd always managed to get valid German passports stamped with a visa from the US Consulate. It was one hundred per cent legal. He'd saved hundreds of lives that way, but he never saved another.

Although Müller seemed tolerably satisfied with these results when they were conveyed to him, he did express a few fundamental misgivings as soon as Hermann and Hagen had concluded their report.

'You've dug up some useful information, granted, but I don't like your style. Violence for the sake of violence is a mug's game.'

'Still,' Hermann said artlessly, 'there's no harm in having fun as well, is there?'

Müller's silence implied he was reserving his comments for later. He proceeded to question the other two teams.

Berner and Bergmann supplied the names of some of Raffael's former friends. 'We've already got two addresses. We'll look them up tonight.'

Norden and Siegfried were able to report that they'd visited Raffael's 'so-called' parents. 'He hasn't been in touch with them for ages. His ex-fiancée died two years ago – suspected suicide.'

Müller pricked up his ears. 'Why "so-called" parents?'

'Raffael was an adopted child, and a handful from the sound of it. His mother put him up for adoption even before she left the maternity ward. Raffael spent his first five or six years in some home or other. We haven't managed to discover his real mother's name and address.'

'Which could be absolutely vital. I'll see what I can do to help. Meanwhile, carry on. If anything turns up in the interim, phone me at once. You can reach me day or night.'

Müller and Wesel in the latter's study:

WESEL: Are you getting anywhere? I hope you've taken steps to see nobody harms the boy.

MÜLLER: We've made a certain amount of progress. How about you?

WESEL: Me? What do you mean?

MÜLLER: I'm referring to Breslauer's release. The moment your boy-friend returns to the fold the Professor moves out. Is it all set up?

WESEL: As far as I'm concerned, certainly. Passport, foreign exchange, exit permit – everything's ready. The only missing item is a US visa. SS Operational Headquarters don't have any pull with the US Consulate.

MÜLLER: If that's all, maybe I can help.

WESEL: You mean you've got connections?

MÜLLER: They're maturing, thanks to our boys' research work. They've unearthed something else that may interest you. While combing sundry homosexual haunts, they stumbled on a couple of SA officers. Here are their personal particulars. They could be of value to Himmler, if not the Führer himself.

WESEL: Let's have a look. Mm, fascinating. Can you prove all this?

MÜLLER: Of course, Brigadeführer. It could come in handy, don't you agree?

Repairing to the cellar, Müller found Breslauer hunched over a book by Waldemar Wesel. It was *Nothing Ventured, Nothing Gained.*

'Grotesque rubbish,' Breslauer observed pityingly. 'Still, you could call it an attempt to drown the stench of war in a perfumed bath of hero-worship. If a man has to die, he may as well have a reason. What's mine?'

'You've no need to invent one, Professor, not any more,' Müller assured him. 'Your days in this place are numbered. You'll be out of here inside a week.'

'What if I don't want to go?'

'There it is again – the good old Yiddisher death-wish! Look, Breslauer, I'm not interested in what you do or don't want. My only concern is to see you safely out of here. I want to save at least one of your kind.'

'And the rest of my kind, as you put it?'

'Some of them have already seen the light and gone. Others will be following as best they can. I'm simply making things easier for you.'

'Yes, but what about the others?' Breslauer persisted. 'What about the ones who don't have a Müller to fall back on? What about the ones who have no money, nobody to take their part, no bank account or organization behind them? Are they going to be persecuted, bullied, eliminated?'

Müller clicked his tongue. 'Really, Breslauer, stop being such a Jeremiah. What are a few pogroms spread over hundreds of years? It's the same old story. A few idiots are biting off more than they can chew. They're bound to choke sooner or later.'

'That I'd like to see, but here on the spot.'

'I don't propose to run that risk, Breslauer. I want to know you're safe. You're my life insurance, and the policy doesn't become valid till you reach America.'

'What am I supposed to do there?'

'Spread the good word. Explain that there are a few decent Nazis – like me and one or two others. Another thing: the Americans think Hitler's invincible and immortal. You can help disabuse them.'

'He'll have to be dealt with here, by his own people.'

'Yes, but not by you and yours. Leave it to us – it's our only chance to save a little face.'

Two days later, following a tip from Müller, Norden and Siegfried drove to Ulm. They parked in a side street near the cathedral and checked the house numbers until they found one that interested them more than the rest. One of the tenants' name cards was inscribed 'Bluhm'.

Maria Bluhm was Raffael's mother, a quiet and unassuming woman who had supported herself for the past twenty years by waiting table at a modest but respectable restaurant.

She opened the door a crack and Siegfried promptly wedged it open with his foot. Norden peered past her into the shabby living-room. 'We only want some information, Frau Bluhm,' he said. 'It's about your son.'

'I don't have a son.'

'Not officially,' said Norden. 'We quite appreciate your position. You had your son adopted but never lost touch with him. Is he here now?'

'Please go away,' Maria Bluhm implored.

'So he *is* here!' Siegfried said.

He threw his weight against the door and tried to barge past her, but Norden restrained him. Courteously, he said, 'I take it you won't object if we have a quick look round?'

She shrugged. 'I can't stop you.'

'That's more like it, Frau Bluhm.' Siegfried flashed her an encouraging smile.

He followed Norden into the living-room, a cramped world of plush and brown varnish, threadbare rugs and potted plants.

Raffael, resplendent in a colourful silk dressing-gown that could only have been a gift from Wesel, was seated over coffee and cakes at a table covered with a white cloth.

'There you are!' Siegfried chuckled heartily. 'Good to see you again, Raffael. Coffee and cakes, eh? Nothing beats home cooking, does it?'

Raffael stared at the two intruders with a mixture of surprise and hostility. 'What do you want?'

'You mean you can't guess?' Siegfried's chuckle became a laugh. 'We came to see how you were and bring you fond regards from you know who, of course.'

'In any case,' Norden added, earnestly and with total conviction, 'we certainly won't ask you to do anything against your will.'

This statement came as a great relief to Frau Bluhm. Her face brightened. 'If the gentlemen would care to . . .'

'Very kind of you,' Norden said. 'Isn't that a poppy-seed cake over there? Poppy-seed cake was a special favourite of mine when I was little. Could you spare some?'

Frau Bluhm hastened to cut an extra-large slice for Norden and a pointedly smaller one for Siegfried. They sat down at the table, Raffael between them.

Raffael glanced apprehensively at Siegfried. 'Who gave you my mother's address?'

'Müller got hold of it.' Norden bit into his slice of cake with evident enjoyment. 'First class, Frau Bluhm. I congratulate you.'

'But what do you want with Raffael?' Maria Bluhm asked, her fears flooding back. 'Are you going to take him away from me?'

'Nobody's going to take anything away from anyone,' Siegfried assured her. 'We just want to straighten things out.'

'You expect me to come of my own accord?' Raffael protested. 'With you? What if I don't?'

'You'll come,' Siegfried said. He sounded unassailably confident.

'Of course you will,' Norden amplified. 'Voluntarily. Because we ask you to.'

Raffael shrank back into his chair. 'You mean you'd take me back by force?'

'Why should we have to? There's a nice warm welcome waiting for you at the other end. Everyone's dying to see you, including Wesel. Besides, all you did was take a couple of days off to visit your mother. That's no crime.'

'This isn't your idea, is it, Norden?' Raffael's suspicions were not so easily lulled. 'Who told you to soft-soap me like this? I bet it was Müller, but why?'

'Because it suits his scheme of things,' Norden said. 'For some reason or other, you fit neatly into his calculations. Wesel accepts that, so make the most of your luck. All right, get dressed.'

Maria Bluhm, writing to her sister:

. . . preyed on my mind for years, having to give up my little boy as soon as he was born, but what else could I do? I had no money and no husband, and his father disowned him. He never had a chance to change his mind – he was killed at Verdun. That nearly finished me, I don't mind telling you.

I wasn't supposed to keep in touch with Raffael, but I did. He used to send me birthday cards and parcels – money too, sometimes.

He even visited me once or twice. Secretly, of course. I was very proud of him. He was a lovely-looking boy and very affectionate, though God knows I didn't deserve it.

Well, one day at the end of April 1934, he paid me another visit. Not just for a couple of hours the way he usually did. This time he stayed several days. I was in the seventh heaven.

Then his friends came for him . . .

The morning of the next day was devoted, under Müller's guid-
ance, to preparations for another 'operational exercise'.

'The object,' Müller announced, 'is to transport someone over-
land to the French coast. The first stage, which starts tomorrow,
will take you from here to Strasbourg, where you spend the night.
The second stage, or Strasbourg-Le Havre, will be completed the
following day. At Le Havre you will ensure that the said person
boards the *Bretagne*, a liner bound for New York. He must be
carefully watched until sailing time. Hagen and Hermann will
provide the advance-guard with Berner and Bergmann acting as
back-up. All of you will travel as German tourists, in cars with
civilian plates. The person in question will be escorted by Norden
and Siegfried. All clear so far?'

'Who is it?' Hagen asked.

Müller's tone was curt. 'You'll find out soon enough.'

The briefing over, Müller dismissed everyone except Norden.

'Well,' he said, 'speaking in the strictest confidence, it's Breslauer. I'm holding you personally responsible for his safety,
Norden. I want him put aboard that ship on time and in one piece.
It won't be easy because he doesn't want to go, but that's immaterial. He's got to go and you're going to see that he does.'

'Can I use force?'

'Breslauer isn't a violent man – far from it – but you can bet
he'll do his best to give you the slip. You'll have to be ready. Are
you?'

'Ready for anything, Herr Müller.'

Two days later, exactly as planned, Müller's consignment reached
Le Havre. The French liner *Bretagne* was due to sail for New
York that evening, and its passenger list included a Professor
Breslauer, for whom a first class cabin had been booked via
Thomas Cook of London.

But Breslauer refused to go aboard. He was sitting in La Marine, a quayside restaurant, eating *Sole bonne femme*. He had also ordered himself a whole bottle of Chablis, but Norden changed this to a half-bottle. Siegfried, sipping Vichy, lurked at a side table near the door.

'There's plenty of time,' Norden said amiably. 'Carry on, Professor. *Bon appétit!*'

'That's very kind, coming from somebody who'd just as soon poison me.'

'My personal inclinations are unimportant, Herr Breslauer. I'm simply obeying instructions. As soon as your hour is up, I'm taking you aboard.'

'You really think it's going to be that easy, Herr Norden?' Breslauer's tone was mildly provocative. 'We're in a foreign country – I might call for help and put up a fight.'

'We have contacts here, you have none. We have valid papers, you don't. You won't get your passport and travel documents till you're safely in your cabin. Besides, Professor, you won't resist. You know you're no match for me and Siegfried, not to mention Hagen and Hermann, who're waiting outside. If we have to, we'll dope you and carry you aboard like a drunk.'

Breslauer nodded with apparent resignation. 'May I have a glass of champagne?'

Norden summoned the *patron*. 'A glass of Pommery for this gentleman.'

'I'm sorry, monsieur, but we only serve champagne by the bottle . . .'

'One glass! You can charge for the bottle.'

Breslauer gazed almost reverently at his glass of Pommery when it came. He held it up to the light but paused before he drank. 'Have you any idea what's behind all this?'

'It's not my business to know. I was told to escort you to a given destination and I did.'

The Professor drank a little of his champagne with evident enjoyment. Then he sat back and sighed. 'Champagne still tastes like champagne here, as opposed to Feldafing.'

'It depends on your point of view,' Norden said indulgently.

Breslauer smiled to himself. 'What do you think may happen if I get to America with your help?'

'I'm not interested.'

'But you should be, my boy.' Breslauer took another little sip. 'As soon as I land in New York I shall tell all I know to anybody who cares to listen. I shall speak the truth about Nazi Germany – about men like Wesel. Are you prepared to take that responsibility?'

'You should know us by now.' Norden thought it advisable to step up the pressure – sailing time was near. 'We've covered ourselves, naturally. You'd have to go further than the United States to escape the long arm of the SS, Herr Breslauer. Better bear that in mind.'

'I shall publicize that remark too,' Breslauer promised, 'when I'm over there. Doesn't that worry you?'

Norden looked unimpressed. 'Not one bit.'

'You seem very sure of yourself.'

'I am. In addition to his best regards, Herr Wesel asked me to convey a farewell message. As soon as you're on board, I'm to hand you a folder. It contains photocopies of the results of a police investigation and an undated warrant for your arrest on a number of serious criminal charges.'

'False charges!'

'Herr Wesel thinks you'd find that hard to prove. If you keep quiet, he says, so will he. If you talk, he'll issue a warrant for your arrest and apply to have you extradited.'

'Typical of him,' Breslauer said scornfully. Almost in the same breath, he added: 'But *you* don't believe this nonsense, do you – *you* don't think I'm a criminal? You can't! I always thought you had a conscience. Don't disappoint me at this late stage.'

All Norden said was, 'Your time's up, Professor. Please get ready to leave.' He turned to Siegfried, who was still lolling near the door. 'Bring the Professor's travel documents. They're in that brown folder in the glove compartment.'

Siegfried hurried out. Breslauer finished his glass of champagne and slowly stood up.

A minute later Siegfried reappeared. With an air of consternation, he walked over to Norden and whispered: 'The brown folder, man – it's empty!'

Breslauer looked incredulous but pleased. He flopped back into his chair and folded his hands like a man at prayer. A faint glimmer of hope dawned in his dark, observant eyes.

From a statement made by Jean-Pierre Brasseur, proprietor of the quayside restaurant La Marine, Le Havre, to Captain Scott of US Military Intelligence:

Believe me, monsieur, I normally have a memory like a sieve. How can I be expected to remember all the girls, pimps and customers who patronize my establishment – not to mention every *flic* and informer, spy and *collaborateur* who ever came here to talk business or enjoy a little glass of something?

But April 1934 – that was different! I shall never forget the day those men arrived. One of them drank nothing but Vichy – I remember that because it made a disagreeable impression on me. Another ordered champagne for his companion but only let me serve one glass, though he paid for the whole bottle.

Then he called a fourth man inside and pushed him into the wash-room. The next moment a shot rang out. I started to call the *flics* but was stopped by the man who drank Vichy.

He shoved a gun in my back. 'Keep out of this, monsieur,' he said. 'A little argument between friends, that's all. Treat yourself to a double cognac at three times the usual price. Drink to our health and put it on the bill.' I ask you, monsieur, how could I forget a thing like that?

'Are you crazy?' Hagen shouted, cowering against the tiled wall. He glared at Norden, who stood near the door with a revolver in his hand. 'You've got a nerve, firing at me!'

'Not at you, Hagen – not yet.' Norden coldly returned his stare. 'If I'd wanted to hit you I'd have done so, you know that. It was merely a warning shot. My first and last.'

'You need your head examined, man! Fancy pulling a gun on a pal because of some stinking Yid!'

Norden gave a thin smile. 'Surely I don't have to remind you of the ground rules? What's involved here is an order, not you or me or some stinking Yid. It's my job to implement that order and nobody's going to stop me, not even you.'

'Jesus Christ Almighty!' exclaimed Hagen. 'Don't give me that old crap, not again. Be practical for a change. Our orders were to get Breslauer to Le Havre. Well, here we are. Now let's tie up the loose ends the way Wesel wants.'

'How do you know what Wesel wants?' Norden said stubbornly. 'My orders were quite explicit. I have to escort Breslauer aboard that ship and hand him a complete set of papers.'

'But God Almighty – don't you see what that stinking Jewish hyena plans to do? He'll shit all over us as soon as he gets to the other end.'

'You can depend on Wesel to have thought of that. His orders were absolutely clear: we're to put Breslauer on board that ship.'

Hagen refused to give up. 'All right, let's. We'll put the bastard on board – we'll even see him down to his cabin. Then we'll kill him. After all, Müller's taught us how to fake a nice neat suicide.'

'Certainly not!' snapped Norden. 'If Wesel had wanted it that way, he'd have told me. And now, hand over Breslauer's papers at once.'

'What if I don't?'

'I'll kill you, just like that. Don't you believe me? All right, give!'

Hagen reached into his breast pocket and took out the thick manila envelope containing Breslauer's travel documents, then tossed it to Norden. It fell short and landed on the tiled floor.

'Pick it up quick,' Norden said inexorably, revolver at the ready. 'And no false moves, otherwise the Wesel Group returns to base one man short.'

'All right, all right,' Hagen said between his teeth. He had to bend double to retrieve the envelope. Then he grinned.

'This time it's your finger on the trigger, next time it could be mine.'

'That's a risk I'll have to take.'

Hagen gave a subdued laugh. 'But I can continue to rely on your team spirit?'

'Of course.'

'You won't rat on me to Wesel or Müller?'

'Completing my assignment, that's all I care about. Can I count on your help?'

'All the way.'

'Then let's get the Professor on board.'

De-briefing conducted by Brigadeführer Wesel and Detective Super-
intendent Müller on the Group's return from Le Havre:

NORDEN: The mission went without a hitch. Breslauer was a
little uncooperative at first, but he yielded to our combined
powers of persuasion in the end.

MÜLLER: So you got him aboard in one piece?

NORDEN: Yes, as instructed.

HAGEN: If I'd had my way, the Jew would have been eliminated.
It was a perfect opportunity.

MÜLLER: Did anyone put you up to the idea?

HAGEN: No, I raised it on my own initiative.

MÜLLER: In defiance of an express order?

HAGEN: Not exactly. No reason why Breslauer shouldn't travel
to the States, but why the first class cabin? A zinc-lined coffin
would have done.

MÜLLER: Your suggestion, Brigadeführer?

WESEL: Certainly not – I'd like to stress that, and I'm sure my
men will confirm it.

HAGEN: I can for one, Brigadeführer.

MÜLLER: What about you, Norden? Did you form a different
impression?

NORDEN: No, Herr Müller, I didn't.

Waldemar Wesel's concluding remarks:

The Le Havre operation has been another outstanding piece of
teamwork, gentlemen. To mark it, I'm granting you another spot
of relaxation. Not at Leopoldstrasse, but at the home of Count von
der Tannen, one of my closest friends. The Count owns a superb
moated castle near Passau. Only those who enjoy his absolute
trust and friendship are privileged to enter its portals. I belong to
that select band. So – now – do you.

I expect you'll be meeting Countess Elisabeth, Tannen's only
daughter. I'm seldom at a loss for words, gentlemen, but even I
find it hard to describe the charms of that incomparable young
woman. You'll understand why when you see her.

From the autobiographical notes of Heinz-Hermann Norden:

Significantly enough, my first meeting with the Countess took place on 1 May 1934 – not a random date in my personal calendar. I suspect that Wesel chose the occasion deliberately, it being my birthday.

My first impression of Countess Elisabeth was one of staggering beauty. She was a living embodiment of perfect womanhood. I confess I felt a strong urge to kneel at her feet.

I did not yield to it because the magic was dispelled by Hagen, of all people, who intruded in the most boorish way. I couldn't tolerate that. What's more, I didn't.

6 The Night of the Long Knives

Count von der Tannen's country seat, the moated castle near Passau, was an imposing amalgam of fairy-tale romanticism and 18th-century architectural refinement.

The wrought-iron gates were flung wide. Beyond them could be seen pale grey marble-chip paths, dense evergreen hedges and groves of trees punctuated by artificial cascades and gently murmuring ornamental fountains. The castle itself, built of luminous dark red stone, conveyed an impression of dignified solidity despite its ethereal lines. Only the windows struck a discordant note, being unexpectedly small and reminiscent of half-veiled eyes.

Immediately inside the gates, wearing a hunting outfit of supple brown deerskin, stood the Count himself, a slim horsemanlike figure with an aquiline face crowned by sleek silver hair. His smile, which was warm and paternal, simultaneously evoked confidence and enjoined respect.

At the Count's feet sat two huge and menacing Newfoundlands of indeterminate age, their languid gaze and lolling tongues in contrast with the sharp white teeth visible when they yawned. These were Ajax and Achilles, the Count's canine bodyguards.

But if the Count cut an impressive figure as he waited to welcome his guests, the girl beside him was stunning. A lissom young woman in virginal white, luxuriant fair hair gleaming like a golden train in the sunlight, an oval face from the pages of an illuminated manuscript – such was Elisabeth, Countess von der Tannen.

As for the ritual welcome that ensued, it not only paid deference to the formal demands of etiquette but had moments of genuine warmth. Friend greeted friend, a father greeted his sons.

Waldemar Wesel deserted his companions and stalked towards the Count, his arms slightly outstretched. The Count took three or four steps, then extended his own arms.

'Waldemar, my dear fellow!' cried the Count. 'Here you are at last!'

'Konstantin,' replied Wesel, 'it's good to see you again!' They gripped each other by the shoulders like masseurs probing for a torn ligament.

With courtly tread, Wesel bore down on Elisabeth, who did not stir from the spot but smilingly proffered her right hand. Wesel grasped it, bent from the waist, and imprinted an elegant kiss.

'You grow lovelier every day,' he said. 'Seeing you as you are now, I can't help thinking of Dante's Beatrice.'

Elisabeth's laugh was silvery – Norden was not alone in saying so afterwards. 'Ah, Uncle Waldi, is that a hint? Would you like to play Dante to my Beatrice?'

Wesel laughed too. So did the Count, no less cordially but with more restraint – the laugh of a hunter in his gloomy forest preserves.

Brigadeführer Wesel then introduced his young officers, all wearing excellently tailored sports suits and thoroughly schooled in the social conventions. The Count received a firm but respectful handshake from each, the Countess a kiss on the hand.

Norden had taken Elisabeth's hand in strict observance of the rules of etiquette that had been drummed into him at Feldafing, chivalrously as opposed to flamboyantly, with the emphasis on gentlemanly reserve rather than virile admiration. He found it hard to do his training justice. He gazed at Elisabeth and stammered, 'This is a – a great pleasure.'

'Pleasure,' Hagen interposed loudly, 'isn't the word for what you do to me, Countess. You're smashing – if you'll pardon the expression.'

This light-hearted tribute was taken in good part by everyone except Norden. The rest of the party seemed to feel the visit had got off to an auspicious start.

'It gladdens my heart,' the Count declared, sounding almost jovial, 'to play host to my old friend Wesel and his men. I trust you won't be disappointed, at least where kitchen and cellar are concerned. The Brigadeführer wishes you to enjoy a few relaxing hours here in the seclusion of my small but still untroubled domain. So welcome, gentlemen. Recoup your strength for the tasks that lie ahead.'

Count von der Tannen commenting on his relations with Waldemar Wesel:

Wesel and I were members of the same regiment during World War I. For a while we fought side by side, as lieutenants, in the same front-line infantry company at Ypres. Although it couldn't be said that we ever developed a really harmonious relationship, shared experience of battle formed a natural bond between us.

In character we were altogether different. Being a strong traditionalist, I subscribe to certain immutable principles. Wesel was more of a revolutionary, despite his philosophical and poetic leanings. He moved further and further into the orbit of that man Hitler, a tendency my very nature forbade me to imitate.

Not that this severed the ties of wartime comradeship. I cannot deny that Wesel went to considerable lengths to help me during those precarious years, though his widespread connections – probably extending to Hitler himself – must have rendered this comparatively easy.

Look at it this way. In those days, a man in my position had to survive as best he could, if only to preserve a family estate acquired over generations. I wouldn't and couldn't come to terms with the Nazis, but I couldn't help welcoming the assistance of an old comrade – assistance given freely, without the smallest political concession on my part.

I had no qualms about entertaining a few of Wesel's closest associates – naturally not – but only on rare occasions. One of them was in 1934, when he visited me accompanied by six young officers – well-bred youngsters. If I understood him correctly, he was training them for special operations of some kind.

I remained fundamentally indifferent to what he meant by this until my daughter Elisabeth became involved. My reaction then was absolutely unequivocal – that's to say, categorically disapproving.

The Count and Wesel had retired to a turret chamber whose only means of access was a circular stairway. The room had two special advantages. Not only could its occupants talk without fear of being overheard, but its four windows afforded a panorama of the gardens, fountains, greenhouses, courtyard and drive.

'Pleasant fellows, those young men of yours,' the Count said thoughtfully. 'Pleasant but young, and youth implies folly'.

Wesel shook his head. 'Not in their case. They only respond to orders. Compared with my outfit, Napoleon's Guard was a nursery-school.'

'Is Elisabeth safe with them?' asked the Count.

'Absolutely safe, Konstantin, as long as she's safe from herself. What do you think?'

The Count gave an indulgent smile. 'She's a very feminine creature.'

'Really, Konstantin! It doesn't matter what she *is* – all that counts is what she represents, and it's your job to see she acquits herself properly. There are six youngsters down there, all burning with idealism. I want your daughter to attract them like a magnet.'

'To be purely practical, six idealists are four or five too many.'

'Don't misunderstand me, Konstantin. I want her to radiate an aura, generate undiluted sex appeal – if possible, react on all my men at once. I want them to look up at her like climbers viewing an insurmountable peak.'

The Count looked sceptical. 'What if one of your men tries to seduce her – rape her, even? They're lusty young fellows.'

'But disciplined, admirably trained.'

'Quite, quite, but what if it were Elisabeth who – shall we say – took the initiative? What if she fell for a couple of them?'

'That, Konstantin, is precisely what mustn't be allowed to happen.' Wesel's tone was earnest. 'It would mean that four or five of my men felt spurned and underprivileged, and that would cause bad blood. I have to keep their engines tuned. Believe me, unrequited romantic love is the supreme spur to heroism.'

'I envy your flights of fancy,' the Count said with a faint smile. 'You're still a dreamer at heart, Waldi, which is more than I can say of our local Party boss. He's making my life a misery.'

'Give me his name and he's fired,' Wesel said. 'If you can recommend a suitable successor, let me know that too. They're only small fry, these local officials. Anything else?'

The turret chamber was an exceptionally snug room. Its pale blue walls were hung with hunting trophies that almost filled the spaces between the four windows. In the centre stood a massive table of gnarled oak, and on it several bottles of red burgundy thick with years of dust. Flanking the table were two high-backed baronial chairs almost as wide as a bed, their ox-hide seats richly tooled.

The two men raised their glasses, not for the first time. Then the Count said, 'This Führer of yours, Waldi – how much longer do you give him? Things are getting shaky, aren't they?'

Wesel brushed the question aside. 'Speculation, my dear fellow – I've heard it all before. Some people gave him two months at most. Now, other equally rash individuals are giving him another couple of years at the outside. They've got no political flair – the Führer will survive them all.'

'Or take them with him to the grave, eh?'

'Don't forget we're dealing with a genius.'

'Even if you're right, aren't the wolves already gathering? Aren't whole packs of them only waiting for a chance to tear him limb from limb? What about the Brownshirts under that ex-captain, Röhm? They say he's getting ideas of his own these days – I've even heard he plans to turn the SA into a kind of people's militia.'

'Anybody can make plans.'

'But isn't the SA a power in the land? Hitler admitted it himself in the *Völkischer Beobachter* a few months ago. "The SA is Germany's destiny and will remain so." Isn't that what he wrote?'

'Of course,' Wesel rejoined calmly. 'The SA will remain our national destiny as long as it proves equal to the task. If not, present assumptions about its future will have to be drastically revised.'

'You seriously think Hitler would dare . . .'

'I know he would.'

'But what about the practical problems, Waldi? The SA can muster nearly two million Brownshirts. Who's going to deal with them? Hitler, the SS – you and your half-dozen? Who else could you count on?'

'All the people who've learnt to read the signs of the times – out of conviction or calculation, it doesn't matter which. I include you among the calculators, Konstantin. You and your contacts on the General Staff. That's partly why I'm here.'

'What do you want?'

'A few hints. A name or two, if I'm lucky. After all, nobody knows the ambitions of your army friends better than you do. I don't imagine they'd take kindly to being gobbled up by Röhm and his Brownshirts.'

'Certainly not!'

'Then they should do something about it. Like giving us some tips about their enemies, their weak spots, their criminal involvements. And tell them not to hold anything back – their future depends on how closely they work with us.'

'So you think Hitler would be prepared to make a clean sweep? Even at the expense of Röhm, his own SA Chief of Staff?'

'He's ready and willing,' Wesel said. 'Just between the two of us, he doesn't have any alternative.'

The Count leant back and closed his eyes, lost in thought. Then he said, 'I could give you five names right away, two near certainties and three possibles, plus another half-dozen prospects in Berlin, Stettin, Königsberg, Cologne and Munich. More information to follow in a few days' time. Would that help? If so, what would it be worth to you?'

'Draw up a list of your friends' requirements, Konstantin. Reliable men only, and against each one make a note of the job he's after – job *and* salary. In our organization, the labourer is worthy of his hire.'

'Waldi,' the Count said with a sigh, 'I don't know what I'd do without you.'

The Group bade a spirited farewell to the moated castle near Passau – spirited but, in the unanimous opinion of its six members, all too premature.

Having shrewdly restricted his men to a stay of three hours, Wesel dangled the prospect of further visits. This was underlined by an approving nod from the Count and an inviting smile from his daughter.

They had been glorious hours indeed, and each man enjoyed them in his own way. Siegfried contrived to make friends with Ajax and Achilles, Hermann waxed knowledgeable about the elegantly proportioned gates, doors and windows, and Berner and Bergmann spent the bulk of their time in the stables, where they appraised the stable-boys with an expert and appreciative eye.

Norden had chivalrously devoted himself to Countess Elisabeth. Walking at a respectful distance on her left, he discoursed on the beauties of nature, beauty as an elemental force, beauty as a romantic ideal. Elisabeth gave a succession of sidelong smiles, but they were not directed at him alone. Hagen, who had appointed himself her joint escort, strolled along on her right with no attempt to maintain a decorous distance. Sometimes, when emphasizing a point, he simply barred her path, ignoring Norden as steadfastly as Norden ignored him.

Before leaving, Norden bent over Elisabeth's hand. 'Meeting you, Countess, has been like the fulfilment of a lifelong dream.'

'How charming,' Elisabeth murmured.

Hagen said his piece a moment later. 'Countess,' he declared, 'you're a knock-out.'

Elisabeth managed to smile at them both simultaneously. Then she withdrew.

One night a few weeks later, Reinhard Heydrich paid a second visit to the Villa at Feldafing. 'Waldi' and 'Reini' greeted each other cordially but wasted little time on preliminaries. The head of the State Security Service wanted an immediate interview with 'our men', and Wesel knew why.

Although the Group had been granted a full night's sleep, they turned out promptly in SS uniform complete with Untersturm-führer collar-badges.

Heydrich shook hands with each man in turn, gazing deep into their eyes. Then he planted his legs apart and hooked his thumbs in his belt.

'Gentlemen,' he announced, 'my time is short and getting shorter. Important decisions are at hand. I came here to discuss preparations with your Brigadeführer, but first I want to transmit a personal message from the Führer. The Führer was extremely impressed by his meeting with you. He made some very favourable comments on your high standard of training, your morale, your unswerving loyalty. The Führer has faith in you, gentlemen. Now that the time of trial draws near, I shall be able to inform him that he can rely on you to the hilt.'

Heydrich performed a second round of handshakes. Two minutes later, without having uttered a word, the six were dismissed to their beds.

After that Heydrich spent several hours closeted with Wesel. Names were mentioned, addresses exchanged and assignments allocated in a businesslike manner. The two men eventually settled on a preliminary list of some five dozen names – candidates for liquidation.

Some days after Heydrich's visit, the Wesel Group attended an afternoon briefing in the library. The only person present apart from Wesel and his men was Müller.

'This time,' Wesel said, 'the key-word is Röhm. Know who I mean?'

A burst of scornful laughter confirmed that everyone did.

Hermann, was as usual determined to go one better than the rest. 'Röhm, first name Ernst,' he recited, 'ex-army captain, 46 years old, notorious homosexual. Took part in the November '23 uprising in Munich, then retired to South America as military adviser to the Bolivian army, returning some five years later. Currently SA Chief of Staff.'

'Correct,' said Wesel, 'and now he plans to eliminate the army and replace it with a people's militia composed of Brownshirts.'

'With the Führer's say-so?' Müller asked.

'No,' replied Wesel. 'That's just it.'

'Against the Führer's wishes, you mean?' Müller seemed tickled by the notion. 'That explains everything. Röhm and his mob are our next objective, right?'

'Precisely right, Herr Müller. And that means you and the rest of the Group are about to be assigned another important mission. Are you ready to take it on?'

'Itching to, Brigadeführer.'

'I was counting on it.' Wesel, who knew Müller's personal file, winked at him. 'You once crossed swords with the SA, didn't you? They had you fired, which was when we found you a slot with us in the SS.'

Müller grinned brazenly. 'But I don't bear malice. All I say is, if somebody's trying to cross the Führer, he needs removing. When's it to be, and where?'

'In the next few days, at the Hotel Hanslbauer in Bad Wiessee. Röhm's planning to hold a staff conference there attended by senior SA officers. The Führer may take a hand himself, and we'll be responsible for his safety. We must be ready when the time comes.'

'We will be,' said Müller.

Operational order issued by Müller to the Wesel Group after preliminary inquiries of a swift but painstaking nature.

MÜLLER: We only have a few days in hand before this SA staff conference at Bad Wiessee. You're going to put in some concentrated groundwork, operating on the CID principle that only a couple of leads in every hundred produce results. I want everything you can dig up on the SA top brass.

Objective No. 1: various dives and rooming-houses regularly frequented by senior SA officers. There are five on the list. Berner and Bergmann, they're your baby. Find out exactly who does what with whom and where, but don't intervene. Surveillance only, please.

Objective No. 2: four addresses, three certain and one probable, also in and around Munich. They belong to boy-friends of Röhm or his closest associates – junior SA men, so you can lean on them a little. Be careful, though, we don't want the alarm going off too soon. Hermann and Siegfried, they're yours.

Objective No. 3: Röhm himself. He's allocated to Norden and Hagen, who'll keep a constant watch on him. His private apartment in Munich is known to us – just opposite the Prinzregententheater – and we also have an accurate layout of his office. What we still need is detailed information about the Hotel Hanslbauer, where this conference is scheduled for Saturday 30 June. We're going to familiarize ourselves with the area till we can find our way around blindfolded. I shall conduct the preliminary reconnaissance in person – for my own amusement, let's say. As soon as I've got an adequate picture of the place, we'll all take a pleasure-trip to Bad Wiessee. Right, Brigadeführer?

WESEL: Right. But I warn you, gentlemen, it's all or nothing this time.

In the late afternoon of the following day, a stranger arrived at the Villa carrying a heavy suitcase.

Müller introduced him to Wesel in the deserted hall. 'This is Herr Grabert, Brigadeführer, the gunsmith I told you about. He works for a firm in Solingen. In accordance with your instructions, I commissioned Herr Grabert to design a special hand-gun – a German-made revolver.'

Grabert eagerly opened his case and produced a bulky object wrapped in black velvet. He unwrapped it and ceremoniously presented it to Müller. 'Your special order, Herr Müller. A unique weapon, though I say it myself. High velocity and one hundred per cent effective. It fires a 10.5 mm. slug.'

Müller took the heavy steel-blue revolver and weighed it thoughtfully in his hand, then passed it to Wesel. He toyed with it too, looking faintly sceptical.

'Let's try it out,' he said.

'Fine,' Müller agreed. 'We'll have it tested by our best shot.'

'Norden?'

'No,' said Müller, 'Hagen. He's got a far more practical approach than Norden, Brigadeführer, which is something you should watch, by the way.'

Hagen was sent for at once. The lights in the Villa's indoor range were turned on and Grabert laid out gun and ammunition with the reverential movements of a priest preparing for divine office.

Hagen had been relaxing on his bed when the call came. Still wearing a brown striped bathrobe, he reached avidly for the gun which Grabert handed him and proceeded to test it for balance. 'Pretty heavy,' he said. 'Still, if the weight's anything to go by, it should produce a fair amount of penetration.'

Splaying his legs, he poised himself on the balls of his feet and took a preliminary shot at the Semitic-looking target. A hole the size of a fist appeared in the figure's stomach. Obviously impressed, Hagen aimed his second shot straight at the head. It disintegrated as if blown apart by a charge of dynamite.

'Terrific penetration,' Hagen observed. 'The gun seems accurate enough, but it's got a kick like a mule. You need plenty of muscle to use it. That makes it our kind of gun. At ten metres, it ought to spray the walls with anyone's grey matter.'

Hagen's work was done. Wesel thanked him and Müller conferred one of his rare nods of approval. Hagen felt privileged. The test firing had been entrusted to him, not Norden.

'Well?' Müller asked, turning to Wesel.

Wesel barely hesitated. 'It's a deal, Herr Grabert.'

'What about the design and production expenses?' asked the gunsmith. 'Will they be taken care of?'

'Not only that,' Müller said. 'You can count on a bonus of several thousand marks. Twenty, Brigadeführer?'

'Twenty-five,' decreed Wesel.

'For a start, Herr Grabert,' Müller pursued briskly, 'we'd like delivery of a dozen guns plus three hundred rounds for each. When can we have them?'

Grabert beamed. 'I took the liberty of bringing six guns and six hundred rounds with me. I can deliver the balance within a month. Will that suit you?'

'Fine.' Müller glanced at Wesel, who wrote out a cheque for a five-figure sum. Before relinquishing it, he impressed on Grabert that the transaction was a State secret. No sketches or blueprints were to be retained by his firm and all repeat orders would require the personal endorsement of Himmler, Heydrich or Wesel himself.

Alone again, Wesel and Müller eyed each other speculatively. 'Well,' Wesel said at length, 'do you really think these custom-made cannons are going to serve a purpose?'

'I certainly do. With production hand-guns, you have to fire off a whole magazine to be sure of doing the trick. This 10.5 magnum has a dumdum effect. The slugs won't just drill some-one, they'll let in the daylight.'

'But won't the use of such an outsize gun be easy to detect? Any reasonably efficient ballistics expert would find it child's play, surely? You might as well leave your calling-card behind.'

'Ah,' said Müller, 'but that could work in our favour, Brigade-führer. It's standard CID procedure to concentrate on tell-tale clues like the use of rare poisons, explosives or weapons.'

'And that could be to our advantage?'

'Certainly. Himmler hasn't got his hands on the whole German police force – not yet, with Göring still bossing the Prussian end – but they're both in the same boat, i.e. ours. They could be persuaded by Heydrich, or the Führer himself if necessary, to issue a general directive stipulating that all cases in which the use of a 10.5 mm. hand-gun is proven or suspected must be immediately referred to a special board of inquiry.'

'To you, in other words.' Wesel chuckled admiringly. 'I presume you're angling for a job with Heydrich's Gestapo?'

Müller nodded. 'Do you mind?'

'No, you're one of us now. The higher you climb the better it'll be for all of us.'

'In that case, Brigadeführer, I hereby constitute myself the board specially authorized to investigate proven instances of the use of such unorthodox firearms. You fix that and I'll do the rest.'

Hagen invaded Norden's quarters without knocking. 'We're going to be at a loose end for the next twenty-four hours, if not longer. Röhm's flown to Berlin, so we don't have to keep tabs on him. We can amuse ourselves till he gets back. Feel like a trip to Leopoldstrasse?'

'Why should I want to go there?'

'There's always Erika – beg pardon, Fräulein Schulze. She's dying to see you again, she told me to tell you. How about it?'

Norden frowned. 'There's our mission to think of. I don't have time for incidentals.'

'Poor old Erika, so she's turned into an incidental! From what I heard, you asked her to marry you – or something like it. Well, why not? You'd make a handsome couple.' Hagen smiled sardonically. 'Let's get going, she's bound to be lying there with her legs open.'

'Keep your vulgarities to yourself, Hagen. Erika's a nice girl, really, but that's as far as it goes. To compare her with, say, Elisabeth – the Countess, I mean . . .'

'Elisabeth's just for show,' Hagen said. 'That's why they keep her in a glass case. She's off-limits to us – Wesel wants it that way.'

'I wouldn't put it past you to try your luck.'

'Flattery will get you nowhere, Norden. As a matter of fact, I'm shouldering some of your responsibilities – I'm taking her to the opera tonight. They're doing *Tannhäuser*. It starts and finishes on the Venusberg – very appropriate eh?'

'Shut your mouth!' Norden snapped, turning pale. 'If you so much as touch the Countess, you'll have me to deal with.'

'You're threatening me again,' said Hagen. 'Watch out, Norden, I may take you seriously one day. One of us won't live to regret it.'

After tapping sundry phones and receiving progress reports from members of the Group, Müller gave Wesel a confidential rundown.

'Berner and Bergmann seem to be doing a good job,' he announced. 'Their visits to three of the spots on the list have produced five more addresses used for immoral purposes by senior members of the SA.

'Siegfried and Hermann are still keeping track of Röhm's playmates. Two of them have already left for the SA staff conference at Bad Wiessee. One has moved into the room reserved for Röhm and the other into the room opposite, which is booked in the name of Obergruppenführer Heines.

'Norden and Hagen are taking a 24-hour break because Röhm has flown to Berlin, where Heydrich's men have assumed responsibility for his surveillance. I smell trouble, though. Not from Heydrich of course – it's our own boys I'm worried about. Hagen just made a date with the Countess – he arranged to meet her at the State Opera in Munich. Five minutes later Norden invited himself along. Neither of them would take no for an answer. I thought I'd better let you know.'

Wesel picked up the phone. 'Get me Count von der Tannen.'

He was put through at once. The Count sounded uneasy.

'I can guess why you're calling, my dear fellow, but what can I do?'

'Precisely what we agreed. I don't want any of my men to receive preferential treatment. In other words, no *Tannhäuser*.'

'I've a good mind to send Elisabeth to some relatives abroad. Either that or marry her off before she gets involved in some reckless escapade. After all, I can't very well play chaperone to my own daughter.'

'No need,' Wesel said thoughtfully, 'but you've given me an idea. Can't you dig up somebody who'll take the job off your hands?'

The Count reflected for a moment. 'My sister Augusta might do. She lives on her late husband's estate in East Prussia, struggling to make ends meet. I'm sure she'd volunteer to help in return for a small fee. Augusta's a real *grande dame* and tough – I'd back her against my Newfoundlands any day. She'll hold your two young stallions at bay. Think you can fix it – the fee, I mean?'

'My dear Konstantin,' said Wesel, 'what are a few thousand marks between friends?'

The latter days of June 1934 proved as strenuous for Wesel's half-dozen as they were instructive. They raced to and fro, fully motorized and in permanent communication via the sophisticated radio-telephones which formed part of their equipment. They shuttled between Feldafing and Wiessee, Wiessee and Munich, Munich and Feldafing.

Raffael, fully rehabilitated after a 'long talk' with Wesel, collated all incoming reports. Müller sifted and assessed them before transmitting them to Wesel, who spent hours on the phone to Berlin, mostly to Heydrich but once to the Führer himself.

Meanwhile, Müller seized every opportunity to familiarize Wesel's men with the 10.5 magnums. Target practice might be held any time, at dawn or at midnight, in any conceivable light and after every conceivable form of exertion. The average score was 10 out of a possible 12. Hagen effortlessly turned in a series of near-perfect performances. So, Müller was gratified to be able to report, did Norden.

Wesel nodded contentedly. 'It's only a matter of hours now. As long as Röhm doesn't back out at the last minute.'

A few hours later, on the evening of 29 June 1934, Wesel mustered his men in the hall. They had never seen him look more resolute. Müller hovered behind him, a shadowy figure in a dark suit.

'Gentlemen,' Wesel announced, 'this is it. Are you ready?'

A volley of affirmatives rang out.

'Very well. Herr Müller, give them their orders.'

Müller might have been reading the weather forecast.

'The Group will prepare to move out in two standby vehicles, both mechanically checked, fully fuelled and radio-equipped.

Brigadeführer Wesel and three men will take the Mercedes, I and the remainder will take the Horch. One of you will drive in each case.

'Constant radio communication is to be maintained between both cars and the central transmitter here in Feldafing, which will be manned by Raffael. Our operating frequency will be changed for the duration of this mission to normal reading plus 150.

'Each man will draw one 10.5 magnum and 30 rounds, which ought to be enough. Reserve ammunition will be carried by me. No sub-machine-guns or grenades, is that clear? Duration of mission: indefinite. It could be over in 24 hours, but other operations may follow in the next few days, so maintain a full alert until further notice. We move out at 01.00.'

It took the Wesel Group less than an hour's drive through the deserted countryside to reach the Oberwiesenfeld in Munich.

They gathered on the edge of the runway. The occupants of about two dozen similar cars had already assembled there and were waiting in silence.

The airfield was cordoned off by a company of uniformed police, none of whom had any inkling of why they had been alerted or whom they were there to protect.

Suddenly, one of the Mercedes limousines disgorged a slender figure of medium height, a round-shouldered man with rimless glasses and awkward, tentative movements. It was Heinrich Himmler, the Reichsführer-SS. He walked over to Wesel.

Wesel went part of the way to meet him. It was a display of formal courtesy, nothing more. The two men saluted and shook hands. Himmler's hand felt cold and flaccid, but Wesel grasped it with every appearance of cordiality.

'I knew you'd be here, Wesel,' Himmler said. 'I always knew the Führer could depend on you in a crisis.'

'Just as he can on you, Reichsführer. After all, the existence of the SS is at stake.'

There was a moment's silence. Then Himmler said, 'These young men of yours – will they do all that's required of them?'

'They will, Reichsführer.'

Himmler nodded with perceptible relief. Peering through his

thick-lensed glasses, he bent a fatherly gaze on Wesel's team, who stiffened to attention. Then he raised his arm and saluted as they stood there like six black statues against the pale line of the eastern horizon.

'What about your unit's special assignment? Are all your men fully briefed – I mean, about the Chief of Staff?'

'We'll kill him if the Führer so directs, him and his entire crew. Two of my men have been detailed to eliminate his aides and another two the members of his personal staff. The remaining pair will deal with Röhm himself.'

'For good, Wesel? I mean, will they have the guts to finish him off? That would probably be the best solution.'

Wesel stared a him with a trace of surprise. 'The Führer,' he said slowly, 'has expressed a wish that Röhm should be taken alive.'

Himmler seemed to recoil.

'Alive? Did he tell you so himself?'

'He instructed someone to tell me.'

'Who – when?'

'Less than three hours ago.'

'But who gave you the message?' Himmler insisted.

'Heydrich,' said Wesel.

That was enough. The Reichsführer really did recoil now. He took two paces to the rear, his face chalk-white in the gloom.

Himmler gave a little cough – he seemed to have caught a chill. After a long pause, he said, 'I see. The Führer knows his own mind, of course, but one can't rule out the possibility of unforeseen developments. For example, there might be no alternative but to shoot the man in self-defence.'

'Of course,' Wesel said. 'One could even precipitate such a situation – say, by delaying matters. If Röhm got a chance to reach for his gun he'd be a dead duck. Is that the kind of unforeseen development you mean, Reichsführer?'

'Well, it isn't altogether beyond the bounds of possibility, is it?'

'No, Reichsführer, but it'll only happen if I receive a direct order to that effect – only if the Führer agrees. Does he?'

'I'm merely saying that it might be best to finish him off quickly.'

'In your view, perhaps, but does the Führer share it?'

'The decision rests with the Führer alone,' Himmler said hastily. 'It was just a suggestion.'

'There's only one thing better than a suggestion,' Wesel said blandly, 'and that's an order. Let's wait for the Führer, shall we?'

A Junkers Ju 52 circled the Oberwiesenfeld airfield and came in to land, its engines snarling as the pilot throttled back. It touched down with a thump of rubber on turf, settled by the tail and taxied to a halt. The time was just before 4 a.m. The sky was still overcast, but June nights were short and the midsummer sun would soon burn away the clouds. The plane squatted on the runway like a dead insect. The hatch opened and some steps were folded down. Almost simultaneously, at a signal from Himmler, two or three dozen men headed for the plane.

The first person to emerge was a giant of a man who moved with surprising agility: the Führer's principal aide. He might have been enjoying the cool clear air of the Oberwiesenfeld. In reality, he was taking stock of the situation. He ducked back into the cabin looking reassured.

Adolf Hitler appeared a few moments later, wearing a brown leather topcoat. Two pairs of hands shot out to take the coat as he pulled it off. Without it he looked small, almost shrunken, but his throaty voice was as resonant as ever.

'There you are, Himmler,' he said, taking the Reichsführer's hand. 'Is everything ready?'

'Yes, my Führer.'

'Good.' Hitler gazed keenly round the airfield. His face was pale and tense and his hands clung to his belt-buckle. He nodded at his chief aide as if for something to do.

The aide whispered a few words to Himmler, who turned and addressed the Oberwiesenfeld in his reedy voice.

'Gentlemen, gather round the Führer!'

At once, three dozen figures converged. Hitler tried to acknowledge their presence without detaching his tremulous hands from their anchorage. He nodded at each man in turn, a gesture of confidence rendered mechanical by fatigue.

Then he caught sight of Wesel and his six men waiting in the background. He approached them, and it was to the Wesel Group that he addressed the words that sealed Röhm's fate.

'This is the darkest day in my life, comrades, but I have never shirked an unpleasant duty. We shall go to Bad Wiessee and mete out stern justice.'

They drove via the Bavarian Ministry of the Interior in Theatinerstrasse, headquarters of one of Hitler's loyal Party veterans. Just as he reached there the sun edged above the Oberwiesenfeld, bathing the Ju 52 in crimson. It was 04.15. Hitler's first act was to summon SA Obergruppenführer Schneidhuber, Munich's chief of police, who was already waiting next door.

As soon as he entered Hitler rushed at him, ripped off his insignia, flung them to the ground and trampled on them.

'You're under arrest,' he screamed. 'I'm going to have you shot!'

Schneidhuber started to protest, but two members of the Wesel Group, Berner and Bergmann, grabbed him and hustled him out of the room. The SS guards lurking in the corridor took hold of the unfortunate man and hauled him away like a sack of potatoes.

Seven or eight other SA officers were similarly disposed of.

'Where to now, my Führer?' asked Wesel, who had observed these proceedings with relish. 'Bad Wiessee?'

Hitler nodded.

Two minutes later a sizeable column of vehicles left the Ministry of the Interior bound for Bad Wiessee, roughly an hour's drive from Munich.

The Führer took the lead, preceded only by a vanguard consisting of the Wesel Group's big black Horch with Müller inside. The other car, manned by Norden and Hagen, followed immediately behind the Führer's Mercedes.

Beside Hitler sat Wesel, who spent the time leafing calmly through his papers: maps, military dispositions for the covering units, special tasks allotted to his own men, lists of those attending the SA conference and particulars relating to the staff of the Hotel Hanslbauer.

Departure from Munich: 05.30. Arrival at destination: 06.25, after a rapid journey in convoy.

Dr Joseph Goebbels, Minister of Public Enlightenment and

Propaganda, described what happened in the dawn hours of this day as 'the night of the long knives'.

The Hotel Hanslbauer was a typical Upper Bavarian building in chalet style, cosily sheltered from the elements by picturesque low-eaved roofs that overhung its numerous balconies. There were a lower-ground and ground floor, two upper floors and a further tier of attic rooms above.

This was where Röhm and his SA henchmen had met to engage – as the official account put it – in 'treasonable conspiracy'. They had arrived the previous day with members of their entourage or – another quote from the official communiqué – 'youthful sodomites'.

The staff conference had opened with a gala banquet consisting of huge roast joints, barrels of beer, mountains of pastries, cases of wine and batteries of schnapps bottles. On the face of it, a victory celebration in advance.

Now they were asleep, blissfully drunk and completely unsuspecting. They slept, in the words of the government press release, 'in communal disorder'. They lolled in armchairs or sprawled on the floor, grunting and snoring their way to perdition like men already dead.

Heydrich had completed the purely administrative arrangements from the Berlin end. A few phone calls sufficed to ensure that Bad Wiessee was hermetically sealed off by police units. A detachment of SS storm troopers waited in reserve near by and elements of Adolf Hitler's Leibstandarte, or personal guard, had been transported to the scene under the command of Gruppenführer Sepp Dietrich.

'If anything goes wrong,' Heydrich had told Wesel, 'it won't be my fault. Still, I know I can rely on you and your men.' He paused. 'Not to mention the Führer himself.'

Hitler's determination seemed to grow as his destination drew nearer. He did not speak for minutes on end, a sure sign of excitement. His lips were compressed and his moustache twitched. Getting out of the car when it pulled up in front of Röhm's hotel, he stumbled and almost fell but quickly recovered his balance. Norden and Hagen stationed themselves on either side

135

of him as instructed.

Hitler strode into the hotel like a man possessed. Norden and Hagen hurried on ahead with Wesel following two paces to the rear.

Just as they reached the central corridor, Berner and Bergmann materialized on their left, revolvers drawn. Siegfried and Hermann, similarly armed, covered the Führer's right flank.

Norden used his revolver-butt to hammer on the door of Röhm's bedroom. It opened. Röhm stood there in a long white nightshirt. He stared at Hitler in astonishment.

'Adolf! You here?'

'Yes, I've come to deal with you!'

'Deal with me?' Röhm looked mystified. 'Why, what have I done? I'm your friend, Adolf – one of your few friends.'

It was a fact. Hitler had been on familiar terms with a mere handful of people in his life, and one of them was Ernst Röhm.

'You!' Hitler screamed. 'You've betrayed me – abused my trust. You've lost the right to live, Röhm.'

Röhm struggled for words. At last he said, 'You can't mean it, Adolf, not after all we've been through together . . .'

'That's enough!' Wesel shouted from the corridor. 'Arrest him!'

Röhm stared at Wesel, thunderstruck, but before he had a chance to retort he was hustled backwards into the bedroom by Norden and Hagen. He received their verbal confirmation of his arrest in incredulous silence.

'Now for No. 2,' commanded Wesel, indicating the door opposite.

Siegfried and Hermann kicked it open. The lights blazed on to reveal two startled figures in a double bed: Obergruppenführer Heines and a youth with skin like silk, both stark naked.

Hitler took one look. 'You might have spared me this spectacle, Heines. It's nauseating.'

The SA general sat up in bed. Almost defiantly, he said, 'But you knew, my Führer – you've known about me for years. Why so shocked all of a sudden?'

Staring wide-eyed at the revolvers of the Führer's escorts, the silken-skinned youth slid out of bed and crawled towards the door on all fours. 'It's love,' he whimpered, 'it's love, you've got to believe me . . .'

A bullet from Hermann's 10.5 blew him apart. Hitler averted his gaze while Siegfried dragged Heines out and consigned him to the Leibstandarte guards.

The first shot had sounded the alarm. Doors burst open and men rushed out, to be gunned down where they stood. Nearly two dozen people lost their lives. Before long, the Hotel Hanslbauer's back yard resembled a slaughter-house.

Only two weeks later the Führer addressed the Reichstag, a parliamentary institution the Berliners had nicknamed 'the Greater German Choral Society' because its sole function was to sing the national anthem after listening to hours of Hitlerian rhetoric. His concluding message was as follows:

'Let it be known, once and for all, that if anyone raises his hand to smite the State, his fate is certain death.'

From statements made by Herbert Hubmann, sometime manager of a hotel in Bad Wiessee:

It was like a bolt from the blue. I wouldn't call it a raid, exactly. I don't say I agreed with them, but some people thought it was essential in the interests of national security . . .

Of course I wasn't indifferent to what happened! On the contrary, I was absolutely horrified. I even took the risk of lodging a formal complaint, and that could have landed me in a concentration camp . . .

Dozens of dead bodies? No, that's an exaggeration, but I did see a few scattered around the rooms and corridors, also the lobby. There were others in the garden and courtyard, but they were quickly carted away in trucks. Besides, the authorities paid a generous indemnity for all the damage. We were also allocated plenty of labour and materials, both of which were scarce at the time.

Anyway, it didn't take long to restore the hotel. Our very next season – that's to say, summer '35 – was an outstanding success. We had plenty of bookings, mostly foreign. I've still got a number of appreciative letters, some from the United States . . .

I'd like to emphasize one thing. Many people jumped to the conclusion that Röhm was shot on the premises, but he wasn't. He was still alive when he left – I want to make that absolutely clear.

Place: a cell in Stadelheim Prison, near Munich. Ernst Röhm, erstwhile SA Chief of Staff and former intimate of the Führer, was lying on a hard plank bed dressed in brown-and-white striped pyjamas. He was sweating and staring at the ceiling.

He did not move when the door of his cell was thrown open. Waldemar Wesel came in followed by Norden and Hagen, who posted themselves at the entrance.

'Röhm,' barked Wesel, 'on your feet!' He was in full SS uniform. The cap with its death's-head badge was pulled low over his eyes. 'I have something to tell you.'

The SA chief propped himself on one elbow and stared at his visitor, smiling contemptuously. 'What could you possibly have to say to me, Waldemar? Your brand of philosophical masturbation leaves me cold.'

Wesel stiffened. 'Kindly don't address me by my first name,' he snapped. 'The Führer has deprived you of that privilege and so have I. I'm here on the Führer's behalf, so I must ask you to conduct yourself accordingly.'

Röhm massaged his sweaty jowls. He peered at his visitors as though trying to gauge what they were capable of.

Hagen enlightened him. 'All right, Röhm,' he said affably. 'Shift that fat butt of yours or I'll leave my boot up it.'

'Do I have to tolerate this kind of thing?' The former Chief of Staff glanced inquiringly at Wesel but saw at once that he could expect no answer.

He sat up, rolled ponderously off the bed and heaved himself erect, swaying a little. 'Did you come here to shoot me?' he asked.

'If you leave us no alternative.' Wesel eyed Röhm with mild disdain. 'Personally, I think it would be a waste of good ammunition.'

Röhm laughed. 'So what are you waiting for? Am I supposed to shout "Long life the Führer!" before you execute me – if you dare to?'

Wesel was unmoved. 'I've drafted a confession for you,' he said, almost conversationally. 'It admits your miscalculations and errors of judgement and expresses your profound regret. You engaged in activities which you now realize were subversive. Are you going to sign?'

'What happens if I do?' Röhm's eyes narrowed. 'Will I be

released? Can I go where I like – South America, for instance? They appreciated my services over there?'

'It's too late for that,' Wesel said implacably. 'There's nothing left for you to do but sign. It'll be your last contribution to the Führer's cause.'

'What if I don't choose to make it?' Röhm's barrel-chest rose and fell rapidly. 'Hitler would never dare have me gunned down in cold blood – not a loyal friend and supporter like me. We fought side by side in the early days of the Movement. He can't have forgotten that!'

'Nor can you,' said Wesel, 'which is what he's counting on. You should be grateful to him, Röhm.'

'He'd never dare liquidate my officers, let alone me.'

'Your fellow-conspirators have already been sentenced to death. The Leibstandarte will shortly be executing them in the prison yard – you can watch if you like. That will leave you. Just you.'

Röhm reeled under an invisible blow. 'You mean – you mean I'm to be killed too?'

'Yes, by somebody in this room.'

An account of events at Stadelheim Prison, near Munich, given by Alfons Sonnenhuber, formerly a senior prison administrator:

Nobody can hold the prison staff accountable for what happened at Stadelheim. Our co-operation was officially requested – it would have been legally impossible to refuse.

The only person empowered to give us instructions was the senior legal authority in Bavaria, in other words, the Minister himself, and he was clearly acting in consultation with the Governor, General Ritter von Epp. Our orders were that one whole cell block should be vacated immediately. At the same time, special units were detached to man the premises, having presumably been sworn in as police auxiliaries.

All that remained for us was to look after the new inmates as regards administration and accommodation. This meant supplying extra latrine buckets, a double allowance of blankets, six-hourly replenishments of drinking-water, and generous food rations – everything in excess of normal standards. We were sticklers for

139

humane treatment at Stadelheim . . .

Yes, a number of so-called executions did take place. Seven or eight senior SA officers were summarily tried and shot – maybe more. The executions were carried out in the rear courtyard, which put them outside our jurisdiction.

We received firm and legally valid instructions to transfer the prisoners to Gruppenführer Dietrich of the Leibstandarte Adolf Hitler. It was the Gruppenführer who actually had them shot.

The prison staff had nothing to do with these executions. From the historical aspect, as it were, I can only contribute the following minor detail, which may be of interest. Gruppenführer Dietrich left before all the SA officers had been shot. His parting words were, 'Got them at last!'

I might add that Herr Röhm, the former SA Chief of Staff, was not disposed of by the Leibstandarte. He survived the executions by two days or so.

Then he was found dead in his cell. He had obviously committed suicide. Such was the official verdict, anyway, and I was bound to accept it. The fact that some press agency disseminated another account of his death is irrelevant. From the official point of view, it carried no weight at all.

The final phase of the Röhm affair came quickly to a head. Hitler gave the order and Heydrich transmitted it to Wesel, hinting in confidence that Himmler, Göring and the army had all brought vigorous pressure to bear. 'They want the Führer to make a clean sweep, so Röhm's got to go. It suits us too, eh?'

'Perfectly,' said Wesel. 'Leave him to me – I'll deal with him.'

'Yes, but not in person. That was the Führer's original idea but I talked him out of it. My reasons should be obvious. Sooner or later, the identity of the person who implements this order may become public knowledge. The Führer finally agreed with me that you must remain on the side-lines. Your kind of work demands a certain anonymity, and we'll be needing your services for a long time to come.'

'Very well. Who gets the job, officially?'

'One of our experts in this field. Brigadeführer Eicke, commandant of Dachau concentration camp. He's a dependable type

– you know him of old. Agreed?'

'Right, I'll stand aside and let him get on with it.'

'No need, my dear fellow.' Heydrich laughed gaily. 'I'd hate to be a spoilsport, knowing how much this means to you. I suggest you assume overall command, brief our friend Eicke and supervise his work. You can bring in anyone else you like – a couple of your men, for instance – just as long as they remain anonymous.' Heydrich chuckled again. 'Well, Waldi, isn't that a compromise after your own heart?'

Stadelheim Prison the same day. Brigadeführer Theodor Eicke presented himself for duty – a sharp-featured man with bushy eyebrows, a prominent nose and deep furrows running from each nostril to the corners of his mouth.

Wesel, escorted by Norden and Hagen, waited for him in the reception area. The two senior officers exchanged a cursory but cordial greeting: Hitler salute, handshake, level gaze.

'Any problems?' Eicke asked briskly.

'None worth mentioning.'

'Good, then I'll finish him off. Mind you, it won't be an unmitigated pleasure. Röhm and I have sunk a few bottles together in the past. He can't carry his liquor like me – we aren't in the same league – but I never held it against him.'

Wesel nodded sympathetically. 'One of my men will go with you. He can relieve you of the donkey-work.'

'He doesn't have to,' Eicke said, 'but I won't say no. All right, let's get it over.'

'Just a moment,' Wesel cut in. 'I've a couple of instructions for you. Please stick to the following procedure.

'Start by handing Röhm this statement I've drafted – it's an admission of guilt. Give him three minutes to sign it. Whether he does or not won't affect the rest of the operation.

'Next, inform him that the Führer has already sentenced him to death but is giving him a chance to take his own life. As an officer, he's at liberty to shoot himself. Put your service automatic on the table and leave him alone with it. Give him ten minutes. I'm almost certain he won't do it – he's a coward at heart.

'That'll leave you no choice. He'll have to be liquidated at once. Any questions?'

Eicke did not take long to put his finger on the single flaw in Wesel's plan. 'You expect me to hand him my gun? The man must be half-way round the bend by now – what if he turns it on me?'

Wesel looked faintly amused. 'It's a physical impossibility. You'll never be alone with him – one of my men will be with you the whole time, and they can both beat a fly to the take-off at ten metres.'

Brigadeführer Eicke scrutinized the two young officers at Wesel's side. 'Which one goes with me?'

Wesel picked an imaginary speck of dust off his uniform, savouring the moment. 'If I select one, it's no reflection on the other.'

Norden could bear the suspense no longer. 'Who's it to be, Brigadeführer?'

'Hagen,' said Wesel.

'Not me?'

'Hagen, I said.'

Eicke set off, followed by his appointed escort.

'Why not me?' Norden persisted.

Wesel stared at him hard. His expression was benevolent but imperious. 'Get this straight, Norden. I give the orders here. There are far bigger things in store for us – far more important assignments for which you'll be even better suited. Is that clear?'

Conjectures, suppositions and opinions voiced by sundry eye- and ear-witnesses.

1. *Eckstein, Wilhelm, prison guard:*

I saw two men go into the cell where Röhm was being held. Then they came out, waited for a while and went inside again. A moment later I heard two shots. Yes, two – I'd swear to it.

2. *Mertens, Josef, judicial officer:*

I also saw the two men referred to. I had no idea who they were, though one looked familiar. From a photograph shown me later, I was able to identify him as Brigadeführer Eicke, commandant of Dachau.

I never saw the other man before or since.

3. *Sonnenhuber, Alfons, senior prison administrator at Stadelheim:*
We received prior notification of Brigadeführer Eicke's arrival through proper channels, from the Ministry of the Interior, the government department responsible for prison administration.

It was further intimated to us that the Brigadeführer was fully authorized to act at his own discretion. In any case, Hitler himself assumed full responsibility for these proceedings in the historic Reichstag speech during which he appointed himself our supreme judicial authority.

4. *Schlegel, Horst, one-time special correspondent of the Party's* Völkischer Beobachter, *now editor of a Munich daily:*
I happened – quite by chance – to be visiting Stadelheim on the day in question. While there I saw Brigadeführer Eicke emerging from a cell in one of the side blocks. Eicke was a stolid and imperturbable kind of man, but I could tell at a glance that he was genuinely shaken. 'Ernst Röhm just shot himself,' he said. 'He died crying "My Führer, my Führer!" It's enough to make a strong man weep.'

5. *Königsberger, Ewald, prison medical officer:*
Ernst Röhm, whose body I was asked to examine, died as a result of a single bullet-wound in the head. His face was so severely mutilated as to be almost unrecognizable – just bloody pulp.

A CID officer who attended the autopsy established that the weapon used must have been of exceptionally large calibre – 10 mm. if not more.

He also discovered a second bullet, not in the deceased's body but lodged in the plaster of the cell wall. It came from a weapon with the calibre of a normal service automatic, e.g. a Walther 7.65 like the one carried by Brigadeführer Eicke.

Do I infer anything from the presence of this second bullet? Why should I? I'm a doctor, not a detective.

Waldemar Wesel mustered his men.

'That, gentlemen, was an admirable piece of work. You're all due for some relaxation, but not till tomorrow. Our Führer wants to see us before the day is out.'

7 Lull before the Storm

Adolf Hitler received Wesel's half-dozen in his study at the Brown House, flanked during the first or strictly formal part of the proceedings by Himmler and Heydrich.

Drawn up in a semicircle round Wesel as they had been on the earlier occasion, the Six gazed reverently at their Führer, proud to have demonstrated their loyalty. Hitler, wearing a plain brown Party uniform whose sole adornment was the Iron Cross First Class, advanced on them like a craftsman benevolently examining the products of his own industry.

He shook hands with them all. His fingers seemed a trifle limp at first, but each vigorous hand-clasp was vigorously returned to the accompaniment of a luminous stare from the magnetic eyes.

From the autobiographical notes of Heinz-Hermann Norden:
I had the honour of meeting Adolf Hitler on many occasions and under a variety of circumstances. Not only at the time of his heroic death, in which I was privileged to play a part, but in earlier years – during hectic victory celebrations, fateful hours of decision, moments of serene contentment.

At the very last, tremors ran through the hands of Greater Germany's greatest son. His body was convulsed with pain, but even in that final hour his eyes – those mirrors of the soul – still glowed despite the infinite grief and suffering that stirred in their depths.

But that day, just after the Röhm coup had been crushed, our Führer shone forth like a star whose destiny it was to illumine the darkest corners of the earth. Whenever he looked at me – and I flatter myself that his eyes lingered on me more than once – I felt transfixed.

'I owe you a debt of gratitude, comrades,' Hitler said solemnly. 'My faith in you has been fully justified. Your services merit recognition. The Reichsführer-SS agrees – don't you, Himmler?'

'Yes, my Führer!' Heydrich was standing a pace to the rear, so Himmler could not see the surreptitious smirk on his subordinate's face. His high-pitched voice sounded almost falsetto. He produced a sheet of paper and cleared his throat, hard.

'In direct consultation with the Führer,' he proclaimed, 'I, in my capacity as Reichsführer-SS, issue the following order: retroactive to June 1st of this year, SS-Untersturmführer Bergmann, Berner, Hagen, Hermann, Norden and Siegfried are promoted SS-Obersturmführer.'

'We thank the Führer!' The ritual response rang out like a Greek chorus.

Hitler smiled and nodded. Then he turned to Wesel. 'Today, Wesel, my special thanks are due not only to a theoretician and propagandist who has also served our Movement as a philosopher. They go to a comrade-in-arms with an exemplary talent for putting his theories into practice.'

Wesel modestly inclined his head. After a momentary struggle for composure, he raised his eyes and fixed them on the Führer's face, so profoundly stirred that even his prodigious gift of language seemed to have deserted him.

The Führer drew nearer. Deeply moved himself now, he announced, 'Brigadeführer Wesel, in consultation with the Reichsführer-SS and on the recommendation of Gruppenführer Heydrich, I hereby promote you to the rank of SS-Gruppenführer.'

Eyeball to eyeball, the two men shook hands and exchanged a formal bow.

'Congratulations,' said Heydrich, sounding almost genial.

That concluded the official part of the audience. Himmler, Heydrich and Wesel retired, the Führer having expressed a desire for personal discourse with his six faithful followers.

They withdrew to the adjoining room, where a circular table was already laid for seven: a snow-white tablecloth and napkins to match, plates and cups of Nymphenburg china, and cut-glass dishes heaped with an assortment of cakes.

The newly promoted lieutenants had been prepared for such an eventuality by Wesel. They stuffed themselves with all the Führer set before them but never removed their eyes from his face. Hitler himself sat back, taking repeated sips of tea. Then he put his cup down and launched into one of his lengthy monologues.

'I feel at ease in your company, gentlemen. I know you understand and trust me – I can sense your devotion to my person. Unfortunately, I cannot always say the same. Good is confronted by evil and decency rewarded with base and unworthy conduct. To be frank with you, this was what I met with from Röhm.

'I trusted the man! I was unfailingly generous to him, I gave him my support and furthered his career. The least I expected was a modicum of loyalty, if not gratitude, but how did he repay me? He insidiously attempted to worm his way into a position of supreme power, at first by devious means, then by a process of direct confrontation which would have culminated in my death. Yes, gentlemen, my assassin had already been hired – a Standartenführer Uhl, now dead.

'Such was the predicament that faced me. My only recourse was to mete out justice with a merciless hand. That was why I decided upon the measures in which you played so active a part – measures that had to be taken if our way of life was to survive its hour of trial.

'But I must tell you something else. We *are* the State. That being so, the law of self-preservation bids us be ready to protect and defend it at a moment's notice. Anyone who stands in our way forfeits his right to exist, convicted by history, sentenced by me, executed by you. I now know – and rejoice in the knowledge – that you are ready to do your duty at all times. Comrades, I thank you!'

Late that night the Wesel Group set the seal on this festive day by celebrating in a manner worthy of their Germanic ancestors. The banquet was attended not only by Wesel but by Müller, to whose special tuition the Group owed so much of its success. Raffael was again playing barman, but his duties presented fewer problems this time because no limitations had been imposed on the type and quantity of liquor to be served. Wesel watched his men with sympathetic interest as they drank themselves into a stupor. He himself was sipping champagne, which he could consume by the bottle without any discernible effect, and Müller was also showing restraint.

'Well, gentlemen,' Wesel said, leaning back in his chair, 'I think we've all earned ourselves a spot of relaxation, but how shall we spend it? Any ideas?'

'What about paying the Count a visit?' Hagen said promptly. He was drinking German brandy. 'I could use a few days at his place. You know – riding, shooting, hunting.'

Norden, who was applying himself to some peat-smoked Irish whiskey, eagerly agreed. 'I know the Countess would welcome a visit from us. She told me so.'

'And me,' Hagen countered.

Wesel smiled faintly and glanced at Hermann.

'A nice long session at Leopoldstrasse wouldn't hurt,' Hermann said. He was drinking North German grain spirit straight from the stone bottle. In response to a nod from Wesel, he turned to Siegfried. 'How about you?'

'I'm not particular,' Siegfried said, uncomplicated as ever. His chosen beverage was a cognac twenty-two years old – exactly his own age.

'It doesn't matter a damn how we amuse ourselves,' Berner said, winking at Bergmann. The Siamese Twins were drinking Scotch-on-the-rocks from a one-litre loving-cup. 'As long as it's all right with you, Gruppenführer.'

Wesel shook his head, chuckling ruefully. 'What an unenter-prising bunch you are! I've put you through the finest possible course of instruction, broadened your horizons, coached you in foreign languages and cultural history. There's a multitude of possibilities open to you – trips to Rome, Paris and London to study Italian fascism, French decadence and British narrow-mindedness. The world's your oyster, gentlemen, but your ambitions obviously don't extend that far. I aim to produce members of the master race, not sybarites, so let's call it a night. Get rid of those bottles – pour the dregs down the drain. Today you can sleep it off, but tomorrow you resume life in earnest – or re-embark on the joys of existence, whichever I decide. Get me?'

Rather unsteadily, the six revellers withdrew. Müller watched them go, amused. Raffael cleared away the débris and was dismissed, leaving Wesel and Müller to themselves. The drawing-room of the villa still blazed with light although a new day was already dawning outside.

The Gruppenführer drew his chair closer to Müller's, likewise the ice-bucket containing his champagne. He obviously meant to create an atmosphere of warmth and intimacy.

'My dear Herr Müller,' he said, resting his right hand on the policeman's left, 'I still haven't had a chance to congratulate you.'

'On what?'

'Your promotion to chief superintendent. Himmler has confirmed it on Heydrich's recommendation – and, I may add, with a little nudge from me too.'

'Very nice,' Müller said suspiciously, 'but what does it mean in practice? Are they putting me back on the active list?'

'Heydrich would welcome you with open arms. You'll soon be right at the top of your profession, Müller, but not just yet. I still need you here, and the Führer's directive states that my requirements take priority. However, I've seen to it that you'll draw double pay out of a special fund administered by Heydrich.'

'That sounds ominous,' Müller said. 'What's the catch?'

'There isn't one,' Wesel replied artlessly. 'You know the members of this unit almost as well as I do, that's what makes you worth so much to me. Have you noticed anything about them lately? I'd appreciate your candid opinion.'

'They strike me as overexcited – almost overwrought about something, but what?'

'The Führer, of course.' Wesel stroked his chin. 'He patted them on the back so hard they think they're supermen. Which they are, in a sense, but there's no need to say so. They've got to be brought down to earth, and fast.'

'But not with a bump,' warned Müller. 'I doubt if shock tactics are the proper treatment for men in their condition.'

Wesel astonished Müller by agreeing with him. 'We must devise an entirely new way of engaging their energies. If you can't think of something, who can?'

'I'd rather not shoulder more responsibility for your men than I have to, Gruppenführer,' Müller said. 'My dossier's thick enough as it is. You could have me arrested any time if I withdrew my co-operation, but why should I?'

'Oh, come, Herr Müller, I'm not trying to pressure you. It's your friendship I want – the friendship of a future head of the Gestapo. Don't bite the hand that's trying to feed you.'

'I couldn't afford to even if I felt like it.' Müller lolled back in his chair, blinking sleepily. 'So you still aren't satisfied with their performance? All right, if there are any snags, I'll do my best to iron them out.'

'Join me in reinforcing our men's morale, Chief Superintendent. I want them equal to any demands made on them.' Wesel frowned suddenly. 'But what was that you said about snags?'

Müller did not reply at once. He took a thoughtful pull at his glass and, with great deliberation, lit a cigar. He was the only inmate of the Villa privileged to smoke.

'I'll tell you as much as I know, Gruppenführer. Frankly, it's Countess von der Tannen. A couple of the boys have developed an intense interest in her, as you know. It could lead to trouble.'

'Have you compiled any information about the Count and his daughter?'

'As a matter of routine – yes, naturally, just as I have about anyone in contact with members of the Group.'

Wesel looked slightly perturbed. 'Anything incriminating?'

'It depends on your point of view,' Müller said soothingly. 'Human failings, if you like. Men of the world like us would smile at such peccadilloes, but not idealists like our men. Everything has to be just right.'

'And isn't it?'

'Not entirely. Not where our young Countess is concerned.'

'Really, Herr Müller! What makes you say that?' Wesel seemed torn between outrage and amusement. 'I've known Elisabeth since she was a baby.'

'She's no baby now.'

'What do you mean? Elisabeth has her faults. She's greedy and ambitious under that virginal exterior – it runs in the family – but even greed and ambition can be exploited.'

'If that was all, Gruppenführer, we might be able to contain the situation. But there's something else. To put it very mildly, the Countess is a slave to her appetites.'

'Really?' Wesel looked as supercilious as a man of the world should. 'I must say, it doesn't show. Is this guesswork?'

'Not at all. I've got evidence – and some of it reads like a nymphomaniac's case history.'

Wesel flinched. He saw at once that this could mean the abrupt demolition of his carefully constructed ideal. 'Damn it, Müller, if what you say is true . . .'

'The young lady could have a thoroughly disruptive effect on unit morale,' Müller amplified, sucking contentedly at his cigar.

Excerpts from a file on Elisabeth, Countess von der Tannen, compiled in June 1934 and found among extant Gestapo records:

Preliminary inquiries disclose that the subject has a violent temper and does little to control it. Recent victims of her disposition include: (*a*) a maidservant repeatedly struck in the face for having spilt tea over a damask tablecloth; (*b*) a horse, ridden to death because of its rebellious behaviour; and (*c*) an Austrian cook who committed suicide because she could not endure the Countess's bullying.

There are many stories of her procoecious and unbridled interest in sex. At thirteen she compelled the Count's head groom, an Italian from Modena, to have sexual intercourse with her, then engineered his instant dismissal by reporting him to her father. Other putative sexual partners have included a French tutor, sundry members of her father's shooting parties, at least two of whom boasted of having had grossly unnatural relations with her *à trois*, a local policeman (swiftly transferred), a gardener (horsewhipped by the Count), two or three neighbouring landowners and four or five of their sons . . .

Wesel unveiled his solution at lunch next day.

'Italy!' he proclaimed. 'That's where we'll go. To Rome, the Eternal City.' He basked in the feigned enthusiasm kindled by this announcement. 'Mind you, we're going to make the most of our visit. Relaxation doesn't mean loafing around. You've only got a few days to work out a suitable itinerary, gentlemen. I don't want our trip to degenerate into a Sunday-school outing.'

Hagen raised his hand. 'What shall we do in the meantime, Gruppenführer?'

'Perhaps we could say goodbye,' Norden said tentatively. He

thought he had put a correct interpretation on Wesel's quizzical glance. 'To our friends.'

'Like the Count?' asked Hagen, meaning the Countess.

Wesel just nodded, but his verbal consent followed swiftly. 'Very well, we'll pay a farewell visit to the castle next week, but tomorrow I shall expect to hear your preliminary suggestions. I want a detailed itinerary from each and every one of you, bearing in mind our object of study, which is fascism Italian style. Let's see if Mussolini's boys can teach us a thing or two.'

Waldemar Wesel turned up at the moated castle near Passau an hour before the farewell lunch party was due to begin. He had announced his arrival by phone and expressed a wish to speak to Elisabeth.

She was waiting for him at the gate, all smiles.

'Everything's fixed, Uncle Waldi – Daddy told me to tell you – but where do I fit into your plans?'

'Didn't your father give you some idea what's expected of you?'

'He certainly dropped a few hints.' Elisabeth steered him towards the rose garden, hugging his arm. 'I'm Daddy's daughter, after all, and he didn't become your friend by accident. You want me to play a cross between a virtuous rustic maiden and an aristocratic damsel in distress.'

'You're a smart girl, Elisabeth.' Her brazen readiness to act the part shocked him, not that he showed it. 'Smart enough not to give me any trouble. Or make trouble for yourself and your father, which amounts to the same thing.'

'I know,' Elisabeth said brightly. 'You and Daddy are partners – and I'm part of the deal whether I like it or not. Well, why should I mind, as long as I can lead my own life?'

'Which you can.' Wesel swiftly qualified this generous assurance. 'But in future, my dear, be more discreet about it. You can seduce your father's entire staff and half the local population for all I care, but my men are off limits.'

She smiled without a trace of resentment. 'I can think of at least two who wouldn't qualify anyway. Berner and Bergmann are obviously queer – isn't that the expression? – and Siegfried's more interested in animals than women. As for Hermann, he wouldn't care *who* he did it with. Countess or barmaid, it's all the same to him.'

'Very perceptive of you, my dear. What about Norden and Hagen?'

'I'd hate to have to choose between them. Hagen's the he-man type, Norden's more a knight in shining armour.' Her voice became dreamy. 'Couldn't I – I mean, they're both *so* attractive . . .'

'No!' Wesel said firmly. 'Neither one nor the other nor a combination of both. In case you didn't know, Elisabeth, most men equate laying a woman with winning a battle, and every winner brags about his conquests sooner or later. That's precisely what I'm determined to avoid.'

'So you want me to be good?'

'I insist on it, if only for your father's sake. You're in the middle of a game, and I make the rules. Are you prepared to observe them?'

She was, or said she was, but Wesel found her next remark disquieting. 'You're a wonderful person,' she murmured tenderly. 'You know what makes people tick, Uncle Waldi. You're the kind of man a girl could look up to. Like Goethe.'

Wesel stared at her in consternation. 'Who?'

'Goethe! You're tremendously alike. He could have written your *Maxims* if he'd been alive today. Added to that, he had an affair with an 18-year-old girl when he was 80. Does that appeal to you, Uncle Waldi? I'm sure Daddy wouldn't object if we got together.'

Although the ground seemed to yawn at Wesel's feet, he leapt the chasm unflinching. 'Very flattering of you, my dear, very flattering indeed. Wishful thinking can be a seductive pastime, but we must concentrate on realities. All three of us – you, your father and I.'

The Count was already awaiting his guests by the time Wesel and Elisabeth joined him at the gate. Soon afterwards the gravel crunched beneath the tyres of three funereal black Mercedes.

'Welcome, gentlemen!' called the Count.

'Delighted to see you all again,' Elisabeth said with maidenly charm.

Preceded by the two Newfoundlands and followed by Wesel, they conducted their guests to the great hall.

There ensued a leisurely meal in the traditional German manner. The Count sat at the head of the table with Wesel on his right. Countess Elisabeth took her place at the other end between Norden and Hagen.

After coffee, the Count declared an adjournment, having politely consulted Wesel first, and the other guests dispersed.

Nobleman and SS general were left alone in the dining-hall over another bottle of Franconian wine. They said nothing for a while. Then the Count leant forward, looking conspiratorial.

'The way Hitler dealt with those Brownshirts! A nice piece of work, Waldi. I congratulate him – and you. He's going from strength to strength.'

'I always told you he would,' Wesel said pensively. 'You and your friends refused to believe me.'

'We hoped he wouldn't make it,' the Count admitted, 'but this latest business has convinced us. Hitler is a man to be reckoned with. What can we do for him?'

Wesel smiled acidly. 'I imagine you wouldn't consider joining the Party?'

'Hardly. In any case, it would be rather late in the day.'

'Of course, there are other alternatives.'

'For instance?' the Count demanded eagerly.

Wesel looked him straight in the eye, seemingly determined to put all – or almost all – his cards on the table. 'This, for example. We take a leaf from the old Prussian General Staff manual: divided we march, united we attack. One or other of us is bound to come out on top in the end, with guaranteed dividends for both parties.'

'What do you mean!' The Count's face clouded. 'This Führer of yours – don't you see him staying firmly in the saddle, at least in the immediate future?'

'Of course I do,' Wesel said, 'except that the immediate future's an unknown quantity. You never know how long it will last.'

'But he always talks about a Thousand-Year Reich.'

'Very persuasively too, but there's never been such an animal in recorded history. It's not beyond the bounds of possibility that his thousand years will be up before we're ten years older.

'And you think we ought to cover ourselves?'

'I never said anything of the kind – not officially.' Wesel smiled.

'There's no need to, between friends like us.'

The Count nodded thoughtfully. 'I'd have to insist on maintaining my standard of living. Could you guarantee that?'

'Absolutely,' Wesel assured him. 'After all, I know you'd never be unwise enough to let me down.'

Meanwhile, Countess Elisabeth was showing her two favourite guests round the castle's rose garden and convincing them that she was a creature from the realm of courtly romance.

One pace away on either side, Norden and Hagen escorted her like twin custodians of all that was virtuous and beautiful. That they kept a wary eye on each other did not for one instant distract them from humble attendance on their lady's wishes.

'Aren't those roses heavenly!' Elisabeth exclaimed. 'I love them when they're in full bloom like this, and sharing them with you makes them seem even lovelier.' She did not look at either of them. 'Both of you, I mean.'

'It's hard to say goodbye,' Norden confided with manly restraint, 'even for two or three weeks.'

'But we'll be back,' Hagen assured her, 'if it's all right with you.'

A heady fragrance filled the air. They had just come to a bed of pale yellow tea-roses. Elisabeth stooped and, after careful deliberation, picked two. They were identical in size and hue.

Gracefully, she rose to her feet. Then, with a gentle smile and a slight inclination of her dainty head, she offered the blooms to Norden and Hagen. They were rapturously accepted.

Raffael, very eager to please of late, handed out passports. They were German passports containing plausible details of each man's date of birth, place of origin and physical data. The photographs had been taken in civilian dress.

The special feature of the passports themselves was that each member of the Group had been allowed to select his own profession. Far from being a random procedure, this had entailed careful preparation, and every cover story had been thoroughly checked with the aid of specialized literature and expert advisers.

The official tally was as follows: one gunsmith – Hagen; one free-lance journalist – Norden; one sales representative – Hermann; one veterinary surgeon – Siegfried; and two film-makers – Berner and Bergmann.

'So we're all set for Rome,' Wesel concluded.

'Just in case any problems arise,' Müller put in, 'I've taken the precaution of getting in touch with the Italian police and our embassy in Rome. Contacts with the fascist authorities are the Gruppenführer's responsibility. I might add that the Duce will be granting him a private interview.'

There was a trace of self-satisfaction in Wesel's smile. His comment on Müller's reference to a forthcoming tête-à-tête with Mussolini was a masterpiece of understatement.

'A special mission for the Führer,' he said casually.

The trip opened with a three-day test of physical and mechanical efficiency organized by Raffael and supervised by Wesel. Müller had been careful to notify the German and Italian traffic police in advance.

Munich-Milan was the first stage, Milan-Florence the second, Florence-Rome the third and last. The participants in this gruelling event, competing as two-man teams in a trio of high-powered cars, roared across mountain passes, down secondary roads and through urban bottlenecks.

'They're driving like maniacs,' Raffael reported gleefully, '– from one insurance claim to the next. So far they've flattened several dozen chickens, crippled four dogs and run over eight cats, though cats aren't covered. They've also reduced two cars to scrap-iron and killed a worker on an olive plantation near Padua.'

'Settle all claims,' Wesel commanded. 'We don't want any complications – it's the end product that counts. I need to know which of our men have a special aptitude for fast and sustained driving.'

Then came an incident which did not escape Raffael's eagle eye and was promptly reported to Wesel. Postcards were written and slipped into a mail-box in Florence. The offenders: Norden and Hagen.

Gruppenführer Wesel, described in his passport as a professor of philosophy, dealt with the matter at once. He met Norden and Hagen at Mario's in the shadow of the Cathedral. Wesel came straight to the point. 'Look, you know I trust you both, but I like to be kept fully informed. Apart from anything else, you may need some fatherly advice.'

'Of course, Gruppenführer.'

'Fine.' Wesel took a sip of blood-red Barbera. 'I gather you've been sending postcards. Who to?'

'Only the Countess.'

'Well, what did you say?'

Hagen to Elisabeth:

This country seems to have a chronic case of sunstroke. The Italians do nothing but doze, drink and gossip. You can't expect much of a flabby race like them, certainly not from the political angle . . .

Norden to Elisabeth:

Most of the cultural relics betray a strong Germanic influence and are well worth seeing. All the same, one can't help feeling profoundly saddened by their deterioration. It's quite incredible, the way they've been neglected . . .

'I've only three comments to make, gentlemen,' Wesel said, 'and they're strictly confidential.

'In the first place, I alone am authorized to communicate with outside parties. All other external contacts must be personally approved by me.

'Secondly, we're here for educational purposes, as guests of our fascist friends. By all means keep your eyes open, but don't jump to any premature conclusions or transmit them in writing – unfavourable conclusions least of all.

'Thirdly, never make derogatory remarks to anyone outside our immediate circle. In public, I shall expect you to display faultless manners. Be civil, courteous and ostentatiously pro-Italian. Even if somebody claims that the Duce is a greater man than the Führer, don't kick him in the teeth right away – and certainly not in front of witnesses.'

The outcome of this three-day ordeal for men and machines came as an undeniable surprise to Wesel.

He had not given Norden and Hagen a chance – they were too temperamentally unsuited to make a good team. His confident forecast had been an easy win for Siegfried and Hermann, but he was wrong. Berner and Bergmann scored a convincing victory. Their times were consistently fast and their reactions so unerring that they overcame every hazard they encountered.

As planned, the race ended outside the Hassler, Rome's foremost luxury hotel at the top of the Spanish Steps. Seen from this vantage-point, the city seemed to sprawl lazily at the beholder's feet.

The foyer boasted oriental rugs, Renaissance tapestries, Tuscan marble, furniture and vases from the finest Roman workshops, and a first-class copy of the celebrated Roman she-wolf with the infants Romulus and Remus suckling happily.

Presiding over the reception desk was a youthful but efficient hotel employee with an excellent knowledge of German. This was anything but fortuitous. The young man's surname was Huber and his first name Francesco – in plain German, Franz.

'Welcome, Professor,' he said to Wesel. 'We've already received a number of telegrams and telephone messages for you – they're waiting in your room. We've put you between Herr Raffael and Herr Müller, as you requested. The other gentlemen have also been given top-floor rooms with bath. And now, please permit me to wish you a pleasant stay at our hotel and an enjoyable time in our glorious city.'

Retrospective remarks made by Francesco Huber, once employed at the Hotel Hassler, now proprietor of the luxury restaurant Chez Francesco in the Via Veneto:

May I begin by clarifying something? Huber's an ultra-Bavarian name, I know, but I'm one hundred per cent Italian by birth and sentiment. My grandfather, who came from Fürstenfeldbruck in Upper Bavaria and was also in the hotel trade, settled in Rome as a young man. He married an Italian girl from Emilia-Romagna – he was a porter at the time, she was a chambermaid. My father Alfredo took out Italian nationality, so I've always regarded myself as an Italian, if not a Roman. So much for that.

But you were inquiring about that party of German visitors. I remember them well, though not with any particular affection. May I be permitted to insert another small but important remark? Thank you.

I was privileged to belong to the management of the Hotel Hassler for several years. It has always been one of the best-known establishments in the business, with a worldwide reputation for excellence. However, no hotelier on earth can pick his clientèle or run a thorough check on their background. He has to be content with superficialities such as valid passports, good financial standing and respectable conduct while on the hotel premises. All these requirements were met by the guests in question.

It did not, however, escape me that they had some rather peculiar friends in Rome. This became clear the very day after their arrival, when they were visited by a Signor Nero, known to insiders as Colonello Emilio Nero, head of a secret police squad responsible to the Duce himself.

Nero introduced the German visitors to his men. I heard rumours of communal banquets and excursions, joint conferences, trips to the beach at Ostia and the famous wine-growing district of Frascati, also to the Alban Hills, where the Pope spends the summer months.

I'm afraid I can't tell you much more. Although they stand out in my mind, you must remember that these Germans represented only a tiny fraction of our clientèle. We had a truly international élite under our roof, then as every summer. A French financial tycoon, a Dutch diamond magnate, big businessmen from Chicago, a globe-trotting English lord, an Arab potentate, and so forth.

There was also a professor from the United States. An extremely quiet, dignified-looking gentleman – Jewish, at a guess. I must say I formed a very pleasant impression of him.

But what really struck me about him – and alarmed me, for some vague reason – was his apparent eagerness to establish personal contact with this party of Germans. His name was Breslauer.

'You here?' Müller took one look at Breslauer and threw up his hands. 'I don't believe it!'

'Yes, it's me.' Breslauer gazed at the policeman with serene and unwavering obstinacy. 'I have to speak to you, Müller, and you're going to listen.' The old man had accosted Müller in the hotel's top-floor restaurant, which offered a breathtakingly beautiful view of the city.

'My God, Breslauer, what brings you here?'

'Simple,' Breslauer said with a gentle smile. 'It was one of those postcards you keep sending me so regularly – for which many thanks, by the way. Your last card mentioned a forthcoming trip to Rome, so here I am.'

'I hope you don't expect me to jump for joy. What's this all about?'

'Knowing me as you do, why bother to ask?'

'You don't know me yet, otherwise you wouldn't be here. I was looking forward to our reunion, Professor – but only when the Führer's thousand years were up. We could have met on each other's home ground, either in the States or Berlin. But here, like this – no!' Abruptly, Müller's appetite deserted him. He pushed his plate aside. 'How did you find us?'

'No problem there, not for somebody who's had a chance to observe your élitist attitudes at first hand. The best is only just good enough for Wesel's men, and in Rome that means the Hassler. I simply checked in and waited for you to show up.'

'You must be crazy!' Müller sorrowfully shook his head. 'You were safe in America. Here in Italy you aren't, so take the next plane out. I'll help you, but this is the very last time.'

'What if I insist on staying?'

'For God's sake, Breslauer! Don't play the martyr, not in this hell-hole – only a Jew would be that idiotic. I won't stand for it. Even I don't deserve a millstone like you round my neck.'

Müller ground his teeth. He'd only just been congratulating himself on the success of the trip. His precautionary contacts with the Italian police authorities were functioning smoothly. Wesel was closeted with Mussolini and his men were out on another of their excursions. And now Breslauer!

'I wish I'd never met you,' he growled. 'Why do your kind have to exist at all? You don't belong in our world so why not stay in your own?'

'Germany's as much a part of my world as yours. We can't abandon it to a man like Hitler.'

Müller's agitation was barely disguised now. He summoned the waiter and demanded his bill before the main course had been served.

'Look, Professor,' he said, 'get this straight. I'm not going to let my one and only character reference sacrifice himself on the altar of some abstract ideal – I'm too self-centred. Why am I so determined to save my own skin? Because I know what goes on inside Germany. Because a certain megalomaniac is planning to realize his ultimate dream – the systematic destruction of alien forms of life, quote unquote. In plain language, the extermination of the Jews. You know that as well as I do, Professor – you've always known it. Germany's no place for a man like you, not the way it is now.'

Müller ordered a large grappa. Breslauer ordered one too.

'My dear friend,' he said thoughtfully, 'do you remember our nocturnal discussions at Feldafing? Do you recall our attempts to interpret the Old Testament? Our thoughts were centred on the concept of the righteous men – or rather, man. If only one had existed, so the Bible tells us, Sodom and Gomorrah might have been spared. Well, that's the situation facing Germany today.'

'Just one man out of the millions who are entirely at the mercy of the system? You're ready to risk your neck for a single exception?' Müller's shoulders sagged. 'I can even guess his identity. It's Norden, isn't it? You seriously plan to stake your life on that Wagnerian idealist?'

Breslauer didn't look at Müller. 'I'd prefer to put it this way. Norden genuinely seemed to be struggling towards some notion of decency. At least he was trying, even if his capacity for methodical thought hadn't matured. Siegfried's instincts were sound and healthy too, especially where animals were concerned. If only for the sake of those two, it might pay me to have one last try.'

'No,' Müller said gruffly. 'You're getting out of here fast, and for good.'

Müller accompanied Breslauer to his hotel room, feeling as if he were escorting a prisoner scheduled for extradition. He settled down with the telephone, but his arrangements were soon interrupted by an incoming call from Siegfried.

'I'm speaking from a café called the Dante,' Siegfried reported. 'It's just at the foot of the Spanish Steps – only a couple of minutes away. It might be a good idea if you dropped by, Herr Müller.'

'Why the hell?' snapped Müller. 'If you can't pay your bill, contact Wesel or Raffael. I'm busy.'

'It is not that.' Siegfried sounded definitely uneasy. 'I think we're going to have a full-scale brawl with some Italian civilians.'

Müller frowned. 'Are you on your own, or have you got some of Mussolini's boys with you?' Siegfried's reply was visibly reassuring. It seemed that Wesel's half-dozen were being entertained by their fascist brethren.

'Then you don't need me after all. Sit back and let your Italian friends show what they're made of. I've got more important things on my mind.'

Müller put down the receiver and turned to Breslauer. 'I'm not letting you out of my sight until you leave. Plenty of Jews are going to rot in Germany, but I'm damned if you're going to join them.'

Müller made all the arrangements. He quickly discovered that a plane was leaving Rome for Paris in three hours, just in time to catch a connecting flight to London. After that came Southampton-New York by sea. All reservations were made on the spot and underwritten by a cash guarantee.

'It's on me,' Müller announced. 'Call it self-indulgence, but I want you out of here, Professor. You wouldn't begrudge me a little peace of mind, would you?'

Breslauer was silently packing his bag. He seemed to spin out every move he made. Occasionally he straightened up and gave Müller an imploring glance, but Müller remained adamant.

Then the phone rang again. This time it was Wesel.

'I've just come from the Duce,' he announced briskly. 'We had a frank, productive and stimulating exchange of views – very gratifying indeed, which is more than I can say for the news that greeted me here. I've just been informed that our men are beating hell out of some of the local inhabitants, down at the Dante. I told them they could do anything as long as they didn't cause bad blood.'

'According to my information they're with your Italian friends. Nero's there too.'

'So what, Müller? Our fascist colleagues don't pack half the punch we do, even though Mussolini's been at the helm a lot longer than the Führer. The police have turned up – ordinary uniformed police. I want you down there now, before they arrest my boys. The results could be catastrophic, so get moving. Let's see if your contacts with the local police are worth anything.'

Müller slammed the receiver down. 'I have to go out for a few minutes, Professor. Keep packing and don't leave the room. Wait till I get back – please!'

It had all begun so pleasantly, so innocently. Accompanied by Emilio Nero and a handful of his men, Wesel's half-dozen had returned to Rome after an excursion into the Alban Hills. They decided on an espresso and an Italian brandy at the Café Dante.

'We wouldn't want you to leave without seeing the place, *camerati*,' Nero told them. 'If you want to know what a real den of decadent intellectuals looks like, visit the Dante while it still exists. It's not so easy for us to stamp these places out. We're in Rome, don't forget, not Berlin or Munich.'

They trooped inside. The Dante cultivated an elaborately old-world appearance. Round tables with marble tops stood everywhere, surrounded by temptingly fragile bistro chairs.

'Well,' Hermann demanded loudly, 'what's so interesting?'

'The customers,' Nero explained.

The six took a closer look. Hagen gave a contemptuous snort. 'What a degenerate bunch.'

'They call themselves artists,' Nero said, spreading his hands eloquently. 'They spend their whole time here, shooting their mouths off about everything under the sun – even about the Duce.'

'Why do you let them run loose?' demanded Hermann.

The task of explaining fell to Mario, Nero's second-in-command, because the Colonello suddenly remembered a prior engagement and vanished.

'They're damn slippery, these self-styled *letterati*,' Mario said.

'No matter how often we try, we never manage to nail them.'

'Well I think it's a disgrace,' Hagen declared. 'Back home in Germany, dissident types like these aren't allowed to exist.'

Berner glanced at Bergmann. 'But we aren't back home,' he said, trying to break the mounting tension.

After a few whispered words to Norden, Siegfried got up and headed for the telephone.

'Why the hell do we have to put up with them?' Hagen was saying belligerently when Siegfried returned to the table.

'The men are slobs,' Hermann mused, 'but some of those girls have class. They're crying out to be screwed. How about it, Mario?'

'We have a saying in Rome,' Mario told him. 'Young girls sometimes, fiancées never, married women always!' He waited for the laughter to subside. 'However, these coffee-house intellectuals don't subscribe to the normal rules of behaviour. They make their own.'

'In that case,' said Hagen, 'let's break a few.' He started to get up, nodding at Hermann.

'Why not?' Hermann said blandly.

'*Dio mio!*' Mario pleaded. 'Please don't, we can't afford to make trouble.'

'Maybe *you* can't,' Hagen said ominously.

By this time, Hermann was on his feet too and spoiling for a fight. The Café Dante was soon engulfed in a storm which, within minutes, left it in ruins. Women screamed, men reeled backwards and cannoned off others, chairs splintered, mirrors disintegrated, someone howled like a beaten dog. Cries for help rang out, blood flowed, bodies and furniture tumbled into the street, glass smashed.

Then the police arrived, closely followed by Müller.

Meanwhile, Waldemar Wesel sat in the hotel lobby, still clad in the dark suit he had worn for his audience with the Duce.

The Gruppenführer was unperturbed, knowing Müller's dependability. He stared into the depths of a large Scotch and soda, musing on his interview with Mussolini. The man was no match for Hitler, he felt certain.

At that moment a shadow fell across Wesel's glass. He glanced up and saw Breslauer. The Professor stood there for several seconds, pale but composed, gazing at Wesel in silence.

Wesel betrayed no surprise. He rose politely and even sketched an infinitesimal bow. 'Join me, Professor,' he said, waving Breslauer into a chair. 'I assume we're both anxious to avoid any kind of scene.'

Breslauer sank into the chair he'd been offered. His face, filmed with sweat, reflected utter exhaustion, but his voice had an unexpected strength and clarity reminiscent of the days before his employment at Feldafing.

'You aren't particularly surprised to see me here.'

Wesel smiled. 'I knew you were in Rome so I expected you sooner or later. If you hadn't come I should have looked you up myself.'

'Who told you I was here?'

'Not Müller, if that's what you want to know, though I trust he'd have informed me of your presence in due course. No, it was far simpler than that. My Group, to whose excellent state of training you contributed so much, is directly under the Führer's command. That being the case, we've all acquired a top security rating – all of us including you.'

Breslauer bowed his head.

'Almost every move you've made in the United States has been watched. Every detail of your return journey to Europe and your stay in Rome has been reported to me. Time of arrival, accommodation, identity of contacts and so on. But that's only incidental.'

'So why do you think I'm here?'

'Not to make my life difficult, I'm sure. You've never tried to do that, being the wise man you are, and you wouldn't succeed now. In England, Switzerland or Holland, perhaps, but not in fascist Italy.' Wesel sounded invincibly self-assured. 'Anyway, Professor, here you are, and I think I can guess why.'

Breslauer studied Wesel intently. 'You can?'

'Of course. You wish to return to Germany. Your motives don't matter. An urge to pursue your studies, maybe, or an emotional impulse of some kind. Perhaps you simply want to get one of your relatives out of the country. Financial considerations could also enter into it – I'd understand if they did. Or again, it's always possible you find your present inactivity tedious.'

'You mean you'd be willing to get me back into Germany?'

Wesel nodded. 'On certain conditions, yes – by all means.'

'What conditions?'

'Frankly, you could be useful to me – very useful. As a special adviser.' Wesel sipped his whisky. 'It just so happens that there's something really big in the offing. It calls for thorough planning, but there are some teething troubles to be overcome before we really swing into action. Please don't ask me what it's all about, but you can help if you want to. I can't think of a better man for the job.'

'What conditions?' Breslauer repeated.

'You return to the fold,' the Gruppenführer said firmly. He'd foreseen this dialogue and rehearsed his part. 'Mine and Müller's, this time on a monthly retainer of four thousand marks, tax-free. You'd be back in Feldafing but not in the cellar this time. I could even allow you a certain freedom of movement.'

'In return for what?'

'More of the same. More tutorials on Judaism, the Jewish way of life, Jewish customs and philosophy. You'd also have to undertake various research projects with a strong practical bias. Your reports would be commissioned by me and submitted to me alone. What do you say?'

'Yes,' said Breslauer.

Müller took in the Café Dante situation at a glance. He threaded his way through a cordon of patrol cars and entered the premises. Inside he saw that a squad of policemen, guns drawn, had herded the trouble-makers into a corner. Wesel's six stood there only slightly the worse for wear and clearly eager to resume hostilities.

Müller introduced himself to the officer in charge, a lieutenant. He proffered two sets of papers, one German and one Italian, together with credentials issued by the Duce's personal secretariat.

'And now, *camerata*,' he said, speaking as one colleague to another, 'I presume you'll allow me to take these men off your hands.'

The lieutenant smiled accommodatingly. 'I'd like nothing better, Commissario, but I don't know if I have the necessary authorization.'

'You can soon find out,' Müller said. 'Call police headquarters and ask for Signor Boni. Just mention my name.'

'*Subito*,' said the lieutenant, well aware of Signor Boni's identity. He nodded at one of his men and disappeared into the manager's office.

Müller turned his attention to Wesel's half-dozen. 'Don't you think you've done enough?' Müller asked cheerfully. 'Feeling robbed of a finale? Don't worry, you'll get one. The Gruppenführer will see to that.'

Not even this announcement seemed to impress the Six. 'But Herr Müller,' Hermann said, 'all we did was carry out a little pest control.'

'And your *fascisti* friends?' Müller asked. 'What happened to them?'

Hermann's lip curled. 'They took off as soon as things got hot,' he said. 'It's only what you'd expect.'

The Italian police lieutenant picked his way back through the débris. He gave Müller a confidential wink and drew him aside. 'Signor Boni sends his compliments,' he whispered. 'He's delighted to be of service, Signor Müller. These men are released into your custody as requested – that is, in principle.'

'Meaning what?'

'You may think it appropriate to come to some kind of arrangement. Financial, I mean.'

Müller got the point. He returned the lieutenant's wink. 'Say no more,' he murmured gratefully.

The manager was sent for. He bustled up, eyes moist and voice throbbing with reproach, but the exchange that followed was another tribute to Müller's diplomacy.

'I'm prepared to compensate you for all the damage sustained,' Müller told him. 'It's not an admission of guilt, of course, merely a contribution to the furtherance of amicable relations between our two countries. The damage will be paid for in full, but only on certain conditions. You and your staff will sign an affidavit that no personal or political provocation occurred and no physical injury was inflicted. It was simply a harmless scuffle, an outburst of youthful high spirits. Are you and your employees ready to swear to that?'

'But of course, *signore!*' the manager said. 'As long as the compensation is as generous as you imply . . .'

'*Ecco tutto!*' the lieutenant called to his men. 'Put away the guns!' He grinned at Müller. 'Beautifully handled, *egregio collega*, if you don't mind my saying so. It has been a privilege to work with you.'

'Likewise,' said Müller. 'You can rely on me to put in a good word for you when I speak to Signor Boni. If you ever come to Germany I'll be happy to return the compliment.' A vigorous handshake, then he turned to his six charges.

'Follow me, gentlemen. Outside, up the Spanish Steps and straight into the Hassler. The Gruppenführer's waiting for you.'

Waldemar Wesel received his élite in the hotel's small conference-room, a panelled chamber embellished with bowls of fresh roses. The long marble table, a choice specimen of Roman craftsman-ship, was flanked by black leather chairs, but nobody was invited to sit down.

Wesel, leaning nonchalantly against the broad window-sill, beckoned Müller over and inclined his right ear. The policeman's whispered report only appeared to enhance his mellow mood.

'Well, gentlemen,' he said, 'you seem to have had an exhilarating time – and why not? As long as you've enjoyed yourselves, why should I count the cost? Two or three thousand dollars are petty cash to us, that's all.'

Every jaw dropped, even Müller's. The Gruppenführer could always be counted on to take them unawares. They stared at him, humbly and gratefully. They'd been expecting a chewing out, and what happened? The grand manipulator displayed boundless understanding.

'Yes indeed,' Wesel went on, 'I only wish you could pursue the path of pleasure a little longer, but I'm afraid that's impossible. There are two overriding reasons why we must return to base at once. One, I have an important message for the Führer from the Duce. Two, Gruppenführer Heydrich has sent word that our ser-vices are urgently required in a matter affecting national security.'

He parried their questioning looks by issuing a stream of directives. In Wesel's company, orders were the answer to everything.

'First, Herr Müller will act as rearguard. His task is to obliterate all trace of our presence here and ensure that the claims of the Café Dante are met in full.

'Secondly, we head for home two hours from now, this time in convoy. Raffael will issue the necessary movement order. Duration of trip: 36 hours, with one overnight stop at Bologna. Berner and Bergmann are appointed billeting officers. They'll go on ahead and arrange accommodation.

'Thirdly, my car will be carrying an additional passenger. Hermann and Siegfried, you're to look after him till we leave. Don't let him out of your sight. The gentleman in question is staying at this hotel – you're all acquainted with him.'

Wesel stared challengingly at Müller. For what was probably the first and last time in his life, Müller looked disconcerted.

'Not – not Breslauer?' Müller said almost inaudibly.

'The same,' Wesel replied triumphantly. 'What do you say to that?'

Müller said nothing at first. He itched to question the Gruppen-führer's knowledge of the Jews in general and this Jew in particular – ask if Wesel realized he had tangled with a man for whom death was an integral part of life, his own death not excluded.

'How did you track him down, Gruppenführer?'

'It was, the other way round, Herr Müller. He came to see me and expressed a desire to return to Germany. I saw no reason to refuse.'

Müller shrugged wearily. 'The decision is yours, Gruppen-führer. So is the responsibility. I'd sooner tell him to go to hell, myself, but I don't know the address. I can only hazard a guess at it.'

8 Finishing Touches

A bare twenty-four hours after the Wesel Group returned to Feldafing from Italy, they were in action once more.

The operation was preceded by some swift but thorough preliminaries. Armed with their special 10.5 magnums, the Group set off before sunrise and reached Berchtesgaden after a three-hour drive.

Their destination was a German Labour Front training centre set in heroic mountain scenery a little above Berchtesgaden itself. Situated still higher was the mountain retreat in which Hitler customarily recuperated from his official labours and, to quote Goebbels's propaganda hand-outs, drew creative inspiration from the beauties of nature.

They were greeted by Heydrich, who welcomed each man with an individual handshake. After taking Wesel aside for a brief consultation, he led the way to a deserted lecture-room.

The dais at the window end was occupied by a large oak table with a thick top. Facing this but below the platform, ten chairs stood in a single serried rank. Against the far wall was a long polished pinewood bench easily big enough to accommodate six men. The walls were bare, the windows spotless and the floor-boards scrubbed.

'Gentlemen,' Heydrich began, 'it is your honour and privilege not only to guarantee the Führer's personal safety but to act as his strong right arm. In view of your absolute allegiance to his person, you will do whatever has to be done here.

'Your task is to mete out an object lesson in respect of the Führer's projected euthanasia programme. This stresses the need to exterminate hereditarily diseased elements such as epileptics, persistent idlers, sex offenders, pacifists, lunatics and any similar undesirables who may still be infesting this great country of ours.

'I regret to say that the Führer's proposals have met with considerable opposition. Not only from the Roman Catholic Church, which has to preserve appearances in order to keep its

169

members in line, nor only from the medical specialists to whom chronic invalids represent a lucrative source of income. No, gentlemen, the opposition I refer to comes from Party members, some of whom hold senior rank.

'Ten of these suspect individuals have been summoned to appear here today. They comprise a Gauleiter, two deputy Gauleiters, four public information officers and three newspapermen, all of them editors of Party-approved publications.'

'May we know their names?'

'Their names are irrelevant – you'll be seeing them in the flesh soon enough. The Führer will demand an explanation of their subversive conduct. When he does, all you have to do is number them from left to right. I'll tell you which numbers to deal with.'

It was all over in less than half an hour. Although no official communiqué appeared, reports of this latest demonstration of the Führer's displeasure spread like wildfire, inside the Party and out.

The ten turned up nearly fifteen minutes before the appointed time, escorted by SS men. Wesel, who took charge of them at the lecture-room door, allotted them chairs in accordance with a prepared list. The whole operation was carried out in oppressive silence – everyone seemed to be wearing crêpe soles.

Heydrich, armed with a list of his own, hovered in the background. Wesel's men occupied the bench, poised and alert, hands near their holsters.

'Let things take their course,' Heydrich told them in an undertone. 'If one of them makes a false move, finish him.'

Then the Führer appeared. He entered the room with a buoyant and resolute step, accompanied by two of his aides. Everyone rose.

Hitler grasped Wesel's hand and shook it warmly. Glancing with slightly narrowed eyes at Heydrich and the Six, he mounted the platform. The big broad table dominated the room like a bastion. Posting himself behind it, Hitler gazed keenly at the ten unfortunates who had been called to account. His eyes travelled slowly down the line.

'Party members!' The first words emerged in a kind of strangled bark. 'I have been informed, though I find it hard to believe, that you have withheld your allegiance in a matter vital to our nation and the Fatherland. For what reason?'

None of the ten spoke. Some bowed their heads as it started to dawn on then what they were in for.

Meanwhile, the Führer had temporarily abandoned his inquisitor's pose for that of a prophet convinced of his historic mission.

'Life is a never-ending fight for survival,' he proclaimed. 'Our existence is governed by a law which decrees that the superior shall transcend the inferior, that the racially pure shall vanquish the dregs of humanity, that the sick must yield to the healthy. Anyone who fails to appreciate this has failed to read the signs of the times and is not one of us. It takes courage to draw the appropriate inference. You seem to lack that courage. Why?'

The ten accused maintained a dejected silence. They flinched when Wesel turned on them.

'Are you deaf?' he snapped. 'What have you got to say for yourselves? The Führer is waiting!'

At which point Adolf Hitler received three apologies. The first man pleaded that he must have misunderstood the Führer's intentions. He begged his pardon and an immediate opportunity to correct any regrettable misapprehension. The statements attributed to him must have been misinterpreted, if not actually misquoted. Two other penitents solemnly declared that they had been subjected to malicious misrepresentation, distortion and denunciation by rivals who coveted their Party posts.

Substantially different arguments were produced – though with due tact and humility – by only three.

The first: 'The whole subject mystifies me, my Führer, which is why I don't feel entitled to make any life-or-death decisions . . .'

The second: 'May I draw the Führer's attention to the need to pay special regard to the Church, in particular the Roman Catholic Church . . .'

The third: 'I mistakenly thought I was following the dictates of my conscience . . .'

From where they were sitting, Wesel's men had tagged the last three speakers 2, 5 and 7, but Heydrich issued whispered instructions to keep a sharp eye on 3, 4 and 9. 'They're our babies – they've been on my black-list far too long.'

Hitler, back in his Führer's role, gathered himself for a final peroration. 'All that can ensure our survival, all that can quell these threats from within and without, is absolute and unswerving loyalty. I am a living example of that quality. I give loyalty, but I demand it in return. The community is all, the individual nothing!'

He raised his hand in the Nazi salute and held it poised for several seconds. Then, almost as if he were fleeing the room, he hurried out.

The menacing vacuum in his wake was soon filled by Heydrich.

'You,' he said jabbing his forefinger at seven of the accused, ' – you can go, and be quick about it. Give thanks to God or the Führer, whichever.'

The seven men scuttled to the exit, eyes downcast, and disappeared without a backward glance.

Only three remained. Three ashen-faced, submissive and imploring figures.

Heydrich nodded at Wesel. 'They're all yours.'

'Right,' said Wesel. 'This is a special assignment for Berner and Bergmann. The rest of you, cover them.'

Heydrich's chosen victims were promptly taken in hand by the Siamese Twins, who slammed them against the nearest wall.

'Hands up, spread your legs. Don't move a muscle!'

Berner supervised the proceedings with his revolver while Bergmann submitted the trio to a swift and dexterous body-search.

Heydrich and Wesel stood expectantly by the window. The other four members of the Group remained on their bench, which commanded a grandstand view of the whole performance.

'They're clean,' Bergmann announced, looking crestfallen.

Heydrich was undeterred. 'What about their briefcases?'

Eagerly, Berner opened each one in turn. Apart from quantities of official-looking typescript, he unearthed the following items: a switch-blade in No. 3's briefcase, a Mauser 7.65 with a full magazine in No. 4's and a stick-grenade in No. 9's.

'There you are,' Heydrich said blandly, 'that's that.'

One of the accused cried, 'I don't know anything about concealed weapons, so help me! They must have been planted!'

Berner kicked him viciously. His head thudded against the wall and bloody bubbles oozed from his mouth and nostrils.

Wesel enlarged on Heydrich's lethal suggestion. 'If the swine attended this conference armed to the teeth, it can only mean they were planning to assassinate the Führer.'

'In that case,' Bergmann cried like a man inspired, 'they've signed their own death warrant. Will you leave them to us, Gruppenführer?'

'With pleasure,' said Wesel, when Heydrich had nodded his consent.

The Siamese twins needed no prompting. After a brief consultation they put the deterrent principle into practice with devastating effect.

Berner and Bergmann took the table behind which Hitler had been standing and inverted it so that the four legs jutted into the air. The Party member with the stick-grenade was spreadeagled and lashed to these with sash-cord and the grenade itself stuffed down his trousers so that it nestled against his genitals.

Heydrich, who had been watching with interest, retreated a little. 'Surely they're not going to detonate that in here,' he whispered to Wesel, ' – not with us around?'

'Don't worry, this is one of our specialities. Berner and Bergmann have run several tests – it works like a dream.'

The table was tilted sideways so that its thick top shielded everyone but the man lashed to the far side. Berner turned to Heydrich. 'There's a double safety factor,' he explained politely. 'The body, for one, plus a tabletop of solid oak. There's no need to take cover.'

Bergmann pulled the pin and stepped back a few paces. Five seconds later an explosion cut short the 'assassin's' screams and reduced him to mangled flesh and bone. The stench of explosive hung heavy in the air.

Next Berner advanced on the Party member whose briefcase had yielded the switch-blade. He weighed the weapon in his right hand. 'Were you really going to use this on the Führer?' he asked, more in sorrow than anger. Simultaneously, he drove the blade into the man's gut and levered it out with the aid of his knee. 'Or maybe you were going to stick it in here?' The knife sank home once more, just to the left of the man's breastbone. He slid down the wall with a liquid scream, incredulity in his eyes, which were fast glazing.

'Very impressive,' said Heydrich, whose predatory face had turned a shade paler. He nodded at Wesel and started coughing into his handkerchief.

Wesel was unmoved. 'Just a couple of samples from our extensive repertoire,' he said, then turned to his twin executioners. 'All right, get it over with!'

Bergmann handed Berner the pistol found in the last briefcase. 'Give the man his Mauser,' he said. 'Cock it and release the safety-catch.'

Berner did so. The man's trembling fingers tightened on the butt. He gazed desperately round the room.

'Right, you bastard,' Bergmann shouted, 'here's your chance. Try and drop me before I blow your brains out.'

The doomed man actually tried. Bergmann, watching his opponent's hand, hit the floor as he fired. The bullet smacked harmlessly into the wall. At the same moment, Bergmann squeezed the trigger.

The man's skull disintegrated.

'Nice work,' drawled Wesel.

There was something almost disquieting about the inactivity that reigned at the Villa in Feldafing during the days and weeks that followed.

Müller continued his lectures on investigative techniques. This time the emphasis was on observation, a generic term covering surveillance, tailing and information-gathering. It also embraced the study of tell-tale clues, their obliteration and falsification.

Painstakingly, the Gruppenführer hammered away at his men's spiritual armour. He was particularly fond of reading aloud from his own works, whether published or in progress, his main objective being to plumb the ultimate potentialities of obedience.

'That man Breslauer,' he was asked, 'are his lectures really relevant?'

Wesel assumed a look of majesty that suggested he had modelled it on the eyes in Anton Graff's portrait of Frederick the Great, a colour reproduction of which hung in the study of any Prussian aristocrat worth his salt. 'Your syllabus covers every subject I deem fit,' he replied loftily. 'I never take any step that hasn't been carefully planned in advance.'

Professor Breslauer lectured them almost daily now. He explored the essence of Judaism, its philosophical foundations, its historical development, its ethical, moral, social and religious postulates, and its practical bearing on self-preservation in times and circumstances like the present.

'Do we really have to sit there and take it?' Hagen protested. 'All that crap he keeps spouting about the Jews being a chosen race – I ask you, Gruppenführer! I just can't listen to the man.'

'Listen to every word he says,' Wesel enjoined all six of them, 'but never let him rile you into rash pronouncements. Examine every point he raises. Discuss it among yourselves and with me.'

'Not with Breslauer himself?'

'No point,' Wesel said. 'You'd never convince him. He's only here to parade his knowledge, and nobody knows his stuff better than Breslauer.'

'We feel like strangling him sometimes.'

'Perhaps, but keep a grip on yourselves. Take notes on every lecture. Afterwards, prepare individual summaries, complete with your own critical observations. These reports must be submitted to me regularly.'

'Is our next operation aimed at the Jews, then?'

'Never mind about that, gentlemen. Patience.'

Further statements made by ex-chauffeur Stephan Sobottke under interrogation by Captain Douglas G. Scott of US Military Intelligence:

The summer and autumn seemed to crawl by, somehow. There wasn't much to do except in the garage – I always kept my cars in tip-top condition. The rest of the time I looked after that professor of ours.

We got along like a house on fire, Breslauer and me. I looked after him as best I could – took his clothes to the cleaners, got his shoes repaired, bought him soap and so on. A decent sort, he was, Jew or no Jew.

He lived in a side wing – I think he was working on a book. Anyway, he was a nice old soul, like I said . . .

Could he move around freely? Well, yes, up to a point – the same as us. We all had to obey standing orders, and they were laid down by Wesel. The basic rule was, nobody went anywhere on his own, so one person could always keep tabs on the other. Why? Your guess is as good as mine, Captain. I was only on the outside looking in.

I remember chauffeuring Breslauer to Munich a few times. Libraries mostly, though he did visit the University and a couple of museums. No, never without an escort. Norden or Hagen were usually detailed to accompany him.

What was the atmosphere like on these outings? Pretty friendly, especially when Norden came along. They talked for hours, him and the Professor. Everything under the sun – history, philosophy, archaeology, religion, art, literature and the rest.

All I can say is, it was a goddamn boring summer and autumn, even if we did go out on the occasional exercise. Like night marches with map and compass after I'd dropped the teams at some god-forsaken spot in the wilds, or seven-day mountain survival exercises without rations – the young gentlemen were ordered to live off the land, which meant raiding some peasant's larder – or any other fun and games the Gruppenführer dreamed up. It wasn't any of my business what they did.

What happened to the Professor? No idea, worse luck – he could tell you how helpful I was. Helpful to a Jew, mark you! And God knows that wasn't easy in those days.

I can't recall anything else of interest. Oh yes, there was one thing: Wesel told me to get hold of a really pure-bred Dobermann with a pedigree a mile long, which I did. His name was Harras – Harras von Hohenheim. That livened the place up, I can tell you.

Wesel had assembled his men in the drawing-room after a body-building Bavarian supper. Presumably in memory of their trip to Rome, he plied them with some fragrant Frascati, a mellow golden wine of which Raffael had brought back several five-litre demijohns sheathed in straw.

The Gruppenführer stared ruminatively into space. 'Gentlemen,' he said at length, 'you've completed a tough spell of training, arduous in theory and exhausting in practice. This is just as it should be, but I'd quite understand if you felt the need for some more relaxation. Let me have your ideas on the subject.'

'You're right, Gruppenführer,' Hermann said. 'Every man feels like a bit of female company now and then.'

'You don't say!' Wesel laughed. 'What do you suggest we do about it?'

'Gruppenführer,' Hagen said gravely, 'if you don't mind my saying so, frankly I think we've grown out of that place in Leopold-strasse.'

Norden was quick to agree. 'He's right. Those girls are not in our class.'

'I suggest a visit to the Count instead,' Hagen proposed, meaning Elisabeth. 'We haven't been there for ages.'

'Shut your filthy mouth!' Norden's eyes flashed. 'How dare you mention the Countess and a brothel in the same breath!'

'I never even uttered her name,' retorted Hagen.

'That's enough!' Wesel barked. 'For certain very definite reasons, both alternatives must be ruled out.' He smiled. 'However, there is a third.'

The Six gave him an inquiring stare.

'Ever heard of Lebensborn – the Fount of Life?' he asked, watching their bewildered faces intently. 'The Fount of Life is an SS institution. Reichsführer Himmler sponsored it personally on the theory that pure Nordic stock must be conserved and propagated by the systematic and scientifically controlled breeding of racially pure offspring, regardless of bourgeois conventions, or narrow religious scruples.'

'What a splendid theory,' Norden mused.

'Great,' said Hagen, 'but it's the practical side that interests me. When do we get to see the inside of one of these stud farms, Gruppenführer?'

'We leave after lunch tomorrow.'

Gathering outside the Villa in holiday mood, they caught sight of a dog – a Dobermann with a glossy black coat and limpid eyes.

They all stared at it with varying degrees of curiosity. Siegfried was the only one to comment.

'What's he doing here?'

Sobottke, who'd just driven one of the Mercedes round to the front of the house, enlightened him. 'He answers to the name of Harras von Hohenheim – got a pedigree as long as your arm.'

'But what's he doing here?' Siegfried persisted.

'He's here, that's all.' The answer came from Raffael, who'd been detailed to drive Wesel's car.

'What a magnificent beast.' Siegfried's tone conveyed expert appreciation. He moved closer.

At that moment, with split-second timing, the Gruppenführer emerged. He was back in his favourite get-up, a stylized Bavarian suit adorned with green piping and bone buttons.

'No outside distractions, please!' he called brightly, looking at nobody in particular, not Siegfried and least of all the dog. 'Kindly concentrate on the job in hand – in this case, Operation Lebensborn. They're expecting us.'

Müller took advantage of the Group's convenient absence to have an undisturbed conversation with Breslauer. This presented problems because the Professor declined to receive him, claiming pressure of work. 'Besides,' he added, 'what is there left to discuss?'

'What indeed?' Müller brushed past the little old man. 'It's pointless talking to you because you're as good as dead.'

Breslauer shrugged, smiling faintly. 'Everyone has to die sometime, but it may take a little while longer to finish me off. After all, I've still got you.'

'I wouldn't bank on it,' Müller said implacably, 'not in your position. I know I got you off the hook once before, but miracles seldom come in pairs.'

Müller finally pierced Breslauer's armour with the aid of a bottle of champagne from Wesel's private reserve. 'I can get you as much as you like,' he said. 'You won't say no, not if I know you.'

He could afford to make such an offer because he possessed duplicate keys to every room in the Villa, even to the Gruppenführer's desk. He also knew the combination of Wesel's safe. There was little risk involved. Wesel wasn't the only man in the Villa assigned to surveillance. Müller had been given a special assignment too, and by no less a person than Heydrich. The security chief believed in double insurance.

It took three glasses of champagne to loosen Breslauer's tongue. 'When you come down to it,' he said, thawing a little, 'Wesel's men *are* an exceptional bunch.'

'They're a collection of well-trained dummies, Breslauer. You know that as well as I do.'

'Training often means temporarily displacing the subject's original personality, Müller. It needn't be permanently successful. There's always a chance of reversing the process, wiping the slate clean.'

'Not with these zombies.' Müller's response was brutally frank. 'Let's take them one by one: Hagen couldn't live without a licence to kill, Siegfried's a fool who clothes his baser instincts in high-flown sentiments, Hermann's criminal propensities are as plain as the nose on your face, and as for Berner and Bergmann – that pair of turtledoves would wipe out the population of Berlin just for kicks.'

'What about Norden?'

'Don't give me any crap about Norden – I know you've got a soft spot for the boy. You can talk culture with him, which is more than you can do with the others.'

'And yet . . . He's got the makings of a civilized person.'

'Honestly, Breslauer! He's a congenital dreamer with his head in the clouds and his feet five miles off the ground, which probably makes him the most lethal of the lot. Don't tell me you came back on account of Norden?'

'You're always asking what brought me back. All right, I'll tell you, but you won't believe me because it conflicts with your scheme of things. My real motive was – well, a sense of guilt, I suppose. It grew so strong I couldn't stand it any more.'

'Very funny.' Müller's forced laugh sounded more like a groan. 'Jews are fair game in Germany, haven't you grasped that yet? They're being exploited, deported and liquidated, but that's only a start – a modest beginning. And *you've* got a guilt complex? You damned fool!'

Breslauer was still smiling. 'I didn't pluck this sense of guilt out of the air, Müller. Very gradually and by devious means, I've come to realize that we all bear a personal responsibility for these

179

symptoms of our age. All of us! Academics, authors, churchmen, journalists, educators, parents, lawyers, policemen – we've all failed.'

'Goddammit, Breslauer! Who the hell do you æsthetes think you are? What are you planning to do, succeed where Jesus Christ failed? The world's a sewer and always has been, certainly for the past four or five thousand years. Murder and betrayal are built into the human psyche – *nobody* can change that.'

'You're entitled to your opinion, Müller, but the real point is this: if people like us throw in the towel, it spells the collapse of a dam founded on morality, faith and conscience. Then and only then do the forces of destruction and corruption come to full flood – only then, not before.'

'And you'd die like a dog to prevent that?'

'If there's no alternative, yes.'

The two cars took 25 minutes to reach their destination, a former country estate re-entitled a 'State Recreation Centre'. Situated on the edge of the grounds was the Lebensborn Institute.

The whole place had an air of supreme cleanliness and respectability. The wrought-iron gate was freshly painted, the smart and soldierly-looking gatekeeper attired in paramilitary uniform, the well-tended garden threaded with pale gravel paths and dotted with boxwood shrubs clipped into neat green spheres. Beyond the flower-beds, bristling with scarlet rose-bushes, loomed the Institute itself.

They were expected. Waiting on the steps was SS-Obersturmbannführer Dr Rolf Harnberg, a short, dapper man with a pear-shaped head and rimless glasses which conferred a resemblance to Heinrich Himmler. He was wearing a pale blue suit and a grey silk tie.

'Welcome, Gruppenführer!' he exclaimed brightly, grasping Wesel's outstretched hand. 'Would your officers like to go into action at once, or shall I begin by saying a few words about the aims and objectives of our establishment?'

Wesel made a gesture that embraced the entire party. 'We're insatiably curious, my dear doctor. Please enlighten us.'

Extracts from Dr Harnberg's introductory remarks, a standard lecture which he himself preserved in written form:

I must draw your attention to the fact that this Institute is still in something of an evolutionary stage. Our work has yet to receive formal recognition. However, being in the process of developing a pilot scheme for duplication on a nationwide scale, we welcome your wholehearted assistance.

The following sequence of events is initiated by the granting of a Fount of Life permit. In addition to personal particulars, this permit embodies a list of scientifically ascertained racial characteristics and the results of a thorough medical examination. In your case, gentlemen, these data have already been extracted from documents made available to us in advance.

Now a word or two about the young women who have entrusted themselves to our care and with whom you are to consummate a union based entirely on free personal choice. I need hardly tell you that consideration has been paid to the æsthetic aspect of these encounters and their hoped-for consequences. All your partners are drawn from carefully selected human material. In other words, they have healthy bodies, beauty of a suitably Nordic cast, and a sound family background. Above all, their racial origins have been exhaustively researched.

In practice, the selection of these women takes the following form. Some of them are childless volunteers who approach us on their own initiative, others are sponsored by Party members or next of kin – sometimes by their own husbands. Each applicant is thoroughly checked for suitable personal conduct and repute, the police being requested to supply a no-criminal-record certificate. If all these conditions are fulfilled, the applicant is personally interviewed and pledged to secrecy. Last of all comes a rigorous medical examination performed by myself.

The selected women and girls receive a solemn guarantee of absolute discretion, free board and lodging while resident on our premises, and generous financial compensation for loss of time or earnings. In the event of a successful union, they are further guaranteed a bonus payment and free admission to one of our excellent maternity homes. Every child of such a union is granted a subsistence allowance payable monthly until its eighteenth birthday. Should a mother decide to relinquish custody of her child, she can entrust it to us in return for an assurance that it will be carefully reared, given a first-class education and ultimately offered a post in the government service.

'What an admirable scheme!' Gruppenführer Wesel nodded his approval of this lecture, though he was not unduly impressed by the lecturer himself. Despite his apparent talent for organization, Harnberg struck him as pedantic – a medical soul-searcher with a far too theoretical approach.

'You say they're a good selection?' Norden asked.

Dr Harnberg looked a little hurt. 'Only the best are good enough for our purposes,' he said. 'Some of our inmates are ladies from the upper reaches of the Party whom their husbands have failed to impregnate.'

'I see,' said Hagen. 'You mean we may be adding a twig to a Gauleiter's family tree? Fine, let's do our duty for the Fatherland.'

'Us too?' inquired Berner, who was standing close to Bergmann. He lowered his voice. 'If there's any way of avoiding it, Gruppenführer, we'd be grateful – you understand.'

'Of course I do.' Wesel's tone was sympathetic but his eyes shone with glee. 'Except, my son, that you aren't here for your own amusement. This is a form of national service, and no conscientious objectors are allowed. Even Raffael's going to do his stuff.'

Raffael grimaced as if he'd bitten on a lemon.

'One more thing, gentlemen,' Dr Harnberg said. 'I should point out that this process consists of four consecutive phases. Total success cannot be guaranteed unless each is strictly observed. Is that clear? Very well, kindly follow me.'

Dr Harnberg conducted Wesel and his men to a balcony room on the first floor for the first phase – inspection. The filmy net curtains afforded a perfect view of the sunlit garden behind the house.

Eight voluptuous young women could be seen strolling, reading, playing ball or sunbathing.

'Genuine beauties!' murmured Dr Harnberg. 'And now, gentlemen, may I ask you to notify me of your preferences so that everything can take its well-ordered course?'

Hagen reacted swiftly. 'The girl at the table on the right, reading a book – that's the one I want.'

'So do I!' Norden said at once.

Wesel immediately grasped the reason. The girl with the book in her hand bore a striking resemblance to Countess Elisabeth.

'No bickering, gentlemen,' he commanded. 'The lady is assigned to Raffael.'

The six men trooped downstairs to the garden but lingered on the terrace. Then, having conducted a last-minute survey and reached final agreement, they resolutely advanced on the waiting females to complete phase two – introduction. The women were just as well rehearsed. They remained demure, barely glancing at their appointed benefactors.

Gallantly, each man bowed to the lady of his choice. No surnames were mentioned, and both parties employed the familiar mode of address customary between card-carrying National Socialists.

'Splendid young fellows!' Dr Harnberg said approvingly. He and Wesel were still following developments from behind the transparent curtains. 'First-class breeding stock. I can hardly wait to see the outcome of their endeavours.'

Wesel stared at him with a hint of scepticism. 'What makes you so sure they'll click? Aren't you being a little over-optimistic?'

'In an hour at most,' Dr Harnberg said confidently, 'perfect harmony will reign. Coffee, cake and fruit-juice work wonders in conjunction with some pleasant background music in the Mozart to Strauss range. In my experience, there's a rapid transition from idle conversation to exchanges of a more intimate and stimulating nature.'

Rapid was an understatement. Only 25 minutes had elapsed when the first couple – Hermann and a young woman alias 'Anneliese' – rose and disappeared into the house. The others were fired by their example. Another ten minutes and the garden was deserted.

'Excellent!' said Dr Harnberg, rubbing his hands. 'I congratulate your men on their devotion to duty. The occasion promises to be a complete success.'

During the third phase – procreation – Waldemar Wesel had

retired to an armchair in the balcony room and was staring at some lines of illuminated Gothic script in a silver frame:

> 'Millions of women
> love the new State,
> sacrifice themselves
> and pray for it.
> They sense,
> in their natural instinct,
> a mission to preserve our nation,
> which they themselves
> have presented with a living pledge
> in the persons of their children.'
>
> *Adolf Hitler addressing the*
> *Reichstag on 13 July 1934.*

'Very apt,' said Wesel, stretching his legs luxuriously. 'A little refreshment would be welcome, Doctor, but preferably not fruit-juice. I don't have to perform myself.'

Harnberg produced a well chilled bottle of Bocksbeutel – a 1933 Randersackerer Teufelskeller Spätlese of outstanding quality.

'If you're interested, Gruppenführer,' he said confidentially, 'I could, of course, arrange something special for you. We've just been told to expect a new patient – the second wife of a Gauleiter, an extremely attractive young woman whose single desire is to present her Führer with children. Between you and me, the Gauleiter can't manage it.'

'Some other time, Doctor. However, do keep me informed of any similar cases – I'm always in the market for stray items of inside information.' Wesel stared thoughtfully into his glass. 'You really think my men will come up to scratch?'

'Of course,' said Harnberg. 'Everything's provided. Our patients' rooms are luxuriously appointed – soundproof walls, lavish bathrooms, record players complete with suitable selections . . . The windows can be darkened to enhance the atmosphere and the beds are five-star.'

'And you think that's enough?'

'You're wondering if they'll suffer from the inhibitions that sometimes afflict men in their more vulnerable moments.' Dr Harnberg smiled the smile of an experienced professional who leaves nothing to chance. 'Snags of that kind, Gruppenführer, are allowed for. I take the precaution of discussing them with the women in advance. In the event of any such problems developing, I advise them to resort to manual or, if necessary, oral stimulation.'

'Good,' said Wesel, not unimpressed. 'So your patients know one end of a prick from the other, eh?'

'In a sense.' Dr Harnberg was at a loss to cope with Wesel's layman's phraseology. He strove hard to devise an apt response but was spared the need because just at that moment a buzzer sounded. The three dots and a dash were reminiscent of the opening bars of Beethoven's 5th Symphony.

'Good heavens!' The Lebensborn director glanced at his wristwatch. 'That means the first treatment is complete. Less than half an hour – a record! Permit me to congratulate you yet again, Gruppenführer.'

Hermann was the first to finish, largely because he had been the first into action. For the Fourth phase – de-briefing – he was ushered into Dr Harnberg's consulting-room by a Fount of Life attendant.

Harnberg was already seated at his desk with the air of a scientist convinced of his own infallibility. Above his head hung another of the Führer's aphorisms, this time from *Mein Kampf:*

> 'The steadfast aim
> of female education
> must be
> the mother-to-be.'

Wesel stood near the window, no less conspicuous for being in the background. His presence invested the interview that followed with a certain solemnity. It also enjoined honesty, sincerity and candour.

Dr Harnberg was eager to complete his questionnaire. 'Obersturmführer Hermann, we should now appreciate your help in listing certain particulars that will be used in the preparation of important medical and genetic records.'

Hermann glanced at his commanding officer and received an encouraging nod.

'Your partner is registered here under the name Anneliese. Is that correct?'

'Yes, and I can thoroughly recommend her. I wouldn't trade her for the best screw in Leopoldstrasse – and I'll put that in writing if you like, Doctor.'

Harnberg remained businesslike. 'So intercourse took place?'

'You bet it did! Twice, as a matter of fact. Once after five minutes and the second time fifteen minutes later.'

Dr Harnberg made the following entries on his form: names, date and times, to wit, 16.05 and 16.20. 'Did an ejaculation occur on both occasions?'

'Yes,' Hermann said modestly. 'I was feeling nice and rested.'

Dr Harnberg made another note: 'Impregnation probable.' He looked up. 'Thank you, Obersturmführer. Only another four weeks and the results of your work will be confirmed.'

This registration procedure was repeated, with the same scholarly attention to detail, six more times. Even Raffael, Berner and Bergmann contributed to the Fount of Life card index. Harnberg was visibly delighted.

'Your men,' he told Wesel, 'are a credit to you.'

Dusk was falling by the time the Group returned to Feldafing. Dew lay heavy on the lawn, promising a cold clear summer night. The temperature had dropped and a log fire was already burning on the open hearth in the drawing-room.

Far from showing any sign of fatigue, the men walked with a springy step and talked in loud voices as though to demonstrate their general well-being. Wesel watched them disembark with bland approval, then glanced up at the terrace.

Harras von Hohenheim was waiting on the top step. The dog stared at the approaching men fixedly, yearningly.

'That animal's still hanging around,' Hagen said. 'Looks as if he wants something.'

'His supper, I expect.' Siegfried walked up to the dog. 'All animals have to eat some time.'

Raffael, prompted by a look from Wesel, intervened. 'The cook has orders to feed him. I'm sure she already has – he's got a gut on him like Falstaff.'

'All the same,' Siegfried said, adopting his vet's tone, 'he doesn't seem happy. He needs somebody to look after him.'

'There's nothing about it in standing orders,' Raffael said quickly.

Led by Wesel, the others strode past the dog without giving it a second glance. Raffael and Siegfried were left alone on the terrace. They stood there in silence with the dog at their feet. Siegfried studied Harras more closely.

'This dog needs a handler,' he said.

Raffael shrugged. 'Maybe, but Wesel never mentioned it. He hasn't said anything either way.'

'So he hasn't expressly forbidden us to take an interest in the animal?'

'No . . .' Raffael spun the syllable out. 'No, not exactly.'

'Well somebody has to look after it. If nobody else wants to, I will.'

As if he had followed every word, Harras licked Siegfried's hand. Siegfried's fingers buried themselves in the fur behind the dog's ears and scratched his neck with a gentle circular motion. Joyously, Harras reared on his hind legs and put his paws on Siegfried's chest.

It was the prelude to a friendship – and a tragedy.

A few days later Müller went into action again, outlining preliminary plans for another special assignment. Wesel stressed the importance of this conference by attending it in person.

Müller spread a map on the table. Examining it with a practised eye, the members of the Group saw that it was a blown-up section of a street map. It showed a row of detached houses set in spacious green expanses dotted with sizeable clumps of trees.

'Our next sphere of operations is Berlin,' Müller announced. 'To be exact, the residential suburb of Dahlem. You'll see that the central complex has been ringed with red pencil. Our objective can be reconnoitred with comparative ease and is readily accessible from all directions.'

Hagen cocked an eyebrow. 'Berlin's not our stamping-ground. What are we expected to do, give a guest performance?'

'More or less,' Wesel said, 'and it's going to be a smash hit.

You wouldn't be getting the assignment if there wasn't a very good reason. Herr Müller will explain what it is.'

'You've got a thorough job of work to do,' Müller said. 'Gory work – dirty work too, not to put too fine a point on it. You're going to stage a raid on somebody's house. An armed robbery, in standard CID terminology. At least, that's the impression you've got to create. Can anyone tell me why?'

Hermann, with his well developed instinct for violence in all its forms, was the first to catch on. 'The police are apt to assume that housebreakings are local jobs. We're going to throw them off by commuting between Munich and Berlin.'

'Right, Hermann.' Wesel's benevolent nod signified that Hermann's Swiss bank account would soon be swelled by a bonus.

'What's our objective?'

'A villa rented by the US Embassy,' replied Wesel. 'The occupant is only a commercial attaché, but he's dedicated to the spreading of Jewish poison. The man not only casts doubt on the legitimacy of the Reich, he vilifies our country and broadcasts accusations against the Führer. He persistently makes trouble for us in the eyes of the world.'

'I see,' Hagen said simply. 'So he's got to go. Is that our assignment?'

'Yes,' said Müller, 'but you've got to bear the following points in mind. The attaché doesn't live alone. He's got a wife and two children – two boys, nine and eleven. Apart from them, there's a German maid, a French cook and an English chauffeur. That makes a total of seven occupants.'

Hermann shrugged. 'A few extra bodies don't matter.'

'All that *does* matter,' Wesel put in, 'is to set a lasting example. We must issue a stern warning to any other foreigners who feel tempted to abuse our hospitality.'

The policeman in Müller clung to practicalities. 'The first thing is to familiarize ourselves with our objective, using the results of preliminary investigations made by our Berlin colleagues. They'll need checking out. Once that's done, we can launch a concentrated effort of our own.'

'Think it over,' Wesel said briskly. 'At our next meeting I shall expect you to produce constructive recommendations. Any more questions?'

Siegfried raised his hand. 'Could Harras take part in the operation – you know, the Dobermann? He's coming on beautifully, Gruppenführer. I've seldom met a dog with quicker reactions. He could easily be taught to attack specified targets.'

Wesel gazed at the Führer's portrait on the wall facing him. 'Our plans make no allowance for a dog, Siegfried. Nobody ever encouraged you to train Harras as a supernumerary member of our unit, let alone issued any instructions to that effect. If you choose to spend time on the animal, it's nobody's business but your own. Do I make myself clear?'

'Yessir,' Siegfried replied smartly, though the true significance of Wesel's remarks escaped him.

After a further series of exercises, Gruppenführer Wesel pronounced his men ripe for another day's relaxation.

Berner and Bergmann were given free rein in recognition of their past achievements. Wesel authorized them to visit any of Munich's homosexual haunts. The only proviso was that they should observe and report on any senior Party officials patronizing the same establishments who were known to them by sight.

In response to his own eager entreaty, Siegfried was permitted to take Harras for a walk in Munich, either in the Hofgarten or – better still – in the English Gardens, which offered greater scope for canine exercise. Wesel's single stipulation was 'Steer clear of that new art gallery they're building – the Führer designed it personally. Don't let your friend cock his leg against it or there could be trouble.'

Wesel turned to Hermann. 'You, my boy, will act as my personal escort for the day. I'm planning to lunch with Count von der Tannen at the Osteria Bavaria, which happens to be the Führer's favourite restaurant as well as mine. I don't want any eavesdroppers or interlopers, get it?'

'Yessir!'

'As for you two,' Wesel continued, smiling benignly at Norden and Hagen, 'I've already fixed you up with a social engagement. You're going to the opera with Countess Elisabeth. Some sentimental trash or other – *La Bohème*, I believe. Anyway, you'll find four tickets waiting for you at the box office.'

'Why four, Gruppenführer?' Hagen demanded alertly. 'The Countess, Norden and me – that makes three.'

Wesel's smile became a smirk. 'The fourth member of your party will be an aunt of the Countess, the Baroness Weitershausen. She used to be lady-in-waiting to the last German Empress.'

'A chaperone?' Hagen ventured, looking faintly amused. 'Does she really have to come along?'

'The Baroness will ensure that you behave like officers and gentlemen.' Wesel chuckled. 'Which is just as it should be, eh?'

'Certainly, Gruppenführer!' said Norden.

Elisabeth's aunt, the Baroness, was waiting for them in the middle of the opera house lobby, a tall, commanding figure with the vocal equipment of a guardsman. Elisabeth looked frail beside her.

Hagen approached her with exaggerated deference, seized her hand and applied it briskly to his lips.

'An appropriate gesture, young man,' she commented icily, 'but a trifle short on technique. You don't take possession of a lady when you kiss her hand, you convey your tender regard for her sex. You don't grab her fingers and haul them towards you, neither do you touch them with your lips. Let's start again from the beginning.'

She then transferred her attention to Norden. He impressed her as far more dutiful, sensitive and eager to please – someone who might in happier days have made an ideal tutor to the imperial household.

'Give me your arm, boy,' she bellowed, and marched off.

The State Opera's former royal box was now reserved for the Führer, his inner circle, foreign dignitaries and members of the Bavarian regional government. The Wesel Group belonged to this privileged élite. The party seated themselves amid the lustrous gilding and rich crimson of caryatids and velvet armchairs.

Before the overture began, the Baroness lodged a few very vocal criticisms: The box was too brightly lit, the balcony rail too high, the orchestra barely visible. Personally, she preferred first-row orchestra seats. At this point the conductor raised his baton.

The opera, as Wesel had predicted, was *La Bohème*. Hagen began drowsing almost immediately. Norden, for whom Richard Wagner alone was sublime, rebelled against any insidious Italian attempt to dilute the profundity of the Germanic world of ideas and emotions. He was almost physically revolted by the opera's Latin decadence.

Countess Elisabeth, on the other hand, seemed engrossed in the music, but was leaning back with an expression of detachment from the happenings on stage. The Baroness started to yawn unashamedly during Act 1, and soon afterwards fell asleep. Elisabeth smiled. Norden felt sure she was smiling at him and glowed with pleasure. Then she leant back still further, and Hagen, who was sitting just behind her, leant forwards as though striving to capture every note.

Without moving the upper part of his body, Hagen put out his left hand. Invisible to Norden, it casually alighted on the back of Elisabeth's chair, slid down and touched her arm, gripped it and clung there. Elisabeth started, then acted as if nothing had happened. Hagen's fingers tightened, relaxed, and climbed the smooth slope to her left breast.

'Your tiny hand is frozen,' the tenor sang. 'Let me warm it into life . . .'

Act I ended and the house lights came on, flooding the box and auditorium with radiance. The Baroness was awake in a flash. 'Poof!' she said loudly. 'That kind of maudlin drivel would send anyone to sleep!'

'I quite agree, Baroness,' Norden said. 'It is a little on the sentimental side.'

'What about you, Countess?' asked Hagen. 'Were you disappointed too?'

Elisabeth looked pensive. 'Not altogether,' she replied in a subdued voice. 'I wouldn't quarrel with my aunt's opinion. She's right – from her own point of view. On the other hand, every performance has its moments if you wait for them. It pays to be patient.'

'How right you are!' Norden cried fervently. 'Just what I was going to say myself.'

A few days later Professor Breslauer went for an evening stroll with Müller across the moors near Feldafing.

'I think I can see a glimmer of light!'

'At the end of whose tunnel,' said Müller. 'Yours?'

'No, I'm talking about Wesel and his men.'

'You're hopeless, Professor. Only someone like you could see glimmers of light in a world of utter darkness.'

'Wesel has asked me if I can recommend somebody competent to acquaint his men with the beauties of modern painting, notably the German Expressionists. As you know, he hung three particularly outstanding examples of Expressionist painting in the library a few days ago. He must have had his reasons.'

'Quite, except that they aren't the ones you're thinking of.'

They had reached the summit of a hill on the edge of the village. The view was serenely beautiful: verdant meadows, groves of dark blue fir against the paler green of isolated birch-trees, and three fish-ponds like eyes gazing mildly at the sky.

'What a magnificent country,' Breslauer said, quite dispassionately. 'Who can resist the appeal of natural beauty? Nobody, in the long run. That's what I'm banking on, Müller, and that's where these paintings come in. A youngster like Norden, with his eagerness to discover a meaning behind his personal existence, can't fail to be impressed by them. Siegfried too, perhaps. Have you noticed how much affection he lavishes on that dog of his?'

'Yes, but only for disciplinary purposes. He's putting an edge on the beast – turning it into a weapon with teeth.'

'You're wrong.' Breslauer spoke with absolute conviction. 'Siegfried loves that dog. I find that another hopeful sign.'

'God Almighty!' Müller exploded. 'Why do you always wallow in wishful thinking? Haven't you fathomed Wesel's basic principle yet? It's not only diabolical – it's brilliant, and perfectly in line with Nazi psychology. You systematically eradicate every scrap of affection, every human tie and emotion. Then, having created an emotional vacuum, you fill it by fixating your victims on a single overriding relationship. With what? Führer, Fatherland and all the other cheap platitudes, of course! The Germans have been harangued till they're punch-drunk, so now they lie back and let it happen. Damn fools! They deserve to be trampled underfoot – that's why I help to stomp on them myself. It may bring them to their senses at the last minute.'

Breslauer shook his head sadly. 'You're an overworked policeman, Müller – your vision's been distorted by the sight of too much blood. You've forgotten something vital, something which asserts its right to exist against all odds: man himself, mankind – humanity!'

'And you think you've found some humanity in this place? You think it can be mobilized by looking at pictures? By training a dog? By listening to your lectures on Judaism? Goddamn it, Breslauer, stop trying to live in a world where you don't amount to more than a pinch of bone-meal. You're as good as dead but you refuse to accept the fact.'

Statement volunteered by the art historian Dr Gustav Penzberg, an expert on German Expressionist painting:

Everything reputed to have happened in those days should be viewed in relative terms. I mean that preconceived ideas should be avoided at all costs. I know the Third Reich produced phenomena such as the Munich exhibition entitled 'Degenerate Art'. People are always citing it, but it was really designed to satisfy the primitive instincts of the herd – or earn some foreign exchange.

In reality, even senior Party officials cherished a genuine appreciation of this type of art. I was privileged to advise a Gauleiter who collected paintings by Paul Klee, and one senior civil servant of my acquaintance was absolutely crazy about Franz Marc. I also negotiated the purchase of three works by Macke for Professor Troost, the Führer's original architect-in-chief.

And I shall never forget an afternoon I spent at a villa in Feldafing, where my knowledge of Expressionism aroused the greatest possible interest. I was able to illustrate the true significance, æsthetic appeal and outstanding merits of this school of painting with the aid of three pictures which, even to a connoisseur like myself, were works of unusual perfection.

The first was a turbulent seascape by Nolde, filled with a ferocious interplay of light and colour. Then came an infinitely touching little child by Paula Modersohn-Becker, in shades of dark brown against the shimmering greyish-white of a birch-tree.

Last of all, a range of buildings fascinatingly dissected into explosive planes of colour that seemed to be rocketing skywards – a masterpiece by Feininger.

I have seldom been blessed with a more attentive, receptive and committed audience than the young men I lectured that afternoon. They wanted to know everything, and I told them all I knew – with considerable enthusiasm, I may add. I should also like to stress that I was treated with the utmost courtesy.

'Well,' Wesel said briskly, after Dr Penzberg had departed, 'there you have it, straight from the horse's mouth. They're a valuable bunch of pictures. The Nolde's supposed to be a prize specimen – Penzberg says it would bring a hundred thousand marks from a foreign buyer.'

He studied each of the six in turn, studiously ignoring the Dobermann sprawled at Siegfried's feet. 'A hundred thousand marks,' he repeated. 'Aren't you impressed?'

'Money's no criterion,' Hermann said, 'not to us.'

'Quite right,' said Wesel. 'Would anyone like to add anything?'

Hagen sneered. 'It looks like somebody's been rolling around in his own vomit. All it does is make me want to puke myself.'

'Anybody disagree?' asked Wesel.

'No,' Norden said cautiously, 'except that it does possess a certain rarity value.'

'Sure,' retorted Hagen, 'the same way as no two assholes are identical. From that point of view, every dog-turd's unique.' Hagen never passed up an opportunity to cross swords with Norden. 'If you want my opinion, the people who perpetrated these abortions were gambling on the perverted taste of a decadent society.'

'Excellently put,' said Wesel. 'Well, gentlemen, what's the logical inference?'

Bergmann glanced at Berner, who was only too ready to help the proceedings along. 'Maybe Siegfried ought to get his dog to piss on them.'

Siegfried indignantly dismissed this suggestion. 'Harras never cocks his leg indoors. Mind you, if the pictures were taken out into the garden and propped against one of his favourite trees, he might be induced to . . .'

'Too leisurely!' Wesel ruled. 'I want an immediate and decisive response – here and now.'

Hagen was the first to grasp Wesel's message. He rose, walked deliberately over to the Nolde, produced a knife from his hip-pocket, flicked it open and cut the picture to ribbons.

Hermann joined his brother officer with alacrity. Borrowing Hagen's knife, he plunged it into the picture by Paula Modersohn-Becker, *Child and Birch-tree*, painted on card in 1904. First he stabbed the eyes of the weeping child, then its slightly out-thrust stomach, then he slashed its arms and legs. And so on, until only the bare frame remained.

Not to be outdone, Hermann picked up the Feininger, flung it to the ground and performed a war-dance on it. Then, with a single mighty kick, he sent its mangled remains flying into the far corner of the room.

Wesel nodded. 'Nothing that isn't ours has any right to exist. And that, gentlemen, is a point that merits our fullest and most wholehearted acceptance. Carry on!'

Preparations continued for their Berlin project, the raid on the villa in Dahlem and its occupant, the US commercial attaché, pronounced by Wesel to be 'an extremely undesirable and subversive individual'.

'The man has just made another nuisance of himself,' Wesel told them. 'He gave a malicious interview to the *New York Times*, which claims to be a newspaper of international standing but is really a capitalist rag run by a gang of Jews. Never mind, what do we care about the sewers of Wall Street? New York's a long way off, unlike Berlin.

'Well, Herr Müller,' he went on, 'how do you suggest we approach this special assignment?'

'There doesn't seem to be any special hurry, Gruppenführer. That gives us scope for thorough preparation. How much time can you allow us?'

'Six or eight weeks if you like – say until the end of December – no later than then.'

'A nice little surprise package for Christmas, is that what you had in mind?'

'Not a bad idea, Müller. It might help maximize the deterrent effect. I accept your suggestion.'

Müller proceeded to outline his plan. It included a number of communal excursions to Berlin – visits to museums, evenings at the opera, concerts, reference work in libraries and a study of the Führer's latest architectural projects.

'And any other form of activity along those lines,' Wesel added. 'We have to be able to prove your trips were made for educational purposes.'

'But the Group mustn't operate as a unit,' said Müller. 'I suggest you proceed separately, using different means of transport but all with the same end in view: a detailed reconnaissance of the premises, immediate surroundings, terrain, disposition and habits of occupants, etcetera. These patrols should be undertaken late at night if possible, round about the time set for the raid. A few minutes either side of midnight might be best.'

'May I ask a question?' Siegfried was having difficulty in controlling Harras, who had suddenly grown restive. He put one arm round the dog's neck and it nestled obediently against his legs. Müller watched the idyllic picture with a frown, then nodded.

'This Berlin assignment – who's to put the finishing touches to it? I mean, which of us will gun the bastard down?'

'I don't suppose that'll emerge till your final briefing,' Müller replied warily. 'Maybe not till you're on the spot. Anyway, it's up to the Gruppenführer to decide who actually pulls the trigger.'

Wesel's eyes narrowed. 'Do I take it that you're anxious to do the job yourself, Siegfried?'

'Yes, Gruppenführer.'

'Why?'

'I hope you'll pardon me for saying so, but I still haven't been actively involved in a major assignment. I've never operated solo.'

'And you're eager to do so now?'

'Yes, Gruppenführer. Please let me prove myself.'

Wesel sat back, staring almost dreamily at Siegfried. He glanced at the dog, but only for a moment.

'I'm a methodical person, Siegfried, as I expect you've noticed. I never neglect any member of the Group. You all possess outstanding qualities, but they differ. To obtain the best possible results, I always have to take those differences into account.

'As for your request, I may very well grant it when the time comes – and with pleasure. I need hardly add that you would have to accept the assignment with no reservation whatsoever concerning any person or thing.'

The final word contained an allusion which only Müller, with his legal training, interpreted correctly. Under a current law – one that dated from the last century but would doubtless endure for centuries to come, given the prevailing German mentality, and might even outlast Hitler's Thousand-Year Reich – the term 'thing' embraced all that wasn't human.

Like an animal. For instance, a dog.

Some days later, after the communal evening meal, Müller invited Norden to join him in an informal discussion. Wesel had departed for Munich with Raffael, ostensibily to call on the Führer. The Group's time-table prescribed a choice of 'indoor recreational activities'.

Berner and Bergmann had retired to one or another of their rooms on the pretext of study. Hagen and Hermann were downstairs in the firing range, testing some specially doctored revolver ammunition. They had filed crosses into the bullets, but with disappointing results: their greater destructive power was offset by reduced accuracy.

Meanwhile, Siegfried was devoting his full attention to Harras, whose training was progressing rapidly. Norden had been planning to immerse himself in some politically edifying literature when Müller buttonholed him.

The policeman offered him some extra tuition, but first he proposed a stroll. 'It's a relief to snatch a breath of fresh air – I sometimes feel it's in short supply round here.'

After taking a turn in the grounds, they headed for Breslauer's quarters. Müller made the suggestion and Norden accepted it with no sign of reluctance – in fact he might almost have been waiting for him to broach the subject.

They found Breslauer at his desk, which was littered with books. His obvious displeasure at Müller's intrusion quickly evaporated when he saw Norden. He greeted his visitors and invited them to sit down.

'We happened to be passing,' Müller said, lowering his bulk into a chair, 'so we decided to drop in. I thought it might be a good opportunity to retrieve that issue of the *Völkischer Beobachter* I lent you.'

Having established a quasi-official reason for the visit, Müller heaved a contented sigh.

'Know something?' he said. 'I don't think I've finished walking off my supper. If you won't miss me too much, I'll do another couple of laps round the garden.'

A minute later they had the place to themselves. The elderly Jewish professor and the youthful representative of the master race sat looking at each other, keenly but courteously.

Breslauer was wearing a thick woollen cardigan. He seemed relaxed. The aureole of thinning snow-white hair invested his domed forehead with a kind of majesty.

Almost half a century younger, Norden sat there like a steel spring, his face illumined by a pair of watchful eyes. His hands were tightly clasped together.

It was Breslauer who broke the oppressive silence. He indicated the jumble of books, newspapers and magazines on his desk. 'The Gruppenführer collected these and put them at my disposal. They all deal with the subject I'm meant to be lecturing you on: Judaism. Are you familiar with their contents, Herr Norden?'

Norden nodded.

'Nothing could be more biased. Are you aware how absurd this material must seem to me?'

'Material compiled by you and your kind, Professor, would probably seem the same to me.'

'True,' said Breslauer, 'but that's just what always depresses me so much. It doesn't matter who runs the world or holds the reins of power, his claim to authority can always be buttressed by some form of evidence – even by some brand of historico-philosophical theory.'

Norden corrected him, politely but firmly. 'I don't think your view of things is altogether accurate, Herr Breslauer, particularly in regard to us National Socialists. Problems of authority don't bother us in the least. Our task is to impose a new and unshakeable ideology.'

'Look,' Breslauer said, extracting a book at random from the pile. 'Here's a treatise on Jewish characteristics – on our allegedly innate lust for money, our sadistic joy at the misfortunes of others, our morbid urge to seduce little children. Do you believe this rubbish?'

'Are you trying to pick a quarrel with me?' Norden countered, controlling himself with evident difficulty.

Breslauer simply stared at him. The question did not seem to merit an answer. He picked up a newspaper, opened it and held it out.

'Here's a product I'm sure you're familiar with. Yes, Herr Norden, it's *Der Stürmer*, a Party-approved paper edited by one of Hitler's oldest cronies. Only somebody with a cast-iron stomach could fail to be revolted by Streicher and his effusions. How about you?'

'*Der Stürmer*'s only fit for lavatory paper, Professor. I don't even deign to acknowledge its existence.'

'But that's precisely what you should do, Herr Norden. Crude and disgusting it may be, but it has a circulation of six hundred thousand. At a conservative estimate, that means two million people read it. How can you shut your eyes to that?'

Norden was unmoved. 'You really must keep a sense of proportion, Professor. If we include persons of German stock resident on what is still technically described as foreign soil, the German race may be estimated to number one hundred and sixty million. What do the two million readers of *Der Stürmer* amount to, on that basis? Roughly one-eightieth of the population.'

'And you don't find it reprehensible to pervert the public on such a massive scale?'

'Necessary, Professor, not reprehensible. It's a kind of adult education course for the intellectually immature. Banner headlines and crude caricatures are what they need.'

'So the end justifies the means, is that what you're implying?'

'If you don't mind my saying so, I think we ought to disregard such trivia. They're far beneath our intellectual level, Professor. You don't have the slightest reason to worry about them personally, so why bother?'

'Because I must always be prepared – even here in this house – to encounter someone who regards me as a typical *Stürmer* Jew: a greedy, greasy, shifty, lecherous and thoroughly unscrupulous individual. Is that how you see me?'

'You know I don't, Professor.'

'But what if you were expressly ordered to treat me as a *Stürmer* Jew – *ordered* to, Herr Norden? What then?'

The Berlin project progressed steadily. Even Müller was satisfied with the results, which included detailed maps based on careful reconnaissance.

'Good work,' he commented, 'We're ready to go to town any time you say, Gruppenführer.'

Wesel nodded. 'Fine, but the timing's important too, as you yourself pointed out. Christmas is just around the corner and we're going to celebrate it.'

Müller, Wesel and the Group were in the drawing-room of the Villa in front of the open fireplace. The fire crackled, flickered and blazed, steeping the Berlin extermination plans in a roseate glow and tinting the faces of all present. Even Harras, who was lying at Siegfried's feet, seemed gentled by the firelight.

It was the dog that now claimed Wesel's attention. Siegfried felt an instinctive pang of alarm. The others looked unconcerned but not wholly uninterested. Like him, they realized the Gruppenführer was limbering up for one of his more spectacular displays.

'That dog,' Wesel said slowly, quietly, ' – the dog you volunteered to look after with no encouragement from me, Siegfried – I don't like the look of him.'

'Dobermanns aren't everybody's cup of tea, Gruppenführer,' Siegfried parried quickly. 'Breeds are a matter of taste, but Harras is a magnificent specimen by any standard. There's nothing the matter with his pedigree, that's for sure.'

Wesel gave Siegfried a sad but sympathetic smile. 'You've missed the point. I'm not disputing the exceptional qualities of an animal you're so obviously attached to, but your affections are of secondary importance. You must trust my judgement, Siegfried, and not only in respect of the human race. In this case my judgement tells me the dog is sick.'

'Sick?' yelped Siegfried, laying a protective hand on the dog's back. Harras glanced up uncertainly.

'That dog,' Wesel declared, stressing every syllable, 'has rabies.' He seemed satisfied he had said all there was to say. 'You understand?'

'No, no!' Siegfried cried excitedly. 'That's impossible!' The others greeted his mute appeal with smiling indifference. He knelt and put his arms round Harras's neck. 'You must be wrong, Gruppenführer.'

'The Gruppenführer – wrong?' said Hagen. 'How do you figure that?'

Hermann's response to the emergency was quite as swift as Hagen's. He quickly grasped the proper course of action. 'The dog's got rabies,' he said. 'If the Gruppenführer says so, that's that, and if the animal's incurably sick it must be put down. Better shoot it at once.'

'No!' Siegfried exclaimed, clinging still tighter. 'It's impossible!'

'What is?' Wesel inquired sorrowfully.

Bergmann looked at Berner, who was quick to take the hint. 'If you find it hard to put the dog out of its misery, Siegfried, we'll do the job for you. That's what friends are for.'

'But Harras hasn't *got* rabies!' Siegfried cried.

'Oh yes he has,' Hagen corrected him brusquely. 'Didn't you hear what the Gruppenführer said?'

The dog whimpered as Siegfried's embrace drew tighter still. He gazed round helplessly, imploringly, only to see it was useless. His eyes flared up one last time, like the fire expiring on the hearth. After that he looked at nobody, not even his dog.

'Don't you understand?' Norden spoke with almost brotherly affection. 'Absolute obedience is the only principle that counts. Anything that's expected of us – merely expected, not even requested or demanded – must be carried out to the letter.'

Wesel summed up. 'We all have our failings, Siegfried. Failings don't matter as long as we recognize them and take ruthless countermeasures. Then, and only then, do we become capable of performing a thorough and effective job – the kind that awaits you in Berlin.'

'Yes, Gruppenführer.' Siegfried removed his arms from the

dog's neck. Harras gave a little whine.

More comments by Driver Sobottke:
You've never heard such a commotion, and all on account of that lousy dog! I delivered it to the Villa and Siegfried looked after it. He wouldn't let anybody else go near the beast, not even when it had to be shot.

Bertha the cook went absolutely crazy when it happened. The fat bitch must have had a soft spot for Harras. She howled like an air-raid siren.

It was the same with old Caspar, the gardener. He had the nerve to complain to Wesel himself!

In point of fact, the whole thing was strictly on the level. Wesel sent for the district vet, and he issued an official certificate. The dog was suffering from rabies so it had to be put down. That's all there was to it.

On 23 December, the eve of the Berlin operation, which had now been rehearsed in every detail, an exclusive dinner-party was held at Horcher's in the Unter den Linden. The host: Reinhard Heydrich. His guests: Waldemar Wesel and the Group.

The immaculately trained staff waited on Heydrich and his privileged companions with every care. Three generals at the next table took the liberty of raising their glasses politely to the two senior SS officers. After the meal Heydrich turned to his fellow-Gruppenführer and murmured, 'Well, Waldi, what say we adjourn to my place for coffee and brandy or a glass of champagne? We can talk undisturbed there.'

Three glossy black Mercedes waited outside. Less than half an hour later the cortège drew up in front of a handsome lakeside villa on the Grosser Wannsee. There, in a long drawing-room, Wesel and his men were greeted by several pots of coffee, six assorted brands of cognac and a dozen bottles of champagne in ice-buckets.

'Make yourselves at home, gentlemen,' Heydrich said expansively. 'A pity I couldn't have introduced you to my wife but we can remedy that omission in due course. For the moment, it's a question of first things first. We must concentrate on this mission of yours, which is only twenty-four hours away. Do you anticipate any problems?'

'None,' said Wesel, indicating Siegfried. 'This young officer will be doing the job with the rest in close support.'

Heydrich walked over to Siegfried. He looked searchingly into the lieutenant's eyes and placed a hand on each of his shoulders. 'Is that so, Obersturmführer?'

'Yessir,' said Siegfried.

Heydrich left the six to their drinks and drew Wesel a little to one side. 'Your men seem in good shape. Think we'll soon be able to use them on something really big?'

'Of course,' Wesel said. 'The Führer hinted that our next assignment would be of supreme national importance. Do you know what his plans are?'

'Not in detail, but I take it you're ready for anything. Are you – even if it means killing Jews like flies?'

'By the thousand if necessary. You can tell the Führer that.'

This assurance seemed to put Reinhard Heydrich in an artistic frame of mind. He went over to the Bechstein grand which occupied one corner of the spacious drawing-room. On it lay his violin. Delicately, he picked up the instrument and fingered the strings to see if it was properly tuned.

Then he began to play – spiritedly, passionately and with the movements of a dancer. His pale face, so reminiscent of a bird of prey, relaxed. The performance lasted nearly ten minutes.

'Magnificent!' said Wesel, as the final note died away. 'Absolutely superb!'

'A Bach suite,' Norden amplified. Of all the members of the Wesel Group, he was – as Hagen had once phrased it – the one with the thickest coat of cultural varnish.

Heydrich lowered his bow with a sweeping gesture and laid the instrument aside. He stood there, deeply affected by his own performance. Then, suddenly alert once more, his chill eyes looked keenly round the room, though his voice retained its musical quality – soft, subdued and caressing.

'That, gentlemen, is yet another aspect of our world, another thread in our great national tapestry. Unswerving faith in the future goes hand in hand with the search for true beauty and an ever-growing desire for the ultimate fulfilment of our noble German dream.'

The same perfection attended all that happened during the midnight hours of the following day.

The weather: cold, wet and overcast. Visibility: very poor, hence little fear of eye-witnesses. A murky Christmas Eve on which illuminated trees peered dimly through the windows.

Aided by the weather, everything went exactly according to plan. Berner and Bergmann covered the rear of the property while Norden and Hagen stationed themselves at the front.

The mission itself was Siegfried's personal responsibility. Wesel had detailed Hermann to accompany him, but only as a safety measure. Hermann's express orders were to intervene only if Siegfried got into difficulties.

There was little fear of this. Siegfried showed every intention of eliminating everything and everyone unwise enough to get in his way. He had armed himself with two of the special 10.5 magnums, all chambers fully loaded, and his trouser pockets bulged with spare ammunition.

'He had to shoot one dog,' Hagen observed gaily. 'Now he's itching to shoot some more. Four legs or two, it's all the same to him.'

'Go on,' Norden protested. 'He's one of us, that's all. He's only doing his duty.'

For Siegfried, the execution of his duty was meticulous. The US diplomat's chauffeur, who opened the door when he rang, received a slug full in the face. The next to die, with a bullet in the region of her navel, was a scantily dressed maidservant who had materialized in the background. The cook met a similar fate. Then came two pyjama-clad children, who stared at Siegfried and Hermann wide-eyed with terror. Siegfried left them to his back-up man, a display of esprit de corps that Hermann was quick to appreciate. He favoured a less noisy technique. Grabbing the boys, he vigorously knocked their heads together as though playing a kind of ball-game, then hurled them at the nearest wall.

Hermann devoted only a few moments to the contemplation of his swift and successful handiwork before hurrying after his team-mate so as not to miss the final act of this macabre performance.

Siegfried, who seemed to have been waiting for him, took a little time over his finale. He could afford to, now that all potential interlopers had been eliminated. Only two of the villa's occupants remained alive.

The diplomat's wife wore a blue silk dinner-gown. She was a skinny bleached blonde, Siegfried noted. Her whole body trembled and her features were contorted into a gargoyle mask of terror. She stood shielding her husband, a plump man whose round face had turned ashen above the collar of his tuxedo. He was also trembling with an intensity that suggested that he was on the verge of soiling his pants.

Behind them stood a traditional German Christmas-tree, all shiny round globes, tinsel festoons and fat white candles. Lamp-light glinted on the star at its apex, sending shafts of radiance in all directions – heavenwards included.

Siegfried's revolver roared twice and only twice. The man and his wife hurtled backwards into the tree. It toppled over, enshrouding them in festive greenery. Siegfried did not falter. His last two shots were fired straight into each face at point-blank range.

Utter silence fell. The flow of blood made no sound. 'That wraps it up,' Siegfried said. He looked pleased with himself.

Hagen, who was standing at the gate with Norden, glanced at his watch. 'All over in seven minutes. Pretty good going.'

Norden merely nodded.

Two cars from Heydrich's department were parked at the next intersection. Wesel sat in one of them. Siegfried hurried over to him and raised his thumb, nothing more. Wesel leant out and patted him on the shoulder – a signal token of intimacy and approval.

'Right!' he said crisply. 'Tempelhof Airport!'

They drove off, leaving Müller behind. He had been entrusted with a special mission of his own, less sanguinary but no less scrupulously planned.

The Führer's personal aircraft, a Junkers Ju 52, was standing on the runway with its engines warmed up. Hitler's pilot sat at the controls and his principal aide was attending to the passengers' needs. Right up front as usual, the Führer was idly leafing through some official papers. He had given orders that take-off be delayed until Wesel and his men arrived.

There was no delay. They turned up several minutes ahead of time, to be greeted just inside the aircraft by Hitler himself.

He began by shaking hands with Wesel, who submitted his report with undisguised pride.

'Mission accomplished, my Führer!'

Hitler nodded approvingly. 'Good. I expected no less of you.'

He proceeded to welcome the other six aboard, first with his right arm raised in the Nazi salute, then with a brief but hearty handclasp. Siegfried, whom Wesel had propelled to the fore, was treated to a long, silent stare.

The Führer greeted Siegfried by name before Wesel could give him a whispered reminder, likewise the other five. Every one of the six names and faces had been filed away in his celebrated memory.

After they had all taken their seats, he turned and addressed them.

'I rejoice in the knowledge that I am surrounded by the most trustworthy of my comrades-in-arms. We have something very important in common, you and I: a ceaseless and implacable confrontation with the truth. I as Chancellor of the Reich, you as my faithful followers.'

They returned his gaze with ardour and devotion. Wesel, who had been graciously allotted the adjoining seat, said, 'Back in the Germanic Middle Ages, my Führer, people used to say that the executioner, too, belonged in the sovereign's train.'

'Very true, Wesel.' Hitler nodded slowly. 'The exercise of power has its darker side. Genuine greatness is inconceivable without unswerving allegiance, because that is the bedrock on which every leader builds. Viewed in that light, the executioners who attended a king, and whom I should prefer to call instruments of the royal will, were the real heroes of their age.'

The Führer's plane took off for Munich, where he planned to spend the festive season in cosy surroundings made cosier by the presence of Eva Braun. He too was a man – even if he did have to play eternal father to the Fatherland, the unwed and exalted idol of a million female devotees of whom none would gladly have relinquished him to another – even if fate had condemned him to lead a public life worthy of the Third Reich's foremost abstainer.

He sat there rapt in thought, sipping mineral water. Although he seldom made alcoholic concessions to his subordinates, he had sanctioned an exception in this case. Wesel's men were permitted to drink his health in German champagne supplied by the family firm of Frau von Ribbentrop, his Foreign Minister's wife.

After a safe landing in Munich and a hair-raising drive to Feldafing, the Christmas festivities were resumed at the Villa.

Raffael and Sobottke were instructed to carry in a tub full of cracked ice and bottles of champagne. Wesel clapped his hands for silence.

'Drink up, gentlemen! As far as I'm concerned, you can hibernate for the next two days.'

This invitation did not apply to Sobottke, who was on standby, nor to Raffael, who received orders to man the principal telephone in Wesel's study. For the time being, the Gruppenführer wanted to be alone with his own.

Logs crackled in the fireplace and champagne flowed. Before long, Wesel's half-dozen were overcome by a mood of dark, drunken revelry.

The Gruppenführer entertained them with colourful tales of the 'Black' Reichswehr, an unauthorized militia which had operated in the days when Germans were just beginning to grasp the true significance of justice, honour and patriotism after their country's defeat in the Great War.

'One of our main activities was the punishment of traitors. This was promptly denounced as lynch law by some of the more Jew-infected papers. To us it represented, as it still does, the responsible fulfilment of our soldierly obligations. The press deluged us with filth, but we were above such things. Because a few spineless judges failed miserably in their duty, we had to take the law into our own hands. We were compelled to pass sentence and carry it out ourselves.

'I shall never forget one summer night in the Rhineland near Cologne, which was still occupied by Allied troops long after the war. Three traitors had to be liquidated at one fell swoop. They'd opened their cowardly mouths wide enough in the past, but they weren't so talkative when we made them dig their own graves with some spades we'd brought along for the purpose.

'One old bastard – a trade union correspondent, I recall – died of a heart attack before we could shoot him in the back of the neck. Captain Berthold, who was in joint command of the operation with me, had a wry sense of humour. "That's one way of saving ammunition," was all he said.'

Wesel's experiences were received with great interest and punctuated by admiring comments. Only Siegfried, whose privilege it was to sit on the Gruppenführer's right, wore a slightly abstracted expression. His first bottle of champagne was empty in less than half an hour. He seemed bent on getting drunk, perhaps for oblivion's sake.

'Of course,' Wesel was saying, 'some of the Weimar police were rabble. They even had the effrontery to arrest one of our men, this time near Düsseldorf. He was going to be tried for murder, and that we couldn't tolerate.

'An armed detachment stormed the prison. We managed to release five of our political comrades, but not him. He'd been transferred to another prison.

'We interrogated the swine of an official who'd ordered the transfer, but he was a fragile physical specimen and died on us, so we went straight to the judge scheduled to try the case. We held a gun under his nose and talked to him persuasively. The verdict fulfilled all our expectations – an acquittal.'

Siegfried rose with a brimming glass held solemnly at arm's length. 'Permission to be excused,' he said thickly. Poker-backed, he left the room but made his exit through the french windows instead of heading for the lavatory. Once outside on the terrace, he walked on through the chill darkness of that Christmas morning, on through the grounds to a clump of fir-trees near the farthest wall. Beneath one of them lay the dog Harras, buried by his master's hand.

Siegfried stood there, as nearly at attention as his drunken state permitted. He raised his glass, put it to his lips and took a sip. Then he poured the rest over the dog's grave.

He rejoined his companions looking immeasurably relieved.

Wesel, who noticed this at once, felt a thrill of satisfaction – his system worked!

'Well, Siegfried,' he said, 'it's good to see you looking so relaxed. You carried out an arduous and exacting mission, virtually single-handed. I appreciate that. You've shown us what you're made of.'

'I only did my duty,' Siegfried said ponderously, reaching for another bottle of champagne, his third. 'For the Führer,' he added.

'Quite so, quite so.' Wesel spoke with more than usual warmth. 'Nevertheless, however selflessly we devote ourselves to the Führer's cause, we can always rest assured that outstanding services will be generously rewarded. Everyone who took part in this operation will find that his personal bank account has been credited with a four-figure bonus. As for you, Siegfried, a brilliant feat like yours merits special recognition – something out of the ordinary. Name it.'

Siegfried shook his head. 'I don't want anything.'

'Not for yourself, perhaps, but wouldn't you like to give somebody else a treat – somebody outside the Group?'

'There's always my mother . . .'

'There you are! You're not only a reliable subordinate, you're a dutiful son as well. Very praiseworthy of you, Siegfried! So what can we do for your dear mother?'

'Well,' Siegfried said hesitantly, 'she's always dreamed of a cottage in the country. Beside a lake . . .'

'Request granted!' said Wesel. The death of a public enemy and six dependants was well worth a country cottage.

Then he glanced at his watch. It was nearly 6 a.m. 'Hagen,' he commanded, 'turn on the radio. There may be something of interest on the early news.'

There followed three minutes of Tchaikovsky's *Nutcracker Suite* reinterpreted by a string orchestra to sound like Johann Strauss. Then came the latest news, preceded by an announcer crisply declaiming the Führer's Christmas message to his resurrected and regenerated, powerful but peace-loving German people.

The next news item read:

'During the night of December 24th, an armed robbery occurred at the home of an American embassy official in the Berlin suburb of Dahlem. Preliminary investigations suggest that it was committed by an international gang of criminals.'

The Villa rang with laughter at this report, but the best was still to come. The announcer continued:

'The Führer and Reich Chancellor has expressed his deep sense of outrage at this atrocity, which he profoundly deplores. He has also instructed the Berlin CID to pursue their investigations ruthlessly and with all possible speed. A special team has been recruited for this purpose and placed under the command of one of our foremost senior detectives.'

'Meaning Müller,' Wesel explained. 'What do you say to that?'

Words failed them. As aspiring professionals, they could only marvel. Planning of this order bathed them in reflected glory. At Wesel's side, they stood poised on the lonely but commanding heights of human existence.

Only a few minutes later, the Gruppenführer's exuberance was somewhat diminished by Raffael. They had retired to his private suite. In the drawing-room, Wesel's half-dozen had launched into a noisy and rather unseasonal rendering of *The Landlady's Daughter*. Their exuberance was lost on Raffael, who looked grave.

'Count von der Tannen telephoned,' he said tentatively. 'He sounded worried.'

'What did he want? Checking up on his investments, I'll bet. I don't know why he bothered. He's safe as long as it pays us to keep him that way.'

'There's more to it than that.' Raffael's concern persisted. 'He wasn't worried about himself, for once. There's a potential split in our ranks.'

'What's that?' Wesel demanded.

'The Count wanted to speak to you urgently, but you told me I wasn't to interrupt your victory celebrations. Knowing I'm authorized to take confidential messages for you, he said it might be best if I prepared you for an unpleasant surprise.'

'What surprise, man? Stop beating about the bush!'

'Well, he seems to think his daughter has been seeing one of our men. They've been meeting in secret, but he doesn't know where.'

'Hell and damnation! It can't be true!'

'It's certainly possible. You've been giving them plenty of rope lately, and there's no definite ban on meeting her out of hours.'

'Which is it, Norden or Hagen?'

'No idea. The Count doesn't know himself, but he shares your suspicions – he assumes it's got to be one or the other. Apparently the Countess refuses any information. Just like a woman, isn't it?'

'This,' Wesel snarled, 'could be absolutely disastrous!'

9 The Last Ordeal

The spring was glorious – the best this century, people said. Just as they used the expression 'Führer-weather' whenever the sun happened to shine in Hitler's vicinity, so they credited him with the advent of an exceptional spring.

Rain and shine succeeded one another in rhythmic alternation, trees burgeoned more luxuriantly than in previous years, the cry of mating cats rent the balmy nights, dogs ran howling after bitches and countryfolk claimed that even birds were laying bigger clutches of eggs than usual.

These phenomena inspired Waldemar Wesel to poetic effusions which he read aloud to his men at supper. One, entitled *Springtide in Germany*, began as follows:

> The earth bids fair to burst,
> sun assails soil without mercy.
> Birds gather in the treetops,
> singing with unquenchable beauty.
> Singing what,
> singing what song
> and for whom?
> For whom indeed?

Wesel's exegesis: 'This is a reference to the forces of Nature. We heed and respect them but refuse to surrender to them. Why? Because we are alive to the indestructibility of existence as long as birds sing, trees grow, flowers bloom and Nature boasts her crowning glory – *Homo germanicus!*'

Although the Gruppenführer liked it when his æsthetic interpretations drew a response from his men, this did not prevent him from keeping their noses to the grindstone. Efficiency being his declared aim, he put them through new tactical exercises, endurance tests and intensive courses on a variety of subjects including foreign languages, criminology, self-defence and, last but not least, Hitlerian philosophy. Spring notwithstanding, he preserved his determination to leave no educational stone unturned.

Conversation between Waldemar Wesel and Count von der Tannen:

WESEL: I have the greatest personal affection for you, Konstantin, as you know. Our co-operation has often paid dividends in the past, from your point of view as well as mine. What I find increasingly disquieting is your daughter's behaviour. She obviously refuses to come to heel. To be frank, I'm alarmed.

THE COUNT: So am I, Waldemar, but Elisabeth's a woman, and that makes her virtually unpredictable. Don't you have any definite evidence of clandestine meetings between her and one of your men?

WESEL: No, even though we've kept a careful watch on them. I can't afford to ask them straight out. One of them might lie to me, and that would be catastrophic – it would destroy the edifice of trust I've taken so long to construct. But I can feel it in my bones: your daughter's already in league with one of them.

THE COUNT: Perhaps, Waldemar, but we don't know for sure. I've worked on Elisabeth for hours, but all I got out of her was that she seems to regard Hagen as a kind of Nibelung character, whereas Norden strikes her as a knight errant. She flatly refuses to reveal which she prefers. They're both nice and Nordic, she says.

WESEL (*irritably*): I don't care, she mustn't be allowed to favour one or the other. That's the rule we agreed and its got to be observed.

THE COUNT: I know, but . . .

WESEL (*deliberately turning up the volume*): Kindly make that clear to your daughter!

Wesel in conversation with Professor Breslauer:

WESEL: I don't propose to contest your views on the nature, significance and future of international Jewry, Professor. I leave that to my men – they're capable of holding their own. However, from what I've seen of their notes on your lectures, you've been trying to persuade them that Germany's fate may hang on that of the Jewish race. What on earth entitles you to make such a bold assumption?

BRESLAUER: Our very existence, for one thing. I'm talking in purely numerical terms, Herr Wesel. There are two or three million Jews living in Central Europe alone, the majority in Western countries and a substantially smaller proportion in the south. At least as many again form part of the population of Eastern Europe, with major concentrations in Poland and Russia. Counting other groups, that makes a total of some eight million human beings whose existence is as impossible to ignore as that of the millennial heritage of the Jewish race, which is primarily evident in cultural domains such as religion, philosophy, literature, music and the sciences . . .

WESEL: But also in trade and commerce, law firms and stock exchanges, doctors' consulting-rooms and dance bands. In other words, no statesmen or men of action, Professor – no great military leaders, no peasants or workers. How can a race of tradesmen and pawnbrokers hope to survive in a heroic age like ours?

BRESLAUER: The Jews, Herr Wesel, have an exceptional capacity for suffering. They're infinitely tenacious and, as the history of the world shows, versed in the art of survival. You couldn't exterminate us even if you started a second world war and saddled us with the responsibility.

WESEL: How dare you make such insinuations, Herr Breslauer! We Germans strive to be a peace-loving and peaceable nation. It's you and your kind who are always provoking us with your presumptuous theory of a chosen race destined to survive till the end of time. Do you think you've got a lien on eternity?

BRESLAUER: Not exactly. Do you?

WESEL: Once and for all, Herr Breslauer, and let this be a final warning: you can improve my men's political education by dishing up any provocative line of argument you like, but never try to persuade them that National Socialism augurs total chaos or that the Führer is a charlatan and public menace. Indulge in that kind of talk and you'll risk your neck a lot sooner than you may do otherwise. Do I have to spell it out for you?

BRESLAUER (*hesitantly but with sombre determination, not resignation*): No . . .

Feldafing. Heydrich reporting on the effects of the Wesel Group's Dahlem operation:

'An even more successful mission than we expected. Its significance hasn't taken long to dawn on Berlin's colony of international parasites – diplomats, journalists, businessmen and so on. They're pretty subdued. All at once, they've stopped peddling slanderous stories about the Third Reich. Even the foreign press is taking a more cautious line, I'm glad to say.'

Wesel simplified this statement. 'So the hacks are keeping their traps shut rather than have them shut for good.'

'All that matters now,' Heydrich said, 'is for Müller to tie up any loose ends.'

Berlin. Müller reporting to Heydrich on precautionary measures undertaken in his capacity as head of an ad hoc CID team:

'After exhaustive inquiries and a large-scale man-hunt, the theory that this raid was carried out by an international gang of thugs seems to be gaining ground. We've detained four suspects so far, all ex-cons. Judging by their criminal records and suspicious behaviour, any or all of them could have pulled the job.'

Heydrich nodded. 'You're working along just the lines we intended, Herr Müller. Keep it up and your prospects could be bright indeed. Have these men confessed yet?'

'They will,' Müller replied simply. 'It's only a matter of time. Interrogation counts for a great deal. While we're on the subject, I'm busy devising a few novel techniques for use on future occasions.'

Munich. Heydrich and Wesel over hors-d'œuvres at the Hotel Vierjahreszeiten.

HEYDRICH: I was able to inform the Führer that the Dahlem operation has achieved all the results we hoped for, thanks to some effective back-up work from Müller. Like me, the Führer sees this as a good omen for the future.

WESEL: In what respect?

HEYDRICH: The Führer will tell you that himself. He wants us to attend a detailed briefing tomorrow morning.

WESEL: I'm ready for anything as long as I'm given a free hand and all the help I need. That includes a first-class assistant – like Müller.

HEYDRICH: You keep your ear to the ground, Waldi. So my interest in Müller hasn't escaped you? Well, you're right. I intend to have him transferred to Central Security and appoint him head of the Gestapo. It can't fail to reflect credit on you – after all, you discovered the man and gave him his start.

WESEL (*firmly*): Maybe later on, but not until I can spare him. Till then he stays with me. Are we agreed?

HEYDRICH: (*ruefully*): We always are.

Berchtesgaden. The Führer's mountain retreat, a combination of fortress and holiday home. Picture-windows in front, secret police-men in the courtyard, a detachment of SS bodyguards housed at the rear. Wammenberg, the Führer's personal cook and valet, politely distributes Nymphenburg china cups and fills them with Indian tea.

HITLER: And now, gentlemen, to come straight to the heart of the matter, we must formulate a final and definitive approach to the Jewish question. May I have your recommendations?

WESEL: I suggest we teach them an object lesson. A deterrent – a symbolic threat to their survival.

HEYDRICH: I suggest we exterminate them.

WESEL: All of them?

HITLER: Every last one!

HEYDRICH: Too much for you to stomach, Wesel?

WESEL: Of course not, but it would be a gigantic undertaking. We're talking about several million people – roughly eight million in Europe alone. How could we get our hands on them from inside Germany?

HEYDRICH: That, Wesel, is a question which needn't concern you. The first step would be to develop an effective pilot scheme.

HITLER: Quite so, but that would require careful planning in itself. How would foreign observers react to such a venture?

HEYDRICH: At a guess, my Führer, precisely as they reacted to the successful operation in Dahlem.

HITLER: Good. The next question is, what about our German compatriots? How would they respond?

WESEL: With all their characteristic dependability, my Führer. In other words, with the conscientiousness that is their birthright – with obedience, discipline and faith in your leadership.

HEYDRICH: You may be right. Extra pressure could be brought to bear in individual cases, but that's just a question of public enlightenment, skilfully and resolutely administered. I gather Dr Goebbels is already working on that aspect of the problem.

HITLER: Good. That leaves one more factor, but I doubt if it's been sufficiently explored: the Jews themselves. How will they react, what can we expect them to do – what are they capable of?

WESEL: I've devoted a great deal of research to that problem, my Führer. It's another of the subjects in which my men have been thoroughly schooled. I've even toughened their intellectual fibre by bringing them face to face with a selected representative of the inferior Jewish race. Our final conclusion is that the Jews are obsessed by a single dominant idea: the inevitability of self-sacrifice.

HEYDRICH: Precisely my own impression. The vermin have learnt from historical experience that they're predestined to destruction – born martyrs and nothing more. We'd only be meeting them half way.

HITLER: If that is really so – and I share your belief – we must take the appropriate action. We shall initiate what I term Plan F. That is its official designation from now on. Only a very small circle of initiates will be permitted to know that it stands for Final Solution.

WESEL (*clearly impressed by Hitler's explicit confirmation of his prior assumptions*): Yes, my Führer!

HITLER (*rising and striking a prophetic pose*): That is my ultimate objective, gentlemen – the final solution of the Jewish question. It is the most secret and important mission with which Providence has ever entrusted me in my capacity as leader of the German people.

He raises his hand in the Nazi salute and hurries from the room. Wesel and Heydrich exchange a meaningful look.

HEYDRICH: A great plan, eh, Waldi? Did it come as a surprise?

WESEL: I was prepared for something big. Even the establishment of a pilot scheme will involve considerable expense, not to mention the recruitment of a large staff.

HEYDRICH: Anything you request in the way of personnel and funds will be approved. The sky's the limit.

WESEL: What about the chain of command?

HEYDRICH: The Führer devised the scheme and I've been detailed to administer it, but you and your men are to form the executive nucleus. It'll be our joint responsibility to achieve the desired result, agreed?

WESEL: Agreed.

Karl Rogalski, civil engineer, under interrogation by Captain Scott of US Military Intelligence.

ROGALSKI: I really can't imagine what you hope to get out of me, Captain. My speciality is high-speed construction. Back in the 1930s I was employed as a junior engineer by the firm I now own.

Most of our major orders at that time were for huts – for the Labour Service, Party organizations and the armed forces, also for holiday camps run by the Strength through Joy association or whatever it was called. Nowadays we erect factory complexes and warehouses designed for quick assembly. Prefabs too, reasonably priced but of high quality – built along American lines. If we can ever be of service to you personally . . .

Did I visit a house in Feldafing during 1935? Yes, I remember the occasion well. Why should it stick in my mind? Because the atmosphere was rather different from what one normally encountered in the Third Reich.

How different? Well, Nazi officials tended to chuck public money around. Expense was no object when it came to government contracts. You discussed a project, produced designs and received the order – then you went ahead. This time it was different.

In what respect? Well, I wasn't doing business with any of your usual self-important little Party bureaucrats – I was up against an eight-man board. Most of them were youngsters, but they couldn't have been more on the ball. They insisted on knowing every last detail.

For instance, full particulars of how we proposed to supply the huts with water and power, washing facilities and sanitation, special regard being paid to the question of fitting as many people as possible into the smallest possible space. To quote you another example, they asked us to submit specifications for a three-tier system of double bunks. Those conferences were a real test of stamina, believe me, but I couldn't help being impressed by my clients. They were the toughest I've ever come up against.

SCOTT: But you landed the contract?

ROGALSKI: Yes, in the face of stiff competition. We got the go-ahead, though we had to work under tremendous pressure. I had those young fire-eaters breathing down my neck the whole time. Maybe that's the only reason why we met all our completion dates.

SCOTT: So you erected this camp in the Bavarian Forest. Do you still claim ignorance of its true function?

ROGALSKI: All we did was build some huts, Captain. It was a training centre of some kind, or so I was told. Mind you, I did have my doubts.

SCOTT: Doubts about what?

ROGALSKI: Well, in spite of all the care that went into its design and planning, the scheme struck me as cock-eyed, some-how. For one thing, it was squeezed into far too small an area. For another, they picked such a godforsaken site. Supplying the place with water and power cost almost as much as the main construction work, but that wasn't my headache. A contract's a contract as long as the money's right, and it was.

Marginal note on the above by Captain Scott:

There you have it. Firm X won a contract to build some huts, site and purpose irrelevant. A contract was a contract – where economic prosperity beckoned, anything went.

Other firms were soon called in. One of them sank power cables, another laid water mains, another supplied interior fittings. Other contractors built roads, installed wash-rooms and latrines, and supplied ovens – ovens of every conceivable size, possibly for the baking of bread or the incineration of garbage on a grand scale. To the firms involved, what real business was it of theirs?

The thing that took shape in the Bavarian Forest was a proto-type – probably unique – of what later became known as the extermination camps. It was an early version of those thousandfold enlargements called Auschwitz or Treblinka.

After a massive German dinner like those traditionally favoured by the huntsmen and warriors of yore, Wesel assembled his men in the Villa's drawing-room. He came straight to the point.

'The preparatory phase is over, gentlemen. From now on we get down to business. Operation F is under way. After our joint ventures, I think it best now to divide the work-load into various individual spheres of responsibility, still under my overall command. The following appointments are listed at random. Their order has no bearing on seniority or precedence.

'Siegfried: preliminary classification of incoming detainees. They are to be divided into "useful" and "useless" individuals, a procedure I shall term "selection".

'Hagen: instant liquidation of useless individuals and organization of the remainder into work units; further liquidations if those able to work prove unwilling to do so.

'Norden: general security. Liaison with escort personnel and camp guards, also responsibility for perimeter defence and the maintenance of secrecy.

'Hermann: complete disposal of the remains of useless detainees by various methods to be tested with the aid of SS personnel from other special service units.

'Berner and Bergmann: administration and welfare of security personnel and guards. They will be directly responsible to camp headquarters, i.e. myself.

'So far so good. I hope I've made myself clear. Apply your minds to these tasks, and please be constructive. I'm always open to suggestions.'

'How much time do we have?' Norden asked.

'Three months of concentrated preparation for Pilot Scheme F ought to be enough. The trial run will cover a period of ten days.'

Hagen asked, 'What sort of numbers are we talking about?'

'A hundred a day,' Wesel replied. 'A nice round number. Extrapolating from the results we obtain, the experts should be able to plan larger-scale projects with a fair degree of speed and accuracy.'

Hermann frowned. 'I worked in a crematorium once, a fairly substantial operation. We could handle up to two dozen cremations a day. But a hundred? That sounds a little over-optimistic, Gruppenführer.'

'That's only one problem,' Wesel said, ' – one among many. They all require careful consideration and they'll get it. We mustn't let a single snag defeat us. By the time we've finished, gentlemen, we'll stage a firework display capable of dazzling the Führer himself.'

Fragment of a letter from Countess Elisabeth von der Tannen to Heinz-Hermann Norden, found among his personal effects in Lugano:
... can only tell you, my dear, that I always think of you with warm affection and cherish a deep admiration for the work you do – for I sense that it's something of national importance.

Although it grieves me that we so seldom get the chance to meet, my thoughts and hopes are with you, ever and always.

And if you should one day complete the task that fate has called you to perform ...

Waldemar Wesel allowed his men ample time to convert his orders into plans of action. They undertook intensive research and drew up development programmes. The Villa at Feldafing turned into a planning office.

Blackboards stood arrayed in the library, masking most of the shelves. They bore diagrams in whole or part, enlargement or detail, and pinned beside them were lists of materials on order, personnel requisitions and financial disbursements.

For the first few weeks, Wesel merely observed the progress of his men's labours with a contented air, but this did not prevent him from launching well-gauged operations of an interim nature.

'Gentlemen,' he said one day, looking aggrieved, 'we've slipped up.'

'Anything I can put right, Gruppenführer?' asked Siegfried. Ever since he'd been obliged to shoot Harras, the world seemed full of people destined to die like dogs.

Wesel shook his head. 'No, the mistake has nothing to do with Pilot Scheme F. I'm talking about that Lebensborn operation.'

'It can't be our fault,' Hermann said. He gave a loud guffaw. 'We did our stuff.'

The Gruppenführer eyed the Six with mild regret. 'I'm not suggesting otherwise. When we go into action, total success is assured. Unfortunately, however, one of the ladies concerned has turned out to be fifty per cent non-Aryan. To be blunt, one of the children you fathered has Jewish blood in its veins.'

'But that's monstrous!' Hagen exclaimed.

Norden's reaction was more judicial. 'The responsibility must lie with the director of the institute, Gruppenführer. He ought to be dismissed at once.'

'Dr Harnberg has already been dealt with,' Wesel said calmly. 'He was expelled from the SS and is now working as a general practitioner in some remote Silesian village. But that doesn't dispose of the problem – *your* problem, Hermann.'

All eyes veered in the appropriate direction, alight with interest. Everyone was curious to see if Hermann, that most imperturbable of men, would show signs of dismay.

Nothing of the kind. He merely crossed his arms and said, 'Who's the one, Gruppenführer – my Fount of Life playmate?'

'So it appears, I'm afraid.'

Hermann shrugged. 'No sweat. Tell me where she lives and I'll clean up the mess.' He basked in the surprise and admiration evoked by his unemotional response.

Wesel handed him a slip of paper.

'Nuremberg, eh?' Hermann said, giving it a cursory glance. 'That shouldn't take longer than two days.'

'You can have 72 hours' leave,' Wesel decreed. 'I need hardly add that the matter must be settled with a minimum of fuss.'

'That goes without saying, Gruppenführer.'

Hermann returned to the Villa after two days only, just in time for lunch. Grinning from ear to ear, he displayed the latest issue of the *Nürnberger Morgenzeitung*. Its Local Reports page carried the following item under the headline 'A Tragic Accident':

While Regional Party Secretary Heiner Starke was attending a staff conference in Berlin, his wife Anneliese and her new-born son Günther yesterday succumbed to coal gas poisoning in the Starkes' Dirckheimerstrasse apartment. All attempts to revive the victims failed.

Mother and child were dead by the time the district medical officer arrived. The municipal gasworks immediately appointed a special board to investigate the case. Its unanimous finding was that the regrettable accident must have been occasioned by gas escaping from a fractured main.

'Good work, Hermann,' Wesel commented approvingly. 'That's what I call prompt and effective action. We must tackle the tasks that still confront us with similar drive and efficiency.'

Interview between Brigadeführer Clausen of SS Operational Headquarters and Captain Scott:

CLAUSEN: Well really! I thought the days of wholesale generalizations were over. It's absurd to brand the whole of the SS just because a few of its members may have been involved in operations of a borderline nature. I ask you – a mere handful out of several hundred thousand! People tend to forget how big the SS was. Even back in 1933 it numbered at least 33,000, and within a few years that figure had grown tenfold. Then there was the Waffen-SS as well – nearly 40 divisions of combat troops. What if there were a few extremists? You can find them anywhere, even in the Church.

What we set out to create was a military élite of the kind all patriotic nations strive to establish. May I remind you, Captain, that even your own great country has its Marine Corps – its Leathernecks? Compared to them . . .

SCOTT: Save your comparisons! I don't see any connection between crack military units and mass murderers.

CLAUSEN: Nobody can accuse us of genocide, not the SS as a whole. I'd like to stress that, if only to preserve the good name of all my SS comrades who died fighting Bolshevism.

SCOTT: Is that all you have to say?

CLAUSEN: It's possible that an infinitesimal number of SS men were involved in incidents some might describe as not wholly creditable, but they were probably members of non-German units – Lithuanian, Latvian, White Russian. Although I was attached to

Operational Headquarters at the time, with special responsibility
for the Waffen-SS, I knew nothing of such matters, I give you
my word of honour.

SCOTT: But you did know a man named Waldemar Wesel?

CLAUSEN: Of course, Captain. I've never denied that I knew
him – fleetingly. I never had any official dealings with him – nor
did I want any. To be candid, I considered Wesel an academic –
a conceited literary hack in uniform – 'Professor Ego', we used
to call him. Himmler didn't like the man either, but he enjoyed
the personal protection of Hitler – and of Heydrich, whom we all
found equally suspect. Wesel and Heydrich worked hand in glove.

SCOTT: I see, so it all boils down to Hitler again. Men like you
were totally in the dark. Compared to your kind, Pontius Pilate
washed his hands in liquid manure.

Meanwhile, advance plans for Pilot Scheme F were nearing
completion at Feldafing. They were rounded off by a series of
conferences in which Müller regularly took part. His task was to
cross-question Wesel's men.

Query: What happens if a detainee cracks up and starts scream-
ing?

Answer: They can scream like stuck pigs – nobody'll hear them.
The camp's completely cut off from the outside world.

Query: Hysteria can be infectious and cause general panic.
How do you prevent that?

Answer: We obey standing orders. Any attempted stampede
must be nipped in the bud.

Query: How? By systematic weeding-out?

Answer: By summary execution in full view of the offender's
fellow-detainees.

These quizzes continued for hours on end. Müller could fire
off any question he liked – nothing seemed in doubt and everything had been rehearsed with the utmost attention to detail.

Müller evinced a certain satisfaction at this display of logical
thinking, which had largely been developed by himself, and Wesel
took some pride in his pupils' swift and unerring reactions. His
pride persisted when Feldafing was invaded by a man who burst
into the Villa like a tank.

Wesel greeted him with a cordial handshake and introduced him to the Six: 'Standartenführer Rauffer of the Central Security Bureau, currently assigned to special duties under the command of Gruppenführer Heydrich. Standartenführer Rauffer is responsible for the external organization of our undertaking – its delivery service, so to speak.'

The newcomer was a rugged-looking man of medium height, with a fleshy red face and eyes like arrow-slits. He began by submitting the Group to a lengthy inspection and clearly liked what he saw.

Rauffer assumed a statuesque pose, legs braced and arms akimbo, but his voice, when it finally emerged, was incongruously weak. 'I've been assigned three main spheres of responsibility,' he piped. 'To take the simplest job first, I have to provide the camp and its inmates with security personnel – guards, to you. Them I've already managed to round up without much difficulty – they're already on stand-by. Next, reliable executive personnel. Most of these have been transferred to my command and their numbers will be up to strength within a fortnight. Third and last, delivery personnel – all hand-picked for emotional stability. As soon as we agree a date, they'll get moving. Our schedule calls for the delivery of one consignment on each of ten consecutive days, each consignment to number no less than a hundred – preferably a few more.'

'Excellent!' said Wesel.

'One last point, Gruppenführer,' Rauffer went on. 'I'm most anxious that my men be well looked after – comfortably housed and fed like fighting-cocks. Has adequate provision been made?'

Wesel glanced at Berner and Bergmann, whose responsibility this was. They walked over to a blackboard adorned with a ground-plan of the camp.

'May I begin by explaining the basic principles of our lay-out?' Berner said. 'At first glance, it looks like an ordinary detention camp. However, it does present a few special features.'

'I'm all for special features,' Rauffer said jocularly. 'Tell me about them.'

'The administration block and the detainees' huts are usually separated by a parade-ground, as they are here, but this parade-ground is extra large and bordered by some additional premises.

The building that resembles a gymnasium is really a soundproof firing range. The factory-like block just beyond could be a blast furnace, which is roughly what it is.'

'Aha, I understand.' Rauffer's squeaky voice brimmed with approval. 'My men will be happy to work there under your supervision. They aren't squeamish. On the other hand, they must be offered some form of outside distraction – that I insist on. What recreational facilities have you provided?'

Bergmann was responsible for this aspect of the scheme. 'All personnel directly engaged in the processing of detainees will have access to a well equipped junior ranks' club. This will incorporate a bar, a billiard-room, a reading-room stocked with the latest newspapers and periodicals, a record-player and wide selection of records, and facilities for games ranging from ludo to chess. There will also be a library containing works of ideological importance as well as reading matter in a lighter vein. Finally, another room will be set aside for the screening of feature films.'

'You don't think that's good enough, do you?' squeaked Rauffer. 'Not for my boys it isn't! Don't forget they'll be staring death in the face a hundred times a day, day in and day out.'

Bergmann was unperturbed. He nodded at Berner, who took up the thread.

'May I draw your attention to the building marked B7, Standartenführer? Obersturmführer Hermann will be in charge of this installation, which we have nicknamed "The Brief Encounter". From opening day onwards, it will be used to accommodate selected female detainees between the ages of 15 and 25 – attractive physical specimens only, of course. They will be available to our men at all times.' Berner gave a discreet cough. 'In separate cubicles, needless to say.'

'Now you're talking,' Rauffer said, rubbing his hands. 'I'll be happy to vet the place in person. There's just one thing I'm not quite clear about, though. How are these Jewish swine going to react to our radical new approach?'

'That,' Wesel said thoughtfully, 'is a subject on which we've been compiling information for some time.' He gave Norden a brooding glance. 'We're fortunate in having a first-rate consultant, but he's on the uncooperative side. There's only one person who can get through to him. Isn't that so, Norden?'

'Up to a point, Gruppenführer,' Norden said. 'I'll work on the Professor continuously from now on, if that's what you want.'

'It is,' Wesel replied simply. The words amounted to an order, and one that was destined to have dire consequences.

Next day, before anything else could happen, an unscheduled item was interpolated in the Group's timetable. They were bidden to attend a 'cultural function', to wit, an afternoon chamber concert at Nymphenburg Castle. The programme was a Haydn-Mozart-Haydn sandwich – 'Musical Gems in Miniature', as the advance publicity phrased it. Its most notable feature: the presence of Count von der Tannen and his daughter Elisabeth, who looked as ravishing as ever.

The Count was virtually monopolized by Waldemar Wesel. The Countess, on the other hand, was permitted to take her place between Norden and Hagen. Immediately behind them sat Raffael, who'd been instructed to keep his ears open.

The sky above Munich shone with almost Mediterranean brilliance, but a hot and heavy wind from the Alps had reduced everyone to a state of lethargy.

The Count looked more exhausted than most. Classical music always threatened to send him to sleep, whereas military marches or the braying of a huntsman's horn sent the blood coursing through his veins. Wesel eyed his friend with a touch of sympathy.

Siegfried listened rapturously to the strains of the orchestra. Haydn impressed him as being close to nature and thus worthy of appreciation by an animal-lover. Hermann stared wearily into space. Berner and Bergmann brushed shoulders occasionally as they swayed to the conductor's beat.

Norden and Hagen barely heard the music. Consumed with mutual mistrust, they exchanged lightning sidelong glances. Between them, Elisabeth leant back in her seat, relaxed, happy and enjoying every minute. Immediately behind her, Raffael was growing restive. He found it almost impossible to eavesdrop with all this scraping in progress.

The final applause was wildly enthusiastic – 'stormy and prolonged', to quote two epithets more commonly applied to the Führer's ovations – though this might have been connected with

227

the fact that it signalled the end of the concert. Afterwards, everybody adjourned to the castle grounds along the well-raked paths: Wesel and the Count, Siegfried and Hermann, Berner and Bergmann, Elisabeth with Norden and Hagen, Raffael bringing up the rear.

Wesel steered his friend purposefully towards a secluded corner. Once there and out of earshot, the two men spoke freely.

Exchange of confidences between Count von der Tannen and Waldemar Wesel:

THE COUNT: I made a remark at a regimental reunion the other night, Waldi. I know it was indiscreet, but it just slipped out. To cut a long story short, I said, 'You can't make a general out of a corporal.' Some people may have thought I was referring to Hitler. What do you think?

WESEL: I think you were extremely careless, my dear fellow. I've known about your gaffe for days. It was not only registered by the Gestapo but leaked to two foreign correspondents. It could appear verbatim in the *Daily Telegraph* or the *New York Times* any day now. You'd have been carted off to a concentration camp on the spot if I hadn't stepped in.

THE COUNT: Thank you, Waldemar. I'm too honest, that's my trouble. If I am, it's largely because you've always appreciated my bluntness and encouraged it.

WESEL: Precisely, my friend. And since we're both being so honest, I can tell you who passed the word to those two foreign newspapermen, one British and one American. It was me. I wanted them to publicize your avowed hostility to the National Socialist régime.

THE COUNT: For God's sake, Waldi! Where does that leave me?

WESEL: In a very bad way – medically speaking. Your state of health gives grounds for serious concern. You need a long spell in a sanatorium, preferably in Switzerland. You shouldn't find it too much of a financial strain, thanks to your substantial account in Basle, not to mention those two parcels of real estate near Interlaken and Locarno.

THE COUNT: What are you driving at, Waldi?

WESEL: Can't you guess? You're going to emigrate. You can plausibly claim that your status as a victim of political persecution left you no alternative, and I'll do my best to foster the impression. Once in Switzerland, you become my personal contact man. Your first step will be to set up a company – Zürich might be the best place – let's say for the exploitation of international patents. Your capital will amount to several million dollars. These funds will be made available to you by me and jointly controlled by us both.

THE COUNT: Waldi! What are you asking me to do?

WESEL: Merely to embark on a new and enviable way of life for our mutual benefit.

THE COUNT: And there's really no catch? I won't be expected to act as a front man for German Intelligence?

WESEL: Not at all. Your sole contact will be me. The arrangement will be known to nobody but us.

THE COUNT: I understand. Any restrictions on how I spend my time?

WESEL: None. Be as extravagant as you like, even if you seem to be damaging the interests of your native land. You can finance anti-fascist agitation, dole out money to refugees – found a left-wing literary magazine, for all I care. Switzerland is teeming with poverty-stricken crypto-Communist writers. You can keep them in pocket-money.

THE COUNT: If I didn't know we were both on the same side, Waldemar . . . It's an exceedingly tempting proposition, I grant you. Naturally, there'd be one or two other matters to discuss first.

WESEL: I know what you mean – you don't mind cashing in but you don't want to run any risks. I appreciate that, which is why I'm going to help you secure the whole of your German assets by temporarily assigning them to members of your family before you emigrate. Every obstacle will be removed, Konstantin, but there's one condition: get your daughter out of circulation. Right now, before she does any lasting damage.

Meanwhile, Elisabeth was strolling the castle grounds with Norden and Hagen under Raffael's eagle eye. They chatted about the music they had just heard, about the glories of the summer afternoon and the harmony that reigned between those who were mentally attuned.

Abruptly, Norden stopped in his tracks. 'Forgive me, Elisabeth, but why has Hagen got his hand on your arm? What does it mean?'

'Keep your shirt on,' Hagen said belligerently. 'She tripped over something on the path and I grabbed her arm, that's all.'

'But his hand's still there, Elisabeth! You let him keep it there!'

Elisabeth turned from one to the other with a look of sorrowful entreaty. 'Please,' she said, gently but firmly, 'please have a little consideration for my feelings. It hurts me when you quarrel. I'm terribly fond of you – both of you.'

'But you can't make up your mind between us?'

'Not yet.' She sighed. 'I'll just have to wait a little longer before coming to a final decision. Till then, kindly don't squabble over me like two dogs with a bone.'

Raffael, who had overheard most of this exchange, submitted a full report to Wesel.

'Know what our pair of supermen remind me of?' he said uneasily. 'Medieval knights squaring up for a duel to the death.'

'They won't have the time or opportunity. I'll split them up.'

'How?'

'No problem. I'm assigning Hagen to Standartenführer Rauffer as of now – that'll keep him busy – and Norden can devote a lot more attention to our tame Jew. We're just coming into the home stretch, Raffael. I can't afford any outside distractions.'

'I loathe that man Hagen!' Raffael confided audaciously. 'He's like a wild beast – always waiting to pounce.'

'In other words,' Wesel said blandly, 'he's useful.'

'And as for Norden! I used to like him, but now I can't stand him. Do you know what he reminds me of sometimes? A frustrated Jesus, that's what!'

'Good God, Raffael, what gives you that idea? It's crazy.'

'Plenty of things are crazy these days, Waldemar, but it doesn't stop them being true.'

The meeting between Norden and Wesel's 'tame Jew' took place the very next day. Conscious that Breslauer's knowledge was based on a lifetime of experience, Norden had primed himself for the occasion with special care.

The Professor received him in his book-lined den, a bent but alert little figure entrenched behind a rampart of dusty volumes.

'Ah, so you've come to have another shot at picking my Jewish brains, have you?' he said cheerfully. I trust you don't expect me to tell you precisely what you want to hear.'

'Don't underestimate me, Professor – or the reverse.' Norden sat down opposite him. 'I've only got a few questions for you this time. Are you prepared to answer them?'

'By all means.' Breslauer leant back in his chair. 'As long as you're prepared to accept a few home truths.'

Norden hesitated for a moment. Then, very slowly and deliberately, he said: 'Can you imagine yourself face to face with death – your own death? How would you respond to such a situation?'

Breslauer shut his eyes as though the light hurt them, perhaps to avoid the necessity of looking at Norden. 'So that's it,' he murmured almost inaudibly. 'Müller warned me what to expect, but I didn't believe him.'

Norden ignored the reference to Müller. 'So you're afraid of death. You'd be scared – ready to confess to anything in order to save your own little spark of life. Am I right?'

'Death,' Breslauer said quietly, 'is an inescapable part of life, except that it seems to have a preference for Jews. My father was a dentist in Hanover – he was attacked and beaten to death while walking his dog. My mother died soon afterwards, apparently of heart failure. My sister Ruth married a sergeant stationed at Frankfurt. Ruth didn't last long either – she committed suicide. My brother Samuel was a salesman. Some militiamen ran him over during a night exercise – a straightforward road accident, according to his death certificate. I was lucky enough to go to university, thanks to my Uncle Benjamin, a cattle-dealer in East Prussia. He got mixed up in a bar-room brawl and was fatally injured.'

'And you accepted all these deaths as a matter of course?' Norden asked eagerly. 'No point in fighting fate, is that your attitude?'

'Fatalism is what you're gambling on, I suppose, you and your friends.' Breslauer stared hard at Norden. 'You actually mean to exterminate us!'

'So you're frightened of the latent Jewish death-wish, Professor – frightened of the inertia and resignation that's become second nature to your race over the centuries. You're afraid they'll let themselves be butchered in droves, like cattle. Well, will they?'

'The Jews' path through history is paved with the bodies of a million murdered innocents. In the East, in Russia, in Spain and Poland, in the Balkans – throughout the world. Other people have always trampled us like insects. Now it's happening here.'

'But this could be the end of the line, Professor. You're in Germany – don't underestimate our thoroughness.' Norden paused. 'Or do you propose to defend yourselves?'

'Violence is alien to us, but I'm half afraid it won't remain so forever. There may come a time when even the Jews refuse to walk like lambs to the slaughter.'

'What about you? Would you be prepared to resist?'

'I would.'

'You can talk!' Norden emitted a mirthless bark of laughter. 'You're in a protected occupation, Professor. You're safe here with Müller looking after your interests – at least, I assume that's what you're counting on. Why try to persuade me that any circumstances could arise in which you'd be ready to risk your life for a racial concept you don't really believe in?'

'You'll know when the time comes, Herr Norden. Much as I dread it, I hope it comes soon.'

Norden drew his revolver, one of the special 10.5 magnums. Without taking his eyes off Breslauer, he put it on the desk and slowly pushed it across.

'The safety-catch is off,' he said. 'All you have to do is pick it up, point it at me and pull the trigger. Even you couldn't miss at this range.'

Breslauer smiled sadly. 'I've never handled a gun in my life. Are you planning to shoot me as soon as I reach for it?'

'I'm unarmed.' Norden half raised his hands to show they were empty. Very quietly, he went on, 'Just assume that a situation did arise in which one of us had to kill the other. *Had* to. What would you do then?'

'Are you looking for death?'

'I'm not afraid of it.'

'Neither am I, Herr Norden, but I shall never deliberately kill another human being – you least of all. I think you know why.'

'I don't want to know!' Norden said fiercely. 'And get this straight from now on: you're my enemy and I'm yours.'

'So the time may come – very soon, from the look of it – when one of us will have to die by the other's hand. Very well, let it be me.'

'There is a third possibility,' Norden said, indicating the revolver in front of the old man.

'You think I should kill myself? Is that what you expect me to do – me, a Jew? How little you know us!'

Norden rose abruptly. Not looking at Breslauer, he turned and walked out.

He left the gun behind. The professor stared at it with tears in his eyes.

Some days afterwards, Wesel made a pre-lunch announcement. 'Gentlemen,' he proclaimed, 'I'm rationing you to half a bowl of soup per person – half a bowl of concentrated beef stock with an egg stirred into it. We don't want your stomachs rumbling. It wouldn't make a good impression on the Führer.'

Norden beamed. 'You mean we're going to see him again?'

'He wants to see *you*. This afternoon, in Munich. That's why I'm keeping you short. If I know the Führer, he'll ply you with loads of pastries and cookies. You'll have to dispose of everything in sight. Any host likes to see his hospitality done justice to, and the Führer's no exception.'

Hitler seemed to be in a mellow mood when he greeted Wesel and his men at the Brown House. He stalked ceremoniously up to them, gazed into their eyes and conferred a handshake on each.

He succeeded yet again in conveying that he knew them all, knew all about them, could never be deceived. He knew the secrets of Nature, the ways of the world, the hearts of his German subjects.

With a grand gesture, he waved his guests towards the tea-table, which groaned beneath a Himalayan range of cakes – almond buns, pastries, cream slices. 'Don't stint yourselves, gentlemen. There are more outside, I trust.' Wammenberg, Hitler's valet, poured tea; Wesel's half-dozen, guests of their supreme war-lord, munched and sipped in devout silence. Hitler watched them contentedly for a while, then rose and beckoned Wesel to the window.

'From what I hear,' he said in a low voice, 'Heydrich views this bold scheme of yours with considerable optimism. I find that an encouraging sign. Heydrich's a realist – he's counting on your men to make a success of it.'

'They will, my Führer!' Wesel inclined his head in the direction of Hitler's ear. 'However, I'm sure they'd be delighted to receive a final word of encouragement from you, my Führer. I don't say it's essential, but it might spur them to even greater efforts.'

Hitler nodded and returned to the tea-table. His throaty voice filled the room.

'Gentlemen and comrades,' he said 'my sole and unalterable ambition has been to serve the German nation and those who belong to it. I have had to contend with a legacy of lies and cowardice from the past, endure the unbridled abuse of treacherous opponents, wade through an all-engulfing morass of malice and misrepresentation. But my major struggle has been with the dark power that lurks behind all these lies, all this corruption. You know the power I mean. The power of Jewry! The time has come to settle with the Jews. They must be eliminated once and for all. Are you ready to do your part?'

Wesel's men rose and formed up facing him, ready and willing. It was a sight that filled the Führer with pride – Wesel too.

Adolf Hitler locked eyes with each man in turn, holding their gaze for seconds on end. Then he said solemnly, 'Comrades, I invite you to address me in the second person singular!'

A silence charged with fervent gratitude wafted towards him. Tears stole into stern male eyes. Two or three of the six gulped hard, Norden hardest of all, Hagen less so.

The Führer put out his hands to them. They gathered round him as though swearing fealty eternal, not only unto death but far beyond.

Adolf Hitler nodded as each man took his hands. His invitation was purely symbolic, for who among them would have ventured to address him in anything but the third person? However fraternal, the use of *du* – 'thou' – was Hitler's prerogative, and he knew when and when not to use it.

A few days after Count von der Tannen left Germany for Switzerland, his daughter followed suit. With Wesel's express permission, Norden and Hagen donned civilian clothes and drove to Munich's main station to see Elisabeth off.

The Gruppenführer had detailed Raffael to accompany them and sent an additional observer in the person of Driver Sobottke. Both were under orders to keep their eyes peeled for details to be included in the full report they would be expected to submit later.

This presented practical difficulties because the train to Zürich via Lindau was packed, especially the first-class section. Here as elsewhere, Norden and Hagen practised a tactical division of labour. One of them got Elisabeth a window seat by thrusting aside an importunate old lady who was about to sit down; the other took care of the baggage. There was little scope for conversation or eavesdropping.

Elisabeth glanced at her watch. 'Herr Hagen,' she said, 'would you be kind enough to get me some magazines? Two or three will do. Perhaps Herr Norden will help me arrange my things.'

A moment later Elisabeth and Norden were together in the narrow corridor.

'We may not see each other for quite a while,' Elisabeth murmured.

'I shall miss you terribly.'

'But you won't forget me, will you, Heinz-Hermann?'

'How could I ever do that?'

'Come and visit me in Zürich,' she said. 'You'll always be welcome. Who knows, you may even want to stay for good. I should like that.'

'You mean it?' Norden blushed scarlet. 'Thank you – thank you!'

'And now, Heinz-Hermann you may kiss me goodbye.' She tapped her forehead. 'Here.'

Norden did so, tremulous with emotion. Then he was dispatched for some refreshments – fruit and a bottle of mineral water. Hagen returned with the magazines, which he deposited on Elisabeth's seat. After that it was his turn for a few minutes' conversation in the corridor.

'No dutiable goods?' he asked, ever practical. 'No unauthorized foreign exchange? Are your papers in order?'

'Everything's in order with me, Dietmar – you should know that by now.'

He grinned at her. 'You can say that again. Still, if any problems do crop up we'll deal with them for you – or rather, I will. That includes any snags your father runs into in Zürich.'

'How much do you know about Zürich?'

'Pretty well everything,' Hagen said. 'I happened to get a look at some files on Wesel's desk. There are big things ahead for you and your father – big things and profitable ones.'

Elisabeth grinned back at him. 'Do you mind?'

'Far from it. You're welcome to all the action you can get, especially if I can have a piece of it myself. I'm ready to take a personal stake in your operation. My Swiss assets are piling up nicely. If we play our cards right, Elisabeth, we're made for life.'

She stared pensively out of the window. In a low, rather hesitant voice, she said, 'You're taking quite a risk, Dietmar. Are you doing it for me?'

'Of course.' Hagen moved closer until his body brushed hers. She didn't draw away, even when he laid a possessive hand on her waist and slid it downwards until his fingers bit into her thigh, firm and assured. 'We're two of a kind, you and me. We belong together – you want it that way and so do I.'

She was standing at the window of her compartment when the train hissed and clanked into motion. The pale blue of her silk dress floated wraith-like behind the glass. Her eyes were suspiciously moist. A snow-white handkerchief fluttered from her hand and drifted to the platform.

Norden rushed to retrieve it. Ardently, he gazed after the receding train, then pressed the scrap of lace to his lips.

Hagen, who was standing beside him, gave a snort of derision. 'You're a sentimentalist, Norden. Strip off the romantic wrapping and what are you left with? Just another woman who wants to get laid. Do the job properly and she'll kiss your ass.'

'What a depraved son-of-a-bitch you are!' Very quietly, in a hoarse, strangled voice, Norden added, 'I could kill you!'

Hagen shrugged. 'Likewise.'

After weeks and months of intensive preparation, carefully staged rehearsals and trial runs, Operation F was at last ready to roll.

The first moves in what was later described as a momentous experiment took place late on the morning of 1 August 1935.

Rauffer's organization delivered the first of ten scheduled consignments. His three trucks disgorged a total of 114 prisoners. Rauffer congratulated himself: nobody had been expecting a preliminary haul of more than 90.

Siegfried took delivery of the first batch just inside the main gate, surmounted by a scroll bearing the words 'To each his own!' in gold lettering on a red background – an apt suggestion of Wesel's.

The SS escorts urged their prisoners to descend with the aid of boots and rifle-butts. This drew a prompt and forceful rebuke from Siegfried. 'We don't want any violence, men. This is a businesslike and orderly process, not a cattle drive.' The guards obeyed his instructions with a growl of protest.

Within fifteen minutes the whole consignment had been chivvied into some kind of order: 56 men, 38 women and 20 children. All eyes were riveted on Siegfried as he prepared to make his selection. The summer sun beat down, coaxing a peaty scent from the forest floor and transforming the birch-trees from which this camp derived its name – Birkenmoor – into shafts of burnished silver. The 114 detainees stood there meekly against a backcloth of sombre brown huts, trampled expanses of sandy soil, festoons of barbed wire and vigilant men in black uniforms.

Siegfried faced them like a captain surveying his crew from the bridge. He singled out 25 of the 56 males and jerked his thumb to the left. They were old men, weaklings and intellectuals. 31 of the 38 women followed them. So did all the children.

Those whom Siegfried had motioned to the left were taken into custody by Hagen and the SS detail under his command. They were conducted in batches across the central area and into the gymnasium-like building. Once inside, they were put up against a concrete wall and liquidated.

Of the three machine-guns installed there, two went into action at once and the third was held in reserve. Where necessary, life was finally extinguished by a bullet in the base of the skull. Total expenditure of ammunition: five rounds per detainee.

Meanwhile, Hermann took over the seven surviving women as founder-members of his camp brothel. Eager for reassurance about the merits of his prospective staff, he forced them to strip in front of him. Any inhibitions were dispelled by an encouraging wave from his revolver. He only had to fire it once, and that was when an unusually stubborn recruit threatened to hurl herself at his throat.

This left half a dozen 'playmates', as Hermann called them. Although perceptibly agitated, they seemed resigned to their fate. He examined their teeth, felt their breasts, prodded their thighs and buttocks. 'Nothing to write home about,' was his considered opinion, 'but they'll do for a start.'

Norden was by this time devoting himself to the 31 male survivors. He requested them to enter the first of the huts – requested, not ordered. His courteous manner had a positively horrific effect on them. They cowered against the clapboard walls, trembling.

'Right, dump your things,' Norden told them. 'The bunks up front are for you – one between two. Elect a hut leader and I'll decide whether to confirm the appointment. The rest of you, split up into three groups of ten. One member of each group will act as foreman. He'll supervise your work. He'll also be responsible for your good conduct, but responsibility brings its own rewards. Efficiency always pays with us.'

Once the working parties were organized, Berner and Bergmann took charge of them. This resulted in the first show of internal dissension. Bergmann drew Norden aside and whispered indignantly, 'What the hell's this – only thirty?'

'That's all there were after Siegfried weeded them out.'

'He must be crazy! We need as many as that to man the boiler-rooms. How are we going to run the kitchens, dig latrines and improve the roads? Wesel even wants us to put in flower-beds!'

'Todays quota is thirty,' Norden said firmly. 'Another couple of days and there could be ninety, maybe more. These things take time.'

The Siamese Twins' misgivings about the output of their 'boiler-rooms' proved largely justified. The five furnaces had to cope with 66 bodies on this first day alone. All the signs were that they would soon be over-extended.

The entire cycle was completed shortly before midnight. 'We just made it,' Bergmann reported to Wesel. 'All the same, Gruppen-führer, this kind of organization doesn't run itself. It's no go unless we get enough man-power.'

Wesel summoned all parties to a late-night conference. 'I'm worried,' he said. 'The incineration process is wasting a vast amount of time. Obviously, our plant doesn't have the requisite capacity.'

Berner raised his hand. 'Five firms were invited to bid,' he reported. 'We hardly bothered about price, just concentrated on efficiency of performance. In this respect, the furnaces installed here were the best.'

'We'll just have to think up something more effective,' Stand-artenführer Rauffer put in. 'How would it be if we delivered the subjects in a pre-liquidated condition? That would simplify matters a lot at this end, surely.'

Wesel looked dubious. 'What do you have in mind?'

'Nothing could be simpler,' Rauffer said confidently. 'Exhaust fumes! Administered in the right strength, they're lethal. All we have to do is seal the freight compartments of our trucks, nice and tight, and pump them full of carbon monoxide. It's child's play, technically.'

Hagen was quick to agree in principle. 'It would save a lot of ammunition too, Gruppenführer, apart from doing away with all the blood, shit and grey matter. One or two of our men started to buckle at the knees – a couple of them actually threw up. Comrade Rauffer's method would be much tidier.'

'Except,' said Siegfried, 'that it would also cut out the selection process. We need able-bodied men to keep this place going. Our orders are clear: we aren't running a funeral parlour, we're sup-posed to be organizing an extermination camp.'

'Well said,' Wesel commented approvingly. He turned to Norden. 'What about the surviving Jews? How are they reacting?'

'I can't tell yet, Gruppenführer. Too early in the game.'

'But I'll have to know soon – their attitude could be crucial. We mustn't let a few preliminary successes mislead us. The question we have to ask ourselves is this: Will they simply give up, or might they one day yield to a fit of bravado? We should deal with them even if they did, of course, but we'd do so far more effectively if we knew what to expect. Try and find out, Norden.'

Hagen stared at his rival with narrowed eyes. 'Far be it from me to cast any aspersions on Comrade Norden, Gruppenführer, but I doubt if he's the man for the job. After all, none of us can claim to have a perfect insight into the Jewish mentality. Only one person has that.'

'Are you proposing to involve Breslauer in this?' Norden snapped. 'My advice is, leave him out of it.'

'Not worried about him, are you?' Hagen's tone was irritatingly bland. 'It almost looks that way.'

'I'm not worried about the man himself,' Norden retorted fiercely. 'I think it would be dangerous to call him in, that's all. He's a shrewd customer – there's no knowing what he'd do.'

'We'll give it a try,' Wesel ordained. 'Let's send for him.'

Late on the third day of the trial run, Müller drove from Feldafing to Birkenmoor Camp. With him, as instructed by Wesel, came Professor Breslauer. They pulled up at the main gate.

Müller asked for Norden, who had been notified of their visit and appeared without delay. He was looking weary but resolute.

Norden put out his hand and the policeman shook it vigorously. Breslauer, who remained in the car, was greeted with an almost imperceptible bow.

'Another hectic day,' Norden told Müller in a low voice, 'hectic but rewarding, in spite of a mass of problems. We're making progress. There's still room for improvement, but we'll get there in the end. If you'll come with me, I'll show you to your quarters. We can discuss things later.'

Müller thoughtfully scanned the surrounding scenery. 'Idyllic,' he said. 'A last look at the beauties of nature, eh? All hope abandon, ye who enter here – isn't that the local motto?'

'It depends on your point of view.'

The policeman drew Norden a little to one side. In a muted but incisive tone, he said, 'Right, Norden, the Professor's all yours. I'm handing him over to you personally.'

'Fine. His services are required here – Gruppenführer's orders.'

The old man was still in the passenger seat. He seemed to be gazing at his hands, which rested on a small suitcase – the one that had accompanied him to America and back, empty of books.

'Look, Norden,' Müller said urgently, 'I'm not only handing him over, I'm holding you personally responsible for his safety. Whatever he gets up to here, and however much of a fool he makes of himself, nobody's to lay a finger on him, understand? Make that clear to the rest of your outfit – every last man. You can rely on me to back you up.'

'I understand, Herr Müller.'

'He's your baby now. I'm sure you'll take good care of him.'

Norden stared at the policeman. 'I will, but what makes you so certain?'

'The fact that you left him in possession of one of our 10.5 magnums. Breslauer, of all people! What the hell were you thinking of, Norden? He can't even fill his fountain-pen, let alone pull a trigger.'

'But how did you find out, Herr Müller – about the gun, I mean? How long have you known?'

'Quite a while.'

Norden's eyes opened still wider. 'Quite a while?' he repeated. 'You knew but you didn't report it, didn't institute an inquiry – didn't even hint at your suspicions? That means you didn't want to. And that, in turn, means we're all tarred with the same brush – you, me and the Professor.'

Müller looked almost pitying. 'Keep your ridiculous insinuations to yourself, man. However outspoken it is, a private conversation means nothing unless it's overheard by a third party. I never said a word and neither did you, got it?'

'Perhaps, but it doesn't preclude the possibility that we're both on the same side.'

Müller laughed aloud. 'Don't ever try and fool me for your own purposes, whatever they are. You're out of my league, Norden.

Of course I made inquiries about the gun you so impulsively left on Breslauer's desk. It wasn't yours, as it turned out, but one reported missing after a three-day mountain survival exercise in January of this year. That seems to imply a degree of premeditation.'

'Maybe,' Norden said with an effort. 'Maybe not.'

'There's no maybe about it. It was Hagen who reported the loss of that gun. You found it, hung on to it and gave it to Breslauer. If he'd used it to shoot somebody, the serial number would have proved he'd done so with Hagen's gun. You were counting on that, weren't you?'

'You've got a mind like a corkscrew, Herr Müller. I'm far more direct.'

'Really?'

Norden abandoned his attempt at self-defence. 'Very well, assume you're right. Let's forget about it, shall we?'

'As long as you've grasped what's expected of you.'

'You've made that clear. Anyway, I don't suppose it's escaped you that I've developed a soft spot for the old man.'

'That,' Müller said brusquely, 'is the only reason you're still around.'

From Captain Scott's research notes:

Violent death was a commonplace in the Third Reich, but there were innumerable cases where only a small and very superficial proportion of the facts emerged like the tip of an iceberg – and not even those facts could be proved in terms of national or international law. We noted down everything that came to light, almost indiscriminately. The following samples are drawn at random from hundreds of similar cases recorded in the early years of the Hitler era:

In Siegburg, a village near Bonn, eleven corpses were discovered in the cellar of a tenement, sparsely covered with coal. The CID assumed them to be the victims of a pathological mass murderer with a grudge against orthodox Roman Catholics.

At four different locations in Hanover – a pond, a storm drain, a vegetable garden and a clump of bushes in a municipal park – fifteen bodies were found in the space of a week. All belonged to

242

members of the 'Red Front', allegedly killed in street battles, bar-room brawls and road accidents.

In Berlin, fire accidentally engulfed a Jewish old folks' home, claiming sixteen lives. In Hamburg, nine bodies were washed up in a single day – all Social Democrats who disappeared during a factory outing. In Stuttgart, seven members of a gathering of Jehovah's Witnesses succumbed to a gas explosion. Stuttgart again, only 24 hours later: four homosexuals horribly murdered in the course of an alleged orgy during which they cut off each other's genitals.

And so on and so forth. Our files on similar incidents ran into thousands. Conjecture, suspicion, but only a handful of cases capable of proof for lack of witnesses prepared to testify.

'What do you expect, Captain?' the General asked me. 'You want the dead to climb out of their graves – if they have any – and swear to the circumstances under which they died?'

'What about the survivors, General?' I said. 'There's such a thing as conscience.'

'Conscience,' he said, 'what's that? The survivors have survived, period.'

'But this was mass murder, General.'

'Oh sure, Captain, but there's nothing harder to prove. You can generally catch the killer when you're dealing with one dead body, especially if it's soon enough after the event. In this case we're confronted by mass graves and mountains of unidentifiable remains. We may suspect who the killers were, but they can't be definitely identified after so many years.'

'Well I'm not giving up, General,' I told him. 'And I'm certainly not dropping this Bavarian Forest inquiry. That's where the so-called Final Solution seems to have started.'

'Are you a Jew, Captain?' he asked.

I shook my head.

'So it's not even that,' he said. 'Then why are you so hell-bent on making trouble for yourself?'

'I don't rightly know, General,' I said. 'Must be a Pavlovian reflex.'

Although we'd received a number of clues to what happened at Birkenmoor Camp, we hadn't gotten very far with our investigation. The only firm leads were as follows: a convoy of three heavy trucks, estimated capacity 30 or 40 persons each, observed heading for the camp every day for a period of roughly two weeks; twelve-foot barbed wire fences and watch-towers; sounds of machine-gun fire; finally, an acrid stench emanating from smoke-stacks like those of a factory. At first sight, the establishment seemed little different from many others of its type. It was a concentration camp, but with a special function of some kind.

On-the-spot research didn't become feasible until 1945 – ten years later. By that time it was almost like tackling an archaeological site, but the experts assigned to the case did estimate from their findings that roughly a thousand people had been cremated there. Modest, compared to the seven-digit total ultimately achieved by Hitler's Final Solution.

But the most important feature was as follows: these mass murders at Birkenmoor Camp antedated the subsequent whole-sale extermination of the Jews by roughly five years – five whole years!

It was shortly after midnight when Norden escorted Breslauer to the administration building, where Gruppenführer Wesel received him with Müller at his side.

The squeaky pinewood floorboards of Wesel's office were scattered with oriental rugs. The desk in the centre was of oak. Behind it hung a mediocre reproduction of Altdorfer's *Battle of Arbela*. The walls were adorned with maps, diagrams and typewritten directives. The windows were hung with heavy black curtains which rendered them almost soundproof.

'Do sit down,' Wesel said politely, waving the new arrivals into a pair of comfortable leather armchairs. Breslauer and Norden sat.

'I'm sorry, Professor,' Wesel continued, focusing his attention on the older man, 'but I can't exempt you from what lies ahead. I need hardly add that iron self-discipline has forbidden us to spare our own feelings. As an *ex officio* member of the Group, you must show the same fortitude.'

'What am I doing here?'

'Didn't Herr Müller explain?'

'I did,' Müller said, 'but the Professor thought it was a bad joke.'

'I couldn't believe it,' Breslauer said.

'I'm afraid you'll have to reconcile yourself to the truth,' said Wesel. 'You've a job to do – probably the most important and almost certainly the last piece of work you'll ever be called upon to perform for us. As soon as it's over you can revert to your former academic status and occupy yourself however and wherever you choose. Under our protection, needless to say.'

'You mean there'll be an afterwards?' Breslauer asked quietly.

'That's guaranteed,' Müller cut in. 'Isn't it, Gruppenführer?'

Wesel nodded. 'There'll be no danger unless it's of your own making. Our men have been instructed to keep an eye on you. Should a situation arise that presents any kind of threat to your personal safety, you'll be extricated at once. Just give us a sign – you know all my men, and one of them will always be close at hand. Norden has personal orders to look after you, so you can rest assured on that score.'

'What am I expected to do?'

'Tomorrow morning, Professor, you'll be surreptitiously introduced into the day's consignment of arrivals. Norden will be responsible for seeing that this is done. Your batch will be lined up in front of Siegfried, who'll act as if he doesn't know you. You'll be assigned to the right-hand group and marched off to one of the huts.'

'What then?'

'Then you buckle down to some of the most intensive research you've ever done – two or three days of it. After that you submit a detailed account of your findings. Is it a deal?'

'Yes,' said Breslauer.

'In that case, Professor, sleep well. Have a good night's rest before you're exposed to the rigours of an existence my men and I have already been obliged to endure for the past three days.' Wesel nodded to Norden, who escorted Breslauer from the room.

Left alone together, Wesel and Müller eyed each other. It was a wary and reflective gaze but not unoptimistic. They were drinking imported Scotch on the rocks.

The Gruppenführer raised his glass. 'He'll toe the line, won't he? I'd like your personal assurance – you know him better than anybody.'

245

'Come off it, Gruppenführer! Who but a Jew knows the Jews? I still find their mentality an enigma sometimes, even now. They're an unpredictable lot.'

'What?' said Wesel. 'Are you suggesting Breslauer may lose his head? A convinced rationalist – a subscriber to the theory of relativity? I don't believe it. If Breslauer decides to make trouble, on his own head be it. It'll be nobody's fault but his if he goes up in smoke.'

'Is that what you're counting on?' Müller asked with barely disguised menace.

Wesel brushed the question aside. 'I always allow for every eventuality. But not that, if it makes you feel any easier.'

Sundry statements relating to Birkenmoor Camp in the Bavarian Forest.

1. *Brigadeführer Clausen of SS Operational Headquarters, under subsequent interrogation:*

I have no knowledge of any such camp. In other words, it never officially existed. Speaking for myself, I never had any direct or indirect dealings with camps of that type. Whatever may or may not have happened there is no concern of mine. My conscience is clear.

2. *Friedrich Hochberg-Walden, landowner:*

At that time my estate included various holdings in the Bavarian Forest, some of them moorland. Although they were virtually useless for agricultural purposes and yielded little in the way of game, I was reluctant to sell on principle. I only reached a compromise after I had been subjected to intense pressure by senior Party officials.

Eventually, I agreed to lease the land. There was no reason why I should have had any qualms. They built roads and sewers and laid power cables – all, so I was credibly informed, in readiness for the construction of a holiday camp.

3. *Christine Rothmund, former official in the State Directorate of Women's Affairs:*

The camp was transferred to us only a few months after its completion. By whom? Some department or other – I forget which. We converted it into a home for unmarried mothers. One thing I do recall: although Birkenmoor Camp was fairly new when we took it over in the late summer of 1935, its general appearance was one of neglect. It also stank. Dreadfully.

Not that this deterred us, of course. We started by cleaning the place from top to bottom, and I'm happy to say we succeeded in creating a nice cheerful atmosphere. It wasn't long before our unmarried mothers felt thoroughly at home.

The Party authorities were extremely generous and helpful, particularly when it came to modifying the numerous camp ovens, whose function we found hard to fathom. They were then used for baking bread. In point of fact, our output was so large we soon started supplying other camps – to their complete satisfaction, I might add. We continued to do so until quite late in the war.

By the seventh day of Operation F, confidential records kept by Berner and Bergmann revealed that it was a very definite success. This was evident from the figures themselves.

The able-bodied working parties, now concentrated in three huts, were 180 strong. With each man working a total of twelve hours daily, the camp had at last begun to meet its targets.

The women selected for service in the camp brothel now numbered 51. According to Hermann, they were proving equal to the demands made on them. It even became possible to raise standards by replacing 19 of the less efficient ones and transferring them to kitchen and sanitation duties.

So far, the extermination figures read: 217 males, 216 females and 199 children of both sexes. The furnaces had coped with only 66 bodies in 12 hours on the first day, whereas Berner's latest report indicated that a similar number had been disposed of in half the time.

Wesel summoned Rauffer, who was responsible for external operations, to discuss these gratifying results at camp headquarters. Rauffer was equally pleased when he heard the figures. Not without pride, he submitted a report on his own sphere of responsibility.

'First let me say that co-operation by local SS units, Party agencies and police forces has been universally good. They've given us a free hand everywhere: Bayreuth, Bamberg, Füssen, Rosenheim, Fürstenfeldbrück, Kempten – you name it. We mounted two raids in Nuremberg and three in Munich, and never hit a single snag.

'Secondly, all our raids have been carried out under police cover. We flushed the rats out of their holes, using prepared lists. No interference from neighbours or tenants. Our worthy fellow-citizens are looking the other way or turning a blind eye – they don't want to know. We've been able to operate in complete freedom.'

Wesel nodded, lolling back comfortably in his chair. 'I can only confirm and amplify what you've just told me, Rauffer. We've had no complaints at all, neither from respectable and un-suspecting citizens nor from interfering foreign diplomats. There hasn't even been a whisper from the self-styled gentlemen of the international press.'

'They don't dare poke their noses into our business,' Rauffer said, 'not any more. Your Dahlem operation scared the shit out of them. Things couldn't be better.'

Hagen sauntered past the work detail engaged on road improve-ments. The main track leading to the ovens was to be widened and reinforced to facilitate continuous two-way traffic by heavy trucks.

Thirty prisoners and three foremen were hard at work, super-vised by six SS guards. They toiled away in baggy, sweat-stained clothes, pallid faces beaded with exertion and eyes downcast.

Strolling casually past, smirking at their docility, Hagen spared them only a cursory glance. Then one man broke away from the apathetic, toiling group. He did not dare rise to his full height but slunk towards Hagen and crouched at his feet.

An SS guard trotted up with his gun at the ready, but Hagen waved him away. 'Leave this one to me,' he said, patting his revolver holster. 'Carry on!'

He stared down at the despairing face. 'Who are you? What do you want?'

'My name's Londoner, sir. I'm a doctor. May I have a word with you?' The man was trembling all over. Detecting a hint of encouragement in Hagen's eyes, he burst into a torrent of speech. 'I've got friends, sir – good friends, rich friends. It would be worth something to them to get me out of here.'

'Are you trying to bribe me?' Hagen said smoothly.

'Of course not, sir – I'd never dare do that! But – well, perhaps if they made a gift, a contribution, a donation to some worthy cause . . .'

'How much?' Hagen asked, outwardly indifferent.

'As much as it takes, sir! Shall we say a hundred thousand marks? Would that do? I'm sure my friends could raise that much.'

Hagen's expression remained dispassionate. All he said was, 'It's worth discussing, but we'd better be quick. You won't be worth shit as a corpse. When could the money be available – and by money I mean cash?'

'Two or three days at most,' the man assured him, slowly straightening up. 'It all depends if I can contact my friends. A phone call or a note would be good enough.'

'I just might arrange it,' said Hagen.

He had laid the foundations of a financial empire. Its objective: a pleasant, secure and auspicious existence with Elisabeth von der Tannen.

She the political refugee, he the clandestine saviour of Jews: a couple to whom the future would assuredly belong if ever Hitler came to grief. And that was a contingency which, after a few days at Birkenmoor Camp, Hagen's sixth sense prompted him not to dismiss.

Back in the administration block, Wesel had opened a bottle of Veuve Cliquot Ponsardin for himself and Rauffer. The late afternoon sun streamed in, alchemizing the champagne into liquid gold. They raised their glasses.

The smile on Wesel's lean face seemed to be directed at himself. 'Everything's going fine. Frankly, I was expecting a few problems. I'd even allowed for an element of danger.'

'From this bunch?' Rauffer roared with laughter. 'The Jews are gutless – why else do you think they let other people walk all over them?'

'You may be right,' Wesel mused, 'but every rule has its exception, or so I thought. A minor upset would have been welcome – something to provide another test of my men's will to succeed.'

'Not a hope, Gruppenführer. Anyone'd think these dregs of humanity were set on exterminating themselves.'

'It certainly looks like it.'

Wesel thoughtfully poured some more champagne. Just as they were raising their glasses again, somebody hammered at the door. Without waiting for permission to enter, Siegfried rushed in. He looked distraught.

'They've mutinied,' he reported breathlessly. 'In Hut No. 3!'

Rauffer turned to Wesel, open-mouthed. Wesel studied his fingernails, but there was an air of tension about him. Mechanically, he put his glass down.

'Mutinied?' Rauffer bellowed. 'In *our* camp?'

Siegfried nodded. A faint look of bewilderment dawned on his face. 'They've refused to turn out for work. They were scheduled to relieve the afternoon shift, transporting bodies to the ovens, but they won't co-operate.'

'*Won't co-operate?*' screamed Rauffer. 'The bastards won't co-operate and they're still alive and kicking? Why weren't they shot instantly?'

'Not so fast.' Wesel spoke with elaborate calm. He bent an almost amiable gaze on Siegfried. 'Emergencies of this kind were built into our plans. In cases of open disobedience, standing orders state that all offenders must be summarily shot. Why wasn't this done?'

'Berner and Bergmann wanted to shoot them on the spot,' Siegfried reported eagerly, 'but Hagen intervened and Norden backed him up.'

'On what grounds?'

'It would have meant shooting Breslauer too – he seems to be the ringleader. Hagen said he couldn't be executed without a direct order from you, Gruppenführer. He also said the job would

probably go to Norden because Breslauer's his special responsibility.'

'Get Norden,' Wesel said briskly.

Norden reported within seconds, Siegfried having left him in the
outer office at Hagen's suggestion. He marched in and snapped
to attention facing Wesel.

'I don't understand it, Gruppenführer,' he said slowly. 'Breslauer must be out of his mind. Shall I segregate him from the
others?'

'What kind of suggestion is that, man?' snarled Rauffer.
'Where do you think we are – in a lunatic asylum? Anyone who
plays the madman must be shot!'

'Segregate him, Norden.' Wesel spoke as though the decision
was a matter of course. 'Then shoot him.'

Norden faltered. 'Shouldn't we consult Herr Müller first?'

'Can't you understand a direct order?' Rauffer screamed in his
high-pitched falsetto.

'My meaning was quite plain,' Wesel said, staring at Norden
with mild reproach. 'Professor Breslauer is to be segregated, then
shot by the officer responsible for his good behaviour. That's
an order, Norden. Do you propose to disobey it?'

Norden stood there stiff as a ramrod. There was no doubt of
his absolute obedience. Head high, he saluted and marched out.

Inside Hut No. 3, thirty men were squatting on the grimy floor-
boards. With sagging shoulders and lack-lustre eyes, they clustered
in a semicircle round the single erect figure who stood facing
them: Breslauer.

Breslauer was the only one to turn and stare inquiringly at
the men who burst into the hut. Hagen stationed himself two
paces away but did not look at him. Berner and Bergmann occupied
the middle ground flanked by a dozen SS men with their pistols
and sub-machine-guns trained on the mutineers. A moment
later, more boots thundered across the bare boards as Siegfried
strode in with Norden.

Siegfried did not return the old man's gaze. A curt gesture,
and two of the SS men flung themselves at Breslauer. Little

more now, it seemed, than a tottering bundle of skin and bones, he was dragged from the hut and into the open air.

They half carried him across the main thoroughfare to the place of execution – the concrete wall where hundreds had already died – and dumped him on the ground like a discarded sack.

Norden had marched stiffly in the execution detail's wake. He dismissed the pair of SS men, who retired with alacrity. They were reluctant to miss the execution of the other thirty prisoners, either from a commendable sense of duty or because members of a firing-squad qualified for extra pay.

Norden bent over Breslauer, who was sprawled at the foot of the wall but making feeble efforts to sit up.

'You want to die, Professor, I know that perfectly well, but why force me – me, of all people – to carry out your death sentence? Why have you lost your will to live?'

'Who would want to survive under a system ruled by insanity?'

'I don't care what you think of the system,' Norden said heatedly. 'It doesn't apply to you. You were never in any personal danger. There's no need to give up, even now. We could say you were temporarily deranged – I'd back you.'

'Me, deranged?' Breslauer said with a flicker of amusement.

Norden ignored this. 'Only temporarily, and you beg the Gruppenführer's pardon. You're in serious trouble, Professor, but an apology might work wonders. Meanwhile, I'd notify Müller – he'd be bound to step in. With Müller on our side, Wesel would have to listen.'

Breslauer managed another smile. It hurt him because the SS men had pistol-whipped him about the head as they drove him from the hut to the wall. He peered into the setting sun through a veil of blood.

With a groan, he said, 'My God, Norden, how different things might have been if we'd met in another age!'

'There's no time for that kind of speculation, Professor. This is your last chance of survival. I *want* you to survive, don't you understand? I'll do my best to save you, but you'll have to give me a little help.'

Breslauer made a renewed attempt to rise. His face twisted with pain as he heaved himself erect against the pitted concrete, spreading his arms in quest of a handhold. To Norden, it was a posture disconcertingly reminiscent of crucifixion.

'Isn't there a saying in your ranks, Herr Norden – that everything must have a purpose, even death? Why should you object if I try to invest *my* death with a modicum of significance by compelling you to kill me? Of all the people here, you're the only one I credit with an ability to recognize what really goes on in this place.'

'You're forgetting something!' Norden exclaimed fiercely. 'I've sworn an oath of absolute allegiance to the Führer.'

'Your Führer will be branded for all time by what he's doing in Germany – indelibly branded, anathematized to all eternity, and you with him. Is that what you want?'

'You're *incapable* of thinking like us!' Norden's protest sounded like the last desperate cry of a drowning man. 'You don't understand us. You refuse to see that we're only doing what history requires us to do. Come what may, Providence will acquit us.'

Breslauer shut his eyes. 'If that's what you believe, shoot me, and be quick.'

Heavy of heart but true to the dictates of his conscience, Norden drew his 10.5 magnum. He pointed it at the chest of the man who half stood, half knelt in front of him. Then he pulled the trigger.

Breslauer collapsed without a sound, as if his teeth were firmly clenched. He jack-knifed, twitched once, and lay still.

Waldemar Wesel received the news of Breslauer's death in silence. Having delivered his report, Norden saluted smartly and withdrew. Wesel did not watch him go. Instead, he refilled Rauffer's glass and his own with champagne.

'Satisfied, Gruppenführer?' asked Rauffer.

'I've no reason not to be,' Wesel replied gravely. 'Breslauer was my only real problem, and a dangerous one at that. No more Breslauer, no more problem. The matter has been disposed of by Norden, my best and most dependable man. Even Müller will have to accept this *fait accompli*, if only because it was Norden who removed the obstacle from our path. It was an exemplary piece of work – a pace-setter for the next thousand years of our Thousand-Year Reich.'

EPILOGUE
IN LUGANO

Detective Inspector Fellini of the Lugano CID was paying another call on HH, the Ascona-based novelist. HH ushered him into his work-room, a kind of studio whose walls appeared to consist of books alone, many of them HH's own.

'Well,' the author said, eyeing Fellini quizzically, 'are you still investigating the death of that man Norden? Have you discovered the motive yet – or the killer?'

Luigi Fellini shrugged, a gesture eloquent of regret. 'The conventional motives for murder – greed, jealousy, passion – can be ruled out.'

'Have you considered the notion of murder for ideological reasons?'

'It's a clear possibility,' Fellini admitted. 'Also, my friend, it would tie in with the picture I've formed on the basis of my own investigations to date. Just try proving it, though, especially when the chances are that German neo-Nazis were responsible.'

'And it's the devil's own job to track them down, you mean?' Having devoted much of his life to such problems, HH had to agree. 'Murders with an ideological background can be a head-ache, even to the most hardened of experts.'

'Of whom you're one,' Fellini said. 'What's more, you're going to help me – I know you will.'

'I'll gladly give you all the help I can, but I don't have extensive records or documents on the subject of war-crimes. Nothing as exhaustive as the archives kept by one of our most determined Central European contemporaries. You know who I mean?'

'Simon Wiesenthal of Vienna?' Fellini shook his head. 'I already phoned him. Names like Norden, Hagen and Siegfried mean nothing to him. They don't appear in his files, which concentrate on the so-called *soluzione finale* of the Jewish question subsequent to 1939.'

'What about Dr Fiola of the Institute of Contemporary History in Munich?'

'I had a long telephone conversation with her, too, but she specializes in Waffen-SS personnel and SS guards assigned to extermination camps in the East, mainly Auschwitz. I gave her the names, but she couldn't make anything of them either.'

'You're a very persistent man, Inspector,' HH said admiringly. 'It must be Swiss thoroughness. Are your superiors suitably pleased with you?'

'I'm in no position to judge.' Fellini grinned. 'I only know I'm a policeman with a case to crack. If the victim turns out to be as shady as his killer, that's none of my business.'

'Ever heard of somebody named Scott – ex-Captain Scott of US Military Intelligence? He was given wide powers to investigate SS special service units after 1945. I had a certain amount to do with him in occupied Germany. He is living in New York now.'

Fellini clasped his hands together. 'Ah, New York,' he said almost reverently. 'That's a place I'd like to visit some day, but it's a little beyond the range of a Swiss police inspector.'

'Can you make a transatlantic phone call?'

'On our budget? Only in an extreme emergency, and this doesn't qualify.'

'That's all right,' said HH. 'Permit me to stand you one. Call it a small token of my gratitude for your country's generous hospitality to an expatriate.'

The Ascona-Lugano-New York connection took only a few minutes. New York came through loud and clear. After a brief exchange of courtesies and a concise situation report, HH mentioned the names that had come to light. Scott's response was immediate: 'I've always wanted to spend a few days' holiday in Ticino. If I can take in a visit to the local morgue, all the better.'

Two days later Scott landed in Milan and was met at the airport by HH and Fellini. An hour's drive brought them to Lugano, where their first joint venture was sampling a dish of fresh mushrooms on *polenta* at Cossi's in Ponte Cremenaga.

Over a double espresso, Scott said, 'I can offer you something to round off the meal, Signor Fellini, but don't get too excited. It may not be worth much in practical terms. What you're dealing with is the aftermath of crimes committed in the name of patriotism, and they're nastier than most.'

'In that case,' HH said, 'I suggest we start by fortifying ourselves with a *grappa nostrana*.'

'Heroes were at work here, don't forget,' Scott said. 'And for every hero there's a tragedy. When heroes kill or get killed, it often boils down to a grossly criminal act – murder, if it ever comes to trial.'

From Captain Scott's research notes:

In 1945 I was assigned to trace the movements of the 'Wesel Group'. Its tracks were half obliterated, so I had to rely on guess-work. After testing the Birkenmoor pilot scheme, the Group appears to have been involved in the following operations:

1. Assistance in preparing for the invasion of Abyssinia by Italy, Germany's partner in the Rome-Berlin Axis. A number of abortive attempts were made to assassinate Emperor Haile Selassie, two of them documented. Hostilities opened on October 3 1935, and the conquest of his backward and feudal country was completed by early May 1936, poison gas being used in the process. The main undercover operations were in all probability directed by Norden.

2. During the Spanish Civil War, Communist attempts to infiltrate the German 'Condor Legion' were suspected. They were crushed by a special service unit acting on orders from Heydrich or Hitler himself. Responsible for a number of executions: Hagen, real name Dietmar.

Still in Spain, the Wesel Group saw combat on various occasions, usually deployed as an assault detachment and presumably for weapon-testing purposes. We do know that later on, when the Condor Legion returned to Germany in June 1939 and held its victory parade in Berlin, each member of the Group received decorations for bravery, Spanish included.

3. It is equally fair to assume that the Wesel Group played a part in the Blomberg-Fritsch affair of 1938. This time, the special talents of Berner and Bergmann were enlisted. Field Marshal Blomberg was accused of marrying a former prostitute. General von Fritsch fell prey to a smear campaign of subtle and sinister perfection. He was charged with homosexual activities. This allegation proved to be unfounded, but too late to save his career.

4. Immediately after German troops entered Austria in March 1938, an SS special service detachment arrived in Vienna with orders to assist the local Nazis, notably Kaltenbrunner. Two of the names that cropped up in the course of our laborious research may be of interest in the present context: Hermann and Siegfried.

5. Between May and September 1938, violent disturbances broke out in the Sudetenland. One of them was the so-called Weisskirchen Massacre, which took place during evening Mass in the local church. Twelve fatalities resulted. The Germans claimed that it was an atrocity committed by treacherous and inhuman Czechs. The Czechs did their best to prove that it was an attack by Germans on Germans – a murderous act of provocation. The authorities tried to compile a list of those involved. Together with eleven others, it bore the names of Hagen and Norden. This document vanished when German troops marched into the Sudetenland on 1 October 1938.

6. On 20 April 1939, Adolf Hitler celebrated his 50th birthday. He marked the occasion by promoting Waldemar Wesel Obergruppenführer and General of the Waffen-SS. Wesel's men – still the same tried and trusty half-dozen – received the rank of Brigadeführer.

7. On 23 August of the same year, Hitler's Foreign Minister, Joachim von Ribbentrop, travelled to Moscow to conclude the historic non-aggression pact with Stalin. Wesel was attached to Ribbentrop's personal staff. Four of the six members of the Wesel Group, who were functioning as bodyguards, can be identified in numerous official Soviet photographs.

8. Probably the showpiece of the whole collection was 'Operation Himmler', a raid on the German radio transmitter at Gleiwitz, Silesia, on the eve of World War II. The Nazis sensationalized this incident for propaganda's sake, denouncing it as 'a brutal and wanton atrocity committed by gangs of Polish thugs'.

The circumstances surrounding this raid were revealed after the war. The raiding party consisted of Germans in Polish uniform and included – no surprise – all six members of the Wesel Group.

I have to admit that it was this seemingly incomprehensible incident which triggered all my subsequent investigations. That enemies should be killed, rival gangsters eliminated and murders committed to order – all these things were as much standard practice under the dictatorships of the 1930s as they still are in the modern world of organized crime. Here, however, I was presented with a phenomenon: the butchering of one's own compatriots for reasons of Machiavellian expediency.

But more of that later. First let me conclude my list – which is surely not a complete one.

9. Immediately after 1 September 1939, during the German campaign in Poland, more special assignments were carried out. Their main objective was to foster anti-Polish terror propaganda by the deliberate mutilation of German corpses. One such example occurred at Mlawa in the Polish interior, where a German paratrooper was found with his belly slit open, his genitals amputated and both eyes put out. This frightful discovery was reported, quite coincidentally, by two SS officers named Berner and Bergmann.

10. Finally, to set a temporary but not unhistoric seal on this collection, we come to the death of Adolf Hitler in his underground command post at the Reich Chancellery, Berlin, on 30 April 1945. Soviet sources hint at the involvement of a man named Norden, though his later movements have proved as hard to trace as the whereabouts of Reichsleiter Bormann, who was reported to have been burnt to death in a German tank. Norden simply vanished – but not, it now appears, for good.

Fellini gave a low whistle. 'That ought to give us something to go on, even at this distance in time. Don't you think so, Signor Scott?'

'No, that's precisely what I don't think.' Scott spoke with a touch of commiseration. 'All these items I just listed for you – they don't amount to more than valid conjecture. Valid but not open to proof. The material witnesses are either dead or reluctant to testify for a number of pretty compelling reasons. Have you ever attended one of these German war crimes trials?'

The Italian shook his head.

'Then you don't know what it means to be subpoenaed. You're a sitting duck, a universal target – for the accused who claim that every prosecution witness is a vindictive muckraker; for the double-edged questions of defence counsel, who call experts to testify that you're mentally disturbed and that their clients – concentration camp guards and similar solid citizens – are one hundred per cent innocent. Finally, you're exposed to the adamantine scepticism of West German judges who find it difficult to conceive that wanton brutality ever constituted a legal norm in their country.'

'If you believe all that, Signor Scott,' Fellini said, 'why did you come?'

'Because I've spent half a lifetime trying to track these people down. I wanted to set eyes on one of them.'

'Even in a morgue?'

'Especially in a morgue,' Scott said grimly.

'We could be in for a long night,' HH observed. 'I suggest we equip ourselves.'

Summoning the proprietor, Signor Cossi, he ordered another bottle of grappa and a big pot of coffee. He also asked Cossi to hang a 'Private Party' notice on the restaurant door in two languages, Italian and German.

Then he turned to Scott. 'I'm sure we can offer you something a little more eloquent than the sight of a body on a slab. How would you like to dip into Norden's autobiographical notes? I suggest you start with the passage relating to Hitler's death.'

HH glanced at Fellini. Deftly, the policeman opened his briefcase and extracted several sheets of paper. He deposited them in front of Scott one by one, like a poker-dealer.

Notes made by Heinz-Hermann Norden and found in Lugano, the second of three extant drafts which display only minor discrepancies:

Not long after his last birthday, which we had celebrated in a fitting manner, the Führer sent for me. He returned my salute and shook my hand. His jaw-muscles were twitching and he seemed to be in considerable pain. Only his eyes retained their unwavering clarity.

'Comrade Norden,' he said, 'my final hour has come, and with it the need for an act of supreme loyalty. I must put one of my most faithful followers to the test – you! Are you prepared to undergo that test?'

'Yes, my Führer,' I replied.

'I have made my last will and testament,' the Führer went on.

'Our enemies are at the gate. For days now, I have been debating whether or not to confront them, gun in hand. I have lived, fought and suffered for the German nation. Under my leadership it scaled the heights of history, only to wilt and wither in the rarefied air of world supremacy. If it fails to survive now, its destruction will be self-induced and richly merited. Too many good men have perished on the field of honour as it is. My dearest wish at this time would be to follow their example and die like the front-line soldier I was so long ago, when my struggle on behalf of Greater Germany began. Would you be willing to accompany me on that final journey?'

'Yes, my Führer,' I said.

'Thank you, Norden, I expected no less of you, but it will not come to that. I have to consider what might happen if I did not die in battle, if I were only wounded – if I fell into enemy hands . . .'

I immediately grasped the terrible implications of what he had said. 'That, my Führer, must not be allowed to happen,' I said. 'Not under any circumstances – never!'

'Nor will it,' he replied. 'It will not happen if you are prepared to do me one last service. I told you that I had summoned you to test your loyalty. Before I do so by giving you the appropriate order, I ask you again: Are you prepared to carry it out?'

'Yes, my Führer,' I said, and we shook hands once more before I left the room.

A little while later I helped to kill him and his wife Eva, preserving them from the indignity of capture and the unseemly attentions of the curious. After they had taken poison, I gave them both the *coup de grâce*. Their remains were carried outside, soaked in petrol and burnt beyond recognition.

I have to confess that the spectacle moved me to tears of profound and overwhelming sorrow.

'Well, Scott,' asked HH, 'what do you say to that?'

'What do you want me to say?' Scott said quietly. 'If you expect me to weep on your shoulder, forget it. Not even Dante could have described the kind of hell that came to light during the final days of the Greater German Reich. I was there when they liberated a couple of the camps. I've never slept since without

263

seeing it again – all of it, in every detail, even now.'

'So you think Norden's notes are irrelevant?' Fellini said.

'Not irrelevant, just useless.'

HH gave a rueful smile. 'You mean they might be dismissed as the egocentric ramblings of a misfit?'

'Norden may strike us as a misfit now, but he fitted in just fine in the old days. He was a small but significant cog in the Nazi war machine. All we know of him suggests that he was a true believer as well – and there's nothing more dangerous than a perverted idealist.'

'But his notes are almost valueless from the legal aspect, Signor Scott,' Fellini said, 'especially as their author can't attest their authenticity.'

'What about witnesses?' HH asked. 'Judging from that list of yours, you must have rounded up dozens.'

'Well over a hundred,' Scott said. 'But what witnesses! An ex-chauffeur who keeps protesting his total ignorance and innocence. A cook, a gardener and a maidservant, all of them disastrously well equipped with verbal umbrellas like "Maybe, possibly, we couldn't say for certain."'

'What about ex-members of the SS or the Party and its various agencies?'

Scott laughed brusquely. 'The ones who claim to have been sheep in wolves' clothing, you mean? All their statements have the same common denominator: in the final analysis, there was only one guilty party – Adolf Hitler.'

'And the surviving victims?'

'They're too often treated like casualties of history – lucky to be alive at all. I quite understand why they're reluctant to run the gauntlet of their memories!'

'Just the same,' said HH, 'you did try and fit the pieces together.'

'Right. I built up a pretty useful picture too. But then came 1954, and the results of my investigations were sacrificed on the altar of international relations – or political expediency, whichever you prefer. I almost got axed myself. Here's a copy of the memo I drafted at the time.'

Memorandum filed by Captain Scott shortly before his retirement from active intelligence work:

1 August 1954, 10.00–12.00 Central European Time. Interview with General James J. Clark, Directorate of US Military Intelligence, Wiesbaden. I presented a summary of my findings to date, classified under ten main headings. I further submitted that this documented account of the activities of an SS special service unit should suffice to warrant the institution of criminal proceedings, even if these came within the jurisdiction of a German court.

After closely examining the documents I had put before him, the General expressed grave misgivings. His exact words, 'We won't get anywhere with this stuff. It'll set us back five years.'

My response, also quoted verbatim, 'So times have changed that much, have they, General?'

General Clark proceeded to enlighten me. The attitude of the United States had always been quite straightforward and un-equivocal – unlike that of our temporary wartime allies, the Russians. The latter were intent on dominating Europe, a political development the United States had to combat with all due vigour. This entailed the acquisition of trustworthy political associates, not to say potential comrades-in-arms, and the sooner the better.

'Surely you don't mean the Germans, sir?' I said.

'Why in hell not?' he retorted. 'The Krauts are the only people who've ever thrown a real scare into the Reds. We have to make the most of our assets, Scott. The least we can do is avoid riling the Germans unnecessarily, and that's just what you're liable to achieve with these petty suspicions of yours, which could never be fully substantiated in any case. I'm afraid I can't allow you to follow them up, not any more.'

Later in the interview, General Clark added, 'There's another reason why I'm putting the bar down. Keep on like this and you'll be stepping on the corns of the State Department. To honest-to-God soldiers like us, Scott, that's Indian territory!'

'What was the General driving at?' asked HH. 'Surely it's absurd to suggest that crimes committed by an SS special service unit could have proved embarrassing to official American circles?'

'Not necessarily,' Scott said, ' – not at the time. Just for now, let's concentrate on the present. Signor Fellini, I'd be interested to know if you've come across a certain name in the course of your investigation. It's one you'd be unlikely to forget: von der Tannen.'

Fellini nodded vigorously. 'We found a large number of letters among Norden's effects, mostly written between 1935 and 1939. They were from a Countess Elisabeth von der Tannen.'

'Just the lady I'm interested in!' Scott sounded pleased. 'Do these letters contain any facts and figures – names, dates, places? What about sums of money?'

'Nothing like that,' said Fellini. 'They're only love letters, all very tender and sentimental but written in a style that suggests the affair was never – how do you say? – consummated. They merely hint that love's young dream may come true at some unspecified time in the future.'

Scott chuckled. 'That sounds like the Countess all right!'

'Do you know her?' HH asked, looking faintly surprised. 'Strangely enough, I met the lady's father some years ago. He was reputed to be an avowed and active opponent of the Nazi régime – he'd got out of Germany well before the war and was living in Zürich. Now he's back on his country estate near Passau. They say he's one of the richest men in the Federal Republic.'

'Rich but deprived,' Fellini added sombrely. 'He lost his only daughter. It just goes to show you that nothing in this world is perfect.'

This drew a bellow of laughter from Scott. 'Christ Almighty, Inspector, what gives you that crazy idea?'

Fellini looked hurt. 'About fifteen years ago,' he said, 'a woman's body was discovered in the San Bernardino district of this canton. She appeared to have been the victim of a climbing accident and was registered as such. Decay was too far advanced to permit positive identification. At first, that is.'

'But the dead woman was later presumed to be Countess von der Tannen?' Scott looked mystified. 'Why?'

'Several weeks later, if not months,' Fellini continued briskly, 'Count von der Tannen turned up and reported his daughter's disappearance. He was told of the discovery of the body and given access to our official records at Bellinzona. Having examined them, he came to the conclusion that it must have been his missing daughter Elisabeth.'

'I'm beginning to catch on,' Scott said with a slow grin. 'Not long afterwards, Norden surfaces in Lugano and takes charge of the anonymous grave.'

'Several witnesses have unanimously stated that Signor Norden tended the grave himself and adorned it with flowers, particularly on three days in the year.'

'Let me guess which ones,' said Scott. 'The first could be 1 May, the date of their first meeting and Norden's birthday. Then 10 October, the Countess's birthday. Finally, the third floral tribute would have coincided with the putative date of the putative Countess's death. Right?'

Fellini was astonished. 'Absolutely right, but what are you implying?'

'That an attempt was made, and with almost lamentable success, to exploit Norden's romanticism. He might have rebelled, which left his lifelong rival no choice but to eliminate him.'

'Is that another guess, Signor Scott, or do you know something?'

'I pursued my investigations privately after leaving the army. A few years back, in a society column, I came across a name I knew. It was the maiden name of a former German countess.'

'A few years back?' Fellini said incredulously. 'Not fifteen or twenty? Unless my English is at fault, that can only mean she's still alive!'

'You bet she is.' Scott savoured the effect of his revelation. 'Alive and living in clover – a baronial mansion on the outskirts of Chicago, a holiday retreat in Miami Beach, a luxury Fifth Avenue penthouse with a superb view of Central Park . . . To the Countess's husband, that's just peanuts.'

'And who's he?'

'A pillar of the industrial establishment. Vice-president of a steel corporation, president of one major bank and director of another two, major stockholder of a press syndicate, an insurance company, a chain store, etcetera. His other interests, so far as I've been able to ascertain, extend to pharmaceuticals, electronics and transportation.'

'His name?'

'James Q. Hagen.'

HH groped for the bottle of grappa but found it empty.

Fellini poured himself some black coffee so hurriedly it slopped into the saucer. Regarding his companions with an indulgent smile, Scott put another sheet of paper in front of them.

Details of an interview recorded by ex-Captain Scott, now military correspondent of a number of influential newspapers including the New York Times *and the* Washington Post*:*

Interview with James Q. Hagen in his private office on the 45th floor of Lakeside Towers, Chicago. It was only granted after several telephoned requests had been reinforced by pressure from some friendly fellow-journalists and the good offices of two US Senators.

The following is a summary of the conversation, which consisted largely of monologues by Mr Hagen.

'Mr Scott, I've become inured – I wouldn't say reconciled – to the fact that certain people regard me as a suitable target for their shady imputations, even in a land of liberty like ours. My origins seem to invite it, I'm afraid. I was born in Germany like Albert Einstein and Wernher von Braun, but what does that prove? I've been a US citizen for over ten years now, and my citizenship goes deeper than the print on a passport – let's get that straight from the start.

'I'm well aware that a number of questionable rumours have been circulated about me – deliberately circulated by a certain party. I should like to stress that they're all totally unfounded.'

'How much of your life has been spent in Germany, Mr Hagen?'

'I lived in Munich until 1939. To be more accurate, in the neighbourhood of Munich.'

'Did you ever belong to a crack military unit?'

'What on earth gives you that idea, Mr Scott? I was a civil engineer in those days – a technician. I worked on a wide variety of projects. Highway construction, housing schemes, plant installation and so on. It's all on record.'

'You also helped to build hutted camps?'

'I took whatever came along. One had to live – or rather, survive, which is just what I and millions of other people tried to do. I didn't have to ingratiate myself with the régime. I was fortunate enough to come into contact with a firm opponent of the Third Reich, Count von der Tannen. My links with him go back well before 1939. They were founded on our common detestation of the unscrupulous methods employed by Hitler and his cronies.

'Then I emigrated to Zürich, where I worked for the Count and various expatriate organizations. I succeeded in helping large numbers of political refugees, Jewish included, to embark on a new and happier life. For what it's worth, I can produce several dozen letters of appreciation and gratitude. Some of the people I rescued went so far as to call me the good angel of the Zürich refugee community.

'The six long years between 1939 and 1945 weren't an easy time for me either, Mr Scott, but I survived them.

'It wasn't until after the war that our international patent agency secured a foothold in the States, thanks to co-financing offers from a number of major US concerns. The Count had opened up these contacts and I had no qualms about exploiting them.

'In 1946 I accompanied the Count to the States. I was his right-hand man by that time. We'd established a close personal relationship in Zürich – so close that he was happy to accept me as his son-in-law. Later on, when the new and democratic climate in postwar Germany encouraged him to return home, my wife and I remained behind in the States.

'I think that about covers it. I'm a businessman, Mr Scott. My wife works for a string of charitable organizations. We're not only American citizens – we feel at home here.'

'Well,' said HH, 'did you leave it at that?'

Scott shook his head. 'Of course not. I used it as one more piece in the jigsaw puzzle I was trying to reconstruct.'

'Were there any other leads?' asked Fellini.

'Sure,' Scott said. 'To give you an example, I came across several references to the name Breslauer. Professor Breslauer was a Jew who seems to have been acquainted with Wesel and Müller. Yes, gentlemen, it genuinely looks as if he was a friend of the notorious Gestapo Müller.'

'A Jew on friendly terms with the head of the Gestapo?'

'Why not? Nothing was impossible in those days. Anyway, I was given access to the Professor's diaries by his nephew, who lives in Boston. They were the usual exile's tale of woe – a lament for loss of liberty, dignity, love, security, familiar things and places – but they did include a couple of sentences which I copied out. I know them by heart:

'"They bear the mark of death on them, but they have yet to sense that death is looking over their shoulder. It will horrify them beyond all measure when they do, and the consequences will be dire."'

'Who did he mean, the Jews?'

'No, the Germans under Hitler.'

'What happened to him?'

'He was a Jew in Nazi Germany,' Scott said, as if that told the whole story. 'I only know he was in contact with the Wesel Group during its early years. He never reappeared after that.'

'I imagine he couldn't,' HH said. 'Norden's notes give some idea why.'

Further extracts from Captain Scott's files:

In mid-September 1939, shortly after the outbreak of World War II, the Wesel Group appears to have been disbanded, presumably because its members were henceforth employed to carry out major assignments on an individual basis. Wesel had solved his most difficult personnel problem, the feud between Norden and Hagen, in an inspired manner. He sent Hagen on a secret mission to Zürich, and thus into the immediate orbit of Count von der Tannen and his daughter. This inevitably provoked Norden's jealousy.

There was only one way of placating him, and that was to invest him with a status nobody could transcend. Norden was assigned to the Führer's personal entourage, an appointment he no doubt regarded as final confirmation that he had always been the best of the best in his élite group.

Berner and Bergmann ended up in the SS Economic and Administrative Section, where they were entrusted with special responsibility for the building of extermination camps. They did an excellent job. Immediately after the war, backed by the huge deposits in their numbered Swiss bank accounts, they founded a successful chain of brothels extending from Mexico City to Rio and Buenos Aires. They both lost their lives when some foreign visitors to one of their establishments went berserk and shot the place up. Rumour had it that they were Israeli agents.

Hermann and Siegfried were transferred to Heydrich's command and performed various special assignments for him. Hermann was acting as Heydrich's bodyguard when the latter's car was ambushed in Prague in 1942. Both men died of their wounds.

In reprisal, all the male inhabitants of a village named Lidice were shot, the women deported to Ravensbrück concentration camp and the children distributed among German families. This punitive operation was directed by a Captain Rostock under Siegfried's supervision.

Siegfried more or less went underground after that. I came across his name another two or three times in the course of my research, always in connection with special assignments carried out for Müller, who was by then heading the Gestapo. Both men disappeared during the last few days of the war. All trace of Müller was lost, but Siegfried may yet be alive.

'I wonder what happened to Wesel,' HH said.

Scott shrugged regretfully. 'That makes two of us. All I managed to discover was that Hitler continued to value his advice until the end. He's listed as a regular attender of staff conferences at the Führer's headquarters.'

'Could he still be alive?'

'I doubt it – he'd be a pretty senior citizen by now. His great and good friend Raffael was found shot in 1944, shortly after the attempt on Hitler's life. I lost track of Wesel from then on, but that doesn't prove anything. A man like Wesel would have been smart enough to keep a low profile, even here in Switzerland, which is where he may have ended up.'

'Count von der Tannen would know. Did you ask him?'

'Did I! You can guess how far it got me. The Count disclaimed all knowledge of Wesel's fate. "The man was a rank outsider," he said. "I regret ever having met him.""'

'So with Wesel officially presumed dead and Norden in the morgue, that leaves just two of the original half-dozen: Hagen and Siegfried.'

'I wouldn't put it quite that way,' the American said cautiously. 'I'd say we're left with Hagen and a guided missile named Siegfried. Not forgetting that grey eminence the Count – after all, Hagen's his son-in-law. My inquiries may have triggered a few alarm bells in the ancestral home.'

'Is that another piece of guesswork?'

'I thought so till you showed me these notes of Norden's. They seem to provide a key to recent developments. Siegfried ran Hagen to earth in the States, and Hagen, with his usual dexterity and lack of scruple, diverted him to another target: Norden. I guess he thought it fair to assume that Norden's literary aspirations would get the better of him sooner or later – that he'd write the story of his life or a history of the Wesel Group. And that, as Hagen must have impressed on Siegfried, was a straightforward betrayal of the oath of secrecy they'd all taken in the past.'

'So Hagen persuaded Siegfried that Norden could be a threat?'

'He was one, to these superannuated Nazis. He was concocting philosophical treatises, dabbling in pseudo-scholarship, romantically tending a grave in Lugano. He may even have tried to trace Hagen himself – we know he made two trips to the States last year. To men like Hagen and Siegfried, what could have been more alarming or suspicious?'

Fellini scowled. 'And they had to settle things here in Switzerland! I call that sheer impertinence. We must do something about it, but what?'

As a former intelligence officer, Scott had a series of practical answers to this question.

'First of all, Signor Fellini, may I suggest you run a check on everybody who's signed in at your Lugano hotels in the past seven days? Concentrate on the upper end of the price range. These ex-Nazis like to live high but they also like a certain degree of anonymity. They might attract attention in one of the smaller hotels, not in a four- or five-star establishment.

'Then, I'd like to see Norden's body. Can that be arranged? Good. Tomorrow will do, or rather today – it's long past midnight. I'll hope to be able to identify him.

'And the burial should take place the day after, at the same cemetery as the unmarked grave attributed to Countess von der Tannen. Can you fix it so he's buried near by?'

'In the next plot,' Fellini confirmed. 'I already allowed for that.'

Scott gave the Italian an approving wink that indicated they were on the same wavelength. 'Finally, can the funeral be publicized? No special coverage, just an item on the local news page. How many dailies do you have in Ticino?'

'Five. Four Italian and one German, the *Südschweiz*.'

'That could be the vital one. Any problem there?'

'None, Signor Scott,' Fellini said. 'I could even arrange for the *Südschweiz* to distribute a few hundred complimentary copies to every hotel and *pensione* in town – for advertising purposes, you understand. Every German-speaking visitor would find one on his breakfast tray.'

'Perfect. You obviously know what I'm driving at.'

Fellini just nodded. 'This man Siegfried – does he know who you are?'

'It's quite possible – I've been on his tail for nearly thirty years. I know precisely what he looks like, thanks to some eye-witness descriptions which tie in with the few photographs I've managed to get hold of. I guess he'd recognize me also.'

'May I see one of these photographs?'

'Sure, Inspector. I'll bring a copy of the best one to the morgue with me – it's an enlargement. You can have if for your files if you like.'

'I'd like a copy too,' HH said, 'for a friend of mine. He thinks he may have come across this Siegfried in the old days.'

'When – where?'

'August 1935, at a camp in the Bavarian Forest.'

'My God,' Scott said excitedly, 'if that's true, he must be talking about the grandaddy of all the extermination camps. You mean somebody actually survived Birkenmoor – somebody who saw Siegfried in action there? He may have seen other members of the Wesel Group, too. Hagen, for instance. Where is this friend of yours?'

'Here in Lugano, visiting his mother. He saw Siegfried the other day, right in the middle of town.'

'This could be the break I've been waiting for all these years! I have to see him – can you arrange it?'

'Only if he wants to see you.'

The three men met a few hours later at Lugano's municipal hospital. The Ticinese police had no official morgue of their own. The Department could certainly have afforded one, but cases of violent death were so comparatively rare that it would have been a needless extravagance.

HH, Fellini and Scott had assembled in a small, sterile room. All three looked pale and weary, thanks to lack of sleep or the fluorescent lighting that bathed the windowless chamber in a bluish glow. At a nod from Fellini, a medical orderly tugged at one of the handles protruding from the wall.

A drawer slid out. In it lay Heinz-Hermann Norden. His white hair looked youthfully blond in the harsh light, and the once distorted features had relaxed. The steel-blue eyes could only be imagined behind his closed lids.

'That's him,' Scott said in a low voice. 'He hasn't changed much in three or four decades, disregarding the more obvious signs of age. It's the kind of face that sets early.'

HH slowly wagged his head. 'And that's the type so many Germans trembled to behold – or worshipped?'

'All dead bodies are a disappointment, signori.' Fellini sounded like a kindly schoolmaster. 'Particularly when you haven't known them in life. They always look small and insignificant – almost without substance. As if they'd never been alive.'

Late that afternoon they met again. They shook hands, then Scott handed Fellini a postcard-sized photograph. The policeman examined it with care.

'So that's Siegfried.'

'Yes, taken thirty-five years ago in Moscow, when Ribbentrop went there to sign the non-aggression pact between Nazi Germany and Soviet Russia. Wesel, Norden and Siegfried were attached to the Foreign Minister's staff, as I told you. The Russians snapped everything in sight.'

'Do you know what the man reminds me of?' said Fellini. 'A Nordic god. He fits my idea of Baldur.'

HH inspected the photograph thoughtfully. 'So that's what he looks like – like a heroic tenor who specializes in the *Twilight of the Gods*. He must have aged since then, but there's something sinister about the face – a kind of mindless intensity.' He turned to Scott. 'You won't like this, but I'm not going to show your photo to the friend I told you about.'

Scott was taken aback. 'What if he has some vital information? He may be able to identify other members of the Group – even Hagen himself. What if he's willing to put his testimony on record, either for me or Signor Fellini?'

'No,' HH said firmly. 'Even if he were, I'd advise him not to. Why should he volunteer for a second dose of hell? It would harm him more than it would benefit you, Scott. Be absolutely objective – what do you hope to get out of all this research?'

'I've spent a lifetime trying to help you Jews,' Scott exclaimed angrily, 'trying to balance your books by proving that these mass killings took place and nailing at least a few of those responsible, and what do you do? You don't want to know!'

'I sympathize with HH,' Fellini said, surprisingly candid. 'The sight of this photo is enough. One can't help fearing such a man, one can only meet him on equal terms – with a gun and the ability to use it. How's your aim, Signor Scott? If you ever meet, his first target will be you.'

Norden's burial took place late in the afternoon of the day following their visit to the morgue. No mourners, no reporters, no priest. Only three spectators: Fellini, HH and Scott. Two lethargic cemetery attendants trundled the coffin to the grave-side on a barrow, unloaded it and lowered it into the waiting pit.

The Ticinese sun beat down. Sweltering heat, withered grass, dusty paths. The cemetery was almost deserted.

There were very few visitors: a woman with a small child, an elderly couple, an old man crouching over a grave. None of them made reliable witnesses of what was about to happen. They must have seen it, but their statements remained sketchy in spite of careful questioning.

HH was staring meditatively down at the coffin in its final resting-place. Inspector Fellini looked tense. He was keeping a wary eye on Scott, whose taut stance suggested that Lugano had turned into a jungle filled with beasts of prey. His arms were crossed, but his right hand nestled beneath his jacket.

It was all over in seconds. Scott caught sight of a man edging cautiously from behind one of the cypresses near the cemetery wall. Fellini spotted him almost simultaneously. They both recognized him.

'Down!' Fellini yelled.

HH stood glued to the spot – paralysed, he said later. Scott, who reacted with lightning speed, drew his borrowed gun and took cover behind the mound of newly turned soil.

Inspector Fellini's lifelong training in the use of firearms was a Swiss tradition. He reacted even faster. Dropping to the ground, he emptied his magazine with the rapidity of a machine-gun.

The man's body jerked violently, several times, as if somebody had kicked him in the chest. Then he collapsed and fell face down, his fingers slowly relaxing their grip on the butt of a heavy revolver.

Scott drew a deep breath. 'That,' he said, 'was Siegfried.'

The head of the Ticinese CID took less than an hour to reach the cemetery from his office in Bellinzona. He nodded affably at all present including Scott, whose part in the affair Fellini had explained by phone.

'It's strange,' he said. 'We pride ourselves on living in the world's most neutral country. Our canton is supposed to be one of the last remaining heavens on earth – apart from a few minor blemishes – and now we suffer this visitation by the dregs of the German master race. Ah well, so be it. We may not have invited them but we'll have to clean up the mess they've left behind.'

He glanced optimistically at Fellini. Not that he had ever told him so, the inspector was his pet subordinate. 'I imagine you have an explanation for what happened here?'

'But of course, Commissario. It was an act of self-defence, I can state that quite categorically. Mr Scott was threatened by an armed man. His gun has been recovered. It's a 10.5 revolver – probably identical to the one used in the Norden killing.'

'No premature assumptions, please,' said the superintendent.

'In any case,' Fellini went on, 'I was forced to open fire. If I hadn't, Mr Scott might be dead.'

'Quite possibly.' The CID chief strove to sound official. 'However, what matters now is to clarify the events leading up to this incident. With your investigative skill and a pair of associates like these gentlemen, Fellini, you can hardly fail.'

Two hours later the course of events had been largely reconstructed. Fellini was able to report as follows:

'The weapon found on the man shot in self-defence – a 10.5 revolver – was the same as that used to murder Norden. Forensic tests indicate a perfect match between the slug found on that occasion and another fired from the dead man's gun under laboratory conditions.

'The man shot in self-defence was registered at the Hotel Paris in Paradiso, a district of Lugano. The Brazilian passport found in his baggage identifies him as Siegfried Adolfo Linz, a sales representative resident in Rio de Janeiro, though another passport left with the hotel receptionist bears the name Sigismund Fried.

'Found on the body of Siegfried A. Linz or Sigismund Fried was a photograph of Mr Scott – a carefully printed enlargement.'

The American asked to see the photograph and examined it briefly.

'This picture could have been taken during my visit to James Q. Hagen in Chicago. I shouldn't be surprised if he videotaped me during our conversation in his office.'

'More guesswork?'

'Sure,' said Scott, 'but I'd take a modest bet on it.' He hesitated before producing his evidence, looking almost bashful. 'The fact is,' he said, 'I'm kind of superstitious. Or sentimental, call it what you like. Whenever there's something really tough ahead of me, I make a habit of wearing my Marine Corps tie – I used to be a Leatherneck before I transferred to Intelligence. I was wearing the tie when I called on Hagen in Chicago – you can see it in the picture. Come to that, I'm wearing it now. Okay, gentlemen, have a good laugh.'

Nobody even grinned.

'To continue,' Fellini resumed, 'Linz or Fried had already booked his return flight, Milan-Zürich, Zürich-Rio. He was all set to go at 16.00 on the 13th.'

HH whistled. 'That means he was at Milan Airport just as Fellini and I were meeting your plane, Scott. He must have spotted us – or rather, he must have recognized you from the photograph Hagen had given him as a precaution, so he deliberately missed his flight.'

Fellini nodded. 'Linz or Fried made a provisional reservation for three days later. He drove back to Lugano and checked in at the same hotel. In case you're interested, the hotel switchboard has no record of any transatlantic call made during the relevant period. However, the central post office in Lugano does. Some-body matching the dead man's description called Lakeside Towers, Chicago. Does that tell you anything?'

'Plenty,' said Scott. 'He was ordered to assassinate me.'

Fellini's smile was faintly apologetic. 'It rather looks like it.'

Three months later HH received a letter from Scott postmarked New York. It opened with the usual courtesies, like many belated thanks for all your hospitality in Ticino, sorry I didn't write sooner and when are we going to get together again?

Right at the end came a PS: 'I thought you might be interested in the enclosed press clipping – Signor Fellini too, and please be sure to give him my best.'

The clipping read:

TWO DIE IN FREEWAY TRAGEDY.

60 miles west of Chicago, careless driving last night claimed the lives of a man and a woman when their car – a custom-built Cadillac limousine – skidded out of control after being reck-lessly overtaken by another driver who has yet to be traced.

The doomed vehicle careered across the central reservation and collided with an oncoming truck owned by Seebohm's Saniware Inc. of Cedar Rapids, Iowa. The truck sustained minor damage only, but both occupants of the limousine died instantly. They had not been positively identified at the time of going to press.

Scott, in a PPS: 'I happened to be in the vicinity, so was able to help identify them as one Mr James Q. Hagen and his wife Elisabeth.

'They were buried at the Garden of Eternal Repose, one of Chicago's most scenically desirable cemeteries. I took the liberty of sending a really impressive wreath. Its red-white-and-black ribbon bore the words:

"Everything has a purpose, even death."'